THE GODDESS'S ILLUSION

CALATINI TALES BOOK 4

KATHERINE DOTTERER

KatSpell Press

The Goddess's Illusion

Cover by 100 Covers

Edited by Susan Bischoff, Lauralynn Elliott

A KatSpell Press Book

- ISBN 978-1-955614-13-9 (ebook)
- ISBN 978-1-955614-14-6 (trade paperback)

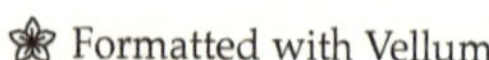 Formatted with Vellum

CONTENTS

About The Goddess's Illusion	1
Prologue	5
Chapter 1	13
Chapter 2	20
Chapter 3	28
Chapter 4	37
Chapter 5	44
Chapter 6	53
Chapter 7	62
Chapter 8	71
Chapter 9	79
Chapter 10	87
Chapter 11	95
Chapter 12	104
Chapter 13	113
Chapter 14	122
Chapter 15	130
Chapter 16	139
Chapter 17	147
Chapter 18	154
Chapter 19	162
Chapter 20	172
Chapter 21	180
Chapter 22	188
Chapter 23	196
Chapter 24	204
Chapter 25	212
Chapter 26	220
Chapter 27	228
Chapter 28	236
Chapter 29	244
Chapter 30	251
Chapter 31	258
Chapter 32	265
Chapter 33	274

Chapter 34   282
Chapter 35   290
Chapter 36   298
Chapter 37   308
Chapter 38   317
Chapter 39   325
Chapter 40   335
Chapter 41   344
Chapter 42   352
Chapter 43   360
Chapter 44   369
Chapter 45   378
Chapter 46   386
Chapter 47   394
Chapter 48   403
Chapter 49   413
Chapter 50   421
Epilogue   433
The Sun-Nymph Bride   439
Calatini Tales   441

About Katherine   443

ABOUT THE GODDESS'S ILLUSION

The Regency-inspired kingdom of Calatini is filled with magic and tender romance. But even in Calatini, magic comes with a cost, and sometimes a curse can become a blessing.

KIT, the young, widowed Countess of Blaine, must remarry. She's already chosen the perfect husband—except she can't stand his kisses. But on Longnight, the Goddess blesses her with a powerful illusion: Kit shall appear a hideous crone until she becomes who she was meant to be. Before anyone from court sees her, she flees to the one person she knows shall help—Mel, the gentleman she loved as a girl who is now a priest for the Goddess.

Mel, the middle son of a wealthy duke but called to serve the Goddess, has been avoiding Kit since discovering her cruel lies separated his brother from the girl he loved. But when Kit begs Mel for his help, he feels compelled to agree for the sake of the devout and tender girl he'd once loved.

But no one can break the Goddess's illusion, not even a wise elf or a powerful seer. So with Mel's support, Kit settles into life at the Goddess's temple. She and Mel continue to clash, and those clashes soon lead to passionate kisses—ones she actually enjoys. But a priest would never marry an unworthy lady like her, and she can't live the rest of her life as a crone.

Somehow, Kit must break her unwanted illusion, forget about Mel, and return to court where she belongs. Yet the Goddess's plans are not so easy to foil, and she has other ideas for Kit and Mel.

THE GODDESS'S *Illusion* **is perfect for fans of** *The Undertaking of Hart and Mercy*, **with the outpouring of magic, fantasy, and clean romance that make the Calatini Tales beloved.**

To Mom—the only pastor whose sermons I always listened to without daydreaming about my latest story, even when my childhood antics being used as examples made me blush.

PROLOGUE

*A*fter Lauds at dawn then organizing the hundred-twenty priests and novices serving at Ormas's almskitchens like he did every morning, Mel strode from the Great Temple's chapter house to finally eat breakfast. However, before he reached the dining hall in the center of the priest quarters, Paul, a rabbity temple priest who'd just been ordained last Longnight, scurried toward him with a note.

Thanking Paul, Mel blinked at his name in Hawke's bold scrawl then continued to the dining hall. A note from his younger brother this early was unusual. Was Hawke writing to explain his peculiar behavior over the past month and at Mother's fete last week? Or was he simply writing about a drastic change in the inheritance Mel had Hawke invest two years ago like Hawke had done his own?

Despite his questions, Mel waited until after he'd fetched breakfast to open Hawke's note. Then he hummed as he read the brief note while stirring three heaping spoons of honey into his tea. Hawke only requested that he visit early today without explaining why. Whatever Hawke wanted to discuss must be urgent but too private to put in writing.

So Mel devoured his breakfast then hurried to Hawke's

townhouse. When Hobb opened the door, he gave the butler a warm smile. "Good morning, Hobb. Hawke requested I visit at once."

Hobb's lips twitched as he ushered Mel inside. "Of course, Priest Melchior."

Mel frowned when the butler left him in the empty morning room. Why hadn't Hobb taken him directly to Hawke like usual? Surely Hawke was ready for visitors since he'd sent that note over an hour ago.

Then he blinked and leapt upright when Hawke and Wren swept into the morning room. Wren was here too? Mel blushed. And why did she and Hawke look disheveled?

Hawke flashed a crooked grin as he sat on the sofa opposite of Mel then drew Wren in his lap. "Thanks for visiting us so soon."

Eyeing them, Mel sat as well. Their intimacy was contrary to Hawke's protests that he and Wren were just friends when Mel and their elder brother Aragon had questioned Hawke at The Gold Griffin a few days ago. What had made Hawke and Wren admit their love at long last?

Blushing, Wren laid her hands on Hawke's. "I suppose you can guess why we requested you visit."

Mel couldn't help chuckling. "You need a priest to marry you. 'Tis about time."

As Wren blushed harder, Hawke merely smiled then replied, "We want a bloodbinding."

Mel nodded. Not surprising Hawke and Wren wanted a bloodbinding that would magically bind their life forces until death. They'd been in love forever, and they didn't need to worry about heirs like Aragon and Aragon's wife Selena did. And although no witch, Mel could still perform the magic required for a bloodbinding, thanks to the Goddess's blessing when he'd been ordained nearly three years ago.

Hawke's eyes narrowed. "And we're only inviting family and

close friends to our wedding ceremony—no matter what Mother wants."

Humming, Mel nodded again. Although the shy Wren would want a small wedding, Mother doubtless wanted all of court to attend since she enjoyed social events. Fortunately for Wren, Hawke was stubborn enough to resist Mother, unlike most. "I'll check when one of the chapels at the Great Temple is free."

Wren shifted in Hawke's lap. "If one isn't free this week, we should marry here instead. We must move quickly to quiet the gossip at court."

Mel frowned. Why would Hawke and Wren finally marrying cause gossip at court? "Gossip?"

As Hawke scowled, Wren wrinkled her nose and replied, "I'm surprised you haven't heard. I thought even the nightmara delegation must be gossiping about my scandalous pregnancy."

Inhaling, Mel stared at them. Wren was pregnant already? An almost imperceptible pang darted through him. With Selena also pregnant, he was the only one of his brothers who wouldn't soon be a father. And he likely never would be since he'd never met a lady he could love who loved him in return, and without love, the Goddess wouldn't approve his marriage. Shoving that aside, he beamed at Hawke and Wren. "Congratulations! Mother and Father and the Keyes must be thrilled, even though you anticipated your marriage vows. But how did court find out?"

When Hawke's scowl darkened, Wren squeezed his hands then smiled at Mel. "Kit overheard our mothers discussing it. Then she promptly told all of court about my scandalous pregnancy."

Mel stiffened, his chest tightening. Since becoming the fashionable Countess of Blaine over six years ago, their alluring, former neighbor Kit had often gossiped—like when she'd told everyone about Selena before Selena's presentation ball since foreknowledge of Mother's plans impressed court. Yet although indiscreet, that gossip hadn't hurt anyone and had probably even enhanced Selena's presentation. But gossiping about Wren's scandalous pregnancy was different. That gained Kit nothing except hurting Wren, the childhood rival Kit adored needling. And hurting Wren hurt Mel's brother too.

He swallowed. The tender girl who'd enjoyed attending services worshipping the Goddess and visiting poor villagers with him would never have been so mean. Marrying Mother's elderly cousin to become the Countess of Blaine and being fashionable at court since her first season had changed Kit beyond all recognition. Or had it been Lord Blaine's death last year that had changed her? He managed a smile. "I'm sorry Kit was so mean."

As Wren shrugged, Hawke grunted then gritted, "Only to be expected, given how she ruined our Longnight kiss eight years ago."

Mel froze. That life-changing Longnight had been when he'd told Mother and Father he meant to become a priest and when Hawke had planned to surprise Wren with a romantic Longnight kiss. But after that Longnight, Hawke had begun pretending he and Wren were just friends. Mel leaned toward them. "How did Kit ruin your Longnight kiss?"

Hawke's pale-blue eyes flared. "Kit told Wren I'd kissed her the day before—a cruel lie. Because of it, Wren assumed I wasn't serious and spurned my kiss with such vehemence I couldn't bear considering her in a romantic light again."

Mel inhaled. That certainly explained Hawke's stubborn insistence he and Wren were just friends these past eight years. How could Kit have been so spiteful and cruel? His heart twisted. And her cruel lie had been *before* she'd become the fashionable Countess of Blaine. Perhaps Kit had never been the devout and tender girl he'd believed she was. He fisted his hands in his priest robes. Or perhaps her vile father had already destroyed that girl by then.

Turning in Hawke's lap, Wren caressed his face. "You should forgive Kit like I did yesterday. After all, she wasn't entirely to blame for our disastrous Longnight kiss. We were both too young and scared to fight for our love."

When Hawke lowered his head to kiss Wren, Mel blushed then leapt upright. He should give them privacy. "I'll write once I find out when a chapel is free."

He strode from Hawke's townhouse but headed to Blaine House rather than the Great Temple. He must confront Kit about her cruel behavior.

THE MORNING after Wren had magnanimously forgiven her for lying about Hawke, Kit woke late with another vicious megrim throbbing inside her skull—her fifth of the nauseating, severe headaches this month. Not activating the witchlights in her chambers or opening the curtains, she gulped a megrim tonic. Hopefully, 'twould help today, even though they didn't half the time. Waiting for the tonic to work, she remained sequestered in her darkened chambers. She hated letting others see her when she was so vulnerable, a remnant of life with Father. Somehow he'd always sensed when she was suffering a megrim and saved his cruelest insults for then.

She sighed as she dropped into her plushest chair. Thank the Goddess her late husband Lord Blaine had been nothing like Father—Lord Blaine had always made sure she had quiet and pampering during her megrims. Familiar tears pricked her eyes. If only she could have been a true wife to him. He'd deserved so much better than her.

She was dozing when her maid Willa touched her shoulder and said, "Priest Melchior Hawke is in the morning room to see you, my lady. Shall I send him away?"

Kit straightened, her sudden movement making blood throb in her head. What was Mel doing downstairs? Since she'd enticed Lord Blaine into marrying her at seventeen to escape Father, Mel had never once visited her. She only saw him at family events—Lord Blaine had been a cousin of Mel's mother, the influential Duchess of Childes. Whatever Mel was here to discuss must be serious. She swallowed then rose. "No, I'll see him."

She made her way downstairs, despite the blinding summer sunshine streaming inside the townhouse stabbing her eyes. Her treacherous heart fluttering like always when she saw Mel even with her megrim, she glided into the morning room and gave him a tight smile. "To what do I owe the honor of your priestly presence this morning? Don't you have some unfortunates to save instead?"

None of his normal kindness warming his deep-brown eyes, Mel rose and scrutinized her. "I had to speak with you first."

Kit tensed at the unusual anger reverberating in his soft words. What of her shameful secrets had he discovered? That Father had always despised and belittled her? Or that the gambling sot had been right to despise his wicked and vulgar daughter? Or that she was still a virgin after five years of marriage and habitual flirting? Feigning nonchalance, she sank into the chair opposite of Mel then gestured for him to sit. "Go on then."

Mel returned to his chair, his handsome face set in stern lines. "Kit, why have you continually attempted to sabotage Hawke and Wren's love?"

Her nauseous stomach tightening, she studied her nails since tossing her head would just exacerbate her megrim. "I'm not sure what you mean."

Mel snorted. "No? Shall we review your latest attempt? You told all of court about Wren's pregnancy, which made her and Hawke's involvement a scandal. Why? Since Wren rarely attends court, gossiping about her gained you nothing."

Kit kept studying her nails as her megrim throbbed in rhythm with her heart. A worthy person like Mel would have remained silent about Wren's scandalous pregnancy, but sharing that the perfect Wren had erred for once had been too tempting for her to forgo. Raising her gaze, she lifted a shoulder. "Telling people amused me."

His jaw clenched, Mel leaned forward. "Like it amused you to flirt with Hawke since you came out of mourning last month? That also gained you nothing."

Eyeing Mel beneath her lashes, she pursed a coy smile. True, although she couldn't resist needling the besotted Wren and the equally besotted Hawke, who had both refused to admit their obvious love until now. A pang darted through her. Wren didn't know how fortunate she was to have her love returned. Unlike hers had been. Not that she loved Mel any longer. That had been a girlhood fantasy.

Clinging to her coy smile as her megrim sharpened, she flicked her fingers. "Flirting with Hawke was a mere lark. I was never seriously pursuing him. My next husband must be wealthy and titled like Lord Blaine—I can't lose the status I gained with my first marriage."

Mel fisted his hands in his dark-brown priest robes. "How can you be so grasping and cold? What happened to the tender girl who enjoyed attending services and visiting poor villagers?"

Kit stilled as Father's derision when he discovered those visits echoed through her. To conceal her initial reaction, she smirked and smoothed the sophisticated gown that flattered her lush curves. Even at home suffering a megrim, she always wore the best. "She grew up."

His eyes turning darker than his coal-brown hair, Mel gritted, "I suppose part of that growing up was telling Wren a cruel lie about kissing Hawke."

She froze, her heart wrenching and megrim throbbing. Of course Wren and Hawke had told Mel that shameful secret. The one she'd *never* wanted Mel to discover. He'd despise her for hurting his beloved brother so. She made herself sniff. "That was just a jest—one I assumed the perfect couple would undo within moments."

Mel stiffened. "Your *jest* turned Hawke into a rakehell. He and Wren would have married years ago if you hadn't interfered."

Suppressing a wince, Kit lifted her chin. Doubtless true, but she wasn't completely to blame. "My jest would have been undone if Wren and Hawke had simply talked to each other."

Mel eyed her, his gaze cold. "True, but don't you feel any remorse for the hurt you caused them?"

She swallowed but impassively returned his gaze. Of course she did. But she'd not admit such vulnerability to anyone, not even Mel. "Remorse doesn't change the past."

Mel leapt to his feet. "Perhaps not, but it does help you atone and prevent you from repeating past mistakes." He stared down at her. "Clearly, the tender girl I believed I knew was nothing but an illusion." He swept a bow. "Goodbye, Lady Blaine."

As Mel strode from the morning room, Kit gazed after him, and the ache in her chest eclipsed her throbbing megrim. She'd been right that he'd despise her once he discovered how wicked she truly was. Exactly like Father did. And now that Mel's good opinion of her was shattered, she'd likely never rebuild it. She fisted a hand above her heart. She never should have interfered with Wren and Hawke's relationship—the cost had been too dear.

Then Kit stiffened her spine. But no sense crying for spilt unicorn water, and Mel's good opinion hardly mattered. He attended court as rarely as Wren did, so his distaste wouldn't ruin her chance to entice a new husband, which she must manage before her stepson Edouard asked Pippa to marry him. She couldn't be a dowager countess once he married. Fortunately, she'd already selected her next husband—the genial Lord Ravenstone. She rose to return to her darkened chambers. She must simply redouble her efforts to catch the rugged count.

CHAPTER 1

Three and a half months later, Kit suppressed the urge to fidget as she waited in the anteroom beside the entrance hall for the Duke of Oakmoor to escort her to the much-anticipated ball that Mel's mother was hosting to open the Long-night season. The rakehell duke had been escorting her to court events since last month when she'd discovered he was finally seeking a wife—thanks to overhearing a conversation between her former favorite Lord Ravenstone and the beauteous Lady Annalise. After overhearing them together, she'd abandoned her pursuit of the rugged count because he and Lady Annalise were secretly in love despite their families being ancestral enemies, and he'd not make an acceptable husband for anyone else.

She smoothed the flattering, arachne silk ballgown that she'd purchased from Celeste's and turned it crimson, like the ripest Goddess laurel apples, using a drop of blood. Although not as kind as Lord Ravenstone, the suave Duke of Oakmoor was a much better match for her even though he was twice her age. Both wealthy and influential, the still hale duke remained in Ormas much of the year since he served on the council as the Minister of Foreign Relations, and he hosted court events often, something she excelled at and enjoyed.

The touch of gray at his temples gleaming amid his brown hair the sole hint of his age, the Duke of Oakmoor strode into the anteroom then swept a deft bow and kissed her hand with a smoldering glance. "I hope I've not kept you waiting too long, Lady Blaine."

Her stomach tightening, Kit freed her hand but fluttered her lashes at the duke as she rose. To catch him, she must play the perfect court lady, always coy yet seeking an alliance rather than love. The infamous rakehell wouldn't appreciate a nagging wife who protested his many affairs. Which she wouldn't be. Smiling, she slid her arm through the duke's. "Not at all. Edouard just left moments ago to fetch Pippa."

The duke chuckled as he escorted her from Blaine House to his carriage. "Of course he did. I suppose it shan't be long before Lord Blaine asks Miss Hawke to marry him."

Since the duke adored intrigue, she moued and claimed, "Yes, although I've been delaying him." Truthfully, her stepson took everything at a deliberate pace, especially courtship. Edouard had clearly liked Pippa, who was also Mel's cousin but on the opposite side, when they'd first met at Aragon and Selena's wedding last year shortly before his father had died, but he'd waited until Pippa's come out this season to quietly court her. Kit tossed her head. "I can't bear the thought of being *just* the dowager countess."

The Duke of Oakmoor chuckled again as he handed her into his carriage. "Perhaps someone shall rescue you by marrying you first."

As the duke sat beside her and draped an arm about her, she forced herself to lean into his embrace despite the chill skittering across her skin. Although older like her late husband, the duke was still in his prime of life and had never married, so he needed an heir, unlike Lord Blaine had. The duke would expect intimacy from her—*he* wouldn't leave her untouched when he discovered his young bride froze like under a stone spell at a mere kiss. Thankfully, the duke would expend his passion with his mistresses once she bore him an heir.

His sandalwood scent making her stomach quiver, Kit swallowed and squeezed the duke's knee. "I'd love if a duke rescued me."

The duke rumbled a laugh and laid his hand on hers. "Perhaps one might."

To curb their flirting before it led to a kiss, she asked, "Are you anticipating the Duchess of Childes's ball tonight?" The duchess's Longnight ball was the first held at court in decades since the season usually ended at Harvestfete over two months ago. However, the felicitous appearance of King Devon's betrothed Lady Kiera and the continued nightmara negotiations had extended the season this year because the council remained in session, and court wouldn't leave Ormas until the most influential nobles did too. Kit tilted her head. "The duchess is sure to have interesting festivities arranged."

Humming, the Duke of Oakmoor nodded. "She does provide interesting amusements at her events, like that play she had her pregnant, soon-to-be daughter-in-law write for her fete celebrating her and the duke's *first* grandchild." He threaded his fingers through Kit's. "Although your events are much more diverting—your water party and fire ball were both unique."

She purred a sultry laugh and made herself caress the duke's palm with her thumb. "Now if only I could manage an air concert or earth rout."

The duke turned and grasped her chin with his free hand. He leaned toward her, his hazel gaze ardent. "I'm sure you shall one day."

Kit froze as her pulse pounded and stomach roiled. Dear Goddess, the duke was about to kiss her for the first time in their courtship. Please let her not turn to stone like she had with Lord Blaine.

But before the duke could lean closer, the carriage halted at Childes House.

As the duke chuckled and released her chin, she managed not to sag but instead eked a weak smile.

The Duke of Oakmoor leapt from the carriage then helped her alight. He kissed her palm. "We'll continue this later. We can't miss the Duchess of Childes's Longnight ball."

Swallowing, Kit fluttered her lashes at the duke. "No matter how much we might long to—missing one of the Duchess of Childes's events would destroy even the most fashionable at court."

The duke chuckled again. "Doubtless true. But perhaps one day we should test that." Then he smiled and escorted her into the crowded ballroom.

The Duchess of Childes beamed at Kit as her husband and the Duke of Oakmoor exchanged greetings. "How gorgeous you look tonight. And such a bold choice too—most ladies are wearing green, gold, or white to celebrate the Longnight season."

Kit lifted a shoulder. True, but the fashionable Countess of Blaine was known for her bold and sultry gowns, and she mustn't disappoint her coterie. They'd abandon her otherwise. "Crimson suits me." Plus, the color of ripe Goddess laurel apples was her favorite. She smiled at Mel's mother. "Has everyone arrived yet?"

The duchess tilted her head. "Nearly everyone except Devon and Kiera, but we'll probably start the dancing without them." She nodded at her three sons and their two wives near the refreshments table. "I'm not certain how long Aragon and Selena, Hawke and Wren, or Mel shall stay. Pregnant ladies tire early, and Mel has duties at the Great Temple in the morning."

Her heart quickening, Kit followed the duchess's nod. Mel grinned between his brothers, who each had a possessive arm wrapped about his pregnant wife. Although Mel was two years younger than Aragon and two years older than Hawke, the three brothers so strongly resembled their father with the same dark hair and strong features that they appeared triplets, except only Mel and Aragon had inherited the duke's dark eyes. Yet Mel was still the handsomest of the three due to the deep compassion that glowed in his heartwarming smile.

As if he could sense her stare, Mel glanced across the ballroom and met her gaze. His grin faded, and the tight expression he'd worn when they'd last spoken flickered across his face. Without acknowledging her, he pivoted toward Wren and Hawke then gave them a warm smile.

She swallowed, her chest twisting. Since Mel had discovered how wicked she truly was over three months ago, he'd ignored her like that at the two other court events they'd both attended. She'd definitely never rebuild his good opinion. She must learn to ignore him like he ignored her. She dragged her gaze back to his parents.

Her brow creased, the duchess eyed Kit. "Do you have another megrim?"

Kit tensed as Mel's father and the Duke of Oakmoor eyed her as well. Of course Mel's perceptive mother had noticed her upset at his distaste. Now her future husband did too and would watch her closer the rest of the evening. She'd best not glance at Mel again so the duke didn't see her reaction and wonder why. He might ask Mel about her, and Mel might reveal some of his distaste. Plus, thanks to Mel's mother, her future husband now knew about her megrims, a flaw she'd not wanted him to learn until after they married.

She managed a blinding smile for the duchess and two dukes. "I feel fine. I'm simply eager for the interesting festivities you've arranged, your grace."

The duchess hummed. "Nothing special tonight—just Longnight reels along with Longnight decorations and desserts."

The Duke of Childes flashed his usual crooked grin. "'Twouldn't do to shock court at the beginning of the Longnight season."

Mel's mother shooed Kit and the Duke of Oakmoor toward the refreshments table, which Mel and his brothers and sisters-in-law had fortunately left. "Go fetch some refreshments before the dancing starts. It shan't be long."

As the Duke of Oakmoor escorted Kit across the ballroom, he scrutinized her, his gaze probing. "You suffer megrims?"

Kit shrugged then murmured, "Only occasionally." In truth, her vicious megrims had increased to around one a week since she'd rejoined court after her year of mourning this summer. Doubtless the stress of acting as the fashionable Countess of Blaine and hunting a new husband as well as the resulting poor sleep was responsible. But surely her megrims would lessen once she was securely married to the duke. She smiled at him through her lashes. "They're hardly worth mentioning."

The duke inclined his head then handed her a mug of spiced cider without asking before fetching a flute of sparkling wine for himself. During their month-long courtship, he'd already learned she much preferred spiced cider to sparkling wine or shokolat. If it had been fashionable, she'd drink it all year long, like she did cinnaspice tea.

As she and the duke glided about the ballroom greeting other guests, she sipped her spiced cider and inhaled its steam. The delicious blend of cinnaspice and apples reminiscent of Goddess laurels soon eased her tension at the duke's near kiss, Mel's distaste, and the duke discovering one of her secrets.

She glanced about the ballroom to find everyone. Mel was still with his brothers and their wives, but they were now beneath the musicians' balcony. She wrenched her gaze free before she could brood then continued checking the ballroom. Their blond hair reflecting the dazzling witchlights, her twin stepchildren Edouard and Elise, who were actually several months her senior, stood near a garden balcony. As they talked and laughed, Edouard had his arm threaded through Pippa's, while Elise lovingly held her husband Lord Farson's arm with their teenage ward Arvan, the Duke of Golddell, between them and Pippa's brothers. Elise and Lord Farson must have brought the young duke since tonight's ball was hosted by family.

The Duke of Oakmoor arched a brow once they finished greeting the temperate Duchess of Wildewall, another of the king's councilors like him, Aragon, and Lord Farson. "Shall we greet your stepchildren next?"

Kit almost winced. Although Elise was always gracious, Edouard had trouble concealing his dislike. Even before she'd enticed their father into marrying her, Edouard had considered her grasping and brazen. And her stepson's deep dislike might give the duke doubts about marrying her, so she attempted to avoid Edouard when with the duke.

Fortunately, the beginning strains of the first Longnight reel began before she could reply.

Handing her near empty mug to a servant, she tugged the duke toward the floor. "We can greet Edouard and Elise after we dance."

The Duke of Oakmoor gave his flute of sparkling wine to the servant as well before leading her to the center of the dancers to form a set with the duke's fellow councilor Lady Ducharme and her husband. Then the duke drew Kit as close as the vigorous reel full of hops and sprightly steps would allow.

She swallowed and resisted the need to pull back to the proper distance. She couldn't protest that the rakehell duke courting her held her slightly too close. Especially given her habitual flirting. Instead, she pursed a coy smile and caressed his arm as they began to dance.

CHAPTER 2

After Aragon and Hawke left to dance the first Longnight reel with the pregnant wives they adored, Mel exhaled then drifted along the outskirts of his parents' crowded ballroom. He didn't often dance at the few court events he attended. Although fun, dancing was mostly an act of courtship, and as a priest, he couldn't woo any ladies devoted to court and being fashionable. So he typically only danced when Mother commanded it.

As he sipped his spiced cider redolent of cinnaspice and apples like Goddess laurels, his gaze drifted to Kit dancing at the center of the ballroom with the suave rakehell Duke of Oakmoor and the Ducharmes. In her crimson ballgown, which must be Hawke's latest find arachne silk from its magical luster, Kit was even more gorgeous than usual—like a vibrant rose amid the leaves and snow of the other ladies' ballgowns. And somehow her ballgown was the precise shade of ripe Goddess laurel apples, even though only priests paid much attention to the small, evergreen shrubs that only bloomed and bore fruit on Goddess-consecrated grounds like temples.

His stomach tightening, Mel clenched his mug when the Duke of Oakmoor deftly pulled Kit against him as they linked arms and spun. The aging rakehell had been dancing too close before, but touching like that was indecent. Yet Kit merely flashed a coy smile as she shifted back to the proper distance. Obviously, she'd found the next wealthy and titled gentleman she meant to charm into marriage. Like with Mother's late cousin Lord Blaine, Kit had chosen another many years her senior.

Mel wrenched his gaze free then tossed back his spiced cider. When he'd last seen Kit at Mother's art gala last month, she'd been pursuing Lord Ravenstone, a genial count who was their age. He eyed Lord Ravenstone dancing with his vibrant mother and the Islayes. Yet 'twas fortunate Kit had quit pursuing Lord Ravenstone. The count was secretly in love with his family's ancestral enemy Lady Annalise Greysnowe. Lord Ravenstone had asked Mel to marry them several weeks ago, but Lady Annalise falling ill had prevented their elopement.

Mel shook his head before heading to the refreshments table for more spiced cider and Longnight desserts. Then he frowned as Lady Annalise, who was whiter than a banshee, slipped into the nearest anteroom with her brother Lord Alexander. The poor lady was clearly still ill—hopefully, she'd not collapse. No doubt Lord Ravenstone would rush to her side if she did, and Mother wouldn't appreciate such a scandal at her Longnight ball, the first at court in decades.

Sighing, Mel devoured his Longnight desserts and returned his gaze to the dancers, but it soon drifted to Kit with the Duke of Oakmoor again. He almost scowled as he wrenched his gaze free once more. He shouldn't find her so alluring now that he *knew* how remorseless and cruel she was. And the devout, tender girl she played when they were young had been the cruelest illusion of them all.

He forced himself to study his brothers and their wives dancing a set together. Aragon and Selena beamed at each other as Selena walked rather than hopped the steps, doubtless the most his heavily pregnant sister-in-law could manage. Romping beside them, Hawke and Wren exchanged heated glances with

Hawke resting a hand against her rounded stomach when the reel brought them close. A faint pang darted through Mel. His brothers were so in love and so elated to become fathers, almost as much as Mother and Father were to become grandparents.

Mel swallowed and turned his attention to his cousins dancing in a set past his brothers. Edouard was laughing with the bubbly Pippa as they danced, despite his frequent gravity since becoming Lord Blaine last year. Dancing beside them, Edouard's twin Elise grinned with her husband Farson, the baron who represented the Golddell duchy and the nightmara on the council. Mel sighed. Nearly all of his family were in love these days, even the ones that hadn't arrived yet—his cousin King Devon and Devon's betrothed Kiera, a longtime friend of Wren's.

Then the first Longnight reel ended, and his brothers and their wives rejoined him beside the refreshments table.

Leaning against Aragon, Selena dimpled and shook her head. "I can't believe how exhausted I am after just one Longnight reel, which I didn't even dance properly."

Hawke's arm draped about her shoulders, Wren wrinkled her nose. "I know. I doubt I can manage another."

As Aragon and Hawke traded frowns above their pregnant wives' heads, Mel smiled at his sisters-in-law then handed his spiced cider and empty plate to a servant. "Perhaps some refreshments shall revive you. I'll fetch some."

He strode to the refreshments table and requested eggmilk punch without spiritwine for Selena and shokolat for Wren. While there, he made himself smile and nod at the Duke of Oakmoor, who was fetching sparkling wine and spiced cider. Doubtless the spiced cider was for Kit since she'd always adored it.

Mel returned to his family then handed Selena and Wren their drinks. His gaze flicked toward Kit across the ballroom near a garden balcony. She was coyly smiling at the duke while accepting her mug of spiced cider. Wrenching his treacherous gaze free yet again, he turned to Aragon and Hawke then waggled his brows to tease them. "If you two want refreshments, you must fetch them yourselves."

Hawke flashed a crooked grin. "A good priest would offer to fetch them for *everyone*."

Feigning concern, Mel sighed and shook his head. "Not if he was concerned about his brothers' sedentary ways."

As Selena and Wren giggled, Aragon snorted and replied, "Sedentary? We just danced a Longnight reel."

Mel tsked. To continue teasing Aragon and Hawke, he claimed, "True, but you both seem out of breath. Clearly, you require more exercise."

Hawke grinned down at Wren. "We'll get some *later*."

As a blushing Wren elbowed Hawke, Mel blushed as well. He couldn't keep teasing his brothers about exercise now, probably Hawke's intention. So he turned to Aragon and asked, "Do you know why Devon and Kiera haven't arrived yet?" As Devon's best friend and part of the council, Aragon often knew the king's plans.

Aragon frowned and shook his head. "State affairs probably delayed them. I hope 'tisn't too serious."

Mel and the others grimaced. Serious like the Magehaven ore exploding again or another poisoning attempt on Kiera. Although none of them dared mention either aloud—the ore explosion had been tragic, so another would be horrible, while only their immediate family and the royal witch knew about the treasonous poisoning attempt. Not even the rest of the council knew about it yet since the royal witch hadn't unearthed the poisoner.

Wren pursed her lips. "I hope Kiera and Devon arrive soon. I've not seen Kiera for over a week, and I wanted to tell her about our Longnight plans at the orphanage."

Mel hummed. Kiera would love hearing about that since she'd been the orphanage matron until she met Devon at his summer masquerade earlier this year. Wren and Hawke had assumed Kiera's duties at the orphanage when she'd left to become the king's betrothed and negotiate the renewal of Calatini's legendary treaty with the matriarchal, horse-like nightmara.

Hawke nodded at the nearby chairs along the wall. "Why don't we sit? We can probably stay longer then."

As the next Longnight reel began, Mel and the others sat and watched the dancers while talking and laughing. Although Mel almost frowned at Kit dancing with the Duke of Oakmoor again—two dances in a row must mean the duke was close to proposing. He forced himself to turn toward his family beside him. Thanks to his duties at the Great Temple, he didn't get to see them often enough, so he should focus on enjoying his time with them, not watching Kit.

But after five Longnight reels, Aragon and Hawke escorted Selena and Wren from the ball, even though Devon and Kiera still hadn't arrived. Alone again since Mother and Father were involved with their guests, Mel drifted about the outskirts of the ballroom once more. He shouldn't stay much longer either—he must organize the priests and novices helping at Ormas's almskitchens before breakfast tomorrow. But he'd eat another plate of Longnight desserts before he left. Such abundant desserts weren't available at the Great Temple.

While he devoured orenge nut sweet biscuits and gingyrbread, he glanced about the ballroom, studying the guests again. Kit was still with the Duke of Oakmoor, although they'd not danced since the first two reels. They were talking with the elderly Duke of Osbourne and the temperate Duchess of Wildewall, who were both councilors like the Duke of Oakmoor, Aragon, and Farson. Kit must be pleased to converse regularly with such influential nobles since that enhanced the fashionable Countess of Blaine's cachet.

His jaw tightening, he turned away to refill his plate. As he did, the crowded ballroom hushed momentarily. He glanced toward the door—Devon and Kiera had finally arrived. Mother and Father greeted them, then Mother shooed the king and his betrothed toward the floor as another Longnight reel began.

That reel was almost over and Mel's plate nearly empty when Mother and Father joined him. Beaming, Mother embraced him and said, "Sorry we've hardly spoken tonight. Are you enjoying yourself?"

Mel returned Mother's smile and lifted his plate as the Longnight reel faded. "Of course. Your desserts are as delectable as ever."

Father chuckled. "You would know, considering you've eaten several plates already. I wish I'd been as fortunate."

As Mel and Father traded grins, Mother shook her head then said, "You can't spend an entire Longnight ball eating desserts. You should dance too."

Mel gestured toward his priest robes. They were the dark brown that priests usually wore, and since he was a community priest, the trim at his collar, cuffs, and hem was brown as well. His plain attire was distinct amid the other guests' finery like a sparrow amid faebirds. Everyone could tell he was a priest at a glance, and that made most ladies at court nervous. Plus, he required a lady devoted to serving others, and many at court were devoted to wealth and influence instead. He shook his head. "You know I can't pursue court ladies."

Mother tsked. "Nonsense. You must simply dance with a lady who knows you and understands your situation." Releasing Father, she grasped Mel's arm. "Come along."

His lips twitching, Father drawled, "I'll wait for you with Alaric and Diana, Caro."

Mel swallowed a sigh as Mother handed his plate to a servant then tugged him across the ballroom. With Aragon and Hawke happily married, she'd only him to focus her considerable attention on, at least until her unborn grandchildren were of marriageable age. Not that her matchmaking attempts would succeed with him. He smiled at Mother. "I'll gladly dance with you or one of my cousins."

Mother continued drawing him across the ballroom. "You really must dance with ladies besides family. How about someone almost family who's known you her entire life?"

He stiffened. Now that Wren had finally married Hawke, 'twas only one other lady that could describe—Kit. And he couldn't dance with *her*. Seeing her across the ballroom was bad enough.

But before he could protest, Mother halted beside Kit and the Duke of Oakmoor, who were now alone. Mother grinned at them. "Why have you two spent most of the evening talking? I can't have court gossiping that the fashionable Countess of Blaine and Duke of Oakmoor hardly danced at my Longnight ball."

As Kit tensed, the duke flashed a smooth smile then replied, "We can't dance together again without gossip flaring, but we prefer enjoying your ball together."

Mother grasped the Duke of Oakmoor's arm. "That shall engender almost as much gossip. Come along, I believe Lady Juliet just arrived." She added over her shoulder, "Mel, you dance with Kit."

While Mother drew the Duke of Oakmoor across the ballroom, Mel and Kit stared at each other, and his heart quickened as her smoky eyes darkened. He shouldn't be eager to dance with the cruel lady she'd proved to be. Then the next Longnight reel began, and he extended his hand. "Shall we?"

Kit's full lips tightened. Was she about to blurt a nonsensical protest like she had at Mother's fete to celebrate Aragon and Selena's child several months ago? To avoid dancing with him, she'd said she didn't think priests danced, when she knew very well he did—she'd seen him dancing at some court events, like Selena's presentation ball. He'd dismissed her protest, and they'd danced together for the first time. A dance he'd enjoyed too much.

Not accepting his hand, Kit lifted her chin. "We don't need to dance."

He leaned toward Kit. Why did she never want to dance with him? Because he was a humble priest with little influence? Or because he reminded her of her futile attempts to sabotage Hawke and Wren's love? "It shall cause gossip if we don't."

Kit tossed her head, her sable hair gleaming in the bright witchlights. "You're a priest. You don't care about gossip."

Mel shrugged. His voice hardening, he replied, "True, but the fashionable Countess of Blaine does." It seemed *all* Kit cared about sometimes.

Kit paled but accepted his hand at last. "Fine. But only if we form a set with the Duke of Oakmoor and Lady Juliet."

He escorted Kit to the floor, and they formed a set with the duke and the royal witch, who were already quarreling. When he and Kit linked arms and spun, her delectable cinnaspice scent surrounded him. He swallowed, his pulse racing. Like her crimson ballgown, 'twas reminiscent of Goddess laurels and tempted him to draw her closer. But that wasn't appropriate, especially with a grasping court lady who only cared about herself.

Instead, he inhaled to settle his pulse then gritted a smile and asked, "So what are your plans for Longnight?"

CHAPTER 3

*B*linking at Mel's question, Kit eyed him as they spun. Was he asking about her Longnight plans because he'd forgiven her wickedness and truly wished to know? Or was he asking to be polite? Her chest twisted at his tight smile. No, he'd not forgiven her. She forced herself to smirk and drawl despite the Longnight reel's bouncing steps, "I'm attending the *many* events at court. Sadly, no one is hosting any events on Longnight itself, so I must spend it with Edouard and Elise like usual."

Mel shook his head, coal-brown hair tumbling against his brow. "There's more to life than attending court and being fashionable."

She almost snorted. For him, perhaps. But she wasn't worthy enough for anything else, and she'd no right pretending to be better than she was. She deepened her smirk. "I suppose *you're* visiting the poor or some such. How noble."

Before Mel could reply, they separated and danced with their opposite partner. Mel's gaze pressing her, she made herself beam and flutter her lashes at the Duke of Oakmoor.

However, unlike during their earlier reels, the duke merely responded with a faint smile, and he didn't pull her against him as they spun. He must be irritated that Mel's mother had forced him to dance with the royal witch. According to court gossip, the two had never gotten along since Lady Juliet had arrived at court thirteen years ago to create then-Prince Devon's protection charm for King Sarastor.

Not wasting her breath attempting to talk during the vigorous reel, Kit kept silently flirting with the duke. She must continue acting the perfect court lady in order to catch him. Then the Longnight reel changed again, and she and the duke returned to their original partners.

His smile not warming his deep-brown eyes, Mel stared down at her while they danced. "You must contact me to perform your wedding ceremony if the Duke of Oakmoor proposes. I've performed all the family weddings since Elise's two years ago."

Kit tensed. Having the gentleman she'd loved as a girl marry her to another wouldn't be distressing at all. Not that Mel knew, or cared, about that. She tossed her head. "Perhaps. Although the high priest of Calatini would be more appropriate, considering the duke's status and position on the council."

Their Longnight reel ended, and Mel bent a brief bow. "As you like, Lady Blaine."

As he strode away, she turned toward the Duke of Oakmoor with a beam, but the duke was glowering after Lady Juliet and failed to notice. Wonderful.

After a moment, the duke's glower cleared, and he smiled at Kit while taking her arm. "Shall we fetch some refreshments after our reel?"

Kit nodded, and as they crossed the ballroom, she glanced toward Mel, who was speaking with his parents rather than devouring another plate of Longnight desserts. Then he turned and hurried from the ballroom. After all, he'd important duties to handle tomorrow—he oversaw all of Ormas's almskitchens, the charity kitchens priests ran in cities to give free meals to any who asked. Fitting for someone who'd visited poor villagers as a boy to give them food and clothes.

When the Duke of Oakmoor handed her a mug of spiced cider, she made herself turn from Mel and beam at the duke again. She and the duke spent the rest of the Longnight ball circulating and didn't dance again. They finally left once three-quarters of the other guests had departed.

As on the ride there, the duke helped her into his carriage then sat with his arm about her shoulders, and she leaned into his embrace despite her quivering stomach. Please let him have forgotten about almost kissing her. To fill the silence, she asked, "What did you think of the Duchess of Childes's Longnight ball?"

Humming, the Duke of Oakmoor threaded his fingers through hers. "Interesting, although I still believe you could do better. Would you like to prove it by acting as my hostess at the charity luncheon I'm hosting the day after Longnight?"

Kit smiled as her heart quickened. The day after Longnight was about charity, so the duke hosting a charity luncheon then was fitting. Although 'twould be challenging too since servants never worked that day and stayed home with their families. Yet hosting a charity luncheon for court was an act of charity even an unworthy lady like her could manage. Plus, she was already familiar with Oakmoor House since she'd acted as the duke's hostess for his soiree soon after he'd begun escorting her to court events.

She squeezed the duke's hand. "I'd love to act as hostess for your charity luncheon."

The Duke of Oakmoor chuckled. "Perfect. We make an excellent team, you and me. Perhaps we should consider making our alliance permanent."

Kit swallowed, her pulse pounding in her throat. Dear Goddess, was that a proposal? 'Twas what she'd pursued the past month, yet now... She stared at her dim reflection in the carriage window. If only she could leap outside into the frigid, black night rather than answer yes. But she must marry someone. Dowagers, especially ones whose stepchildren didn't like them, had little security once their late husband's heir married. Some even returned to their father's house—although she *never* would.

Suppressing a shudder at living with Father and his drunken cruelty again, she caressed the duke's palm with her thumb. "I'd be interested in a permanent alliance with you, your grace."

His grin hungry, the duke drew her into his lap. "But first..."

She froze. Oh, Goddess; oh, Goddess. He truly meant to kiss her this time. Her stomach roiled. She couldn't deny him after all her flirting. Hopefully, 'twouldn't last long.

The Duke of Oakmoor bent his head and captured her lips in a soft kiss. No doubt he was an expert given his many affairs. Yet she had to force herself to remain still and not shove his chest and jerk free. As the duke's kiss continued, his sandalwood scent stung her nose, and her lungs burned since she couldn't relax enough to breathe. Please let him stop soon.

Eventually, the duke drew back with a faint frown furrowing his brow. His eyes narrowing, he scrutinized her. "Are you suffering a megrim?"

Making herself breathe, Kit fluttered her lashes at the duke. She must assuage his concern about that kiss. Otherwise, a gentleman as passionate as the duke would never marry her. "Just drained from the Longnight reels and by the late hour."

The duke kept scrutinizing her for a torturous moment, then he smiled and drew her against his chest. "You must rest then."

Swallowing, she remained limp in the duke's embrace while he rubbed her back. Telling him she'd rather sit alone would only reawaken his suspicions. As his heart thundered in her ear, tears pricked her eyes. Like with Lord Blaine, she'd frozen as if under a stone spell when the duke had kissed her. Why couldn't she react like a normal lady? What was wrong with her?

She almost snorted. At least 'twas one thing Father had been mistaken about. She was nothing like her "whore of a mother" who Father insinuated had seduced him into marriage. She couldn't even manage to enjoy a mere kiss with the greatest rake-hell in Ormas.

When the carriage halted at Blaine House, Kit exhaled and slid from the Duke of Oakmoor's lap.

As she was about to alight, the duke grasped her wrist then pressed a kiss against her palm. "I'll fetch you after dinner tomorrow—tonight, rather—for the Nolans' Longnight charity auction."

She inclined her head. "Until then."

Before the duke could reply, Kit escaped into Blaine House. Thankfully, Edouard had left the Longnight ball an hour before, so he was probably already abed. Otherwise, he'd surely comment on her disquiet. And she couldn't handle that right now.

RISING EARLY despite her late evening, Kit had Willa help her into a favorite morning dress of deep rose wool then sashayed downstairs. The breakfast room was empty when she entered. Good, a few moments of peace. She took some bacon before filling a bowl full of porridge and seasoning it with cinnaspice, honey, and dried apples. Then she poured herself cinnaspice tea and stirred in a spoonful of honey.

She exhaled as she sipped her cinnaspice tea and inhaled its fragrant steam. Goddess, so delicious. She smiled into her cup. She adored cinnaspice more than Mel adored desserts. A love she'd discovered thanks to her dear husband. Lord Blaine had noticed how she enjoyed spiced cider, so their first Longnight together, he'd given her every cinnaspice gift he could find—tea, candies, seasoning, soap, and scent. That had been the best and most thoughtful Longnight gift anyone had ever given her. Six years later, she still used those cinnaspice items every day.

After her first cup of cinnaspice tea, she poured herself another then began her bacon and apple-cinnaspice porridge.

She was almost finished when Edouard strode into the breakfast room.

Edouard nodded at her without speaking then poured himself a brimming cup of kahve before filling his plate with eggs, beefsteak, and tubers. Her stepson didn't enjoy mornings. He didn't even talk to his beloved twin until after his first cup of kahve. So she and Edouard remained silent as she finished her porridge.

Once Edouard began his second cup of kahve, Kit smiled at him over her cinnaspice tea. "Did you enjoy the duchess's Longnight ball?"

Edouard grinned despite the early hour. "Very much. Dancing reels with Pippa is incredible."

A pang darted through Kit as she sipped her cinnaspice tea. Edouard was so in love with Pippa. He was definitely his father's son—Lord Blaine had been the same about Edouard and Elise's mother. Pippa was a fortunate lady. Kit nodded at Edouard. "I noticed you two spent most of the ball together. How soon until you propose?"

Edouard grimaced into his kahve. "Not as soon as I'd like." Drinking his kahve, he eyed Kit. "I noticed *you* spent the entire ball with the Duke of Oakmoor. How soon until the aging rakehell proposes or makes you his mistress?"

Kit almost snorted. "If the duke wanted me as his mistress, he'd have attempted to do so long before now." Not that his attempts would have succeeded with her since she couldn't even kiss him without freezing. "And he obliquely proposed last night. So don't fret; I'll be another's problem soon enough."

Smiling, Edouard set down his kahve and began eating. "Good." He shuddered. "Your ability to spend money is astounding."

She tossed her head. Not that complaint again. "I only spend the generous allowance your father provided me in his will."

Edouard pointed his fork at her. "Yes, but you spend every last coin."

Kit lifted a shoulder. True, although not entirely as Edouard assumed, and she'd never spend so much if he hadn't plenty of funds. "Are you saying your estate can't afford it?"

Frowning, Edouard devoured his beefsteak. "Of course it can. But you should be more prudent with money." He snorted. "And keep better track of it. My bookkeeper and I were reviewing the accounts recently, and none of your receipts match your expenses."

She stilled. So Edouard had finally noticed that. Although wealthy after marrying Lord Blaine, she'd been unable to forget a lifetime of parsimony. She'd proudly attempted to return her excess allowance to Lord Blaine, but he'd just shook his head and told her 'twas hers. She'd hired a young bookkeeper willing to work for reduced rates and had him anonymously donate her excess allowance to charities. She still did so, yet she'd never told anyone, not even Lord Blaine. Telling anyone would be tantamount to boasting how worthy she was, which she wasn't. A worthy lady would donate *all* her allowance to charities rather than merely the excess. Besides, the fashionable Countess of Blaine had a reputation to maintain.

She made herself flash a blinding smile and sip her cinnaspice tea. "Nonsense. No doubt 'tis just an accounting error."

Edouard raised his eyes skyward. "Precisely my point. How Father could have wed a lady as frivolous as you, I'll never understand."

Clinging to her smile, Kit shrugged. 'Twas *good* the Duke of Oakmoor was so close to proposing. She simply must learn to accept his kisses—and more—without freezing.

Before her argument with Edouard could continue, Elise breezed into the breakfast room with a grin. "Morning!"

As Edouard sighed like always at his twin's exuberance during breakfast, Kit hid her smile behind her cup. Unlike Edouard, Elise adored mornings and always rose early. Opportune since her husband Lord Farson did too. Every morning,

Lord Farson rose just after dawn to go riding, often with Elise and their ward Arvan joining him. Yet once or twice a week, Elise ate breakfast with Edouard instead to give Lord Farson and the young Duke of Golddell time alone as well as spend time with her twin.

Edouard sipped his kahve while Elise sat beside him with a plate of eggs, bacon, and several slices of toast. He asked, "How are Farson and Arvan?"

Elise chuckled as she slathered butter on her toast. In addition to mornings, she adored bread, especially with butter. "Congratulating themselves on their cleverness. They 'convinced' me to remain home since 'twas 'too cold for ladies' so they could visit shops after their ride to purchase Longnight gifts for me."

Her throat aching, Kit finished her cinnaspice tea. Elise was fortunate that the gentlemen in her life loved her enough to play such tricks. But Elise deserved such happiness. She was gracious to everyone, even the younger lady who'd enticed her father into marriage. She'd make a wonderful mother once she and Lord Farson finally had children.

Edouard arched a brow at Elise. "How do you know Farson and Arvan's plans?"

Smiling, Elise nibbled on her buttered toast. "The usual way. Seanian's valet told my maid so I could go along with Seanian and Arvan's ruse." She turned to Kit. "The Duchess of Childes's Longnight ball last night was such fun, and your ballgown was stunning."

Edouard snorted. "Expensive, more like."

Kit smirked at him. Although not as much as he assumed, thanks to her secret agreement with Celeste. Her maid Willa was Celeste's daughter, and she'd ensured that Celeste's artistry had caught the duchess's eye, making Celeste the most sought-after dressmaker in Ormas. So Celeste charged her significantly less than her other patrons. She shrugged. "All fashionable ballgowns are expensive."

Elise nodded, her grin as bright as her blonde hair. "Mine

certainly was. But that also means my maid earns more when she sells it after I give it to her." 'Twas how most ladies, including Kit, disposed of their old gowns.

Edouard sighed. "True enough, I suppose."

Smiling at Kit, Elise leaned forward. "I saw the Duke of Oakmoor stuck close to you last night. Does he intend to escort you to the Nolans' charity auction tonight as well?"

Kit smiled back, warmed by Elise's interest. "Yes, he's fetching me after dinner."

Elise nibbled her second slice of toast. "How exciting. The Duke of Oakmoor has never attended to an eligible lady so closely before. He *must* be ready to propose." She beamed at Kit. "Don't worry about his rakehell past overmuch. Seanian has served on the council with the duke for years and says he's more serious than he pretends. Once the duke falls in love at last, he'll make an excellent husband."

Kit swallowed. Surely the Duke of Oakmoor didn't seek love from her, just an heir and a wife who ignored his affairs. 'Twas why she settled on him, in addition to his wealth and influence. She'd never risk loving anyone again—love had only made her vulnerable and foolish.

She rose before Elise could encourage her further. "Yes, the Duke of Oakmoor is perfect for me. I'll leave you and Edouard alone to talk. Until later."

Then she sashayed from the breakfast room to prepare for seeing the duke tonight. Somehow, she must counteract her frigid reaction to his kiss. Hopefully, without encouraging another.

CHAPTER 4

The morning after Mother's Longnight ball, Mel attended Lauds at dawn and organized help for Ormas's almskitchens before eating breakfast. Then he returned to his chambers to finish his plans for the almskitchens over the Longnight season. He was about to open his door when his married friends Deacon and Sarah left their chambers across the hall. Most of his neighbors were married because this wing of the Great Temple's priest quarters had housing with multiple rooms. He only lived here because High Priest Theodag, who led all the priests in Calatini, insisted the son of a wealthy and influential duke needed more than a single room.

Sarah smiled at Mel. Like him, she was a community priest, the most common type of priest, so she also wore priest robes with brown trim. Yet instead of the almskitchens, she served at a prayer house called Peaceful Minds, which was fitting given her tranquil demeanor and soothing voice. She asked, "So how was your mother's Longnight ball?"

Mel almost sighed as dancing with Kit and her flirting with the Duke of Oakmoor flashed before him. He made himself return Sarah's smile. "Mother's Longnight ball was very festive—full of Longnight reels, music, and desserts."

Deacon chuckled and straightened his priest robes, which had ivory trim indicating he was a witch priest. He served as a clerk at Charmed Blessings, the holy witch shop that provided magical supplies for worshipping the Goddess. His normally ascetic face creased with laughter, he arched his brows at Mel. "And how many of those desserts did you devour?"

Mel shrugged. "Only several plates. But I left early last night because of my duties here." To deflect his friends from the Longnight ball, he asked, "Are you going to Charmed Blessings and Peaceful Minds?"

Deacon and Sarah both blinked and eyed him. Doubtless they were wondering at his needless question. Then Sarah replied, "Of course."

Nodding at Mel, Deacon took Sarah's arm. "We should go so we're not late. We'll see you at dinner tonight."

When Deacon and Sarah began down the hall, Mel exhaled then slipped inside his chambers and sat at the small table in the center of the room to finish those plans for the almskitchens. They'd little money to spare for frivolities, but some festive decorations and desserts would help make the Longnight season special for the parishioners who needed the almskitchens. He wrote out instructions for street children to create paper snowflakes as decorations this year because the man who'd donated evergreen branches had died recently. Decorations settled, he turned to the desserts the Great Temple prepared for the almskitchens on festival days. Using his list from last year, he jotted down how many Longnight sweet biscuits they'd need for all the almskitchens.

Finishing his plans close to noon, Mel attended Sext in the nave of the main temple and heartily sang the carols praising the Goddess. How he loved caroling—'twas why he always tried to attend Sext, the service that featured mostly hymns. Although since the service was midday, his duties at the almskitchens and family events sometimes prevented him from attending.

After Sext, he proceeded to the dining hall for luncheon. He gave his list of almskitchen Longnight desserts to the head kitchen priestess Esther then ate his heaping bowl of fish chowder. He sighed as he devoured his bread with honey and finished his well-sweetened tea. If only kitchen priests would prepare desserts for every meal. But most priests didn't adore sweets like he did.

Following luncheon, Mel headed to the Great Temple's Center of Learning where he taught two groups of second-year novices about the various charities community priests ran. Since these two groups would end their lessons the day before Longnight, he handed out the novices' rotation of service assignments for the next eleven days. He answered their questions before saying he'd see them for their final lesson. Then he dismissed them, and the novices thundered from the study like a herd of galloping unicorns.

While Mel was gathering his papers to leave, High Priest Theodag strode into the study, his priest robes' gold trim that indicated his rank glittering. He grinned at Mel. "Your novices appear as eager as ever. You've a way of inspiring others to serve those less fortunate."

Mel shrugged. Not always—once Kit had quit visiting poor villagers with him because her father had discovered their visits, he'd never been able to convince her to resume them. A shame since she'd appeared to enjoy their visits, although perhaps that had been an illusion given how she'd hurt Hawke and Wren without remorse. He quirked a wry smile at the high priest. "I can only inspire those that wish to help others, which most novices do, your excellency."

His grin fading, the high priest tsked. "They all should if they wish to become priests. Fortunately, our rigorous training removes most who don't, and the Goddess's approval at our ordination examinations removes the rest."

Mel nodded. Due to both, only around a quarter of novices ever became full priests. Beneficial since many of the failed novices assumed being a priest would be easy because parishioners paid for all their needs.

Another grin illuminating his austere countenance, High Priest Theodag leaned toward Mel. "But a priest possessing the gift for inspiring others should serve the Goddess by more than overseeing Ormas's almskitchens. He should train as my successor so he can oversee all of Calatini's priests once I retire or return to the Goddess."

Mel suppressed a grimace. Not that suggestion again. Since he'd become a full priest three years ago, High Priest Theodag had hinted he should train to become the next high priest of Calatini. And recently, the high priest's suggestions had practically become sermons. Yet Mel had continued to refuse because the Goddess had called him to spread her love through charity, not by leading others.

He sighed but offered the high priest an apologetic smile. "Except the Goddess hasn't called me to become the next high priest of Calatini, and until she does, I must still refuse to train as your successor."

Now frowning, High Priest Theodag shook his head. "Yet you're the most suitable candidate by far. Not only did the Goddess bestow a Goddess laurel apple upon you during your ordination examination, but many of the high priest's duties involve handling court, and since you're an influential duke's son and a third cousin to the king, you'd excel at that."

Mel couldn't help coughing a laugh. "Any skill I have for handling court doubtless comes from Mother, not Father or being Devon's cousin."

The high priest chuckled as well. "True. The Duchess of Childes is a powerful and clever lady." He leaned toward Mel again. "One you've dealt with your entire life, so handling Calatini's court and many priests would be easy for you."

Mel repeated his earlier sigh. Why must High Priest Theodag keep harping about this? He was worse than Mother. To redirect the high priest, he replied, "Perhaps. Tell me, how is Kiera's education initiative progressing?"

Straightening, High Priest Theodag beamed. Since Mel had involved him at Kiera's behest two months ago, the high priest had been eager to help implement her momentous initiative to make basic education mandatory for all children in Calatini. He said, "Ready to start after the Longnight season like we hoped. Nearly all the priests who shall act as teachers have received their books and resources from Lady Kiera's people. And those few still awaiting their materials in the remote regions of Calatini shall receive them within the next week."

Mel smiled. Soon the poor would receive the education they needed to improve their lives. "How marvelous." He nodded at the high priest. "My apologies, but I must return my papers to my chambers before Vespers. Good afternoon, your excellency."

After inclining a slight bow, he strode from the study before High Priest Theodag could mention him becoming the next high priest of Calatini again. He visited his chambers then attended Vespers in the nave of the main temple. The garrulous pulpit priest Fitzwilliam, the high priest's great-nephew, wasn't speaking tonight, so the sermon was brief, as were the liturgical prayers thanking the Goddess. A relief because Vespers preceded dinner during the shorter days since the service was held at sundown.

In the dining hall, Mel fetched dinner then sat near the wall. He was eyeing his Longnight trifle when Deacon and Sarah joined him. He should really eat his regular food first. As he began his stewed chicken with vegetables, he greeted his friends.

Once they'd talked about their days, Deacon smiled at Mel over his half-empty bowl. "This morning, we didn't have time to finish discussing your mother's Longnight ball. Did she attempt to matchmake like you feared?"

Mel swallowed as dancing with Kit flashed before him like it had earlier. He made himself shrug and eat his chicken. "Not exactly, although she did make me dance with Lady Blaine."

Unless among family, he always referred to Kit by her title since her marriage—'twas only proper.

Her laden spoon halfway to her mouth, Sarah stilled and arched her brows. "Having you dance with an eligible widow sounds like matchmaking to me."

Although tensing further, Mel shrugged again as he began his Longnight trifle. He never should have mentioned his concerns about Mother's matchmaking to his friends. They saw it everywhere now. "If so, 'twas futile because Lady Blaine isn't an appropriate wife for a priest. She's too devoted to being fashionable and only considers herself."

Deacon and Sarah traded a glance, then Sarah murmured, "Isn't she the lady who used to visit villagers with you when you two were young?"

Mel jerked a nod. Amazing Sarah remembered that. He'd only mentioned Kit helping once, when first describing those charitable visits to his fellow novices years ago.

Deacon hummed then said, "Surely a lady who would do that wouldn't consider only herself."

Mel gripped his spoon. Except her cruelty toward Hawke and Wren proved she did. "Lady Blaine has changed beyond recognition since we were young." To distract Deacon and Sarah from Kit, he shared what the high priest had told him about Kiera's education initiative, and they discussed that for the rest of dinner.

Yet as they returned to their chambers, Sarah asked, "Shall you attend more court events over the Longnight season?"

Mel grinned. "No, none of my family are hosting events. Although I shall be celebrating Longnight itself with them for once." Something he'd not enjoyed since entering his novitiate.

His parents, Aragon, and Selena usually returned to Childes Castle after the season ended at Harvestfete. Even Hawke and Devon, who both lived in Ormas, visited his family's estate for Longnight, so none of his family remained during the holiday season. Yet because his duties kept him in Ormas, he'd always celebrated Longnight at the Great Temple, only seeing his family through a mirror call. But this year, everyone was still here.

Deacon and Sarah returned his grin, and Deacon replied, "How wonderful." Since Deacon's family lived in Magehaven and Sarah's in Oakmoor, which were farther away than Childes, both of his friends understood his excitement.

After saying good night, Mel entered his chambers then sat at his desk to prepare for tomorrow. He read the reports about today from the many almskitchens. Then he studied his lists of priests and novices helping tomorrow and assigned everyone to an almskitchen. He preferred keeping around half of the staff at each almskitchen the same and half different from day to day.

He leaned back in his chair. Since he didn't have teaching duties in the afternoons, he should visit various almskitchens starting tomorrow. Although the daily reports from the almskitchens helped him oversee them, nothing replaced visiting them in person. And talking with the parishioners there was always illuminating and motivating.

Everything ready for tomorrow, Mel read Zariste's *Practical Applications of Theology* for several hours then went to bed, well before Nocturns at midnight. Since he rose early to organize the almskitchens, he rarely attended that service.

He smiled as he drifted to sleep. Tomorrow would be another full day of serving the Goddess through his various duties, and he'd his first Longnight with family in years to look forward to as well. He was fortunate to be so blessed.

CHAPTER 5

When the Duke of Oakmoor escorted her to the Nolans' Longnight charity auction, Kit coyly smiled at him despite the megrim throbbing behind her left eye. But as the duke began wrapping an arm about her in his carriage, she purred a laugh and slid from his embrace. Then she drawled the excuse she'd devised to prevent further kisses, "Upon reflection, allowing a rakehell of your reputation to take such liberties is *much* too dangerous."

The duke chuckled with a wicked grin. "True, I suppose. Although most widows are freer with their favors."

She sniffed and folded her hands in her lap. He would know —he'd doubtless seduced every fast widow at court. "Well, I'm certainly not one of them. And if I was, I doubt you'd have mentioned making a permanent alliance."

Eyeing her, the Duke of Oakmoor arched a brow. "That depends on if you were free with everyone or just me."

Kit flashed a blinding smile to conceal her tension. "But how would you know the difference?" She arched her brows at the duke. "You want to be certain your heir is yours, don't you?"

The duke inclined his head. "Of course."

She fluttered her lashes at him, exacerbating the throbbing behind her eye. "So 'tis good that I'm not free with my favors."

The Duke of Oakmoor captured her hand and threaded his fingers through hers. "Yes, but I still want a wife who returns my passion."

Kit swallowed and forced herself not to stiffen. A lady who froze at a mere kiss would never return a rakehell's passion. Yet she must marry, and surely she could pretend to enjoy intimacy until she bore the duke an heir. She squeezed his hand. "And so I shall—once we're wed."

The duke laughed and returned her squeeze. "You're a cruel and clever lady, my dear Lady Blaine."

She lifted a shoulder. "You'd not be interested in me if I wasn't." To distract the duke from passion, she said, "I was thinking about your request to act as your hostess. Did you simply want me to greet guests like I did before, or did you want me to plan the luncheon as well?"

Smiling, the Duke of Oakmoor caressed her palm with his thumb. "Plan it so we can enjoy one of your unique and diverting events."

Kit nodded, her megrim sharpening. She'd thought as much. Doing so would be challenging since the duke's charity luncheon was only two weeks away, and everything must be prepared beforehand since the servants wouldn't be working.

As his carriage halted before Nolan House, the duke added, "I'll send you a list of guests tomorrow as well as inform my housekeeper and butler that you'll be contacting them about arrangements."

Then the Duke of Oakmoor escorted her inside to the charity auction. Many from court had donated items, including the duke, Mel's family, and her stepchildren. The bidding was fierce yet full of cheer, although the outrageous prices most items reached made her shudder. She'd rather be thrifty and donate her excess money directly. Yet she'd the Countess of Blaine's reputation to uphold, so she bid on several items either frivolously fashionable or donated by the most influential at court. Thankfully, she didn't win anything she'd bid on, although the duke won several items.

As the duke escorted her home, she said, "Congratulations, your grace, on winning those exquisite paintings and Orandian scrying bowl."

Taking her hand like before, the Duke of Oakmoor inclined his head. "'Twas a worthy cause—Sandlane Orphanage."

Kit hummed. Supporting orphanages like Lady Kiera's had become *remarkably* fashionable since the former orphanage matron had become their future queen. "Do you have a specific cause you wish to support with your charity luncheon?"

The duke studied her with a suave smile. "No, surprise me."

She almost sighed as her megrim throbbed fiercer. Meaning whatever she chose would be a test, just like planning the charity luncheon was. Lovely. Not that she could manage planning anything tonight. But hopefully, her megrim would have faded by tomorrow so she could start.

At Blaine House, the Duke of Oakmoor escorted her inside. "I'll collect you tomorrow for the Escanas' Longnight story evening." He kissed her palm. "Go rest, my lady. You look pale."

Kit suppressed a grimace. Doubtless because her head felt as if an ogre was crushing her skull. However, she simply nodded and said good night. She headed upstairs to her chambers then gulped a megrim tonic before collapsing into bed.

THE FOLLOWING MORNING, Kit rose late due to exhaustion from her vicious megrim. But at least her head no longer throbbed once she woke. When she headed downstairs, Edouard was leaving to fetch Pippa to show her the new piece he'd acquired for the art collection of tenth-century masters his father had started, so Kit enjoyed breakfast alone. After that, she retreated to the morning room to plan the Duke of Oakmoor's charity luncheon. She must be available if anyone called on her.

Eyeing the blank paper on the writing box in her lap, she sipped a cup of cinnaspice tea. What would be diverting enough to amuse court, while still being easy to do without servants? In addition to raising money, it should involve Longnight since the charity luncheon was the following day, which began the second half of the Longnight season.

Kit tapped her pen against her lips. Perhaps when the guests arrived, they should each draw a task for the luncheon, like serving food, pouring drinks, or performing Longnight carols. She should be able to devise enough tasks for everyone, especially if she requested the servants not set the tables and leave the prepared food in the kitchen with a preservation spell to keep everything fresh.

After listing the tasks she could devise quickly, she finished her cinnaspice tea. But how to involve money and amuse court? She straightened. Each guest could pay three gold to receive their task, and if they didn't want that one, they could pay again for another draw. They could also trade tasks with other guests, but the trading guests would each need to pay for that. Once all the tasks were assigned, the guests would serve and eat luncheon then play Longnight games. The guests could be assigned to groups based on their task—she must give each of the groups clever names. To raise additional money and stimulate excitement, the groups could wager on the Longnight games, but the money won would be donated.

Kit smiled as she wrote out her plans. That should raise plenty of money for whatever charity she chose and would be different enough to amuse court. Now what charity should she choose? She poured herself another cup of cinnaspice tea. Although an orphanage would be fashionable, the Countess of Blaine must choose something ahead of fashion. How about Goddess's Refuge, the family refuge on Our Lady's Way? Most at court had probably never heard of the largest family refuge in Ormas, but 'twas a charity she regularly funded because of her childhood with Father.

That evening on the way to the Escanas' Longnight story evening, she described her plans for the charity luncheon to the Duke of Oakmoor then said, "Since the guests shan't have money on them, you and I shall keep track of everyone's donations as well as their tasks to prevent illicit trading."

The duke nodded and kissed her hand. "Sounds perfect. Court shall love it." He arched a brow. "But what made you choose to support Goddess's Refuge?"

Kit shrugged with a blinding smile. She mustn't let the duke realize her support was personal—she'd kept her father and childhood secret from court. And although Mel's and Wren's families would suspect her reasons for supporting the family refuge, they'd not tell anyone. "Everyone is donating to orphanages now, thanks to Lady Kiera. And the poor or veterans are too obvious. This charity is worthy yet original."

The Duke of Oakmoor hummed as the carriage halted at Escana House. "So it is."

The duke escorted her inside, and distracted by the merry reading of Longnight stories, he didn't ask about his charity luncheon or the family refuge again.

OVER THE FOLLOWING WEEK, the Duke of Oakmoor continued escorting Kit to Longnight court events every day. Court was giddy to celebrate Longnight in Ormas for once, so hosts were throwing every Longnight-themed event possible, like caroling, story evenings, pastry feasts, and games parties.

The Longnight merriment dominated the events—until gossip spread that young Lord Morwynne had assumed his mother's position on the council and had her magically confined to their country estate because she'd gone mad. When Kit first heard the gossip, she snorted into her cup of spiced cider despite her pounding megrim. The once Lady Morwynne was mad as a fox, more like. Doubtless the devious and manipulative former councilor had committed a crime that King Devon and Lady Kiera didn't wish to reveal. Kit concealed her smile. She and the erstwhile countess had never gotten along, so they'd not invited each other to their events, which had titillated court gossips. Now, their petty feud had ended without any effort on her part.

Yet the scandalous gossip about Lord Morwynne's mother was eclipsed a few days later by the news that Lady Kiera and the nightmara queen-heir Lady Moonbud would be renewing the Nightmara-Calatini Treaty soon. At long last—the nightmara negotiations had continued months longer than normal, which had begun to worry some at court since the treaty was vital to Calatini's southern defense.

The day after the news about the treaty, Elise hosted a ladies' luncheon celebrating the upcoming nightmara negotiations. Not surprising since her husband Lord Farson was councilor for the Golddell duchy and the nightmara.

As Kit was leaving for Elise's luncheon, Edouard leapt into the carriage after her. Quirking a smile while he settled across from her, he arched a brow. "What, no Duke of Oakmoor?"

She sniffed. "Of course not. Your sister is hosting a *ladies'* luncheon." Which thankfully allowed her respite from flirting with the duke while deflecting his kisses. She narrowed her eyes at Edouard. "Why are *you* attending?"

Grinning, Edouard chuckled and leaned back in his seat. "I'm not, but someone has to keep Farson and Arvan company—as far away from the ladies as possible."

Kit pursed her lips. Edouard wouldn't be almost beaming to see his brother-in-law and the young Duke of Golddell. "Liar. You're attending to see Pippa."

A faint blush darkening his cheeks, Edouard shrugged. "Can't I do both?"

She shrugged despite the pang darting through her. "I suppose." Then she turned to stare out the window. Thank the Goddess she and the Duke of Oakmoor were almost betrothed.

Even if constantly flirting and preventing his kisses wore on her. Surely he'd propose after she successfully hosted his charity luncheon, which she would. Once they were betrothed, perhaps she could convince the duke to have a short betrothal—he was no longer young, after all.

When Edouard escorted Kit inside Golddell House, Pippa was lingering in the entrance hall. Edouard dropped Kit's arm and strode straight to Pippa, who beamed and grasped his extended hands. Those two would doubtless be wed before next season. Please let her and the duke be as well.

Kit made herself sashay past the loving couple to join the other ladies. When she did, she glanced about the drawing room. Who should she join? Not Mel's mother and Lady Keyes—the duchess might quiz her about the Duke of Oakmoor and would see too much. And not Lady Kiera—their future queen was talking with the two remaining female councilors, the Duchess of Wildewall and Lady Ducharme.

Then Kit frowned when she spotted Elise along the far wall with Lord Farson's maternal great-aunt, Lady Gilbert. The elderly lady was thumping her cane while she spoke, and Elise's usually bright smile was brittle. The baroness had doubtless cornered Elise some time ago, so Elise needed rescuing.

Accepting a mug of spiced cider on her way, Kit sashayed toward Elise and Lady Gilbert. As she approached, Lady Gilbert was saying, "...too selfish. They delay doing their duty—"

Before Lady Gilbert could finish her tirade, Kit drawled, "Because duty is so dreadfully dull."

Lady Gilbert scowled at her. "That sort of attitude is precisely the problem." She turned her scowl on Elise. "Doubtless you feel the same."

Elise lifted her chin. "No, but—"

Lady Gilbert thumped her cane. "Then why haven't you born Farson children yet?"

Kit glared at the elderly baroness. Anyone with eyes could

see how Elise yearned for children. To scold her about that was cruel. "Have you asked Lord Farson that?"

Blinking, Lady Gilbert snorted. "Of course not."

Kit smirked back. "Perhaps you should." Lord Farson would blister his great-aunt for tormenting his beloved wife. She threaded her arm through Elise's. "Come, Elise, the Duchess of Childes wanted to speak with you."

As they glided across the drawing room, Elise murmured, "Thanks. Lady Gilbert wouldn't quit lecturing me about children again."

Kit squeezed Elise's arm while they joined the duchess and Lady Keyes. If only she'd wisdom that would hearten Elise. Although even if she did, offering it mightn't be prudent. Advice coming from a childless stepmother several months younger might nettle even the normally gracious Elise.

During their conversation with the duchess and Lady Keyes, a maid brought Elise a note that made her smile like a smug sphinx. After murmuring a reply to the maid, Elise called the ladies to luncheon. Amid many toasts to Lady Kiera, the rest of the luncheon passed smoothly. Even the feuding Lady Greysnowe and Lady Ravenstone didn't quarrel—possibly because Elise had wisely placed them at opposite ends of the dining room.

After luncheon, Kit returned to Blaine House alone since Edouard remained behind with Pippa, who'd never joined the ladies. That evening, the Duke of Oakmoor escorted Kit to the Blakeleys' Longnight soiree, and afterward, her face ached from all her coy smiles and sultry glances. Yet she managed a blinding grin when the duke asked to escort her to the traditional Longnight play the following evening.

When she and the duke arrived for the Longnight play, she purred a laugh at his quip about the crowd before stilling at Mel fetching refreshments directly before them. The duke kept walking, which spurred her forward. But in her haste, she stumbled and dropped the duke's arm then collided with Mel.

Her heart fluttering like it never did for the duke, Kit straightened and stepped back with a polite smile. "Good evening, Priest Melchior. I'm surprised to see you attending such a *frivolous* event."

CHAPTER 6

$\mathcal{H}$is pulse swifter than it should be from Kit stumbling into him, Mel set down the cups of mentha tea he was fetching for Selena and Wren then straightened his priest robes before answering Kit's sardonic quip, "Devon invited me to attend, and the traditional Longnight play about the Goddess choosing her Winter Queen isn't frivolous." Managing a smile, he nodded at her escort. "Good evening, your grace."

The Duke of Oakmoor returned his nod as he recaptured Kit's arm. "Good evening, Priest Melchior. You should attend my charity luncheon the day after Longnight with the rest of your family. We're supporting one of the family refuges you priests run—Goddess's Refuge, I believe—and Lady Blaine is planning my luncheon, so it shall be diverting too."

Mel swallowed. No doubt it would be. Kit had a talent for hosting court events—not that he'd attended many of them, but Mother had described them in thorough detail. His stomach hardened. For Kit to be planning the duke's luncheon, the duke must have proposed. Since Mother hadn't mentioned their betrothal, Kit and the duke must be waiting until the luncheon to announce it. Clinging to his polite smile, he nodded at the duke again. "Thank you for the kind invitation, but I'm usually busy with my duties at the Great Temple the day after Longnight."

Her eyes narrow, Kit purred a laugh and squeezed the Duke of Oakmoor's arm. "I'm afraid Priest Melchior doesn't approve of my events. Too frivolous. He only attends them if they're family events and his mother forces him."

Mel sighed and shook his head. True, but not because of Kit personally. "My duties as a priest don't allow me time to attend many court events, including yours, Lady Blaine." When she sniffed, he added, "I'd gladly attend this one if I could. Not only are your events spectacular, but Goddess's Refuge is a most worthy cause. You chose it, I imagine."

As the duke's brows rose, Kit stiffened but flashed a blinding grin. "Only because 'twas a cause none at court had supported yet."

Frowning, Mel eyed Kit and the duke. She'd not told her betrothed about her unfortunate childhood? Such secrets weren't conducive to a healthy marriage. Was she afraid the duke wouldn't love her if he knew about her past? 'Twasn't as if her degenerate drunkard of a father was her fault—unlike the cruel lie she'd told Wren about Hawke. He made himself smile at Kit. "Regardless of your reason, you chose your charity wisely." He turned to the duke. "I'll send you a donation, even though I can't attend."

The Duke of Oakmoor nodded. "Kind of you. Although I'd expect nothing less from a priest." He drew Kit closer with a warm smile. "Shall we head up to my box? I don't wish to miss any of the Longnight play. I've heard the play's Winter Queen is superb."

Her lips coy, Kit looked up at the duke through her lashes. "Yes, please." Then she and the duke nodded farewell before threading through the crowded theater.

Mel stared after them for a moment then shook himself. He should return to the royal box. He didn't want to miss the play either.

When he strode into the royal box, he blinked. Only his brothers and their wives were there. Devon, Kiera, and Lady Annalise still hadn't arrived yet. Hopefully, they'd arrive before the play began.

Hawke's arm about her shoulders, Wren turned to face him. "Mel, there you are. The crowds downstairs must be hideous. Fetching our tea took ages."

Nestled against Aragon, Selena dimpled. "Except he hasn't any tea. What happened?"

Mel winced. He was a poor brother-in-law for forgetting his pregnant sisters-in-law's tea.

Before he could apologize, Hawke snickered then drawled, "Fetching your tea took so long that Mel got thirsty and drank them."

Aragon shook his head. "Mel would have fetched more if he had." He arched his brows at Mel. "What actually happened?"

Mel suppressed a grimace. This was all Kit's fault. "Someone stumbled into me. While conversing with them, I set down the teacups to repair my appearance, but I forgot your tea after our conversation." He glanced at Selena and Wren. "I'm sorry. Did you want me to fetch some more?"

Chuckling, Selena waved toward the two seats beside her. "No, 'twould take too long." Once he sat, she asked, "Who was this someone who distracted you?"

Thankfully, Lady Annalise gliding into the royal box forestalled his answer. Paler than at the Longnight ball, she sank onto the chair beside him then smiled at Aragon and Selena. "Are you eager to hold your child in your arms?"

Aragon and Selena beamed at each other, then Aragon replied, "Very."

Selena rubbed her vast stomach. "I'm almost as eager to be done being pregnant."

Lady Annalise's cerulean eyes flickered, but before she replied, Devon and Kiera bustled into the box with their guards.

Kiera headed straight to Wren, and after a moment, Aragon rose to talk with Devon, and Lady Annalise joined Wren and Kiera.

Ignoring the other conversations, Selena studied Mel and rubbed her stomach again. "So *who* was it who distracted you? The duchess would be ecstatic if 'twas an eligible lady."

Mel tensed. Kit was no longer eligible, and she'd not distracted him because he wanted to marry her. "Unfortunately for Mother, 'twas merely Kit and the Duke of Oakmoor. Their invitation to his charity luncheon distracted me. Kit arranged to support Goddess's Refuge, but she lied to the duke about why."

Selena hummed and nodded. "Not terribly surprising. Having a vulgar, drunkard father wouldn't enhance Kit's fashionable reputation."

Not letting his hands clench, he leaned toward Selena. "But surely she should tell her betrothed the truth."

Selena's brows rose. "I doubt they're betrothed yet. Kit would have ensured all of court knew about that if they were." She glanced at Aragon and Devon still talking. "I'd better fetch Aragon. The play is about to start."

As Selena waddled away, Mel turned and studied the crowded theater. His gaze was drawn to Kit and the Duke of Oakmoor in the duke's box. They sat so close that she was almost in his lap. Although she didn't mind from the smug and sultry smile curving her lips. Despite Selena's doubts, they *had* to be betrothed, and given the duke's rakehell reputation, he'd probably made love to Kit too.

His jaw tightening, Mel forced himself to face the stage. Soon, everyone returned to their seats, and the Longnight play began with the play's Lady Winter, the future Winter Queen, gliding onstage. As she rescued unloved children across Damensea and gave them a home in her ice palace, she almost appeared a true arctic elf and was as superb as the duke had said. By the time she met the girl playing the Goddess in disguise, Mel was relaxed and smiling.

He chuckled at Lady Winter's bewilderment after the girl completed three tasks that each should have taken a lifetime within three days. The Goddess's works and love were awe-inspiring, even more so when coming from such an unprepossessing girl. He'd have reacted the same if he'd been Lady Winter.

Then Lady Winter questioned the girl, who admitted to being the Goddess before transforming into her adult self in a puff of smoke. Mel peered at the adult player. She appeared remarkably like the girl—either they were related, or the player had been disguised as a girl with an illusion spell. No wonder this Longnight play was called one of the finest in Ormas.

He leaned forward as the Goddess asked Lady Winter to become her first avatar for gifting hope and love to children amid the darkness of winter. Being called in person like that must have been wondrous. Although the Goddess had called him in his heart, he'd never met her in person—most didn't since the gods had ascended to the heavenly plane several millennia ago. Now, gods only manifested in their corporeal form on their holy days, although they rarely did. So the closest he'd come to meeting the Goddess had been her presence suffusing a Goddess laurel at his ordination examination.

He grinned when Lady Winter accepted the Goddess's offer and stepped into a door of light to be reborn as the Winter Queen. Then just after midnight on Longnight morning, the Goddess's first avatar emerged through the same light at the heart of the Great Temple in Oress. She gave the Goddess a butterfly of ice and light representing her deep love and hope, then the Goddess proclaimed her the Winter Queen to the awestruck priests surrounding them.

Uplifted by the magnificent play, Mel said farewell to his family and Lady Annalise then strode to the Moon Chapel of the Great Temple, where Nocturns was held at midnight to celebrate the mysteries of the Goddess. Although he couldn't stay up that late, he spent an hour at the chapel in joyful prayer before heading to bed.

MEL'S CHEER from the Longnight play continued the following two days. He couldn't help his broad smiles as he visited several almskitchens then met with his two groups of novices for their final lesson where they developed plans for their future service work. Not even High Priest Theodag suggesting again that he become the next high priest of Calatini dampened his mood.

Even so, he was relieved when Paul scurried toward him during the high priest's near lecture with a note from Devon. He said farewell to the high priest then returned to his chambers to read Devon's note. Even if commonplace, notes from Calatini's king were best read in private.

Once he did, his brows rose. Devon was asking him to meet at Hawke and Wren's townhouse for dinner? He must want to discuss something secret. But what? Devon and Kiera had been embroiled in several secret situations recently. Kiera's poisoner, Lady Morwynne, had been unearthed and convicted of treason —not that most of court knew 'twas why she'd been magically confined to her family's country estate. The Magehaven ore had been stabilized although not fully counteracted yet, but Mel wasn't a witch who could help resolve that situation. And yesterday, Kiera had negotiated the best treaty with the nightmara that Calatini had ever had.

He hummed. Perhaps Devon wanted to celebrate Kiera's triumph with just family. If so, Mother would be irritated Devon hadn't asked her and Father to host his private celebration. Mother adored hosting events as much as Kit did.

To arrive for dinner on time, Mel didn't attend Vespers. Instead, he prayed his thanks to the Goddess as he strode to Hawke and Wren's townhouse. When he entered their drawing room, Wren was scowling and flushed with Hawke beside her telling Longnight jests, no doubt to calm her.

While Mel sat, Aragon and Selena joined them. Since they appeared alone, Mel asked, "Where are Mother and Father?"

Aragon shook his head. "Devon only invited us."

A dimple quivered in Selena's freckled cheek as they sat near Mel. "We had to tell your parents we were dining in our chambers then slip out the servants' entrance. It reminded me of the lengthy months we were betrothed."

Mel and his brothers chuckled, although Wren leapt upright, her scowl darkening. Pacing along the wall, she gritted, "How *selective* the king has become of his company lately."

As Hawke winced, Mel, Aragon, and Selena stared at Wren. What had made her so furious with Devon? Doubtless it involved Kiera.

Before they could ask, Devon strode into the drawing room, and Wren flew across the room much faster than a pregnant lady should. While everyone gaped at her, she slapped Devon and snarled, "How dare you never tell Kiera you loved her and truly wished to marry her? As soon as I can hold a pen without breaking it, I'm starting that satiric play about you I promised if you hurt her."

Mel exchanged a wide glance with Aragon and Selena as Hawke captured Wren and drew her against his chest. Quiet and kind, Wren was never violent—not even to Kit, who'd cruelly lied to her about kissing Hawke.

Devon held up his hands. "I know I should have told Kiera, but I was afraid she'd flee if she knew our betrothal wasn't just to negotiate with the nightmara. I thought showing her my love would convince her I was sincere. Although I *never* imagined she'd flee in the middle of the night as soon as she renewed the nightmara treaty. But I've a plan to fix that."

Mel blinked. Kiera had thought her betrothal to Devon was fake? No wonder Wren was upset for her friend. He frowned. But how could Kiera believe that? She and Devon were so perfect together, even if she'd once been a poor orphanage matron of common birth. Plus, the nightmara had accepted her, and with their power over the dreams and the mind, they'd never accept a fake future queen.

Hawke still restraining her, Wren humphed and crossed her arms. "Explain, *your majesty*."

Devon gestured toward the dining room and flashed a beseeching smile. "How about we eat first?"

Mel nodded along with everyone but Wren. Food should calm the furious pregnant lady. After a delectable dinner where he and Wren split an entire Longnight trifle, they all returned to the drawing room.

Sitting beside Aragon and across the room from Wren, Devon sighed and said, "My plan to convince Kiera to return and marry me is to confess everything, tell her I love her, then beg her to marry me in a bloodbinding on Longnight."

As Wren relaxed and began to smile, Mel gaped at Devon then asked, "Longnight as in tomorrow or next year?"

Devon lifted a shoulder. "Tomorrow afternoon. Would you mind officiating the wedding ceremony here?"

Mel nodded. "Of course not." Although if High Priest Theodag found out, he'd *insist* Mel become his successor after wedding the king and queen. 'Twas usually the privilege of the high priest of Calatini.

Devon beamed and turned to the others. "Could the rest of you act as our witnesses?"

After everyone nodded, Wren shifted in her seat beside Hawke, her face scarlet. "I apologize for slapping you, your majesty. Violence is wrong, and I've never resorted to it before, but I was so furious for Kiera, and pregnancy has made me... volatile, it seems."

His smile gracious yet wry, Devon shook his head. "I can understand your fury on Kiera's behalf, especially after I swore I'd not hurt her." He grinned at Wren. "Now enough about that; let's discuss the details for tomorrow."

Once they finalized everything for the secret royal wedding

ceremony, Mel hurried back to the Great Temple with a grin. Tomorrow would be a most exciting Longnight. Even more than he'd imagined at the start of the Longnight season. Perhaps one day he'd be as fortunate as his brothers and Devon.

CHAPTER 7

In the dark and silent hours after midnight on Longnight morning, Kit jerked awake from a nightmare about Father slapping her and sneering that she was a whore unworthy of marrying any gentleman. Her eyes still shut, she shuddered and rubbed her face. A coalescence of Father's cruelty over the years, doubtless inspired by her upcoming betrothal to the Duke of Oakmoor. What a perfect way to begin the new year. Hopefully, she could return to sleep—otherwise, she'd likely suffer a megrim later.

Then the air in her chambers stirred. Surely not Willa since even the most diligent maid was asleep at this hour. She opened her eyes and suppressed a scream.

Four ladies were peering down at her in a circle around her bed. Although her chambers were dark, the ladies were wreathed in light, and their presence almost hummed in the silence. One lady was a radiant arctic elf with fathomless blue eyes and a waterfall of white hair. The next was a smiling lady with kind green eyes and sleek blonde hair arranged in a loose chignon. The third was an intense lady wearing trousers who had glowing gold eyes and spiky brown hair. The final was a spirited lady with dark-brown skin, piercing brown eyes, and black hair tied in many tiny braids.

Gaping at the four glowing ladies above her, Kit swallowed. "Who—who are you?"

The lady wearing trousers snickered, although the others merely tsked. Then the smiling lady shook her head and replied, "For such a devout little one, you don't remember your lore, do you?"

Kit snapped her gaping mouth shut. Devout? She wasn't devout. A pang darted through her. Not since she was twelve when Father had made her see her dream was impossible because she wasn't worthy enough.

Quirking a smile, the arctic elf leaned closer. "Forgetting the truth happens to mortals sometimes when they ignore the calling."

Her skin prickling at their intense stares, Kit blinked at the ladies. The calling?

The dark-skinned lady bobbed a nod. "Yes, it twists them. I would know."

Kit began to glare. Must the mysterious ladies be so cryptic?

Cocking her head, the lady wearing trousers eyed Kit. "People would be much better off if they boldly pursued their calling."

Kit set her jaw. Enough of this. Leaping from bed, she strode across her chambers then swirled to face the ladies with her hands fisted on her hips. "*What* are you talking about?"

The four ladies swept after her and circled her again. As the dark-skinned lady waved her hand and witchlights illuminated the room, the arctic elf smiled at Kit and asked, "What day is today?"

Kit frowned. How did that answer her question? "Longnight."

The smiling lady chuckled, her green eyes gleaming. "And what *type* of day is that?"

Kit frowned harder. What did that matter? "One of the four festivals of the Goddess."

Behind her, the lady wearing trousers snorted. "And *who* can appear on those days?"

Kit whirled to face the sardonic lady. Did she mean...? Kit eyed the lady wearing trousers closer—given her coloring and swooping movements, she *could* be a were-eagle. Kit turned and glanced at the other ladies again. The first *was* an arctic elf, while the others could be a soul healer and a spirit witch. And all of their coloring and dispositions matched that from religious lore. But why would *they* bother visiting her?

Laughter curving her lips, the dark-skinned lady arched her brows. "Now do you realize who we are?"

Swallowing, Kit nodded as her hands fell to her sides. "You're the Goddess's female avatars." She faced the arctic elf. "The Winter Queen." She faced the smiling lady, doubtless the soul healer. "The Spring Queen." She faced the were-eagle wearing trousers. "The Summer Queen." She faced the dark-skinned lady, who must be the spirit witch. "And the Autumn Queen."

The Spring Queen beamed. "You remember your lore, after all. I knew you would."

As the Winter Queen nodded, the Summer Queen snickered behind Kit. "You two are such optimists. I didn't think she'd ever understand."

The Winter Queen and Spring Queen narrowed their eyes at the Summer Queen, but the Autumn Queen laughed and said, "Only because you've no patience."

Her head whirling, Kit stared at the Goddess's female avatars. Were they bantering like ordinary ladies? She gulped a breath. If only she could sit down without them towering over her. She stiffened her spine. No, she mustn't reveal such vulnerability. She crossed her arms over her chest. "Now that I know who you are, why are you *here*?"

The four avatars glided closer until they completely surrounded

Kit. Then the Winter Queen cupped Kit's cheek, her hand as warm as her gentle smile. How unexpected. The Winter Queen said, "The Goddess sent us because you've strayed from your path."

The Autumn Queen nodded. "So you've not become who you were meant to be."

Kit stiffened and recoiled from the Winter Queen's hand. She'd become the best an unworthy lady could be. "What are you talking about?"

The Spring Queen touched Kit's chest above her heart. "If you think about it here, you'll know."

As Kit recoiled again, the Summer Queen sighed behind her and asked, "Could we get on with casting the Goddess's blessing?"

The other avatars nodded. They all linked hands, and a white glow appeared about Kit as the fragrance of cinnaspice and apples perfumed the air. Humming, they began circling around her, and the glow brightened and fragrance thickened. During their third circle, Kit shut her eyes against the blinding light and dizzily gulped the heavy cinnaspice-apple air. Then the light piercing her eyelids flared before it and the fragrance vanished, and the four avatars quit humming.

A smile in her voice, the Autumn Queen said, "You can open your eyes, Kit. Your blessing is cast."

Kit did and glanced at the three avatars she could see. They were no longer holding hands, but they still closely surrounded her. She swallowed and asked, "What did you do?"

The Summer Queen swooped across Kit's chambers and turned the cheval mirror to face her. "This."

Kit yelped at the crone reflected there. 'Twas no blessing! She desperately patted her face and hair, and although they felt as young as ever, the crone in the mirror did likewise. The avatars must have cast an illusion making her appear ancient and ugly. "Change me back!"

As the Summer Queen rejoined her fellow avatars, the Spring

Queen patted Kit's shoulder and said, "You shall when you become who you're meant to be."

Whirling away from her hideous reflection, Kit blinked back the tears burning her eyes. She was nothing without her youth and sultry beauty. How could she entice anyone into marrying her now, especially a suave rakehell like the Duke of Oakmoor? She glared at the Goddess's avatars. "I *am* who I'm meant to be." Except for the missing husband.

The four avatars laughed. Then the Winter Goddess smiled at Kit and replied, "If you were, the Goddess wouldn't have sent us."

Kit clasped her hands together above her chest. Somehow she must convince them to give her back her normal appearance. "I beg you; please, *please* revoke this curse."

The Autumn Queen shook her head, her tiny braids flying. "Only you can do that by becoming who you're meant to be."

Kit swallowed as her tears burst free and scalded her cheeks. "I don't understand."

The Spring Queen beamed at her. "Listen to your heart, and the Goddess shall guide you."

Her blue eyes gentle, the Winter Queen kissed Kit's forehead. "You have all you need, my child."

As the Winter Queen stepped back, the Summer Queen clapped Kit's shoulder and added, "Simply remember to be bold and believe in yourself."

Kit glared at the four avatars. She believed in herself just fine. Some things were impossible, no matter how much you wanted them. Although they probably couldn't remember that—they'd left behind their mortal flaws behind millennia ago when they'd been reborn as the Goddess's avatars.

But before she could protest further, the four avatars smiled at her again then vanished. And the witchlights the Autumn Queen had cast vanished with them.

Blinking at the sudden darkness, Kit stumbled over to her dressing table and managed to light the lantern there. She sank into her dressing chair then held her hand mirror before her face. She shuddered. Definitely hideous. No one here or at court could *ever* see her like this.

She set the mirror face down on the dressing table. What was she to do? She couldn't sequester herself in her chambers until she broke the curse. Willa would eventually see her and insist on involving Edouard. Kit snorted. How Edouard would laugh to see the stepmother he disliked like this. He'd say that her face finally matched her character.

She nibbled her lip. She must leave Blaine House. But where could she go? Looking like this, she couldn't access her allowance as Lady Blaine. And even if she could, her generous allowance wouldn't extend to renting a townhouse in Ormas. That meant she must stay with someone, but who? None of Lady Blaine's coterie were genuine friends—if they agreed to help, they'd merely gossip about her at court.

Kit sagged and rubbed her chest. The only ones who'd ever been truly kind to her had been Mel's and Wren's families. Any of them would shelter her if she asked and not tell anyone. She winced. Yet how could she reveal her haggish appearance to the always elegant duchess and the oh-so-perfect Wren? So she couldn't stay with them.

She gulped a breath. But what about Mel? He *was* a priest and always eager to help those less fortunate. Although he'd not forgiven her wickedness toward Wren and Hawke, he'd surely shelter her and help break her curse. Her lips twisted. And as her childhood attempts to flirt with him had proved, he didn't care a whit about her appearance.

Kit straightened. She'd head for the Great Temple after breakfast. But first, she must prepare and get some more sleep to prevent a megrim. She rose and locked her door to stop Willa from entering. Then she began to pack. She packed her megrim tonic as well as her cinnaspice scent and soap—no one would believe she'd left willingly without them, and she'd need them in the coming days. She hunted in her wardrobe for suitable clothes, but her gowns were much too ostentatious for a crone, although she did pack her simplest arachne silk gown since she could turn it any color. Yet with its magical luster and flattering cut, wearing that every day would attract notice. Fortunately, Willa was about the same size, so she could request several of Willa's dresses to wear most days.

Packed except for her maid's dresses, she began writing out notes to arrange her sojourn. She wrote to Edouard requesting her allowance be sent to her bookkeeper. Then she wrote to her bookkeeper asking her allowance all be donated to the usual charities, except for Willa's wages. Finally, she wrote to the Duke of Oakmoor providing instructions for his charity luncheon and explaining that urgent business had called her away but she'd return soon. She grimaced. Her note wouldn't prevent the duke from pursuing another lady as his wife, but maybe she'd break the curse before he settled on anyone.

Everything prepared, she doused her lantern and crawled into bed. Wrapping her covers about herself, she drifted into a fitful slumber. She woke hours later when Willa rattled her door and called, "My lady, your door is locked. Are you all right?"

Squinting at the winter light streaming through her windows, Kit rubbed her eyes. She'd slept much later than she'd expected. Perhaps that meant she'd not suffer a megrim from lack of sleep. She exhaled. She'd best calm Willa before her maid alerted the entire household. Thankfully, like her physical self, her voice remained unchanged by the Goddess's illusion. "I'm fine, Willa. I simply wanted time alone to celebrate Longnight. Could you fetch me a breakfast tray and leave it outside my door?"

Once Willa left, Kit slid from bed then prepared to dress. At her maid's return, she said, "I must leave to tend some unexpected business, but all of my gowns are too elaborate. Could you bring me several of yours?"

After a long pause, Willa replied through the door, "Of course. How many should I pack for myself?"

Kit sighed. "Unfortunately, you can't join me. Visit Celeste while I'm away." Staying with her mother should keep Willa occupied. "My bookkeeper knows to send your wages there until I return."

Her voice worried, Willa asked, "Are you certain I can't join you, my lady?"

Kit grimaced. Willa would be horrified if she saw the crone illusion afflicting her once gorgeous mistress. "Yes, I must go alone. But don't fret; I'll be fine." She knew how to take care of herself thanks to her childhood without a maid because Father had always drunk and gambled away all their money. As Willa sighed but began to leave, Kit said, "I'll have some notes for you to post when you return. And could you pack my extra megrim tonic as well as my cinnaspice tea, seasoning, and candies?"

After Willa agreed and left again, Kit cracked open her door then checked no one was watching before grabbing her breakfast tray and leaving her notes for Willa. She devoured all her breakfast then paced while waiting for Willa to return. Once Willa did, Kit thanked her and told her to enjoy her stay with Celeste. Then she dressed and packed the other dresses and cinnaspice items Willa had brought before donning a warm black cloak and slipping from Blaine House through the servants' entrance.

Until she was away from the fashionable areas near the palace, she kept her head lowered and ensured her cloak completely covered her face. No one must see her and guess she was Lady Blaine.

At the Great Temple, she rapped on the discreet wooden door to the priest quarters. Please let Mel be here and not out visiting the almskitchens or his family.

The view panel slid open, and suspicious eyes peered at her through the slim opening. "Yes?"

Kit swallowed. "I'm here to see Priest Melchior Hawke." When the priest acting as porter snorted, she blurted, "Tell him 'tis Kit."

The priest's eyes narrowed. "You'll have to wait. He's out."

As the panel slammed closed, she bit back a protest. Clearly, the porter wouldn't listen. No doubt he assumed she was one of the poor from the almskitchens seeking to thank Mel. She'd just have to wait until Mel returned.

Kit wrapped her cloak tighter to keep herself warm then settled on her bag to wait. Hopefully, Mel would return soon.

CHAPTER 8

After Lauds, organizing the almskitchens, and breakfast, Mel strode to his family's townhouse to join them for Longnight. Yesterday evening, Mother had sent a note asking him to act as their first-foot, the first Longnight visitor who arrived around midmorning with traditional gifts to bring good fortune for the year. Mother had even sent him the first-foot gifts, writing that he likely wouldn't have time to get them himself. Which he hadn't.

When Perkins opened the door with a grin on his usually formal face, Mel wished the longtime family butler happy Longnight before joining everyone in the drawing room. His parents, their best friends Wren's parents, Aragon, and Selena were sitting and laughing around the winter palace, an enchanted ice sculpture that held the small Longnight gifts they'd exchange. "Happy Longnight." After everyone echoed him, he asked, "Where are Hawke and Wren?" Devon was doubtless at the orphanage with Kiera.

Mother and Wren's mother Lady Keyes beamed at each other, then Mother replied, "At the orphanage. We'll join them at their townhouse in the afternoon for Devon and Kiera's wedding ceremony."

Suppressing a laugh, Mel traded a wry grin with Aragon. Not surprising Mother had already discovered that and insisted on attending. She'd always treated Devon like a beloved nephew —except she'd not dared to matchmake the king like she had Aragon and Hawke.

Father arched his brows at Mel. "Why don't you pass out the first-foot gifts before your mother begins rhapsodizing about the wedding ceremony?"

Wren's father Sir Alaric chuckled. "Otherwise we'll never have time to eat our Longnight feast before heading to the orphanage, and I'm famished."

As Mother and Lady Keyes narrowed their eyes at their teasing husbands, Mel smiled and began extracting first-foot gifts from his satchel. He handed Mother the jar of salt, Father the bag of coal, Aragon the flask of spiritwine, and Selena the tin of Longnight sweet biscuits. "May these bring you all good fortune in the coming year."

Dimpling, Selena shook her tin. "Wise of you to give the pregnant lady the sweet biscuits."

Father flashed a crooked grin. "You should check that there are more than one or two left. Mel had them since last night."

Mel grinned back as he sat beside Selena and Aragon. "I'd not eat a first-foot gift, although I admit to being tempted." He turned to Selena. "But if you're opening them now, I'll gladly take one."

Everyone laughed at his jest, then Mother said, "How about we open our Longnight gifts instead? We can eat the sweet biscuits at the Longnight feast." She glanced at Sir Alaric. "Someone is famished, after all."

Mel and his family laughed again before swiftly exchanging the small Longnight gifts they'd gotten each other. Unlike some families, they cared more about enjoying time together on Longnight, rather than exchanging elaborate gifts. Which had made celebrating without them the past seven years lonely, even though attending all the Longnight services at the Great Temple, especially Sext with its many Longnight carols, had been plea-surable. And witnessing the usual ordinations and infrequent investitures, both always held on Longnight after Sext, had been uplifting as well.

After exchanging gifts, he and his family headed to the traditional Longnight feast of venison, wild boar, roasted root vegetables, fresh orenges, and Longnight cake. Along with the first-foot sweet biscuits, which Selena handed out before they devoured their feast—they enjoyed good food almost as much as spending time together. And since 'twas Longnight, he allowed himself to eat his Longnight sweet biscuit and cake first then eat another slice of Longnight cake afterward, even though everyone began jesting again about his love of desserts.

Midway through their feast, a note from Devon arrived, asking them to meet at the orphanage for his and Kiera's wedding ceremony instead of Hawke and Wren's townhouse. So once Mel and his family finished eating, they took two carriages to Waterstreet Orphanage with his parents and the Keyes taking the first one.

Once Mel settled in the backward seat across from Aragon and Selena, he grinned at them. "So how did Mother discover Devon and Kiera's *secret* wedding ceremony?"

As Selena giggled, Aragon sighed and replied, "She waylaid us as soon as we returned from Hawke and Wren's townhouse, quizzing us about what Devon wanted."

Mel almost laughed. Poor Aragon and Selena. Withstanding Mother's quizzing was practically impossible.

Aragon quirked a wry smile. "Fortunately, after you'd left Hawke and Wren's, I asked Devon if I could invite our parents and the Keyes to his wedding ceremony. Mother would ensure she and Father attended anyway, and they do everything with Wren's parents."

Mel did laugh at that. How true.

Dimpling, Selena rubbed her vast stomach. "But Devon didn't seem upset about inviting them. Doubtless he expected that, and he trusts them not to gossip." She nestled closer to Aragon. "I'm going to use the carriage ride to take a nap so that I've enough energy for the rowdy orphans."

As Selena shut her eyes, Mel and Aragon fell silent to not disturb her rest. Even so, the ride to the orphanage was enjoyable because he was with family.

At the orphanage, Aragon roused Selena, then they and Mel strode to the dining hall with Mother, Father, and the Keyes. They gave the orphans small Longnight gifts, which the children tore open with gleeful shouts. 'Twas wonderful to see the poor orphans' joy this Longnight.

While Mel and his family exchanged Longnight greetings with Hawke, Wren, Devon, and Kiera, the nightmara queen-heir Lady Moonbud arrived with Lady Annalise leaning against her. Poor Lady Annalise was whiter than ever—definitely ill but still determined to attend her friend's wedding ceremony. They'd better begin before she collapsed.

Once Kiera darted over to Lady Annalise, Mel murmured to Devon, "Shall we start your wedding ceremony? Are we holding it here?"

Eyeing Kiera and Lady Annalise as well, Devon hummed. "We're holding it in the library. Unfortunately, having the orphans attend risks gossip spreading about our secret marriage. Besides, they're too engrossed with their Longnight gifts." After Mel chuckled, Devon added, "I'll fetch Kiera."

Mel smiled after Devon. His cousin was clearly eager to make Kiera his wife at last. Too bad Devon and Kiera would have to hide their marriage until their public ceremony.

Except for the royal guards who remained to mind the orphans, all the adults plus young Miss Weston headed to the library. Fitting fifteen guests, including one horse-like nightmara, into the orphanage's tiny library was a struggle, but they managed, and Mel began the wedding ceremony with an opening prayer.

Beaming at Devon and Kiera, Mel read the sacred words and

spoke about marriage before another prayer asking the Goddess to bless their marriage. He crowned them with evergreen garlands and led them through their vows. Then he performed his second bloodbinding ceremony ever—'twas good he'd performed Hawke and Wren's three months ago before attempting Devon and Kiera's. 'Twouldn't do to botch a royal bloodbinding ceremony. He tied their left hands together and cut their palms before pressing their bloody palms to their marriage tokens, a strand from their protection charms, to bind their life forces together.

As Devon and Kiera slid their protection charms onto their left wrists, Mel said a prayer over them then announced to the guests, "I present to you King Devon and his wife Queen Kiera."

He and the guests beamed and laughed as Devon pulled Kiera against him for a passionate kiss. 'Twas fortunate their protection charms included a contraceptive strand—otherwise Calatini's throne would have an heir along the way before the kingdom officially had a queen. Eventually, Devon and Kiera quit kissing so they could sign the matrimony certificate.

Then everyone returned to the dining hall, and Devon regaled the orphans with the tale of his pursuit of Kiera. Moments after he finished, a loud thump echoed from the back of the dining hall.

Mel and the others whirled to face Lady Annalise collapsed on the floor. He and half the adults surged toward the fallen lady to help, while Hawke and the other adults diverted the orphans with Longnight caroling.

Wren and Kiera were frantic for their ill friend, and they agreed to summon the veiled witch—the powerful Rhiannon descendant who'd provided Wren's glamour spell and Kiera's enchanted masquerade costume as well as given a prophecy to help neutralize the Magehaven ore after its deadly explosion.

Lady Moonbud mentally called the veiled witch, and young Miss Weston attempted to use her magic to sustain Lady Annalise with little success. Then the veiled witch arrived and revealed Lady Annalise was under a virulent curse before whisking the unconscious lady back to her witch shop atop Lady Moonbud with Miss Weston accompanying them.

Once their friend was gone, Wren and Kiera exchanged worried frowns. Nibbling her lip, Kiera murmured, "I hope the veiled witch can break the curse before 'tis too late."

As Wren swallowed while rubbing her rounded stomach, Devon drew Kiera close with a tender smile, although his brow was furrowed as well. "We all know how incredibly powerful the veiled witch is. I'm certain Lady Annalise shall be fine."

Mel nodded and straightened his priest robes. Even so, someone should inform Lord Ravenstone about Lady Annalise's collapse and the curse so he could support her. Mel hummed. And since he was the only one here who knew about their secret involvement, he must leave at once.

He smiled at Wren and Kiera to hearten them. "Devon's right, but you can also pray for Lady Annalise while attending Longnight Vespers with the orphans." When they nodded, he continued, "Which reminds me; I must return to the Great Temple."

Wren frowned at him. "I thought you were joining us at the nearby local temple then for drinks at our townhouse after the orphans are abed."

He swallowed a sigh. He'd meant to, but Lady Annalise's collapse forced him to miss the rest of his family Longnight. "I wish I could, but I've been gone for too long already."

Selena waddled over with Aragon's arm wrapped about her. "We should go as well. I thought I could last until drinks later, but I'm too exhausted. I'm sorry."

Wren grimaced. "Don't be. I'm tired as well. I think we'll cancel drinks tonight. None of us are in the proper mood after Annalise's collapse, anyway."

Mel and the others soberly nodded, then Mel turned to Aragon and Selena. "Do you mind if I ride back with you?" He could get to Ravenstone House much faster by carriage.

Aragon smiled at him. "Of course not. Do you want us to drop you at the Great Temple?"

Mel shook his head. 'Twould take longer to reach Lord Ravenstone. "I'll walk from the family townhouse to the Great Temple." After a detour to Ravenstone House.

Mel, Aragon, and Selena said farewell to everyone then headed out to the carriage. Before climbing inside, Mel asked the driver to drive as swiftly as possible. And because the streets were mostly empty since 'twas Longnight afternoon, the carriage raced across Ormas in half the usual time.

After the carriage halted, Mel waited until Aragon and Selena entered the family townhouse before running to Ravenstone House. Fortunately, he wasn't out of breath when he rapped on Ravenstone House's front door since he was accustomed to walking everywhere. So when the door jerked open, he managed a warm smile and evenly asked, "Could I see Lord Ravenstone, please? I've an urgent matter to discuss with him."

The butler blinked at Mel. Then his gaze flicked across Mel's priest robes. He blurted, "My apologies, holy sir, but Lord Ravenstone, his mother, and the Greysnowes galloped to Goddess knows where not long ago."

Mel exhaled. For Lord Ravenstone and his mother to be galloping off with Lady Annalise's family, they all already knew about her collapse somehow. The two feuding families who'd been enemies for centuries wouldn't act together for anything less serious. With their support and the veiled witch's magic, Lady Annalise's curse would soon be broken, and Lord Ravenstone would ask him again to perform their wedding ceremony —hopefully, with her parents' blessing this time.

Mel smiled brighter to reassure the Ravenstones' anxious butler. "Lord Ravenstone must be already handling my urgent matter." He nodded at the butler. "Have a happy rest of your Longnight."

He returned to the Great Temple with a smile. Today had been an even more exciting Longnight than he'd expected. And thanks to the Goddess's mercy, everything would resolve as it should. But midway back, he sighed. If only he could rejoin his family for Longnight Vespers, but he'd likely not reach the orphanage in time, and explaining why he'd left would be difficult without betraying Lady Annalise and Lord Ravenstone's involvement.

Mel was about to enter the priest quarters to spend the hour before Vespers in his chambers when Kit's sultry voice called, "Mel, at last. I thought you'd never return."

He frowned. What was Kit doing *here*? Shouldn't she be at Blaine House or Golddell House with Edouard and Elise? Sighing, he turned toward Kit then froze. An old woman wrapped in a black cloak and a servant's dress stood there. He peered closer. Although the old woman appeared so ancient that a strong breeze would topple her, she possessed Kit's smoky eyes.

He strode toward her. "Kit, is that you? What happened?"

The elderly-looking Kit stared up at him, her gaze shimmering with tears. She swallowed then began to reply, but before she said a word, she began to sob.

His chest squeezing, Mel gathered Kit into his arms. Even as a girl, she'd rarely revealed such vulnerabilities to anyone. A defense against her despicable father, no doubt. And that shell had become a glittering, unbreakable diamond since she'd become the fashionable Countess of Blaine. He kissed Kit's now white yet still silky hair, inhaling her delectable cinnaspice scent. "Tell me what happened."

CHAPTER 9

Mel's embrace and kiss making her heart clench, Kit buried her face against his chest and sobbed harder. His tenderness was precisely what she needed right now. Although once she'd calmed, he'd doubtless return to his earlier distaste toward her for interfering with Wren and Hawke's relationship.

The door behind them creaked open, and the priest acting as porter coughed. "Do you know this beggar, Priest Melchior?"

As she stiffened and jerked away from Mel, he glowered at the porter and replied, "Of course I do, Dirk. How long did you make her wait outside in the cold?"

Before the porter could answer, she tugged on Mel's arm. Appearing a crone was bad enough, let alone sobbing all over his chest on a public street. 'Twas fortunate no one could recognize her as the fashionable Countess of Blaine. "Never mind how long I waited. Could we talk somewhere private?"

Mel eyed her then inclined his head. "We can talk in my chambers." He threaded his arm through hers as if she was still a gorgeous court lady. "Shall we?"

Tears burning her eyes again at his consideration, Kit nodded and grasped her bag with her free hand. She couldn't let all she possessed be stolen by street thieves because she was upset.

Mel escorted her inside then through the warren-like priest quarters. Eventually, he halted before a plain door, no different from any of the rest, and ushered her in. "Here we are. Why don't you sit down? I'll prepare some tea to warm you. Just regular, I'm afraid. I don't have any cinnaspice tea."

Chilled from her hours-long wait in the frigid air, she remained wrapped in her cloak as she settled at the small, wooden table in the center of the room. "I've some in my bag."

Chuckling, Mel strode to the cabinets and counter along the wall. "Why aren't I surprised?" He set a kettle of water on a fire plate, an enchanted disc used to prepare food outside a kitchen. He murmured the word to activate the fire plate then returned to her. "Do you want your tea or regular tea?"

Kit silently extracted her cinnaspice tea and set it on the table. As Mel prepared their tea, she glanced about his chambers. Although austere, they were full of sunlight thanks to the three windows and were larger than she'd expected. In addition to this general room, there were three others—likely two bedrooms and a refreshing room. Perhaps he shared his chambers with another priest.

Once their tea was done, Mel sat beside her and pressed her hot teacup into her still icy hands. "Drink." After she added a spoon of honey and began to drink, he began stirring three heaping spoons into his, which normally would have made her smile. "Now tell me what happened."

Sipping her fragrant cinnaspice tea, she inhaled then described the appearance of the Goddess's female avatars in her chambers and how they'd cursed her with the hideous crone illusion.

His eyes wide, Mel stared at her after she finished. Eventually, he murmured, "So what do you intend to do?"

Kit grimaced and set down her empty teacup. "Break the curse, obviously, but I need assistance and a place to stay while I do." She leaned toward Mel with a beseeching smile. "I know you despise me since discovering my wickedness toward Wren and Hawke, but I desperately need your help, Mel. Shall you provide it?"

Mel sighed. "I don't despise you, Kit. Your thoughtless cruelty and lack of remorse did disappoint me, however. I believed better of you."

Her chest squeezing, she tossed her head. Only because he was so worthy himself. "Not all of us can be compassionate priests for the Goddess."

Frowning into his teacup, Mel drained his tea. "No, but the devout, tender girl I believed you'd been never would have hurt anyone like that."

Kit winced. Except she wasn't worthy enough to have been that girl, just like Father had always said and her cruel lie had further proved. She lifted her chin. "We've digressed. Shall you shelter me and help me break the curse?"

Humming, Mel eyed her. "Of course I shall, although I'm not sure you need either. The Goddess made you appear old for a purpose, and you shouldn't attempt to circumvent her. Plus, anyone in the family would help you if you explained what happened, so why hide here instead of remaining at home?"

She shuddered then glared at Mel. How could he not understand? "*No one* else can see me like this, not even your precious family. And I don't have time to 'become who I was meant to be'—whatever that means. If I don't break this curse soon, the Duke of Oakmoor shall never marry me."

Mel stiffened. "He would if he loved you."

Snorting, Kit crossed her arms. "Not all marriages are about love. This one would be about the duke having a fashionable wife to enhance his suave reputation and provide him an heir."

Mel gazed at her, his jaw tight. "Such an empty marriage would make you unhappy."

She glared back. Must he lecture her about love and marriage? He'd never even courted anyone. "Enough about that.

We must devise a plan to break my curse. While waiting for you to return, I decided we could start by visiting witch shops. Surely one of them can remove the crone illusion."

Mel sighed. "We can visit my friend Deacon across the hall. He's a witch priest and works at Charmed Blessings." He glanced at the clock on the mantel. "But tomorrow. Everyone is heading to Longnight Vespers now. We should leave as well."

As Mel rose, Kit remained seated. The more devout at court would attend Longnight Vespers at the Great Temple since 'twas the first day of the year. "I told you—no one can see me like this."

Shaking his head, Mel returned their teacups to the counter. "People shall see you when you visit witch shops."

Kit grimaced, her stomach tensing. "True, but that's necessary to break my curse."

Mel flashed a warm smile, doubtless to hearten her. "Eating is necessary too, and dinner is directly after Longnight Vespers."

Her heart fluttered at his warm smile—the first he'd given her since he'd discovered how she'd hurt Wren and Hawke. She'd thought that lost forever. But she couldn't risk anyone from court recognizing her. She swallowed then lied, "I'm not hungry."

Mel snorted. "Liar." He beckoned her. "No one shall know 'tis you. Come to Longnight Vespers and dinner. There shall likely be spiced cider."

Kit swallowed again. She'd not eaten since breakfast, and spiced cider would be delicious. "No."

Tsking, Mel straightened his priest robes. "Must you be so stubborn?"

When she stared back without replying, Mel sighed then strode toward the door.

She leapt upright. She'd almost forgotten. "Before you go, we must settle where I can stay."

Turning to face her, Mel gestured toward the right door. "You can stay in my spare room."

As Mel left, Kit exhaled and sank into her chair. Thank the

Goddess he didn't share his quarters with another priest and was kind enough to let her stay with him. She didn't trust anyone else while she looked like this. Without her youth and sultry beauty, she'd no defenses and was of little use to anyone.

She carried her bag to her new bedroom and unpacked. Her meager belongings filled the tiny room. Then she flopped on her bed and attempted to nap after her stressful day, but her stomach gnawing her insides wouldn't let her.

Two hours later, Mel rapped on her door. "I brought you some food, even though I shouldn't have. It just enables your stubbornness."

Kit darted to the table in the general room and fell on her repast like a starved tygris on a doe—and the massive felines who ruled the Tsarkan grasslands weren't polite eaters. Mel had even brought her spiced cider and Longnight cake. Midway through dinner, she beamed at him. "You can have half my Longnight cake if you like."

Mel shifted in his seat beside her. "No, I had plenty in the dining hall." He paused then said, "At dinner, I began thinking about the family's response to your disappearance. Everyone shall worry if we don't explain."

She suppressed a snort as she gulped some spiced cider. Most of his family would be relieved rather than worried. "In my note to Edouard arranging my allowance, I wrote I'd be gone awhile. So they'll know I left willingly."

Mel frowned and tapped a finger on the table. "That's not enough of an explanation. How about you write Edouard and Mother that Longnight inspired you to reflect on your life, and I can contact you if needed?"

She slowly nodded. Writing that would lead his family to assume she was on a retreat at one of the many prayer houses near the Great Temple. Not a bad excuse.

Mel sighed. "I don't like misleading them, but since you refuse to tell them what happened, this explanation shall ensure they don't worry. And if you follow the Goddess's guidance, 'tisn't even a lie."

Kit scowled at him as she finished her Longnight cake. She was breaking the crone illusion, not following some cryptic guidance. But to avoid quarreling after he'd been so kind, she simply replied, "I'll write them now if you've pen and paper."

She wrote Mel's family then fell into bed and sank into a dreamless slumber. Today had been the longest Longnight day ever.

The following morning, Kit rose late and dressed. She was more refreshed than she'd been in months, and without a mirror here, she could almost forget the crone illusion afflicting her— except whenever she glanced at herself. She grimaced at her hands, which appeared gnarled and spotted with age.

Burying her hands in her skirt, she left her bedroom to find Mel. He was already out, although he'd left her a note on the table, stating he'd be back with breakfast after organizing the almskitchens. She hummed. His duties began early. While she awaited his return, she made herself a cup of cinnaspice tea.

She sighed as she sipped her tea. If not for the crone illusion, she'd be preparing to host the Duke of Oakmoor's charity luncheon in a few hours. Hopefully, her instructions would be enough for the duke to host it without her.

Kit had just prepared a second cup of cinnaspice tea when Mel finally strode into his chambers with two laden trays. While setting the trays on the table, he said, "I wasn't sure what you wanted, so I brought some of everything."

She smiled at him. How like Mel. "The porridge, please. 'Tis the easiest to season with cinnaspice."

Mel chuckled and handed her the porridge. "I suppose you had some of that in your bag too."

Kit shrugged. "I brought all my cinnaspice items with me. No one would believe I'd left willingly without them." She fetched her shaker of ground cinnaspice and seasoned her porridge.

When she handed Mel the honey after adding a spoonful to her porridge, Mel arched his brows and eyed her. "Are you certain you don't want more honey?"

She concealed her smile behind her teacup. "I don't need an entire pot of honey for my porridge—unlike some people."

Mel flashed a rueful grin as he stirred his three spoons of honey into his tea. "True." Once they began eating, he said, "We'll visit Deacon this morning about your illusion, but in the afternoon, I must begin teaching my two new groups of novices about charities. So I can't help you then."

Kit nodded. Mel was truly as busy with his duties as he'd claimed. Her throat tightened. And she'd simply added to his load. "Perhaps your friend can break my curse this morning."

After breakfast and Mel returning their dishes to the dining hall, he escorted her across the hall and rapped on the plain door identical to his own.

A smiling priestess wearing brown priest robes over her simple green dress opened the door. Her voice soothing as a babbling brook, she said, "Morning, Mel."

Mel returned the priestess's smile. "Morning, Sarah. Is your husband in?" He gestured toward Kit. "My old friend Kit is visiting me and must speak with him about a spell."

Kit almost snorted. Thanks to the Goddess's illusion, she appeared his "old" friend in more ways than one.

Sarah beamed at her. "A pleasure, Kit. How do you know Mel?"

Kit swallowed. She couldn't outright lie to the affable priestess. "I knew him as a boy."

Nodding, Sarah turned back to Mel. "Unfortunately, Deacon has already left for Charmed Blessings."

As Kit tensed at more people seeing her, Mel smiled at Sarah and said, "We'll visit him there then. Thanks."

Mel escorted Kit through the Great Temple to Charmed Blessings and straight to the ascetic priest in the center of the busy room, surely Deacon. Engrossed with assisting patrons, the other priests didn't even glance at them.

While Deacon finished helping a patron select a small shrine for home worship, she studied the witch priest. Unlike Mel's and Sarah's, Deacon's priest robes were trimmed with ivory, as were the other priests in the holy witch shop. The trims on priest robes must indicate something.

Once Deacon said farewell to his patron, Mel stepped forward and greeted him then introduced her and explained she wanted to discuss a spell.

Deacon turned to her with a not-quite smile. "What type of spell?"

Kit lifted her chin. Deacon was nowhere as affable as his wife. "An illusion spell cast on me against my will. I want it broken."

Deacon's brows rose. "I see. Let me take a look." The witch priest flicked his fingers and muttered a probing spell. Then he gasped and jerked back. "I can't break a spell cast by the Goddess's female avatars. And even if I could, 'tis blasphemy!"

CHAPTER 10

Mel sighed at Deacon's outburst. He'd expected no one could break the Goddess's illusion, but Kit had been so distressed when begging for his help. Her heartrending sobs and desperate pleas had made him ache to take care of her, even though he was still disappointed with her for hurting Hawke and Wren. He'd been unable to refuse her, if only for the sake of the tender and devout girl he'd once known.

While Mel sighed, Kit glared at Deacon with her fists clenched at her sides. "I can't live looking like this for the rest of my life."

Deacon stared down at her. "Then you better follow the Goddess's guidance. Holy curses don't break until you learn what she wants to teach you."

As Kit bristled further at Deacon's dismissive tone, Mel suppressed a grimace. Although true, saying it that way was sure to provoke Kit. What was wrong with his friend? Deacon was nowhere as personable as his wife, but his reply was harsher than usual.

Before Kit could reply and inflame their quarrel, Mel asked Deacon, "What else can you tell us about the illusion? And can you see Kit's true appearance beneath it?"

Deacon shook his head. "All I can sense is the illusion itself and that the Goddess's female avatars cast it."

Kit sniffed. "Surely you sense more than that."

Mel winced as Deacon scowled at Kit and snapped, "No, and most witches shall sense even less. I can only sense so much because I'm a priest of the Goddess."

Mel grasped Kit's arm as she opened her mouth to retort. He'd best separate her and Deacon before they started a feud like the Greysnowes and Ravenstones had centuries ago. He smiled at Deacon. "Thanks for examining Kit's illusion. I'll see you later." Then he hustled Kit from Charmed Blessings.

Kit remained silent as they strode back to his chambers, but as soon as they entered, she burst out, "Your *friend* wasn't very helpful."

He sighed and headed to the fire plate to heat some water. Perhaps a cup of her adored cinnaspice tea would calm Kit. "I'm sorry. Although brusque, Deacon told us all he could."

Swishing about the room, Kit snorted. "Nonsense. He just disliked me for some reason, so he refused to help. We must visit some other witch shops to remove this hideous crone illusion."

Mel set her tea on the table. "Come have some cinnaspice tea." When she dropped into her chair, he sat beside her. Clearly, until she saw other witch shops couldn't help either, she'd not quit attempting to circumvent the Goddess's purpose. A purpose that the Goddess had sent her avatars to bring about—Kit didn't seem to realize how rare and wondrous that was. Swallowing a sigh, he smiled at her. "We could visit the veiled witch tomorrow."

Kit frowned back over her teacup. "Who?"

He almost grimaced. Right, Kit wouldn't know about the veiled witch since she wasn't close to Wren or Kiera. "She's a witch near Waterstreet Orphanage who provided Wren's glamour spell and Kiera's enchanted ballgown." To prove the veiled witch's ability to discern spells, he added, "She also saw the curse killing Lady Annalise."

Kit blinked at him. Then she shook her head. "Even so, I doubt a witch from a poor neighborhood near the docks shall be enough. We should visit some of the fashionable witch shops instead."

Mel sighed. Of course Kit would insist on visiting fashionable shops. But hopefully, she'd believe them when they told her they couldn't break a spell from the Goddess.

Humming, Kit sipped her tea. "But which fashionable witch shops? Although I adore Charms and Nonsense, they only handle magical trinkets with minimal magical costs, so they shan't help. Perhaps Mirage since they sell illusion and glamour spells. Or Esrever since they specialize in nullifying spells."

He shrugged and rose. "Either shall do, although I don't think I can accompany you for a few days. I need to rearrange my duties to have enough time to leave the Great Temple." When Kit sighed but nodded, he said, "'Tis almost time for Sext and luncheon. Shall you join me?"

Kit set her jaw. "I'm not leaving your chambers until we're visiting Mirage or Esrever."

Mel frowned at Kit. So stubborn. She might need to visit all the fashionable witch shops in Ormas before she believed they couldn't help her. "Very well."

He strode to the main temple for Sext, and the Longnight carols cheered him like always. Then he headed to the dining hall to eat luncheon. Yet when he arrived, he couldn't make himself eat there. Instead, he fetched two trays and returned to his chambers. Although she'd deny it, Kit was too fragile to be alone so much, as her wrenching sobs in a public street yesterday had proved. And his duties meant he'd be gone the entire afternoon.

When he entered his chambers, Kit straightened her slumped shoulders and stared at him, her eyes shimmering with tears. Yes, definitely too fragile. She murmured, "You brought luncheon."

Mel nodded then set a tray before her and sat.

As they began their hearty pea soup, Kit said, "I'm surprised you didn't bring any dessert."

He suppressed a sigh. "Kitchen priests typically only prepare desserts for dinner. I brought extra bread so we can eat some with honey."

Kit's lips quirked. "How horrible for you to be so deprived of desserts. No wonder you devour them at the few family events you manage to attend."

A blush warming his neck, Mel shrugged. "I don't mind missing desserts to serve the Goddess."

Kit's gaze darkened. "No, I suppose you don't." She studied her pea soup for a moment. "At Charmed Blessings, I noticed all the priests there had ivory trim on their priest robes, unlike you and Sarah. I assume the trim indicates something."

He couldn't help a smile. Not surprising Kit had noticed that within a day of staying at the Great Temple. "Yes, they indicate rank and duties. Novices wear no trim, while elder priests wear white, bishops red, and the high priest gold. Community priests like me wear brown trim to match our robes so that parishioners remain focused on us being priests rather than our abilities. Witch priests wear ivory, worship priests purple, scholar priests blue, temple priests gray, death priests black, and warrior priests orange. And if priests belong to multiple groups, they wear multiple bands of trim."

Kit frowned. "I hope I can remember all that. What are warrior priests? I've never heard of them."

Mel nodded as he poured honey on his second slice of bread. "Most people other than priests haven't. They're extremely rare— none are in Ormas right now, although I believe one is helping handle the Magehaven ore crisis. Warrior priests are basically holy knights who travel across Damensea defending the inno- cent and righting wrongs with their warrior skills."

Kit inhaled. "I can see why they're so rare. Learning warrior skills in addition to priestly duties must be demanding."

Finishing his bread and honey, he shrugged. "I believe most

of them are warriors before they become priests." He glanced at the clock on the mantel and sighed. "I should go so I'm not late for my classes. Do you want to come listen?" 'Twould prevent her from sitting and brooding alone.

Kit glowered at him as she stacked their dishes and trays. "Why do you keep asking me to join you? I told you *multiple* times that no one else can see me like this. I'm only emerging for the witch shops because I must."

Mel frowned back while collecting the stacked trays and dishes. Kit had always been prideful about her sultry beauty, but she was being ridiculous. Under the Goddess's illusion, no one could possibly recognize her as the fashionable Countess of Blaine. "I keep asking because remaining alone in my chambers shall bore you."

Crossing her arms across her chest, Kit sniffed. "I'll be fine."

He suppressed a snort. "As you like. I'll see you at dinner."

After returning their trays to the dining hall, Mel taught his two groups of second-year novices, and his irritation from quarreling with Kit faded. The novices were invariably an endearing mixture of eagerness and nerves during their first class. So he was smiling when he fetched dinner after Vespers.

Kit brightened upon his return. She'd been as bored as he'd suspected she would be. He must continue asking her to join him on his duties. If anyone asked, he could say she was an old friend acting as his assistant. He'd give her some tasks so 'twould be true.

They'd only eaten a spoonful of their chicken stew when Kit leaned toward him. "Have you figured out when we can visit Mirage or Esrever yet?"

He sighed. Her impatience was understandable after remaining in his chambers most of the day, but still. "No, I haven't had time to check. But I should be able to figure it out tomorrow."

Kit sagged then pointed her spoon at him. "You'd better do that soon so I quit interfering with your duties."

Mel swallowed as weight squeezed his chest. His gaze on his Longnight sweet biscuits, he murmured, "I don't mind you staying with me."

Kit leapt upright. "You shall if I'm here much longer."

He stared after her as she swept to her bedroom then firmly shut her door behind her. Her boredom had made her even more prickly than normal. He glanced at her barely touched dinner. He'd not return it to the dining hall in case she calmed enough to eat in a bit. Which she did an hour later.

The following morning, Mel was striding from the Great Temple's chapter house after organizing the almskitchens to fetch breakfast for him and Kit when Paul scurried toward him. The rabbity temple priest said, "That lord who visited you last month is here again to speak with you. He's in the nave."

Mel thanked Paul then went to meet Lord Ravenstone in the main temple. Hopefully, the count's visit meant he'd happy news. He smiled at Lord Ravenstone. "How's Lady Annalise? We were all worried after she collapsed at the orphanage."

Lord Ravenstone beamed. "She's recovered from the curse, and her parents support our marriage now, so we no longer need to elope."

Mel returned Lord Ravenstone's grin. Ending the centuries-long Greysnowe-Ravenstone feud with a marriage was perfect. "What wonderful news. I assume you're here to ask me to officiate your wedding ceremony."

Lord Ravenstone leaned forward, still grinning. "When's the soonest you're free?"

Mel smiled. Lord Ravenstone was clearly as eager to marry Lady Annalise as Devon had been Kiera, and ending the feud was too important to delay. If he shifted his duties, he could manage to officiate, although that meant Kit would have to wait a bit longer. Please let her not be too upset. He hummed. "How about three mornings from now in the Harvest Garden? The chapels are surely occupied."

Lord Ravenstone rubbed his beard. "Just after breakfast would be best. Our parents want to keep our marriage secret until they can host a ball at the end of the Longnight season."

Mel coughed a laugh. How dramatic. "Do you want a blood-binding?"

Lord Ravenstone smiled. "No, we've no need of one, although we do have two sets of wedding tokens—hair spirals and rings."

His brows rising, Mel eyed Lord Ravenstone. Most with titles or their heirs didn't risk bloodbindings because bloodbound couples could only have children together, making heirs impossible if one was infertile. Yet how the count had refused was odd. Perhaps breaking the curse had already bound him and Lady Annalise. Mel inclined his head. "I'll make sure to include both sets of wedding tokens."

Lord Ravenstone swept a bow. "My deepest thanks, Priest Melchior. We'll see you in three days."

Once Lord Ravenstone strode from the nave, Mel fetched breakfast and returned to Kit. While they ate, he told her about the upcoming wedding ceremony.

Kit simply nodded then asked, "When can we visit Mirage?"

He shifted in his seat. "After the wedding, I'm afraid."

Stiffening, Kit swallowed then lifted her chin. "I see."

Mel winced. Postponing helping her to help someone he barely knew had hurt Kit. "Ending the Greysnowe-Ravenstone feud is important and mustn't wait." Besides, visiting witch shops wouldn't actually help Kit.

Kit flashed Lady Blaine's blinding court smile. "Of course."

Kit didn't speak much for the rest of breakfast and quietly returned to her bedroom afterward. Over the days before the Greysnowe-Ravenstone wedding ceremony, she remained quiet and didn't even quarrel with him much. Yet she still refused to emerge from his chambers, even though he kept asking her to join him every time he left.

At breakfast before the wedding ceremony, Kit was pale, her face pinched, and she picked at her porridge. She must be suffering one of her vicious megrims—doubtless because she'd not gotten fresh air and had been brooding for days.

Mel eyed her with a frown. She looked wretched. What if her megrim worsened, and he wasn't here to help? Although she'd protest, she must attend the wedding ceremony. When she pushed away her half-eaten porridge, he set his jaw. "All done? We should head to the Harvest Garden for the wedding ceremony. Wear your cloak—'tis freezing."

Kit shuddered. "No. I've a megrim."

Squeezing her hands, he drew Kit upright. "I thought you might, but 'tis why you must join me. You're too ill to remain alone."

Her lips tightening, Kit blew a sigh. "I always remain alone when suffering megrims like this one."

Mel wrapped Kit in her cloak then his to make sure she'd be warm enough. "But at home you've a maid to tend you. Here you don't." When she dully stared at him without retorting like she usually did, he drew her into his arms and kissed her brow. "If you sit along the back wall, most shan't notice you—they'll be engrossed in the wedding ceremony anyway. And if you don't speak, no one shall recognize your voice."

Kit sighed again. "Very well."

He ushered her to the Harvest Garden and settled her on the stone bench in the back. "Are you warm enough?"

Kit lifted a shoulder. "I suppose."

Mel frowned, but before he could probe further, Lord Ravenstone and Lady Annalise arrived along with their families and a few wedding guests. So he squeezed Kit's shoulder then turned to greet them with a warm smile.

CHAPTER 11

*W*hen Mel left to welcome Lady Annalise, Lord Ravenstone, and their wedding guests, Kit sighed and leaned her throbbing head against the wall behind her. Thankfully, 'twas cloudy today, so the daylight wasn't too bright, although colors possessed the garish edge typical during her megrims. She shut her eyes. Please let this wedding ceremony end soon so Mel would let her return to his chambers. She'd only agreed to attend because she could tell he'd not relent until she did, and thanks to her vicious megrim, she hadn't the energy to fight.

Chilled despite her two cloaks, she kept her eyes shut as the cheerfully chattering guests spread about the Harvest Garden. She relaxed when the air suddenly turned balmy. Then she stiffened at Wren thanking Lord Ravenstone and his mother for casting a warming spell. Why must *Wren* be here? Her clever childhood rival would doubtless recognize her as easily as Mel had.

Removing her cloaks, Kit peered at the others in the garden through her lashes. Wren and Hawke were beside King Devon and Lady Kiera. Behind them stood a dappled midnight nightmara mare and a black nightmara stallion—likely Lady

Moonbud and her mate since Lady Annalise had become acquainted with them during her nightmara rides with Lady Kiera. Near Lady Annalise and Lord Ravenstone were her parents and brother as well as his mother, and the two mothers giggled together, while the gentlemen grinned.

Kit blinked. What had engendered that change? Surely not their children's marriage, which they would have forbidden just last week. Perhaps it involved Lady Annalise's curse that Mel had mentioned.

The chattering guests quieted once Mel began the wedding ceremony with an opening prayer. When he began speaking about love and marriage, her heart twisted. From his beam, he truly believed all that. But why wouldn't he? Most of his family was happily married, and he and his family all loved each other, so love had never made *him* vulnerable or foolish.

Her head pounding, she lowered her gaze. Bile burned her throat at her ancient-looking hands resting in her lap. 'Twas so unfair that everyone else was so happy while she was cursed to appear a crone for Goddess knew how long. Burying her hands in her skirt, she glowered at the others in the garden. Wren had married the gentleman she'd loved forever, and no one seemed to care he'd made her pregnant beforehand. King Devon had fallen in love with a poor commoner, yet all of court adored her and couldn't wait until she became queen. And Lady Annalise, a secret soul healer, had formed a forbidden soulbond with her family's ancestral enemy, but somehow their parents now supported their marriage.

Kit inhaled a hissing breath as Mel crowned Lady Annalise and Lord Ravenstone with gardenia garlands. If not for the Goddess's illusion, she'd have successfully hosted the Duke of Oakmoor's charity luncheon a few days ago, and he'd have proposed by now. True, she didn't love the duke like everyone here loved their spouses, but at least she'd have wealth and status.

She almost snorted when Lady Annalise and Lord Ravenstone donned rings *and* hair spirals as their wedding tokens. How excessive. Most couples only had one set of wedding tokens. Then Mel announced them, and Lord Ravenstone kissed the new Lady Ravenstone amid cheers. Kit gritted a smile. They were so blessed.

While Mel had them and their two witnesses—Lady Kiera and Lord Alexander Greysnowe—sign the matrimony certificate, the other guests began talking again, although King Devon silently eyed his betrothed across the garden like a lonely griffin.

Releasing Wren to clap King Devon's shoulder, Hawke chuckled and drawled, "You'd best quit gazing at Kiera like that until after your public wedding ceremony on Plantfete, or everyone shall guess the truth about you two."

Kit blinked and eyed them. What truth? That the king was mad for his once mysterious mermaid? But all of Calatini knew that.

While King Devon grumbled at Hawke's teasing, Wren glanced about the garden, and her gaze met Kit's.

Swallowing, Kit jerked her gaze free. Then she tensed as Wren headed toward her. Why was Wren approaching an unfamiliar crone?

Wren sat beside Kit, her hands resting on her rounded stomach. Wren was rotund for a lady five months pregnant. She smiled at Kit. "How do you know Annalise and Lord Ravenstone?"

Her blood throbbing inside her skull, Kit swallowed again. Wren would recognize her voice if she spoke, but if she remained silent, Wren would become suspicious and possibly draw attention to the crone who'd snuck into her friend's secret wedding. Rasping and deepening her voice to disguise it, Kit muttered, "I don't. The priest made me attend."

Wren's brows rose. "Mel did? Why?"

Kit simply shrugged. Talking further or explaining that she was staying with Mel might make Wren suspect the truth. Although she was too nice to gloat, Wren would surely be amused that the Goddess had cursed Kit to appear a crone. Especially after she'd lied about Hawke kissing her and spread gossip about Wren's scandalous pregnancy at court.

Wren hummed and leaned closer, her brow furrowing. "Have we met before? You look familiar. Have you ever visited Waterstreet Orphanage?"

Kit froze. Oh, Goddess.

Before she could manage a reply, Mel strode over with a warm smile. "Wren, I see you've met the lady acting as my assistant. Hawke sent me to fetch you."

Wren wrinkled her nose but rose. "I can fetch myself. He's no doubt alarmed because I sat down. As if I was ill instead of merely pregnant."

Kit exhaled once Wren returned to her husband. Thank the Goddess Mel had distracted Wren. Kit arched her brows at him. "Acting as your assistant?"

Mel quirked a smile. "If I can ever get you to leave my chambers, you can help with my duties so you would be." He eyed her. "How are you feeling?"

Grimacing, she rubbed her temple. Her head was pounding worse than ever, likely thanks to the daylight outside and encountering Wren. "Drained. Can I return to your chambers to rest now?"

Mel drew her upright. "I'll escort you."

As they began to leave, Lord and Lady Greysnowe swept over and waylaid them. Lady Greysnowe beamed at Mel and said, "Thank you so much for officiating Annalise and Dare's wedding. You must attend our ball celebrating their marriage at the end of the Longnight season. Your assistant—is it?—is welcome too."

Mel smiled at the Greysnowes. "I'll be glad to attend." He glanced down at Kit, clearly waiting for her to accept their invitation as well. When she frowned back, he sighed then said, "Excuse me, my assistant is tired, and I must escort her to her bed."

When Mel ushered her into his chambers, he helped her sit at the table then closed all the curtains and dimmed the lights. "Do you have any medicine?"

Kit grimaced. She'd taken her megrim tonic when she'd gotten up, but it had done little. Not surprising given how vicious this megrim was. Yet she could probably risk another dose. "In the brown bottle in my bedroom."

Mel fetched her megrim tonic. "I'll prepare some tea and a cold compress for you."

She gulped her tonic then shut her eyes. Despite her megrim, warmth flooded her chest at his solicitude. "Thanks, Mel."

Soon Mel pressed a teacup redolent of cinnaspice, gingyr, and khamomile into her hands. Then he wrapped a cold compress scented with lavender and mentha about her head, covering her eyes too. "I brought a plate of crackers and sweet biscuits as well."

Smiling up at his voice, Kit sighed as she sipped her tea and nibbled her crackers. Mel made a better maid than Willa.

Once she finished, Mel removed her cold compress and laid his hands on her shoulders. "Take a few deep breaths."

Her shoulders tingling at his touch, Kit inhaled and opened her eyes. "What are you doing?"

Mel murmured, "The massage Father gives Mother whenever she suffers a megrim. I had him teach me as a boy. He taught me the tea and cold compress recipes too. As soon as you began staying here, I ensured I'd everything prepared."

She blinked back her sudden tears. He was always so thoughtful. Even to her after he'd discovered her wickedness. She shut her eyes and inhaled deeply as instructed.

When she exhaled, Mel pressed down on her shoulders, and he repeated that for her next few exhales. Then he squeezed her neck several times before sliding his fingers in her hair to press and rub her scalp.

Almost purring, Kit leaned into his massage. Goddess, that felt *amazing*.

Too short a time later, Mel extracted his hands from her hair to stroke her forehead from the center outward a few times. Then he rubbed her temple in gentle circles before continuing along her jaw line. His hands resting on her shoulders again, he asked, "How do you feel?"

She smiled without opening her eyes. Her megrim was still there, but its throbbing was muted after all his ministrations. "Better, thanks. Although I'm drowsy now."

Mel helped her rise. "How about you take a nap? While you're sleeping, I'll rearrange my duties so we can visit Mirage tomorrow."

Opening her eyes, Kit beamed at him. "Really?"

Escorting her to her bedroom door, Mel nodded. "Rest now. I'll fetch our luncheon once you wake."

Kit smiled and curled on her bed then drifted into slumber. Mel was the best. And although she didn't deserve his tender care, she couldn't help reveling in it while it lasted.

AFTER BREAKFAST THE FOLLOWING MORNING, Kit grinned and leapt upright when Mel returned from taking their dishes back to the dining hall. Her megrim had vanished overnight, and they were finally about to visit a witch shop that could remove the Goddess's illusion. She and Mel strode from the Great Temple, but she halted just outside the door. No carriage awaited them. "Wait, are we *walking* to Mirage?"

Mel arched his brows. "Of course. I don't have a carriage, so I walk everywhere unless Mother sends one—usually to ensure I attend her chosen family event as commanded."

Kit gaped at him. The fashionable witch shop was nowhere near the Great Temple. "But it shall take at least two hours to walk to Mirage."

Mel nodded. "Why do you think I had difficulty rearranging my duties to leave?"

She pursed her lips. She'd simply assumed he had too many

duties. "Doesn't the Great Temple have carriages? Surely we could take one."

Mel grasped her arm and propelled her forward. "They're all being used for temple business. Besides, walking is healthy."

Kit sighed. True, but she'd not walked a long distance since marrying Lord Blaine. Using a comfortable carriage had been such a relief after growing up with Father's ancient carriage that was often broken because he'd drank away the funds to repair it.

She and Mel walked in silence the rest of the way to Mirage. Near the Great Temple, no one eyed a priest and a crone walking together. But as they approached the fashionable witch shop, more and more people stared at them. A blush burned her cheeks at everyone's curious stares. So embarrassing, but at least they didn't encounter anyone influential from court.

Kit exhaled when they entered the sleek and bright illusion witch shop. Mel close behind, she strode past exhibits of decoy charms, invisibility cloaks, projected scenes, and other illusions to speak with the nearest clerk. She smiled at the exotic young witch. "I require your help removing an illusion spell cast on me."

Flicking her fingers, the girl murmured a probing spell. Then she frowned. "What illusion? I can't sense one about you."

Kit stiffened. Could Deacon have been right and not merely refusing to help? "There is one, I promise. Could I see the witch shop's owner, please?"

The girl sighed but fetched an older, even more exotic witch. That witch repeated a probing spell then shook her head and said, "I'm sorry, but I can't sense an illusion spell about you either."

As a lump clogged Kit's throat, Mel smiled at the witches then gave them each a gold coin and said, "Thanks for checking."

Kit frowned while she and Mel returned to the Great Temple. Why must the Goddess's illusion be so complicated? She worried her lip. Hopefully, the witches at Esrever, who were accustomed to nullifying spells, would sense more.

At luncheon, she leaned toward Mel and asked, "When can we visit Esrever?"

Mel sighed. "Not for a few days at least. I'm behind after performing the wedding ceremony yesterday and visiting Mirage today."

Kit echoed his sigh. She mustn't act ungrateful after all his tender care since she'd arrived. Yet remaining hidden in his chambers all day was as boring as he'd warned. Mel didn't even have many interesting books to read—most of his tomes were on theology or other serious matters. Yet she'd begun reading them anyway.

Mel had just left to return their dishes to the dining hall when a spritely knock sounded on his door.

She blinked. Who could that be? When another knock sounded, she frowned and slowly opened the door.

Sarah beamed at her. "Afternoon, Kit. I finally had off from Peaceful Minds today, so I stopped by to talk." She lifted the basket in her hand. "I brought spice buns."

Her mouth watering at the sweet rolls made with cinnaspice and honey, Kit smiled and waved the affable priestess inside. At least Sarah's dismissive husband wasn't with her. "'Tis too bad Mel isn't here."

As Kit began preparing cinnaspice tea, Sarah chuckled and set her spice buns on the table. "He *can* devour an insane amount of desserts. When he returns, I'll give him the two I brought to bribe him to leave for a while. We ladies need time alone to truly get to know each other."

Kit sighed while she poured their tea. She'd never had much success with that. Unlike Wren, who'd formed deep friendships with Lady Kiera and Lady Ravenstone, she only had superficial relationships with fashionable ladies at court. However, she smiled at Sarah as she handed the priestess a cup of cinnaspice tea. "I'll enjoy getting to know you."

Sarah grinned and sniffed her tea. "Is this cinnaspice tea? I've not drunk that in ages."

Humming, Kit sipped her cinnaspice tea. "I always do. I adore anything cinnaspice."

Sarah laughed. "'Tis fortunate I made spice buns then." She sobered and leaned toward Kit. "Deacon told me about the Goddess's illusion on you."

Kit almost winced. Hopefully, Deacon hadn't told anyone else. Gossip at the Great Temple about a spell from the Goddess might reach court, and given the timing, court might correctly connect it to Lady Blaine's disappearance.

Frowning, Sarah sighed. "He was rather agitated when he mentioned it, so I hope he wasn't too curt with you."

Kit suppressed a snort but made herself shrug. Sarah clearly knew her husband well.

Sarah tsked and shook her head. "I can see that he was. I'm sorry. He was just shocked to see a spell from the Goddess, and perhaps a bit jealous. Spells cast by the Goddess are *extremely* rare, as are holy manifestations, so even most priests haven't enjoyed them."

Kit studied her cinnaspice tea. Plus, her determination to break the Goddess's illusion had horrified the ascetic priest. "'Twas merely the Goddess's avatars who cast my illusion."

Sarah waved a hand. "That amounts to the same thing." She smiled at Kit. "But I hope you don't hold my husband's ill-temper against me. I'd love to become friends with Mel's 'old' friend."

Her chest warming at Sarah's kindness, Kit returned the priestess's smile. "I'd like that." She winked. "Especially if you bring more spice buns."

CHAPTER 12

When Mel entered his chambers after returning the luncheon dishes, he halted and blinked at Kit and Sarah laughing together at his small table. 'Twas an unexpected development. But a good one—the warmhearted priestess would make Kit more comfortable staying here, so Kit might actually leave his chambers.

Still grinning, Kit and Sarah turned to face him, then Sarah waved toward a plate of spice buns and said, "Afternoon, Mel. I brought you two spice buns, if you promise to leave to eat them."

Almost drooling, he snatched the plate. Sarah enjoyed baking in the temple kitchen on the days she wasn't at Peaceful Minds, and her desserts were always delicious. "I'll take myself off then. Have fun."

Kit and Sarah laughed again as he strode from his chambers. He devoured his spice buns in the study where he taught as he waited for his first group of novices to arrive. Sarah's spice buns were as delicious as he'd expected.

After teaching his second group of novices, Mel hurried back to his chambers. Perhaps Kit would join him at Vespers and dinner after her afternoon with Sarah.

Yet when he asked Kit, she frowned at him and said, "No."

He sighed. Must she be so stubborn? "Surely you can't still be worried about people seeing you. You just spent the entire afternoon with Sarah."

Kit tossed her head. "She's different."

Mel sighed again but left for Vespers. He really shouldn't keep bringing back dinner, but Kit was stubborn enough to let herself starve rather than relent.

Over the following days, Kit continued refusing his invitations to join him and leave his chambers, yet she beamed when Sarah visited again.

Like before, Sarah bribed him to leave with two desserts, cinnaspice apple trifles this time, but as he shut his door behind him, Deacon snorted from his and Sarah's door across the hall then drawled, "I see that woman is still staying with you."

Gripping his trifle bowls, Mel frowned at Deacon. "*That woman* is called Kit, and must you act so dismissive toward her? She's done nothing to deserve it."

The ascetic priest's face tightened. "Except for not appreciating how the Goddess blessed her with the avatars' visit and that illusion. Why would the Goddess do that for someone who plans to defy her?"

Mel forced himself to quit gripping the trifle bowls before he broke the glass stems. He should have realized Kit's "blasphemy" was what had riled Deacon. He shrugged. "I don't know why the Goddess chose to bless Kit, but I'm certain she has a reason." He laughed with a rueful smile. "Maybe 'tis as simple as because Kit is too stubborn to listen otherwise."

His eyes narrowing, Deacon grunted. "What *is* her appearance under the Goddess's illusion?"

Mel swallowed and studied his cinnaspice apple trifles. What could he say that wasn't a lie yet didn't reveal Kit's identity as Lady Blaine? She'd never forgive him if he inadvertently revealed that. "Quite different, except her eyes are the same."

Deacon humphed. "She sounds much younger than she appears." When Mel managed a shrug, Deacon scowled. "'Tisn't appropriate for a young lady to stay with you unless she's your wife or family, Mel."

His neck heating, Mel shrugged again. Kit was almost family, but saying that would definitely reveal her identity. "She's an old friend in need with nowhere else to stay. I couldn't turn her away."

Deacon narrowly eyed him. "Well, you should make other arrangements before too long." He paused then grudgingly added, "Sarah would probably be happy to have her stay in our spare room."

Mel stiffened, his chest tightening. "No. Kit would be hurt if I made her leave."

Deacon snorted as he opened his door. "Fine. I'll see you later."

Mel strode to the study he used in the Center of Learning to eat his cinnaspice apple trifles and wait for his novices to arrive. Deacon was right that he must help Kit end the Goddess's illusion, even though he'd liked having her staying with him, despite all her stubbornness. If he rearranged his duties, he should be able to escort her to Esrever tomorrow morning. Hopefully, after that, Kit would quit attempting to circumvent the Goddess's purpose and follow her guidance instead.

AFTER BREAKFAST THE FOLLOWING MORNING, Mel and Kit headed to Esrever, which was just as far from the Great Temple as Mirage. Yet Kit still practically ran to the dapper clerk as soon as they entered the witch shop, disregarding the tidy shelves of spell ingredients, magical accoutrements, and magical tomes.

Kit smiled at the clerk. "I've an illusion spell afflicting me that I need removed."

The clerk inclined a half bow. "Of course, venerable lady." Clearly missing Kit's scowl at that honorific, the witch flicked his fingers and muttered a probing spell. Then he blinked and repeated his incantation, much louder this time. Afterward, he frowned and shook his head. "I'm sorry, lady, but I can't sense any spell glowing about you. Whoever cast your illusion spell must have warded it against magical sight and is more powerful than me. Perhaps you should consult an elf or a Rhiannon descendant, if you can find one."

As Kit's shoulders sagged, Mel gave the dapper clerk a gold coin. "Thanks for your assistance." Then he escorted Kit from the fashionable witch shop.

While they returned to the Great Temple, he kept glancing at Kit, who remained silent the entire walk. From her tight lips and set jaw, she was disappointed but still determined to consult more witch shops. Too bad.

Yet unlike after visiting Mirage, Kit didn't ask him about visiting another witch shop at luncheon. Perhaps she was reconsidering that. So he made sure not to mention visiting witch shops either.

Kit continued brooding over the following two days, although she still didn't mention visiting any witch shops. To distract her, he said at dinner on the last day of the Longnight season, "You should join me at the Greysnowes' ball tonight. You can wear the arachne silk you said you brought."

Kit gaped at him, her spoonful of venison stew halfway to her mouth. "Absolutely not. Someone at court might recognize me."

Mel arched a brow. Maybe mentioning her childhood rival would motivate her. "Wren didn't recognize you at Lord and Lady Ravenstone's wedding."

Kit snorted. "Barely." When he began to protest, she sniffed. "Besides, the cut of my arachne silk gown is too flattering for a crone."

He shrugged as he finished his venison stew and began his bread custard. "Wear a shawl over it, and no one shall notice."

Kit raised her eyes skyward. "That gown isn't meant to be worn with a shawl. Besides, I'm not attending a ball at court until I break the Goddess's illusion. Quit asking."

Mel sighed. When would Kit realize that her ancient appearance wasn't hideous and she could let people see her? "Very well."

After dinner, he bundled in his warmest coat then said farewell to Kit before leaving, although she only muttered a reply without looking at him.

On his brisk walk to Greysnowe House, Mel frowned and studied his breath misting in the frigid air. Somehow, he must convince Kit to do *something*. She couldn't hide in his chambers forever. Perhaps he could ask Hawke for advice about what witch shops they could visit. Hawke had visited many of the fashionable ones in Ormas while hunting his mysterious lady, who'd actually been Wren disguised by a glamour spell.

After greeting the Greysnowes, Mel strode straight through their boisterous guests to Hawke and Wren beside Devon and Kiera. "Evening, are Aragon and Selena here?"

Devon shook his head. "Aragon said Selena is too exhausted so late in her pregnancy to attend an evening event."

Wren wrinkled her nose. "I can understand that. Hawke and I shall leave directly after the announcement."

Kiera squeezed Wren's hand. "I'm certain that shall be soon."

Mel frowned at Wren, who looked weary with pale skin and shadows beneath her hazel eyes. His pregnant sister-in-law definitely wouldn't last long tonight. He'd better ask Hawke about witch shops now. He turned to his brother with a bland smile. "I need to consult with a witch, but I'm not having success finding any that can help. Any suggestions?"

His brows rising, Hawke hummed. "I'd start with the veiled witch—she's an incredibly powerful Rhiannon descendant."

Wren nodded and rubbed her rounded stomach. "A seer, according to Annalise."

Mel almost sighed. A Rhiannon-descendant seer could help Kit with the Goddess's illusion if any witch could. Yet how could he convince Kit to visit after she'd already refused because she only trusted fashionable witch shops?

Devon twisted his powerful protection charm about his left wrist. "I could arrange an appointment with Lady Juliet if you like."

Mel grimaced and shook his head. Kit would never consult with the royal witch, who was an influential member of court.

Kiera sipped her sparkling wine. "There's also the wood elf at Over the Walle. She might deign to help."

Mel slowly nodded. Over the Walle was a fashionable witch shop, so Kit would be willing to visit. "I think I'll start there. Thanks."

Hawke leaned toward him. "But why do you need to consult a witch?" He flashed a crooked grin. "Mother shall be elated if it involves an unwed lady like my visits did."

Mel shrugged and straightened his priest robes. He couldn't truly explain without breaking Kit's trust. "I'm just helping someone in need."

Hawke chuckled, his pale eyes gleaming. "I notice you didn't deny helping a lady."

As a blush heated Mel's neck, Wren prodded Hawke with her elbow. "Cease tormenting your brother. He's a priest, so no doubt he meets many in need who aren't eligible ladies."

Mel was about to nod and echo that when Kiera shushed them then said, "The Greysnowes are about to make their announcement."

As the excited crowd quieted and turned to face the Greysnowes at the front of the ballroom, Devon sighed and drew Kiera closer, while Hawke did the same with Wren. Devon said, "I hope this doesn't get too rambunctious."

Beaming at his guests, Lord Greysnowe said, "Thank you all for attending our ball celebrating our only daughter's recent marriage."

Their son Lord Alexander almost snickering beside them, Lady Greysnowe gestured toward an anteroom near the musicians' balcony. "Without further ado, our daughter and her chosen husband, with her new mother-in-law."

The entire ballroom, except for Mel and his family, gasped as Lord and Lady Ravenstone glided from the anteroom with the grinning Dowager Lady Ravenstone behind them. The ballroom remained silent as they joined the Greysnowes and the two mothers embraced. Then chatter erupted, and the crowd surged toward the Greysnowes and the Ravenstones.

Wren shuddered. "Oh my. We can't greet Annalise through all that."

Kiera shook her head. "Yes, we'd better wait."

Mel smiled at them. "How about we enjoy desserts while we wait? Who else wants some?" He chuckled when Wren brightened and bobbed a nod. After the others shook their heads, he left to fetch desserts for him and Wren.

He was returning with two laden plates when Mother, Father, and the Keyes waylaid him. Mother beamed at him and said, "Mel, I didn't know you were attending tonight."

He shrugged. "The Greysnowes invited me as thanks for performing their daughter's wedding ceremony, and I thought I should attend to support them ending the Greysnowe-Ravenstone feud at last."

Father flashed a crooked grin and nodded at Mel's plates. "They might not have invited you if they knew how many desserts you eat."

Mel grinned back then turned to Sir Alaric and Lady Keyes. "One of these plates is for Wren. Your daughter adores desserts as much as I do right now."

Once everyone chuckled at that, Mother leaned toward him. "Before you return to Wren, I wanted to ask you about Kit. Except for that note stating you could contact her, none of us have heard from her since she vanished on Longnight. Is she all right?"

Mel forced a calm smile. "She's fine. Just busy." Busy hiding in his chambers.

Mother pursed her lips. "Which prayer house is Kit staying at? I'd like to visit to check on her."

He swallowed. "I don't think Kit wants any visitors right now." Before Mother could reply, he nodded at his parents and the Keyes then said, "Excuse me. I must get Wren these desserts."

Mel hurried back to Hawke, Wren, Devon, and Kiera. After he and Wren devoured their plates, the two couples went to greet Lady Ravenstone so Hawke and Wren could leave. He fetched another plate of desserts then joined Edouard, Pippa, Elise, and Farson. After everyone exchanged greetings, Edouard eyed the crowd still engulfing the Greysnowes and the Ravenstones. "Goddess, 'tis madness. I don't think I want a ball celebrating my betrothal or marriage."

Elise giggled and winked at Pippa. "You're not the only one with a say in that, Edouard."

Pippa squeezed Edouard's arm. "I wouldn't mind having a ball, but I agree nothing like this one."

Mel smiled as the courting couple beamed at each other. 'Twas amazing they'd not announced their betrothal yet.

Elise turned to Mel. "Edouard mentioned you can contact Kit. How is she? Vanishing when she was about to host a court event isn't like her at all."

Mel almost grimaced. Not more questions about Kit. "She's fine. She just needed to vanish for a while."

Edouard nodded. "I'm glad she's well and no longer staying with me. Monitoring her spending was draining."

Mel frowned at his cousin. Edouard had never understood Kit's unfortunate situation as a girl and always been too harsh on her.

Farson inclined his head toward the Duke of Oakmoor. "Does the Duke of Oakmoor know you can contact Lady Blaine?"

His stomach hardening, Mel shrugged. "Kit didn't mention writing him, and 'twould be awkward for me to tell the duke if she didn't. Besides, 'tisn't as if he'd proposed yet." When Elise frowned and opened her mouth to speak, he smiled at everyone and said, "I should go greet Lord and Lady Ravenstone then leave. I've duties at the Great Temple in the morning."

He fought through the crowd still surrounding the couple and smiled at them. "Congratulations. Your marriage shall be the gossip at court for ages."

Lord Ravenstone grimaced. "'Tis even worse than after the nearly fatal duel between me and Alex. And there isn't the king's summer masquerade to distract everyone this time."

Lady Ravenstone sighed. "I'd beg to leave if our parents weren't reveling in all this." Her ice-perfect face softened. "But seeing our mothers giggle and plot triumphs together is too wonderful to deny."

Mel gave the couple a bracing smile. "Just remind yourself the ball shall be over soon, and when it is, you can return home together."

Lord Ravenstone grinned at his wife, who blushed. He murmured, "I can hardly wait for that."

Blushing too, Mel said farewell then strode back to the Great Temple. As soon as he returned, he must discuss visiting Over the Walle with Kit. Please let that hearten her. Yet when he entered his chambers, she was already abed.

So at breakfast the following morning, he asked, "Did you want to visit Over the Walle in a few days about the Goddess's illusion? Apparently, the owner is a wood elf."

Kit brightened as she stirred cinnaspice and honey into her porridge. "I'd forgotten about Over the Walle. I'd no need to visit a witch shop for magical creatures. But surely an elf can help me. Their powers and understanding of magic are far superior to that of any human witch."

Mel smiled at Kit, his chest warm at her first true smile in days. "I'll rearrange my duties today and let you know when we can visit."

CHAPTER 13

Kit couldn't help smiling as she and Mel headed to Over the Walle a few mornings later. Even the curious stares as they approached the fashionable witch shop couldn't bother her. Elves lived for centuries and were renowned for their wisdom and magical prowess, so the wood elf at Over the Walle could definitely break the Goddess's illusion. She'd finally be free after appearing a hideous crone for over two weeks.

When they entered the exotic witch shop, she swept past the jars of ambrosia, sachets of faedust, bags of stardust grain, and other supernatural supplies to curtsy before the brunette wood elf wearing a merlin robe who was perched in the back of the shop. "My lady elf, I must beg for your succor."

Her dark-green eyes probing, the elf scrutinized Kit for a long moment. Then she quirked a smile and waved toward the tall stools before her. "Sit, please." Her gaze flicked to Mel. "Both of you."

Kit swallowed as she and Mel climbed atop the stools. Please let the elf deign to help.

The wood elf cocked her head, and the merlin feathers braided behind her pointed ears brushed her face. "So what brings an ancient lady with a young voice and one of the Goddess's priests to my witch shop?"

Kit glanced at Mel, who nodded at her to start. She inhaled a bracing breath then replied, "An illusion cast by the Goddess's avatars."

Her winged brows rising, the elf leaned forward. "How intriguing. Spells sent by the Goddess are exceedingly rare." She reached toward Kit. "May I?"

Kit nodded, and the wood elf grasped her chin. As the elf's slitted eyes dilated, the air surrounding Kit warmed like a summer afternoon, and Kit suppressed a shiver. Although no witch, she could still sense the elf's potent magic brushing her skin.

After a moment, the elf exhaled and released Kit's chin, and the air cooled while the feeling of magic dissipated. The elf smiled then murmured, "What a wondrous illusion. Not even I can see your true appearance, although I can see you have an illusion about you. Yet the illusion is limited to your physical appearance—you still feel and sound like yourself, and your aura is not disguised either."

Kit and Mel frowned at each other. What did that matter?

The wood elf chuckled. "For whatever reason, the Goddess must have wanted those who know you to still recognize you, as well as anyone who can read auras like seers, soul healers, and most magical creatures."

Tensing, Kit swallowed. Did that mean the new Lady Ravenstone and the nightmara had recognized her at Lady Ravenstone's wedding? Surely they'd been too distracted to notice a crone sitting in the back of the Harvest Garden. She made herself smile at the elf. "Are you able to break the illusion?"

The elf shook her head. "Unlikely. Since I cannot see your true appearance, I cannot see the entire illusion. Attempting to unravel it blind would be unwise. I might harm you or make the illusion permanent without intending to do so."

Her ribs clenching, Kit sagged on her stool. If even an elf

couldn't help her, then who could? Tears pricked her eyes as she studied her gnarled-looking hands in her lap. She'd still no inkling what the Goddess's avatars meant by becoming who she was meant to be.

Reaching out and squeezing Kit's hands, Mel asked the wood elf, "Do you know another we could consult?"

As Kit blinked back the tears now burning her eyes at Mel's tender concern, the elf sighed and said, "You could visit the veiled witch at Rhiannon's Veils near the docks. She is a powerful seer—perhaps as powerful as Rhiannon herself was." The elf chuckled. "Most elves would not admit this, but the veiled witch's power far exceeds mine. However, I am a mere dabbler in magic, not a lore master who has dedicated my life to studying it."

Raising her gaze, Kit inhaled. The veiled witch had been the witch Mel had mentioned before—the one who'd provided spells for Wren, Lady Kiera, and Lady Ravenstone. If an elf recommended her too, the veiled witch *must* be powerful despite her shop's poor location. "Thank you, my lady. We'll consult the veiled witch next."

The wood elf inclined her head as Kit and Mel slid from their stools. After Mel handed her six gold coins, the elf said, "Good fortune to you."

As Kit and Mel returned to the Great Temple, Mel eyed her. "Are you all right?"

She flashed a blinding smile to conceal her upset. "I'm fine. When can we visit the veiled witch?"

Mel sighed. "In a few days, I hope."

Kit echoed his sigh but didn't protest. Mel was helping all he could, and if she'd listened to him, she'd have already visited the veiled witch. She fisted her hands in her cloak. But please let the veiled witch be able to break the Goddess's illusion when they could visit her at last.

· · ·

The following morning, Kit awoke with a burgeoning megrim behind her right eye. Her first in two weeks—a record in recent months. Doubtless this megrim was caused by yesterday's upset and her poor sleep because of it. She crawled from bed and drank some megrim tonic before meeting Mel for breakfast. Fortunately, the pain wasn't excruciating yet, so she could feign she was fine until Mel left to visit some almskitchens. As they'd discussed last night, he'd not return until dinner to ensure he'd have time to visit the veiled witch with her in a few days.

Once Mel left, she closed the curtains and sank into a plush chair before his bookcase, but despite that and her tonic earlier, her megrim continued to grow.

Not long before luncheon, a familiar spritely knock sounded on Mel's door, so Kit sighed and forced herself to rise and let Sarah enter.

Blinking, Sarah peered about Mel's nearly dark chambers. "Why are all the curtains closed?"

Kit dropped into a chair at the table and rubbed her throbbing temple. "I've a megrim. I suffer them every so often."

Sarah winced as she sat across from Kit. "Oh, you poor dear. I hope 'tisn't too bad."

Managing a smile to reassure her new friend, Kit shrugged. She'd suffered worse, but 'twas bad enough.

Eyeing her, Sarah leaned forward. "Is there anything I can do?" When Kit shook her head, Sarah sighed then continued, "I stopped by to see if you wanted to join me for luncheon in the dining hall since Mel is out. But I doubt you feel up to that, do you?"

Kit shook her head again. Even without her megrim, she'd not have felt up to that.

Sarah rose. "I'll leave so you can get some rest, but I'll return with some luncheon later."

Her head pounding and stomach nauseous, Kit made herself nod before returning to her earlier chair by the bookcase. She dozed until Sarah returned with chicken soup and bread. After eating, she settled back in the bookcase chair and napped until Mel shook her awake hours later.

Mel narrowed his eyes at her. "You've a megrim. For how long?"

Lowering her gaze, Kit shrugged as her blood throbbed behind her eye. "Since this morning."

Mel humphed. "Why didn't you tell me?"

She shrugged again, resisting the urge to fidget. "I didn't want to further delay our visit to the veiled witch."

Mel tilted her chin until their gazes met, and she swallowed at the concern darkening his deep-brown eyes. He murmured, "Visiting a witch, no matter how powerful, isn't worth letting yourself suffer."

Her pulse quickening at Mel's touch despite her megrim, Kit grimaced up at him. "Enduring the Goddess's illusion is suffering too."

Releasing her chin, Mel sighed. "'Tisn't at all the same."

Mel strode to the cabinets then prepared tea and a cold compress before massaging her like he had during her previous megrim. Afterward, he made her eat some more chicken soup and helped her into bed. He tucked the covers about her and brushed the hair from her throbbing forehead. "Rest well, Kit."

She managed a tremulous smile before succumbing to slumber. And unlike the previous night, no restless dreams disturbed her sleep.

WHEN KIT and Mel walked to Rhiannon's Veils several mornings later, she twisted her hands in her cloak. Hopefully, the veiled witch would provide more help than the wood elf had. She swallowed as Mel opened the witch shop's weathered red door and ushered her inside.

Kit glanced about the dim chamber, grimacing at the pervasive incense. Please let it not give her a megrim. Then she blinked. The inside of the witch shop was nicer than she'd expected given its location and weathered door. However, unlike most witch shops, the dim chamber was mostly empty—with just glass beads over the rear door, a table, two chairs, and several cabinets holding spell ingredients, magical accoutrements, and other bizarre objects. She sighed. Also unlike other witch shops, no clerk awaited them. Where was the veiled witch?

As if thinking that had summoned her, the veiled witch sashayed through the glass beads. She certainly matched her appellation—black veils concealed her hair and most of her face, giving her a mysterious air. As the glass beads tinkled behind her, the veiled witch stilled and studied Kit, and her exotically lined eyes widened. "I can guess why you've come to see me. But I'm afraid I can't help you revoke the Goddess's illusion."

Mel inhaling sharply beside her, Kit gaped at the veiled witch. Her powers were potent indeed. "You can see the Goddess's illusion without casting a probing spell? Can you see my true appearance as well?"

The veiled witch flicked her fingers, jingling bracelets and tiny bells. "Of course. I'm a Rhiannon-descendant seer." Her gaze turned to Mel. "Which doubtless you already know, considering your escort is Lord Beza Hawke's priest brother and King Devon's cousin."

As Mel nodded, Kit stiffened, and the back of her neck prickled. Had the veiled witch recognized her as the fashionable Countess of Blaine as well? Shoving that aside, she gritted a beseeching smile. "If you're so powerful, why can't you remove the Goddess's illusion?"

A sigh undulated the witch's black veils. "Because only the gods or the gods' chosen avatars when infused with the gods' powers can cast or revoke holy spells. And even if I could, I wouldn't defy the Goddess by ending her illusion. She blessed you to appear ancient for a reason."

Fisting her hands at her sides, Kit glared at the veiled witch.

"Appearing a crone is no blessing. And Mel's witch priest friend called it a *curse*."

The veiled witch tilted her head. "Holy curses and holy blessings are essentially the same, except holy curses initially seem negative, while holy blessings appear positive from the start. The gods aren't evil or cruel, unlike the black witches who cast ordinary curses, so holy curses aren't either. Any harm holy curses do is to help the cursed person grow, and that growth is what breaks their curse. They simply must follow the guidance their god provided."

Kit sagged, weight crushing her chest. 'Twas what Deacon had said about ending the Goddess's illusion. The disapproving priest hadn't simply been refusing to help, after all.

Mel wrapped his arm about her and squeezed her shoulders, and warmth eased the weight crushing her. Then he asked the veiled witch, "Can you at least help Kit understand what she must do to break the Goddess's illusion herself?"

Leaning into Mel's embrace, Kit slanted the veiled witch a pleading glance. "Please, madam witch. All the Goddess's avatars told me after casting the crone illusion was that 'twould end when I become who I'm meant to be and that I had everything I needed. But I still don't understand what to do."

The veiled witch nodded then set a large quartz bowl on the table and added crystalline water from an opalescent leather flask. Sitting, she beckoned Kit. "Come sit."

Kit swallowed and made herself leave Mel's arms to sit across from the veiled witch.

Extracting a needle, the veiled witch reached for Kit. "Your full name and your hand, please."

Kit swallowed again but gave the veiled witch her hand. "Katherine Elizabeth Sutton Gernand, the Countess of Blaine."

Humming, the veiled witch pricked Kit's finger and allowed three drops of blood to fall into the large quartz bowl, turning the crystalline water pink. The dim witch shop hushed like the quiet before a thunderstorm as the veiled witch peered into the pink water. Somehow, her potent powers were more eerie coming from her than from a magical creature like the wood elf. Perhaps because the veiled witch was clearly human.

Eventually, the veiled witch returned her gaze to Kit, her dark eyes probing. "Have you found sanctuary at the Great Temple yet?"

Shifting in her wooden seat, Kit waved toward Mel standing behind her. "Yes, in Mel's spare room."

The veiled witch inclined her head, her black veils fluttering. "Then you're in precisely the right place to grow as the Goddess intends. Participating in temple life shall show you the way."

Kit wobbled a nod as Mel squeezed her shoulder. Why would participating in temple life show her the way? She wasn't worthy enough to belong at a temple. Yet a Rhiannon-descendant seer couldn't be mistaken, so she must stay at the Great Temple.

The veiled witch circled her hand over the large quartz bowl, and Kit's three drops of blood rose from the once-again crystalline water. Then the veiled witch flicked her fingers, and the blood vanished.

Inhaling at that additional display of powerful magic, Kit allowed Mel to pull her upright. Then she swept a deep curtsy as he handed the veiled witch nine gold coins. "Thank you for your wisdom and advice, madam witch."

Holding her gaze, the veiled witch nodded back. "Remember that another's truth isn't yours unless you make it so. And the Goddess's avatars were right that you have everything you need. Just listen to your heart, and you'll hear the Goddess's guidance."

A shiver prickling her skin, Kit swept another curtsy. So eerie.

Once they stepped out in the bright winter sunlight, Mel arched his brows at her. "What did the veiled witch mean by that last advice?"

She forced a shrug as Father's cruel insults echoed through her like the whispers of bitter ghosts. Those words she'd proven true long ago. "I'm not certain."

His eyes narrowing, Mel studied her for several moments then asked, "Why do you think the veiled witch suggested you participate in temple life?"

Kit frowned and shrugged again. What possible purpose could *she* learn at the Great Temple? "Perhaps participating in temple life shall show me ways to make supporting the Great Temple fashionable at court."

Mel inclined his head. "I suppose that makes sense. So how did you want to start participating in temple life? We could attend Sext together then eat luncheon in the dining hall."

She swallowed but stiffened her spine. Everyone would see her as a crone then, yet if she must participate in temple life to break the Goddess's illusion, continuing to hide was futile. She must simply remember to disguise her voice and move like an old lady would. She nodded at Mel. "Very well."

Mel grinned and squeezed her arm. "Wonderful. You'll love it. Sext is my favorite service—hymns are a perfect way to praise the Goddess."

Warmed by Mel's grin, Kit smiled back as they returned to the Great Temple.

CHAPTER 14

As he heartily sang the hymns at Sext, Mel glanced at Kit to check how she was enjoying the service. Although she sang quietly, probably because she wasn't familiar with the songs like he was, she was at least singing. And she was standing straighter than she had at Rhiannon's Veils and almost smiling. Good, attending Sext had heartened her as much as he'd hoped. Just like when she'd been a girl.

He grinned at Kit after Sext ended. "What did you think?"

Kit smiled, still gazing at the raised sanctuary of the main temple that held the massive, gold-veined white marble statue of the Goddess behind the matching altar covered with gifts from parishioners. "I'd forgotten how moving attending regular services worshipping the Goddess was." She glanced about the nave, whose white limestone with green and gold ornamentation glowed in the midday sun streaming through the many stained-glass windows. "Especially amid all this splendor."

His chest warm at her smile, Mel took Kit's arm and escorted her from their foldable chairs at the end of the back row. The Great Temple *was* a stunning tribute to the Goddess that had taken over a century to build, although legend said its splendor was nothing compared to the Goddess's Great Temple in Oress that had been razed during the Stone Wars by a crazed chimera. He squeezed Kit's arm. "When is the last time you've visited the main temple?"

Kit tilted her head. "Elise's wedding almost three years ago. We were always at Blaine Castle when we attended Longnight Vespers." Just before they left the nave, she sighed and glanced back at the altar and the Goddess's statue. "I should have attended services sooner, but 'tisn't fashionable to be overly pious, and I had a reputation to maintain."

He almost grimaced as they strode through the covered walkways toward the dining hall. Perhaps freeing Kit from her fashionable reputation, in addition to breaking through her stubbornness, was why the Goddess had blessed Kit with an illusion. "Well, you no longer need to worry about that."

Kit blinked. "I suppose that's true."

To distract Kit before she could brood, Mel waggled his brows and asked, "Are you hungry after all our walking today? The food is plentiful in the dining hall, although I'm afraid there's no dessert at luncheon."

Her smoky eyes gleaming, Kit chuckled. "So you've mentioned. That deprivation must truly bother you."

He smiled at her allowing him to distract her. Hopefully, 'twould continue. He shrugged to continue their banter. "I make do with bread and honey."

Kit chuckled again. "Very noble of you."

Then they entered the dining hall, and as they fetched spicy pork stew, bread, and tea, the head kitchen priestess Esther, who he'd known since they were novices together, beamed at him and handed him a pot of honey like always. "Afternoon, Mel. Who's this?"

Before he could reply, Kit rasped in a deep voice, "Just a humble visitor here to witness the Great Temple's many glories."

Her gray-trimmed priest robes stilling, Esther eyed Kit, who flashed a bright grin in return before tottering to the back of the dining hall.

After shrugging at Esther with an apologetic smile, he followed Kit then sat beside her and arched his brows. "What was that about?"

Taking his pot of honey to add a spoonful to her tea, Kit sighed and shook her head. "I think 'tis best if you don't introduce me to anyone—or mention I'm staying with you. If gossip spreads about a Kit staying with you, people might realize I'm Lady Blaine."

Mel frowned at Kit as he reclaimed the honey and liberally sweetened his tea. Even though she was participating in temple life like the veiled witch advised, Kit was still hiding. "I doubt it. Few outside the family know we were close as children, and the Great Temple is a different world than court."

Kit tore her bread into tiny pieces. "I don't want to risk it. Besides, I want to observe for a bit before truly participating in temple life."

He sighed but nodded. At the Great Temple, Kit *was* like a weredolphin on land for the first time and needed time to find her legs. And she despised appearing vulnerable thanks to her childhood enduring her cruel father's "tender" care. His jaw tightening, he began his spicy pork stew. He'd just have to keep encouraging her to participate until she was ready to do so.

After luncheon, they returned to his chambers for his papers, then Kit joined him while he taught the two groups of novices about the history behind prayer houses. However, she sat in the back corner and said nothing, so doubtless the eager novices didn't even notice her.

As they returned to his chambers, Kit shook her head and asked, "Do all the novices you teach possess so much energy?"

Mel chuckled. "Usually. They're all so young and eager to serve the Goddess. They make me feel old sometimes."

Kit raised her eyes skyward. "Mel, you're only six years or so older and possess more energy than those puppies. You're just forever running about helping everyone else—including me."

Almost blushing, he shrugged. Why did Kit sound so

amazed about that? He couldn't not help her. "I get that from Mother no doubt."

Prodding his arm, Kit snorted outside his chambers. "The duchess isn't the only reason."

Mel shrugged again and opened his door then blinked at the note adorned with Mother's elegant script inside the threshold. Paul must have slid it under the door rather than interrupting his teaching. The rabbity priest avoided that unless 'twas imperative since he'd always disliked enduring lessons.

As Mel bent to grasp Mother's note, Kit asked, "What's that?"

He opened the note. "A note from Mother, oddly enough." His brows rose as he read. "Inviting us to a family luncheon the day after tomorrow." The last time Mother had done that, she'd informed him and Hawke of Aragon and Selena's pregnancy.

Kit blinked at him. "Us?"

Mel nodded. "Mother wrote that I should bring you along." When Kit stared at him, he handed her Mother's note. "Here, read for yourself."

Once she did, Kit pursed her lips. "Why did your mother invite me to a family luncheon that Wren and Hawke shall surely attend? Hawke detests me for what I did to Wren, and his glares would ruin luncheon." She shook her head and returned Mother's note. "Not that I can attend looking like I do. You'll have to tell the duchess I can't see anyone at present."

He sighed but tossed Mother's note and his papers on the table. Encouraging Kit to attend a family luncheon would be futile when she wouldn't even let him introduce her here. "Shall we head to Vespers? 'Tis about to start."

Kit nodded, and they returned to the main temple. During Vespers' lengthy prayers thanking the Goddess, he darted glances at Kit. Unlike at Sext, a faint frown furrowed her brow. No doubt she didn't feel grateful for the Goddess's illusion right now. So he didn't ask how she enjoyed the service but simply escorted her to the dining hall for dinner.

They'd just begun eating their beefsteak stew with dumplings when Deacon and Sarah strode over to join them. Although Deacon frowned while they sat across the table, Sarah beamed at Kit and said, "I'm so glad you could join us tonight."

As Kit smiled back then she and Sarah began sharing their days, Deacon humphed and eyed the chattering ladies. He muttered to Mel, "What made *her* finally emerge?"

Mel sighed. Perhaps if he revealed Kit was no longer defying the Goddess, Deacon wouldn't be so harsh. "Kit decided circumventing the Goddess's illusion was impossible, so she's participating in temple life to understand the Goddess's guidance."

Deacon snorted into his beefsteak stew and dumplings. "We'll see how long that lasts. Temple life is harder than people realize —especially a spoiled court lady."

Frowning at Deacon, Mel glanced at Kit and Sarah, who were both still engrossed in their conversation. Doubtless Deacon had guessed Kit was from court given she was an old friend of a duke's son. Mel leaned toward Deacon and lowered his voice to ensure neither lady overheard, "Kit understands suffering better than most at court."

To quit discussing Kit before he revealed too much, Mel asked Deacon about his day at Charmed Blessings. Deacon had just finished describing a merchant's wife buying the holy witch shop's entire supply of miniature Summer Queen shrines for her eldest son's wedding ceremony when Kit tugged on Mel's priest robes.

After he lowered his last bite of spice cake and turned toward her, Kit said, "Sarah asked if I'd join her at Peaceful Minds tomorrow, so you'll be free to perform your duties without me for most of the day."

He nodded. The prayer house would be a good place for her first taste of temple life outside the Great Temple, particularly with Sarah. And if that went well, he could probably get Kit to visit some almskitchens soon. The girl who'd joined him visiting poor villagers would enjoy doing the same in Ormas. He smiled at Kit. "I don't mind you joining me on my duties, but you'll have fun with Sarah."

Kit beamed at him before turning back to Sarah, and the two ladies began chattering again. 'Twas wonderful to see Kit so cheerful after days of her brooding in his chambers.

THE FOLLOWING MORNING, Mel woke Kit to attend Lauds, and she joined him without protest. She spent most of the dawn service in the Sun Chapel staring at the many Goddess laurels in pots before the windows. With their showy white flowers and small apple-like fruit at the same time nestled amid their lush dark-green leaves, the Goddess laurels were an awe-inspiring sight. Plus, their cinnaspice-apple fragrance perfumed the air, and cinnaspice was one of Kit's favorite things.

He smiled at Kit once Lauds ended. "Did you want to go look at the Goddess laurels?"

Sighing, Kit shook her head. "Perhaps another time. You must organize the almskitchens, and I must meet Sarah."

Mel nodded then escorted her from their pew at the back of the Sun Chapel. "Did you want to join me in the chapter house or have me escort you to the dining hall? I can meet you for breakfast once I'm finished."

Kit hummed. "I'll join you."

So Mel organized the almskitchens in the chapter house with Kit watching before they headed to breakfast. Kit had barely finished her cinnaspice porridge before Sarah swept in and whisked her from the dining hall.

Mel smiled after them. He must write a list of charities he should visit with Kit later. He'd returned to his chambers and was about to start his list when a firm knock interrupted him.

He opened his door then stilled at High Priest Theodag. The high priest had never visited his chambers before. Why now? Had the high priest somehow discovered Kit was staying here?

He waved for the high priest to enter. "Good morning, your excellency."

The gold trim on his priest robes glittering, High Priest Theodag strode inside. "Good morning, Mel. You've not been around for more than services lately. Is everything all right?"

Swallowing, Mel managed a calm smile. "Just busy. My family was here for the Longnight season this year, so I'd events outside the temple to attend." And he'd been spending time with Kit in his chambers whenever possible.

The high priest rubbed his jaw. "Of course. I suppose you've not heard the news then." When Mel shook his head, the high priest continued, "Elder Priestess Agnes has decided to retire and return to Blackham."

Mel nodded. Elder Priestess Agnes, who'd led the community priests of Calatini for nearly forty years, was older than his parents, perhaps around Wren's father's age. Not surprising she'd decided to retire. "She'll be sorely missed. Who's in line to replace her?"

High Priest Theodag frowned. "No one really, which is why she waited so long to retire. But with your gift of inspiring others to serve those less fortunate, I thought you might do well as the elder community priest of Calatini."

Mel blew a sigh. Becoming Calatini's elder community priest was nowhere as bad as becoming the kingdom's future high priest, but 'twas a lot of additional responsibilities, and he was already busy. "I don't know..."

The high priest leaned toward him. "Please, you're our best candidate by far." He exhaled. "Although your acceptance does mean I must find another as my successor."

Mel almost snorted. *That* would be a relief. But how could he take on additional responsibilities, particularly while Kit was staying with him? "Is there truly no one else?"

High Priest Theodag shook his head. "Can *you* think of anyone?"

Sighing again, Mel grimaced. Most of his fellow community

priests had no inclination or skills to lead others. He was content in his duties too, but thanks to growing up watching Mother, he'd the skills to lead others, which was why he'd been organizing the almskitchens since he'd been ordained. And leading the community priests would still involve spreading the Goddess's love through charity. He straightened. So somehow he must make becoming the elder community priest of Calatini work.

He nodded at the high priest. "Very well, I'll train as Elder Priestess Agnes's successor."

A beam brightened High Priest Theodag's austere face. "Wonderful. I'll inform Agnes of your acceptance. She's agreed to remain in Ormas until your investiture next Longnight, and the two of you can figure out how your duties must shift to accommodate your new position."

Mel swallowed but nodded. Once the high priest strode from his chambers, he sank into his chair at the table. In addition to working with Elder Priestess Agnes and his other duties, he must still help Kit find her purpose and end the Goddess's illusion. Please let him have time for everything. He couldn't fail the poor parishioners, the Great Temple, or Kit.

CHAPTER 15

$\mathcal{K}$it smiled at Sarah's grin as the priestess ushered her into Peaceful Minds. Her friend was so excited to show her the prayer house, especially since she'd admitted to never visiting one. She glanced about the entry room of the prayer house—witchlights cast soft light on the pale-blue walls, gentle music came from the enchanted music box in the corner, and a small waterfall babbled down the far wall. A priestess with Sarah's tranquil temperament would adore serving here.

Sarah waved Kit toward the hall. "At Peaceful Minds and other prayer houses, we strive to help people find peace and well-being so they can better connect to the Goddess through prayer. But because there are many paths to achieve that, we do much more than just lead prayers and provide retreats for those needing reflection."

Light suffusing her, Kit nodded for Sarah to continue. Sarah's joy in her purpose was so lovely. Perhaps one day she'd feel the same.

Sarah led her to a small chapel with a white marble altar and statue of the Goddess. "Some find peace in a chapel." They returned to the hall, and Sarah nodded at a closed door to her left. "Others require silence." She led Kit to a room redolent of cinnaspice and apples from the Goddess laurel in the corner. "Others scent."

Kit inhaled the heavenly fragrance. Although not a temple, the prayer house must count as Goddess-consecrated ground for the Goddess laurel to be blooming and bearing fruit.

Sarah led her to a conservatory full of verdant trees, wooden benches, and tiny songbirds. "Some must return to nature." They continued to a luxurious bathhouse with steaming pools amid white and blue-green tiles. "Or soak in warm mineral water." They headed to a quiet room where a priestess poured tea in an elegant ritual for those waiting. "Or drink tea." She led Kit to several small rooms where priestesses, healers from their gold torcs and green trim on their priest robes, massaged people. "Or through touch."

Tingling flooded Kit as Mel's tender massage during her megrims echoed through her. Touch *could* be very soothing.

Sarah nodded at several small rooms, half with closed doors. "Others need to talk and hear advice to achieve peace." They continued to two large rooms opposite of each other. The first held a priestess sitting cross-legged on the floor instructing those sitting around her to breathe deeply. The second held a priestess leading people in flowing movements. "Whereas meditation or movement helps others." Sarah smiled at Kit. "So what do you think of Peaceful Minds?"

Kit smiled back. "'Tis wonderful. The peace here is tangible, so I imagine you help many, many people." When Sarah beamed, Kit asked, "I didn't see any priests here. Is that normal?"

Sarah hummed. "Most who serve at prayer houses *are* priestesses, even at Peaceful Minds—the largest prayer house in Ormas since 'tis near the Great Temple. Elder Priestess Agnes, the elder community priestess of Calatini, oversees Peaceful Minds, although she relies on her assistant Priestess Dorothea to manage it due to her other duties." Sarah lowered her voice, "I suspect Dorothea shall completely run Peaceful Minds once

Elder Priestess Agnes retires next Longnight. Thankfully, such heavy duties aren't mine. Running a prayer house would be much too stressful for me."

Kit inclined her head. Even leading priests would have conflict, which would upset her affable friend. Sarah wanted to include everyone and ensure they got along.

Straightening, Sarah arched her brows at Kit. "Where would you like to start? I typically counsel people, but 'tis private, so you can't accompany me."

Kit smiled. Not surprising 'twas Sarah's duty here. "I'll wander for a bit, if 'tis all right."

Sarah waved a hand down the hall. "Of course. I'll find you for luncheon."

Kit wandered Peaceful Minds, spending some time in most of the rooms, except for the bathhouse, counseling rooms, and massage rooms. She'd be much too vulnerable participating in those rooms. Then she ate luncheon with Sarah, but bored with being idle, she didn't return to wandering afterward. Instead, she volunteered to fetch water and towels for the people performing movements.

When she and Sarah returned to the Great Temple in the late afternoon, she couldn't help smiling. The peace from the prayer house still suffused her. However, when she joined Mel in his chambers, she stilled at the faint frown furrowing his brow. "What's wrong?"

Mel sighed and looked up from the note he was reading. "Nothing really. I just agreed to become the next elder community priest of Calatini, but I'm concerned about completing all my duties. Elder Priestess Agnes wants to meet tomorrow to discuss everything, yet I can't thanks to the family luncheon."

She eyed him. Mel would be a superb elder community priest, although he was right to fret. He was already too busy. Yet saying that wouldn't hearten him, so instead she nodded and said, "Surely you can meet the following day. And perhaps you can find some guidance from the Goddess during Vespers."

Like the previous evening, she and Mel attended Vespers then ate dinner with Sarah and Deacon. And although Mel remained cheerful throughout, she could tell he was still fretting.

When they returned to his chambers, Mel exhaled as they sat in the chairs before his bookcase. "I almost forgot. When he visited, High Priest Theodag asked about my recent absences. I didn't mention you, but he might return to discuss my new position, and he'll notice you if he does."

Kit swallowed, twisting her hands in her skirt. She'd never dared to meet High Priest Theodag at court because of his austere and trenchant reputation. But the high priest had regular contact with court and would know about Lady Blaine's sudden disappearance, so she mustn't let him see her. If he discovered the unworthy Countess of Blaine was hiding in his temple with one of his priests, he might evict her, and she'd nowhere else to go. Plus, the veiled witch had said she must stay at the Great Temple to break the Goddess's illusion. But Mel would protect her as best he could, so she should remain with him as much as possible, even if that meant joining him at family events.

When Mel prepared to leave the following morning for his family luncheon, Kit leapt upright as well. Risking his family discovering her crone illusion was better than risking the high priest discovering it. At least she knew Mel's family would take pity on her—even Hawke despite his anger. "Do you mind if I join you for your family luncheon?"

Mel grinned at her. "Of course not. Plus, you *were* invited."

She grimaced. "I'm not revealing that." On purpose, at least.

Sighing, Mel took her arm and escorted her from his chambers then out to his parents' waiting carriage. She relaxed as they settled on the forward seat. The carriage meant only his family would see Mel with a crone.

When they arrived at Childes House, Mel's mother sailed over with the duke close behind. After embracing Mel, the duchess said, "You're the first to arrive other than Diana and Alaric." She turned to Kit. "Who's this?"

Mel pursed a tight smile. "The lady who's recently begun acting as my assistant. We usually eat luncheon together, so I didn't think you'd mind if I brought her."

As the duchess's brows rose, Kit swept a deep curtsy. Deepening her voice, she rasped, "Call me Kay." 'Twas similar enough to Kit that she'd remember to answer to it, but hopefully different enough that no one would realize her identity.

Mel's parents glanced at each other then nodded at her. The duchess said, "A pleasure." She turned back to her son. "Were you able to convince Kit to attend?"

Kit blinked at the duchess. Why was Mel's mother asking after her?

His shoulders stiffening, Mel didn't glance at Kit. "She said she can't see anyone at present."

Kit swallowed to ease her aching throat. Deceiving his family clearly troubled Mel.

The duchess frowned. "Is Kit truly all right?"

Mel nodded, still not looking at Kit. "She just wants to avoid people from her old life right now."

Kit almost blushed when the duke flashed a crooked grin and replied, "Except for you."

Shrugging, Mel straightened his priest robes. "I'm a priest. 'Tis different."

Kit suppressed her echoing nod as his parents exchanged another glance. Fortunately, before they could probe further, Aragon and Selena entered the drawing room. Goddess, Selena appeared about to give birth at any moment. Why *had* the duchess arranged a family luncheon right now?

As Mel's parents fussed over Selena, Kit muttered to Mel, "Why did your mother ask about me?"

Mel sighed. "Mother is fond of you. She asked about you at the Greysnowes' ball too, as did Elise. Your sudden disappearance worried them, especially since you've not contacted anyone afterward."

Her chest squeezing, Kit studied her old-looking hands. They'd actually cared enough to worry? When she and Mel returned to the Great Temple, she should write to reassure them. She grimaced. She should write the Duke of Oakmoor too, informing him she wasn't returning to court soon. Although the rakehell duke had likely begun courting another, 'twasn't right to not formally release him.

Before long, the rest of the luncheon guests arrived—Wren and Hawke, King Devon and Lady Kiera, Elise and Lord Farson with Arvan, and Edouard and Pippa with Pippa's two brothers.

Everyone headed to the family dining room, and once the gentlemen served the ladies oyster soup, the duchess beamed at her guests. "No doubt you're wondering why I arranged this luncheon. I would have done so sooner, but Hawke and Wren only told us and the Keyes last week."

Her spoon halfway to her mouth, Kit glanced at Wren and Hawke then their parents. Wren smiled with a blush darkening her cheeks, while Hawke flashed a proud grin, and all four parents beamed.

The duchess continued, "Hawke and Wren are having *twins*."

Congratulations swept about the table, but King Devon and Lady Kiera just smiled while Elise paled slightly. Since Lady Kiera was close friends with Wren, doubtless she and the king already knew. And although too gracious to cry, Elise was likely upset because she wasn't pregnant after nearly three years of marriage.

Once the congratulations quieted, Aragon grinned at his mother. "I'm surprised you aren't hosting another fete to celebrate. Why should Selena and I be the only ones to enjoy one?"

As the duke and Sir Alaric chuckled, the duchess and Lady Keyes grimaced at each other. Then the duchess replied, "Hawke made us swear not to before they told us."

Everyone laughed at that, except Elise, who only managed a tremulous smile.

Kit lowered her spoon as she eyed Wren and Hawke smiling at each other, her heart aching. If only she could enjoy a deep and lasting love like theirs. She forced herself to eat her oyster soup. But she never would.

When the servants brought the next course, she blinked at the mug of spiced cider they gave her instead of wine.

Mel winked at her. "I thought you'd prefer it. 'Tis still winter, so requesting spiced cider isn't unusual."

She smiled back as warmth filled her at Mel's kindness. "I do, thanks."

While she sipped her spiced cider, she glanced about the table. Hopefully, no one realized Mel's new assistant preferred Lady Blaine's favorite drink. However, everyone except Mel's mother was too distracted to notice. Kit tensed at the duchess studying the spiced cider with narrowed eyes. She'd better avoid Mel's perceptive mother later.

So when the ladies withdrew to the drawing room after luncheon, she made sure to remain across the room from the duchess. Fortunately, the gentlemen soon joined them, and everyone began toasting Wren and Hawke again.

As Hawke insisted they toast Aragon and Selena for having the next heir to the duchy, Kit frowned at Elise slipping from the drawing room. Lord Farson was attempting to persuade young Arvan to return his sparkling wine and take a flute of lymonade instead, so not even he noticed his wife's departure.

Kit handed Mel her sparkling wine. Elise shouldn't be alone right now. Kit muttered, "I'll be back. Excuse me."

Before he could reply, she bustled after Elise into the morning room.

Elise whirled to face Kit, her shoulders hunched and usual grin missing with tears shimmering in her blue eyes.

A lump clogging her throat at Elise's upset, Kit embraced her stepdaughter. "Everything shall be all right."

Elise stiffened before beginning to sob, and Kit drew Elise to a sofa and held her hands as she cried. Poor Elise. She yearned so for a child of her own.

Then after a hesitant knock, Edouard stepped into the morning room, without Pippa beside him for once. "Elise?"

As Elise turned away, Kit narrowed her eyes at Edouard and said, "Go fetch Lord Farson."

Edouard jerked a nod then fled.

Her lips trembling, Elise wiped her face. "I'm sorry for crying all over you. I don't even know your name, and I'm being ridiculous."

Kit squeezed Elise's other hand. Although she couldn't offer advice as herself, advice from a crone rather than a too young stepmother shouldn't nettle Elise. "You can call me Kay. And you're not being ridiculous. 'Tis hard to see everyone else enjoy what you yearn to have but don't."

Elise blinked, her gaze still glassy with tears. "How did you know that I crave to have children too?"

Kit shifted on the sofa. Elise hadn't said why she was upset, had she? To excuse her slip, she murmured, "I *am* acting as Mel's assistant."

Elise exhaled. "I suppose he must have told you." Her shoulders sagged. "I feel so mean for being unable to properly celebrate Hawke and Wren's happy news."

Squeezing Elise's hand again, Kit smiled at her. "Once you compose yourself, you shall." Elise was too gracious not to—unlike herself.

Before Elise could reply, Lord Farson burst into the morning room and pulled Elise into his arms. "Forgive me for not noticing your distress."

As Elise began crying into Lord Farson's chest, Kit slipped from the morning room and smiled at Edouard, who was hovering outside the door. She patted his arm. "Elise just needs time alone with her husband."

Edouard frowned as they began back to the drawing room.

"Do you think so? I've never seen Elise so miserable before, not even when Mother died."

Kit nodded to reassure Edouard. "Yes, but if you want to help Elise, you could bring her some fresh bread and butter in a quarter of an hour."

Edouard brightened. "Devouring that does always cheer Elise. Thanks." He strode away, doubtless heading to the kitchen.

Then Kit rejoined the others in the drawing room, and Mel returned her sparkling wine with arched brows and asked, "What was that about?"

CHAPTER 16

$\mathcal{A}$ ccepting her flute of sparkling wine, Kit gave a faint shrug and answered his question, "Elise needed comfort."

Mel smiled at Kit, his chest warming. And she'd rushed to help—exactly like the tender girl he'd known would have. Perhaps that hadn't entirely been an illusion, after all. Just buried. "'Twas kind of you to help."

Her fingers clenching on her flute, Kit tossed back her sparkling wine. "Not really." She glanced at him through her lashes. "Could we return to the Great Temple? I want to leave before your mother corners and quizzes me."

He nodded. Mother's persistent quizzing would distress Kit. Plus, although he'd arranged for Sarah to teach his two groups of novices this afternoon, he should return to the Great Temple to prepare for his meeting with Elder Priestess Agnes tomorrow.

But when he and Kit began to leave, Mother glided over with Father. She gave them a warm smile. "Are you leaving already?"

Mel returned Mother's smile. To shield Kit, who'd stiffened beside him, he replied, "I've duties at the Great Temple. I just agreed to train as the next elder community priest of Calatini."

As Mother beamed, Father clapped his shoulder and said,

"Congratulations! You'll make an exceptional elder community priest." Father chuckled. "Although 'tisn't the position we were expecting. High Priest Theodag seemed determined to make you his successor."

Mel almost grimaced while Kit stiffened further. Of course the high priest had mentioned that to his parents. "Fortunately, he's abandoned that now since he needs me as the elder community priest."

Although still beaming, Mother sighed. "Your promotion is wonderful news, but I suppose you'll be busier than ever now. I hope you can still manage to attend some family events." She turned to Kit. "And you must join him."

Her eyes demurely lowered, Kit curtsied and rasped, "Thank you for inviting me, your grace."

Mother hummed. "We're glad to have anyone Mel likes join us." When Kit's gaze flew to meet hers, Mother peered at her then smiled. "No matter who they are."

As Kit paled and froze, Mel squeezed her arm to reassure her before smiling at Mother and Father. "We really must go. We'll see you soon." Then he escorted Kit from his parents' townhouse and into their carriage.

Kit collapsed on the forward seat, her face white and drawn. "Oh, Goddess, your mother knows. *Already.* I never should have attended today."

While the carriage rumbled toward the Great Temple, he threaded his fingers through Kit's. Mother guessing her identity wasn't surprising. Mother was perceptive and had always paid special attention to Kit due to Kit's unfortunate childhood. He rubbed her palm with his thumb to comfort her. "Mother shan't tell anyone other than Father, so your secret is safe."

Sighing, Kit leaned against him and rested her head on his shoulder. "I suppose. Perhaps I can convince her that she was mistaken when I write her this afternoon."

Mel swallowed, his pulse quickening as Kit's delectable cinnaspice scent washed over him. "You're writing Mother?"

Kit sighed again. "I decided I should when you said she and Elise have been asking about me. I don't want them to worry."

Warmth suffusing him, he squeezed Kit's hand. There was his tender girl again. As they fell silent, he continued caressing her palm, and Kit kept leaning against him. He should really shift back to a proper distance. Yet he never did, so he and Kit spent the rest of the carriage ride almost embracing.

Once they returned to his chambers, Kit wrote her letters while he began reviewing his notes for his meeting with Elder Priestess Agnes. As they rose to leave for Vespers, Kit asked, "Could you send my letters for me?"

Mel nodded, and Kit handed him three letters: one to Mother, one to Elise, but the third... His stomach tightened. "Why are you writing to the Duke of Oakmoor?"

Kit shrugged. "When I fled Blaine House, I wrote the duke that I'd return soon, but 'tis clear now that I shan't, so I must formally end our almost betrothal."

He exhaled, his stomach easing. "I see. That must be distressing."

Kit's gaze lowered. "Less than it should be, considering I was prepared to marry him."

Mel leaned toward her. Surely given all her blatant flirting and their obvious intimacy, she'd *wanted* to marry the duke. "What do you mean?"

Shaking her head, Kit set her jaw. "I don't wish to discuss it, and it hardly matters while I still appear a crone. I can't marry anyone looking like this."

He sighed. A gentleman who loved Kit wouldn't care about her illusion. Yet saying that would only distress her, so instead he asked, "Ready to attend Vespers? I'll give your letters to Paul at dinner afterward."

AFTER ORGANIZING the almskitchens and breakfast the following morning, Mel headed to Peaceful Minds to meet Elder Priestess

Agnes with Kit accompanying him. When they arrived at the prayer house, Kit murmured, "I'll go wander during your meeting. Find me once you're done."

He nodded then headed to the elder priestess's study and knocked on the open door. Hopefully, this meeting wouldn't take long. "Good morning, Elder Priestess Agnes."

Her hair whiter than Kit's under the Goddess's illusion, the wizened elder priestess wearing brown-and-white-trimmed priest robes glanced up from her papers and beckoned him to enter. "Good morning, Priest Melchior."

Smiling, he sat in a chair before Elder Priestess Agnes's orderly desk. How did she manage to be so tidy with all her duties? His desk would look nothing like that. "Mel, please." He handed her the list he'd prepared. "I wrote out all my current duties so we can decide how to handle them."

The elder priestess's brows rose as she read. "You must love keeping busy. Continuing all these shall be impossible with your new position."

Mel sighed and shifted in his chair. "I know. I thought perhaps Sarah could take my teaching duties. She enjoys covering for me."

Elder Priestess Agnes hummed. "'Tis a good start, but I think we'll need to find another to organize Ormas's almskitchens as well."

His throat tightening, he leaned forward. "I'd prefer continuing to do that. I've provided charity to those less fortunate since I was a boy."

The elder priestess pursed her lips. "Organizing and leading community priests in addition to that shall be too much."

Mel set his jaw and waved his hand to indicate the prayer house. "You run Peaceful Minds in addition to being the elder community priestess of Calatini."

Elder Priestess Agnes sighed and shook her head. "In name only, and 'tis one prayer house, not twenty-four to forty-eight almskitchens depending on the season."

He held the elder priestess's gaze. "I'll manage." He was his mother's son, after all.

Sighing again, Elder Priestess Agnes set down his list. "As you like, but consider who should replace you in case you must relinquish organizing the almskitchens." She handed him some papers. "Here's a list of the local temples and our community programs in Ormas. You'll begin your training as my successor by visiting them all and familiarizing yourself with the priests serving there."

Mel nodded as he perused the eight-page list. The elder priestess had helpfully grouped them by type and sorted them by location. 'Twould take at least two months to visit everywhere.

Elder Priestess Agnes laced her hands together on her desk. "Once you finish that, I'll train you on the other aspects of my position, and you'll assume my duties soon thereafter. I want you to have at least six months acting as the elder community priest of Calatini while I'm still here to advise you."

He repeated his earlier nod. A sensible plan. "How often did you want to meet?"

The elder priestess tilted her head. "Once a week or so, but feel free to stop by whenever you've questions."

Smiling at her, Mel rose. He must return to his chambers to study the list and decide which he should visit first. "Thank you, holy lady. I'll visit next week with an update on my progress."

He found Sarah at the counseling rooms and asked her to take his teaching duties, and his warmhearted friend readily agreed. Then he wandered the prayer house to find Kit. He blinked when he found her in the tea room. Under the tea priestess's careful eye, Kit was kneeling and gracefully performing the elegant tea ritual as if she too was a tea priestess who'd been doing so for years.

He grinned as Kit began handing people tea with a radiant yet serene smile. She'd clearly forgotten she appeared ancient. Visiting the prayer house and helping others was good for her.

Doubtless why the veiled witch had said Kit must participate in temple life to discover the Goddess's purpose for her, even though she'd return to court once she did.

After Kit finished, she rose and glided over to him, and they returned to the Great Temple. As they walked, he told her about his meeting and plans to visit the various local temples and community programs in Ormas.

Kit cocked her head. "Do you mind if I join you? I don't think I can remain alone in your chambers anymore."

Mel grinned at Kit. "I'd love if you joined me." His pulse quickened when she beamed back. Then he asked her what she'd done at Peaceful Minds during his meeting, and they discussed that the rest of the walk.

When they returned to his chambers, he handed Kit the two letters just inside the threshold sent to him for her. "Mother and Elise wrote you back already, it seems."

Grinning, Kit sat at the table to read her letters, while he sat beside her to study his lengthy list of places to visit. He sighed. At least he needn't visit the almskitchens since he was already familiar with those. He glanced at Kit. Except he still wanted to visit at least one with her since she'd enjoy it. Perhaps later in the week he could take a day to show her Lady's Way Almskitchen, the one closest to the Great Temple.

When Kit sighed and dropped her letters, Mel arched his brows at her. "What did Mother and Elise write?"

Kit rubbed her temple. "The duchess scolded me for disappearing then ordered me to tell her where I'm staying so she could visit. Elise invited you, me, and 'Kay' to luncheon in a couple weeks. Somehow, I must decline them both without slighting them."

He eyed Kit. Was she getting a megrim? No, her face wasn't pale and pinched like when she suffered those. She was just troubled. "Mother shall persist until you relent, and should you refuse Elise after her recent upset?"

Kit worried her lip. "If I wear a concealing veil and gloves, perhaps I can meet the duchess at Peaceful Minds. And you're right about Elise—I'll accept her luncheon invitation. Although how I'll manage being two people at once, I don't know."

Mel tsked. Kit's stubbornness was blinding her to sense. "'Twould be easier to simply tell them about the Goddess's illusion."

Kit scowled at him. "Absolutely not." When he began to protest, she leapt upright. "We'd better hurry if we don't want to miss Sext."

He sighed but followed Kit. Hopefully, he could get her to see sense before she met with Mother or Elise again.

OVER THE FOLLOWING FEW DAYS, Mel visited several local temples and community programs across Ormas with Kit. She never spoke much while among others, although she quietly helped once she studied her surroundings, acting much like the priests they visited. Yet whenever he remarked on her willingness to help, she dismissed his words, saying she was simply bored and needed something to do. Each time, he shook his head at her refusal to admit she cared, probably because it didn't match the fashionable Countess of Blaine's reputation, but he didn't say anything further.

When they headed to Lady's Way Almskitchen an hour before noon one morning, he grinned at Kit. How long would it take her to throw herself into helping? "I can't wait to show you Lady's Way Almskitchen. 'Tis the one I served at before I began organizing all of Ormas's almskitchens."

Kit arched her brows. "Shouldn't we be visiting another community program instead? Surely you're familiar with this one."

He shrugged as he ushered her into the almskitchen's busy and sweltering kitchen. "I thought you'd enjoy visiting." He waved toward the eight cooks and one baker diligently preparing food. "Here are the morning helpers preparing hearty soup, bread, and herb tea. They start cooking straight after breakfast and continue until the evening helpers relieve them at noon."

Her eyes widening, Kit glanced about the kitchen. "How many do you serve a day?"

As they began toward the serving room, Mel hoisted a pot of barley soup, while Kit took the tray of bread beside it. He smiled at her helping before he'd even finished showing her around. "Almskitchens are open from several hours after breakfast through dinner, and each serves around a thousand a day."

Kit blinked. "No wonder those helpers were so industrious." Then they entered the loud and chaotic serving room, and she gaped at the long queue of poor parishioners awaiting food. The crowd was a mixture of men, women, and children in ragged clothes, many holding containers to take their soup home. "Dear Goddess."

He set his pot of soup on the table then collected the empty pot beside it. Once Kit did likewise with the bread, they returned to the kitchen. "'Tis much more hectic than visiting poor villagers, isn't it?"

Shaking her head, Kit chuckled as they collected more soup and bread. "Very. Everyone who helps here must have enormous endurance. 'Tis fortunate I'm not the crone I appear to be."

Mel grinned at Kit, his chest light. Had she just jested about the Goddess's illusion? Yes, helping others was definitely good for her.

CHAPTER 17

Once they finished carrying all the prepared food in the kitchen to the serving room, Kit relieved a priestess serving mentha tea, while Mel relieved the priestess serving soup beside her. As she poured countless cups of tea and served them to the poor parishioners with a cordial smile, her chest squeezed at their plight. From their creased and gaunt faces as well as their threadbare and meager clothes, 'twas clear they all had so little and desperately needed the free meal the almskitchen provided every day.

She clung to her cordial smile with each new person she served tea. Her childhood with Father had been wretched, but at least she'd always had enough to eat—unlike these poor people. And her struggle to break the Goddess's illusion and return to court seemed selfish compared to their struggle to simply feed their families. They were willing to wait over an hour for just soup, bread, and tea, and they did so with little fighting and were incredibly grateful when they received it.

While she served tea, she kept glancing at Mel beside her, and her heart would warm every time. His deep compassion shone in his smile as he greeted the poor parishioners and served them soup. Just like it had when they'd visited poor villagers together as children. He was truly the best and kindest of gentlemen. And the people he served could sense it too—when he served them, they'd straighten and smile as if relieved of a heavy burden. 'Twas what made him such an excellent priest. No wonder the Goddess had called him.

Around midafternoon, Mel beckoned for two novices to relieve them. "We should eat luncheon before we faint from hunger."

Kit frowned at the long queue of poor parishioners still awaiting food. They needed food so much more than she and Mel did. Yet if she and Mel fainted, they couldn't help anyone, so she nodded and followed him.

As they devoured their barley soup and bread, Mel grinned at her. "Thank you for serving today. I can't imagine most court ladies would throw themselves into helping like you have."

Swallowing, Kit shrugged and lowered her gaze. She wouldn't have either if the Goddess hadn't made her appear a crone. But Mel was so worthy that he always assumed the best of others. "Wren would have, and so would Lady Kiera. And no doubt your mother and the other ladies in your family as well."

Mel tilted her chin until their gazes met. "Just because they would help too doesn't make yours any less commendable."

Her face tingling at his touch, she stilled at the warmth darkening Mel's deep-brown eyes. He'd not looked at her so since she was a girl, back before Father had made her see how wicked she was and before she'd proved it by cruelly hurting Wren and Hawke. Something Mel would doubtless remember soon. Swallowing again, she freed her chin. "We should return to helping."

Mel frowned. "You've barely eaten half your soup. Once you finish, we can return."

Kit finished her soup, and they returned to serving the poor parishioners and continued until the almskitchen closed around dinner. Then they headed back to the Great Temple and devoured dinner before returning to Mel's chambers.

She was writing to Elise at the table beside Mel when a knock sounded on his door. From its firm tone, it likely wasn't Sarah, so Kit darted into her bedroom. She stiffened and swiftly shut her door when Mel said, "Good evening, your excellency."

Gulping, she pressed against her bedroom door. Please let High Priest Theodag not have seen it close or notice her letter to Elise on the table. Her ornate handwriting was nothing like Mel's. She strained to hear his conversation with the high priest, but only indistinct murmurs penetrated the heavy door.

Moments after the murmurs quieted, Mel knocked on her door and said, "You can quit hiding now. High Priest Theodag left."

Kit slipped from her bedroom like a nervous angelcat after a thunderstorm. "What did the high priest want?"

Mel shrugged. "To check on my progress training to become the next elder community priest of Calatini." He grimaced. "And like Elder Priestess Agnes, he suggested I quit organizing Ormas's almskitchens."

She eyed the faint lines beginning to crease Mel's face. Even before agreeing to become the next elder community priest, he was already too busy, but now he was slowly exhausting himself. "Perhaps they're right."

Frowning at her, Mel set his jaw. "Once I become familiar with my new duties, I can manage to organize the almskitchens while leading community priests."

Kit sighed. And Mel called her stubborn. But not wanting to argue about his excessive duties, she asked instead, "Did High Priest Theodag mention the crone who's been accompanying you?"

Mel dropped back into his chair. "No, so I doubt he's heard about you."

She exhaled and settled beside Mel again. Hopefully, that good fortune would last. She couldn't leave the Great Temple until participating in temple life showed her how to break the Goddess's illusion. Only then she could return to court where she belonged.

. . .

OVER THE FOLLOWING FEW DAYS, Kit continued joining Mel on his daily visits to local temples and community programs, including when he met with Elder Priestess Agnes at Peaceful Minds again. Although 'twas draining to always be so busy, she couldn't stop and risk High Priest Theodag discovering her in Mel's chambers. Plus, she did enjoy quietly helping where needed. And since she appeared a crone, she needn't worry about tarnishing Lady Blaine's fashionable reputation by being too nice.

In addition to joining Mel, she began wandering about the Great Temple in the mornings before breakfast while he organized the almskitchens. Despite his growing exhaustion, he didn't require any assistance with a duty he'd been performing for years, and the quiet gave her time to reflect and settle herself. Invaluable when she spent the rest of the day busy helping others with Mel.

One morning after they'd attended Lauds, Kit lingered in the Sun Chapel when Mel left to organize the almskitchens. She'd been attending the dawn service with him for eleven days, but she'd still not examined the many Goddess laurels before the windows. Although the holy shrub with verdant leaves, white flowers, apple-like fruit, and heavenly fragrance had always fascinated her, even as a little girl, she couldn't approach the Goddess laurels with others around. Someone would surely prevent her from tainting them with her unworthy presence.

Once the Sun Chapel was empty, she drifted to the Goddess laurels. Lacing her hands behind her back to avoid touching them, she bent and inhaled. She sighed as their cinnaspice-apple fragrance filled her lungs. So delicious. Her cinnaspice scent was fool's gold in comparison.

A faint chuckle echoed through the Sun Chapel. Then a gentleman murmured, "There's nothing like the fragrance of Goddess laurels, is there?"

Her pulse skittering, Kit whirled to face the gentleman around Mel's parent's age behind her. Wearing plain priest robes with no trim, he studied her with probing eyes. If not for the kindhearted smile softening his austere face, she'd flee at once.

She swallowed. Yet how could she answer him? The distinguished priest, who was too old to be a novice despite wearing no trim, wouldn't be pleased to find her messing with the Goddess laurels. If she still had her youth and sultry beauty, she'd flutter her lashes with a coy smile to disarm him. But such flirting would appear ridiculous from a crone. She'd have to be straightforward instead.

She managed a tremulous smile and rasped, "I've always adored the heavenly fragrance of Goddess laurels."

The priest hummed and continued studying her. "Not many besides priests pay much attention to Goddess laurels."

She snorted a laugh. "I'm no priestess, but the priest at the temple I visited as a girl had an exquisite Goddess laurel that anyone couldn't help but notice."

Humming again, the priest strode beside her. "Sometimes they notice us back—a tiny part of the Goddess always dwells inside them. 'Tis why they only blossom and bear fruit on Goddess-consecrated grounds and why they have both at the same time, unlike other temperate plants. 'Tis also why we can call her presence into them when we need her direct advice, like during ordination examinations." He caressed the Goddess laurel closest to him.

Kit gasped as the verdant shrub quivered like an eager puppy. Then its glossy, leathery leaves wrapped about the priest's finger while its fragrance flooded the Sun Chapel anew. The Goddess laurel definitely noticed the priest, whoever he was.

The priest smiled at her. "Go ahead and touch one. Goddess laurels aren't fragile."

She gripped her hands behind her back. If she touched the

Goddess's holy shrub, 'twould shock her like an angry djinn. "No, thank you."

His smile warm, the priest beckoned her with his free hand. "Anyone can touch Goddess laurels. The Goddess loves all her children, not just priests."

Kit eyed the Goddess laurel before her. Could she really risk touching it? Her heart quickened. Perhaps if she kept her touch brief. Gulping a breath, she reached toward the Goddess laurel and brushed the edge of one dark-green leaf.

The Goddess laurel rustled as if dancing in a summer breeze, and its cinnaspice-apple fragrance swamped her. When she sharply inhaled, the Goddess laurel rustled again, and one of its ripe, deep-red apples fell into her hand.

Gasping, she leapt backward and swung toward the priest. She knew she never should have touched the holy shrub. "I'm so sorry. I didn't mean to hurt it."

The priest chuckled. "You didn't. The Goddess bestowed that Goddess laurel apple on you. An honor usually only priests get to enjoy."

Kit gaped at the priest. She wasn't worthy of such a thing. She thrust the Goddess laurel apple at him. "You should have it."

Shaking his head, the priest closed her fingers about the apple-like fruit. "Goddess laurel apples only come to those meant to eat them." He smiled at her. "Go ahead and eat it."

She inhaled and studied the ripe Goddess laurel apple. It *did* smell impossibly tempting—like the richest cinnaspice and apple dessert. And the priest *had* given her permission. Licking her lips, she bit into the deep-red fruit. She whimpered as its juicy, sweet yet spicy flavor flooded her mouth. 'Twas *better* than any cinnaspice and apple dessert.

The priest laughed. "I imagine 'tis the best food you've ever tasted. They say not even the melissae's ambrosia is as sweet, although Goddess laurel apples can't cure any ill like ambrosia."

Nodding, Kit took another bite and whimpered again. Oh, Goddess, so delicious.

Cocking his head, the priest smiled. "But only bestowed Goddess laurel apples taste sweet. Picked or stolen ones taste bitter and make the eater vomit. 'Tis why we never bother to cook them—each Goddess laurel apple only tastes good to the one person meant to eat it."

She finished the Goddess laurel apple and couldn't resist licking her fingers like an uncouth street child.

But the priest merely grinned and patted her shoulder. "Do you need me to escort you home? Eating a Goddess laurel apple can make you giddy."

Kit returned his smile. "No, I can manage, but thank you." Besides, 'twas best if the older priest didn't realize she was staying at the Great Temple with Mel.

She bobbed a curtsy then swept from the Sun Chapel to meet Mel in the dining hall.

When she joined Mel, who'd already fetched breakfast for both of them, he stared at her. "Kit, what's wrong? You appear flushed."

She sank beside Mel with a deep sigh. Then she beamed at him and replied, "The most extraordinary thing just happened in the Sun Chapel."

CHAPTER 18

*M*el leaned toward Kit. From her radiant grin, whatever had happened couldn't have been bad. "What extraordinary thing?"

Kit glanced about the dining hall then murmured, "While examining a Goddess laurel, one of its apples fell into my hands. The priest with me encouraged me to eat it, and 'twas *delicious*."

He nodded as the exquisite flavor of the one the Goddess had bestowed upon him three years ago flooded his mouth. "Bestowed Goddess laurel apples always are." He chuckled. "For days after mine, desserts tasted like porridge without honey."

Kit tilted her head. "I can imagine. When did you eat yours?"

Mel sipped his well-sweetened tea, now bland after remembering his bestowed Goddess laurel apple. "During my ordination examination." He shook his head. "Which caused quite a fuss. Most priests enjoy at least one Goddess laurel apple during their lives, but rarely during their ordination examination. That blessing, in addition to being the son of a duke, is why High Priest Theodag began asking me to become his successor."

Stiffening, Kit swallowed. "You'd make a wonderful high priest of Calatini."

He sighed. "Except the Goddess has called me to spread her love through charity, not by leading others. If anyone else could serve, I'd not even become the elder community priest of Calatini."

Kit eyed him for a lengthy moment. "You're too virtuous, Mel. 'Tis doubtless why the Goddess blessed you with a Goddess laurel apple during your ordination examination." Her gaze lowering, she stirred her porridge. "But I can't understand why she'd bless *me* with one."

Aching to wrap Kit in his arms, Mel fisted his hands in his priest robes to remain still. For all her apparent assurance, she never believed she was enough. Doubtless thanks to her despicable father's cruel insults. "The Goddess loves you."

Kit grimaced. "Then why did she destroy my life with this hideous crone illusion?"

He tilted Kit's chin until their eyes met, and his pulse quickened. "Did she? Or did she free you from it?" When Kit blinked, he forced himself to release her chin. He should really stop touching her like that. "And even with the Goddess's illusion, you're not hideous."

Kit stared at him. "Only you would say that."

Mel shifted in his seat as his neck warmed. "Nonsense." He gestured toward their untouched breakfast. "We'd better eat. My meetings with the community priests who specialize in performing services for parishioners shall start soon."

Kit nodded and began eating her porridge. "I thought worship priests led services."

He shook his head as he devoured his eggs. "They lead the four daily services worshipping the Goddess as well as festival services. Community priests perform services meant for parishioners, like birth blessings, weddings, and funerals."

Her mouth quirking, Kit finished her porridge. "So 'tisn't odd that the family has asked you to perform all their wedding ceremonies. I suppose King Devon and Lady Kiera shall have you perform theirs as well."

Mel tensed and drained his tea. "Wedding the king and queen is the privilege of the high priest of Calatini."

As he collected their dishes, Kit scrutinized him with a faint frown. "Why do you appear almost guilty about that?"

While they strode from the dining hall, he glanced about to check no one could overhear then muttered, "Because I performed their bloodbinding on Longnight before their upcoming public wedding ceremony, and if High Priest Theodag finds out, he'll *insist* I become the next high priest of Calatini."

Kit gaped at him then chuckled. "I suppose King Devon's haste isn't surprising, considering his ardent behavior since he met Lady—Queen Kiera." Sobering, Kit slanted him a glance beneath her lashes. "I swear I shan't reveal their secret marriage and bloodbinding. I've not gossiped about anyone since telling court about Wren's pregnancy."

Mel stared at Kit, his chest lightening. Out of remorse for the hurt she'd caused Hawke and Wren?

Kit's lips twisted. "Besides, who could I tell here, looking like I do? Not that anyone would believe an unfashionable crone if I did."

He sighed. No, Kit hadn't refrained from gossiping out of remorse. She'd probably refrained because Hawke and Wren's blissful marriage had made her appear foolish before court. "Regardless, thanks for your discretion."

Before Kit could reply, they reached his chambers, and she retreated to a chair before his bookcase as he met with Oliver, a venerable death priest that many at court called on after deaths in their family. Death priests, who wore black trim indicating they were distinct from other community priests, specialized in funerals and grief counseling, and Oliver was the best in Ormas.

When Oliver's eyes scrutinized Kit, Mel distracted the death priest by asking about his recent funerals. She'd be distressed if Oliver recognized her, and he might since he'd performed Lord Blaine's funeral a year and a half ago. Despite the Goddess's illusion, Kit's mannerisms were the same unless she was attempting to disguise them, and the death priest was almost as perceptive as Mother.

After Oliver left, he met with Winifred, a motherly community priestess who performed most of the weddings and birth blessings for court. Like Oliver, Winifred was the best in Ormas —not surprising since she was Oliver's daughter. But Winifred likely wouldn't recognize Kit since Lord Blaine had married Kit in Childes and they'd not had a child together. So Mel let Winifred eye Kit for a bit before asking about her recent services.

Then he met with several other community priests who specialized in performing services until he and Kit attended Sext then ate luncheon, where Kit asked insightful questions about the nine priests he'd met with earlier. After luncheon, they returned to his chambers for more meetings before Vespers and dinner.

While they ate dinner with Deacon and Sarah, Paul darted over and handed Mel a letter from Aragon. Mel grinned as he read. Selena had given birth to a girl this afternoon, and Aragon was ecstatic that his daughter had been born on his natalday. As were Mother and Father—Mother had already arranged a family luncheon to celebrate in a few weeks.

Kit leaned toward him. "What is it?"

Still grinning, he handed her Aragon's letter. As she read, he turned to Deacon and Sarah, who were eyeing them. "Aragon's daughter Isabel Charlotte was born this afternoon."

Both Deacon and Sarah smiled, then Sarah said, "How exciting."

Her mouth wistful, Kit returned Aragon's letter. "The 'best natalday gift ever'? Your brother is clearly besotted with his new daughter already." She tilted her head. "But why did he and Selena name her Isabel instead of Charlotte after the duchess?"

As Deacon and Sarah blinked at Kit, Mel chuckled and finished his apple-crumb dessert. "Isabel was Selena's mother's name, I believe. Mother shall simply have to settle for being second for once."

Kit hummed. "She's too elated about her first granddaughter to care. Though I'm surprised she's waiting four weeks to host a family luncheon to introduce Isabel."

He quirked a wry smile. "Despite Mother's love for social events, she *did* give birth to three sons, so she knows how long Selena and little Isabel need to rest before meeting anyone."

After Kit chuckled at that, Sarah leaned toward her. "You must know the Duchess of Childes quite well."

Kit stilled. "Mel and I *are* old friends."

When Deacon snorted and Sarah narrowed her eyes at her husband, Mel asked to distract them, "Sarah, how is teaching my former groups of novices going?"

Sarah beamed at him. "Extremely well, and I love teaching them."

Mel nodded, and he and Sarah discussed that with Deacon adding the odd comment until Kit silently finished her apple-crumb dessert. As he and Kit returned to his chambers, he said, "I imagine your dessert was bland after your Goddess laurel apple this morning."

Blinking, Kit pursed her lips. "I hadn't noticed."

He squeezed Kit's arm to hearten her. "You know Sarah shan't care if she discovers you're Lady Blaine. You should tell her."

Kit frowned. "Perhaps..."

Mel swallowed a sigh. Meaning Kit probably wouldn't. If only she would. Having another friend who knew the truth would comfort her.

OVER THE FOLLOWING FEW DAYS, Mel continued meeting with community priests specializing in performing services. These meetings went faster than his visits to local temples and community programs because he didn't need to leave the Great Temple. However, he leapt from bed the morning he and Kit were visiting Goddess's Refuge. 'Twould be good to go outside for the first time in days.

But he stiffened when Kit drifted from her bedroom. Her face was pale and pinched—she must be suffering a megrim. He strode over to the cabinets and prepared her megrim tea and cold compress. "Perhaps you should remain here to rest today."

Kit sighed and rubbed her temple. "No, 'tisn't a vicious one, so my megrim tonic might work today. I don't want to miss visiting Goddess's Refuge."

Mel tsked as he handed Kit her tea and cold compress. Although the family refuge doubtless touched her heart because of her unfortunate childhood, she shouldn't make herself suffer. "I could visit there another day."

Wrapping her cold compress about her head, Kit grimaced. "The priests are expecting you. I'll manage."

He frowned at Kit. Stubborn lady. "I'll bring back breakfast then give you a massage before we go. Hopefully, that shall ease your megrim."

As Kit began her tea, he strode to the dining hall and fetched breakfast. He seasoned her porridge with honey and cinnaspice like she preferred before giving it to her. Once they'd eaten, he rubbed her shoulders, neck, and head to ease her megrim. Like the previous times he'd massaged Kit, his hands tingled and heart quickened at touching her so intimately. As she sighed and relaxed into his massage, he frowned at himself. He was only touching her to ease her megrim, and 'twasn't appropriate for him to enjoy it.

When he finished massaging Kit, he rested his hands on her shoulders and murmured in her ear, "Are you certain you shouldn't remain here to rest?"

Kit turned and smiled at him, her face no longer pale and pinched. "My megrim is practically gone thanks to you."

Mel jerked backward, his pulse throbbing. They'd been much too close—almost close enough to kiss. "I'm glad I could help. But if visiting the family refuge becomes too much, let me know."

Kit rose. "It won't. We should go before the priests think you forgot your visit."

Swallowing, he made himself offer Kit his arm like usual. Although he shouldn't risk touching her again, she might be hurt if he didn't.

As they strode from the Great Temple, Kit squeezed his arm. "I'm eager to visit Goddess's Refuge. I've never been."

Mel slanted her a glance. Why hadn't she? Perhaps she'd only heard about the charity recently. "Did you discover the family refuge when hunting for charities for the Duke of Oakmoor's Longnight charity luncheon?"

Kit grimaced. "No, I discovered Goddess's Refuge during my first season in Ormas, but visiting a family refuge wouldn't suit Lady Blaine's fashionable reputation. Plus, my interest might lead people to pry, and they'd learn about Father."

He sighed at Kit's devotion to remaining fashionable. Yes, that definitely explained her continued refusal to admit she cared. "I see. How did you discover Goddess's Refuge then?"

Kit shrugged with a cool smile. "I had my bookkeeper create a list of charities in Ormas."

Mel eyed Kit. For someone eager to visit, her nonchalance about discovering the family refuge was odd. "Did Lord Blaine have you handle his donations to charities?" Many husbands did.

Her gaze lowering, Kit muttered, "Not exactly." When he kept staring at her, she added, "But I had to spend the excess of the generous allowance Lord Blaine provided me somehow."

He blinked. Kit hadn't squandered that maintaining the Countess of Blaine's fashionable reputation? "Excess?"

Kit coughed and shrugged again. "I'm excellent at economizing thanks to growing up with Father, but Lord Blaine didn't want my excess allowance back, so I anonymously donated it to charities instead. I still do."

Mel halted to gape at Kit. "Then why has Edouard grumbled

about your spending since he became Lord Blaine?" His cousin generously supported multiple charities himself.

A faint blush darkened Kit's cheeks. "He doesn't know how I spend it. No one does. I never even told Lord Blaine."

Tilting her chin so their gazes met, Mel leaned toward Kit. "Why hide that from your husband and his heir? Edouard wouldn't have resented your spending if he knew you were donating to charities."

Kit swallowed and licked her lips. "Telling anyone would have been boasting, and I always spent my allowance on myself first."

Tingling warmth flooding him, he leaned closer. Kit buried her tender heart so well even she forgot it, but her secret donations revealed how kind she truly was. When her eyes deepened to the same sable as her hair before the Goddess's illusion, he stiffened and dropped Kit's chin. What was he *doing*? "We should get to Goddess's Refuge."

CHAPTER 19

*H*er heart pounding, Kit gulped a breath as she and Mel resumed walking. Had he almost *kissed* her? She glanced at his blank face. Surely not. Although he'd said she wasn't hideous, not even Mel would want to kiss a crone, especially her—he'd never wanted to kiss her when she'd flirted as a girl and still had her sultry beauty. Plus, he was too restrained to kiss anyone on a public street.

The remnants of her megrim tightened. But even if Mel had kissed her, she'd surely freeze to stone like when Lord Blaine and the Duke of Oakmoor had. So 'twas good Mel would never want to kiss her. Shoving all that aside, she set her jaw. She should be focusing on visiting Goddess's Refuge for the first time, not pondering kissing Mel.

When they entered the family refuge, which was busy like an almskitchen yet almost as calm as a prayer house, Mel strode straight to the lively priestess playing with three young children. "Morning, Jemima."

Straightening, Jemima grinned at Mel. "Morning, Mel." She turned to Kit with a warm smile. "Who's this?"

Kit blushed. Doubtless the priestess assumed she was a

parishioner in need of the family refuge. To disabuse that, she rasped, "I'm Kit, an old friend of Mel's joining him on his visits."

Jemima nodded, her wild curls dancing. "Nice to meet you. I'm Priestess Jemima, and I run Goddess's Refuge. Let me return the children to their mother, and I'll show you both around." She turned to Mel. "We've made some improvements since you visited a few months ago."

The children darting about her, Jemima bustled to a tired woman with haunted eyes, who grinned when her giggling children mobbed her. The woman still loved them, despite whatever their father had done to her.

Kit swallowed, her chest squeezing. Hopefully, the family refuge could help the woman escape and start over with her children.

Smiling at Kit and Mel, Jemima led them down the hall. "Since you've never visited, Kit, let me describe what we do here at Goddess's Refuge. We provide temporary protection and support for families escaping abuse, mostly women and children, although some men need us as well." Jemima's lively face sobered. "A crucial mission, given one in three women suffer abuse during their lives, and one in ten suffer more intimate abuse. Many who come to us are escaping violence, but verbal abuse is no less pernicious."

A chill skittering across her skin, Kit suppressed a wince as Father's habitual cruelty echoed through her. She inhaled when Mel threaded his fingers through hers and squeezed her hand. Although they rarely discussed it, he knew how familiar she was with abuse and instantly sought to comfort her. Her eyes pricking at his tenderness, she returned his squeeze.

Her gaze flicking to their entwined hands, Jemima gestured to a room where several priestesses and a priest were meeting with various women. "While providing refuge, we help those suffering abuse decide how to build new lives by providing counseling to empower them, legal advice to protect them from their abuser, and training to ensure they can support themselves and their families."

Kit clenched her free hand, and her faint megrim surged as she studied the women. Like the woman earlier, many appeared haunted and tired with gazes that darted about the room, and some sported bruises or other injuries. Thank the Goddess the family refuge was here to help them escape the abuse they'd suffered. She gave Jemima a weak smile. "A very noble cause."

Jemima hummed, her eyes scrutinizing Kit. "So it is."

Stepping between them, Mel smiled at Jemima. "Now that you've shown us around, where do you want us to help?"

Jemima blinked. "Why don't you join the priestesses minding the children like you usually do?" Smiling, she turned to Kit. "Even when we were novices, Mel had a way with the children here, which helps them see not all men are like their fathers."

Kit's heart twisted. Of course Mel did—not only was he compassionate and perceptive, but he'd experience with her as a girl.

Eyeing Kit again, Jemima cocked her head. "You should come talk with some of the women. Having a venerable lady who understands their suffering shall hearten them."

Kit swallowed a sigh. Not surprising that a priestess who worked with abused women every day could sense her troubled childhood with Father.

Mel arched his brows at her, clearly asking without words if she was fine separating.

Her chest warming, she squeezed Mel's hand then released him. "Find me when 'tis time to leave." Once he strode away, she faced Jemima, who was still scrutinizing her. Another blush heated her cheeks. Could the priestess sense she wasn't the crone she appeared? Jemima didn't have ivory trim on her priest robes, so she wasn't a witch priest able to sense the Goddess's illusion, but Mel's behavior might have betrayed the truth, particularly if they'd known each other since they were novices.

Kit flashed a blinding smile. She mustn't let Jemima probe further. "Shall we go?"

Kit spent the day talking with various women at Goddess's Refuge. All of their stories made her throat ache and faint megrim tighten, but she listened with a cordial smile then offered what little comfort and advice she could. Many of them almost smiled when leaving her.

As they returned to the Great Temple before Vespers, Mel slanted her a penetrating glance. "So what did you think of Goddess's Refuge?"

She smiled at Mel. He was still concerned about her even after seeing so many who'd suffered more. "'Twas heartrending to see all those abused women, but I'm glad they've the family refuge for support. The money I've donated over the years has been well spent. I just wish I'd done more and visited sooner."

Mel nodded, still eyeing her. "Perhaps you can visit again to help more."

Kit smiled and squeezed his arm. "I think I shall." The women could use more help, even from someone like her, and visiting while appearing a crone would cause little comment. And if she took care to wear plain dresses and take multiple carriages, she could continue visiting once she broke the Goddess's illusion and returned to court.

Mel returned her smile. "I'm glad. Helping them might help you end the Goddess's illusion."

She blinked. "I'd not considered that, but it might." She blushed when Mel's smile warmed like it had earlier, although he didn't lean within kissing distance like before. Burying that, she murmured, "We'd best hurry so we're not late to Vespers."

OVER THE FOLLOWING FEW DAYS, Kit and Mel visited local temples and community programs across Ormas, including several family refuges. Those visits always made her throat ache, yet she offered what help she could. The morning they were to visit

Elise for luncheon, Mel headed to Peaceful Minds to meet with Agnes, but Kit wandered the Great Temple instead. She could use a respite.

Somehow she found herself in the Sun Chapel again and drifted to the Goddess laurels. Like before, she bent to inhale their heavenly cinnaspice-apple fragrance, and her chest lightened.

The distinguished priest chuckled behind her. "Back, I see. Although I suppose 'tisn't surprising. Ignoring the call of Goddess laurels is almost impossible, especially once you've tasted their apples."

Not startled like last time, Kit turned to face the priest. "You make Goddess laurels sound addictive."

Wearing the same plain priest robes, the priest strode beside her. "Addictive? No. The Goddess's presence inside them helps reaffirm our relationship with her. And doing that strengthens us and brings us peace." He scrutinized her. "You feel that, don't you?"

She nodded. Although unworthy of being a priestess, she still felt that strength and peace. No wonder Goddess laurels had always fascinated her. She'd assumed 'twas their cinnaspice-apple fragrance.

A kindhearted smile softened the priest's austere face. Then he leaned toward her. "Until your visit last week, I've not seen you at the Great Temple. Are you new to Ormas?"

Swallowing, Kit lowered her gaze to the nearest Goddess laurel. She couldn't lie to the priest, yet she couldn't admit the full truth either. "No, I've lived in Ormas for years."

The priest hummed. "So why have you just started visiting the Great Temple?"

She twisted her ancient-looking hands in her skirt. "My situation changed, and I live closer now." She made herself smile at the priest. "I must go—I've matters to attend." She darted a curtsy then hurried from the Sun Chapel before the distinguished priest could quiz her further.

When she returned to Mel's chambers, she penned a note to Elise about today's luncheon. Soon after, he returned as well, and they headed to Golddell House. As they walked, she asked, "How was your meeting with Agnes?"

Mel grimaced. "Good, although she mentioned—again—finding another priest to organize the almskitchens." His jaw set. "I've been handling everything fine so far."

Kit eyed Mel. Except the lines creasing his face were deeper now, and every evening, he struggled to remain awake to complete all his duties.

Mel arched his brows at her. "Have you decided how to handle being two people at luncheon today?"

She waved her note to Elise. "I wrote as myself that I'm no longer up to attending." She blew a sigh. "I hope Elise shall be satisfied with just Kay."

His mouth flattening, Mel nodded, and they fell silent for the rest of the walk.

When they reached Golddell House, Elise leapt from the sofa where she'd been sitting between Lord Farson and Arvan. She beamed at Kit and Mel. "Afternoon. Where's Kit?"

Stiffening, Kit handed her note to Elise then rasped, "She couldn't attend. She wrote a note explaining." When Elise frowned while reading the note, she added, "She was very sorry to be unable to attend today. She'd been looking forward to seeing you."

Elise sighed and glanced between Mel and Kit. "Is Kit truly all right? She's not one to hide—unless she's suffering a vicious megrim."

Mel glanced at Kit, clearly indicating she should answer. So Kit said, "She's fine. She just isn't up to seeing anyone right now."

Thankfully, before Elise could reply, Edouard shuffled into the drawing room.

Elise frowned at her twin. "Where's Pippa?"

Edouard's face tightened. "She refused to attend."

Kit blinked. Pippa had joined Edouard everywhere since her

come out. Why would she suddenly refuse the gentleman she loved who adored her as well?

Elise tsked. "*What* happened between you two?"

His shoulders stiff, Edouard shrugged and poured himself a spiritwine then downed it. He rarely drank spirits, and never so fast. Edouard turned around with a frown. "Nothing that you can help with, so quit asking."

As Elise began to protest, Lord Farson grasped her arm. "We should eat luncheon before Arvan expires from hunger. Growing boys, you know."

Elise sighed but allowed her husband to escort her from the drawing room.

When Mel offered Kit his arm, she shooed him toward Arvan. She must talk with Edouard. "You join the Duke of Golddell. Lord Blaine shall escort me."

Mel smiled at her, then he and the gangly young duke strode out, discussing what dessert was for luncheon.

She turned back to Edouard, who'd poured himself another spiritwine. Something was *definitely* amiss. She murmured, "Drinking yourself into a stupor shan't solve whatever happened between you and Miss Hawke."

Facing her, Edouard snorted then tossed back his spiritwine. "No, but it allows me to forget for a time."

When Edouard reached for the spiritwine decanter again, Kit frowned and blocked him. Lord Blaine had been so kind to her, and she owed it to him to protect his son, even if that son didn't like her. "Such thinking leads to becoming a drunkard. Not a pleasant sight. I'd know—my father is one. He's lost everything to drink. And he's cruel with it too."

His pale-blue eyes blurred, Edouard blinked at her. "Your father is still alive?"

She tensed. A crone's father would be long dead. To distract Edouard from her loose tongue, she asked, "What happened between you and Miss Hawke?"

Edouard glared at her. "What's it matter to you?"

Setting her jaw, Kit held her stepson's angry gaze. "I want to help, and you clearly need to talk."

Edouard sagged and quit glaring. "That's right; you're Mel's assistant. You probably want to help everyone like him. But nothing you can do shall help."

She tsked. Edouard could be just as stubborn as Mel. "Perhaps not, but talking shall make you feel better." When Edouard snorted, she added, "Sometimes you need an outside perspective."

Edouard humphed. "I suppose you're practically a priestess, so I can trust you not to gossip."

She almost winced. She wasn't anything like a priestess. But since that would encourage the reticent Edouard to talk, she simply nodded.

Edouard exhaled and dropped on the nearby sofa. "After the Longnight season, Pippa and I quarreled, and she's been furious with me since then. She stopped accepting my escort and began avoiding me at court events. She quit attending family events too —except for the duchess's luncheon. No matter how furious, Pippa couldn't skip *that*."

Kit hummed as she sat beside Edouard. He and Pippa must have had *some* quarrel. "What did you and Miss Hawke quarrel about?"

Edouard stared at his hands. "That I hadn't proposed during the Longnight season when I'd implied I would." His voice broke. "Pippa accused me of not truly loving her."

Kit frowned. Edouard took everything at a deliberate pace, but he never failed to fulfill a promise. "'Tis obvious to everyone you adore Miss Hawke, although I can see why she might doubt it if you implied you'd propose and didn't. Why didn't you?"

Edouard grimaced, clenching his hands. "When I asked for Sir Julian's blessing just before the Longnight season, he said I must wait until Pippa's natalday in spring to propose. *And* that we must have a year-long betrothal to ensure our feelings are genuine."

Pursing her lips, Kit shook her head. Doubtless Sir Julian had insisted on those restrictions because Pippa was just eighteen. Yet neither was necessary—Edouard and Pippa were more in love than a pair of griffins, who were renowned for their devotion to their lifelong mates.

Edouard ran his hand through his blond hair. "But unfortunately, I'd already implied that I'd propose before I spoke to Pippa's father, so she was upset when I didn't."

Kit drew a sharp breath. "You didn't explain why you delayed, did you?"

Edouard shifted in his seat. "I couldn't further strain Pippa's relationship with her father, and I didn't realize telling her 'twasn't time yet would hurt her so."

Snorting, Kit raised her eyes skyward. Such a patronizing excuse would have hurt any lady. "Why are gentlemen such idiots?" She poked Edouard's arm. "Of *course* 'twould hurt Miss Hawke."

Edouard winced. "I know that now. But afterward, Pippa wouldn't let me apologize and explain."

Kit leaned toward Edouard. Please let him listen to her. After all, she didn't appear like his disliked stepmother, just a wise crone who assisted Mel. "You must do something dramatic—something not like your prudent self—to convince Miss Hawke to listen. Then you must tell her Sir Julian insisted you delay."

Swallowing, Edouard eyed her. "You think that shall inspire Pippa to forgive me?"

Kit nodded. "If you're dramatic enough and grovel sufficiently." Her chest squeezing, she poked Edouard again. "Don't squander the deep love you and Miss Hawke share. Not everyone is fortunate to enjoy a love like that."

Edouard brightened and leapt upright. "I'll go visit Pippa now and beg for her forgiveness."

Rising as well, Kit laid a restraining hand on Edouard's arm. Such impetuosity wasn't at all like him. "Perhaps you should wait until after luncheon. You just drank two snifters of spir-itwine without eating."

Edouard blinked. "Sir Julian wouldn't approve if I arrived to see his daughter tipsy, would he?"

Kit swallowed a laugh. "No, he wouldn't. Let's join the others in the family dining room."

Edouard nodded, and as they strode to the family dining room, he beamed and squeezed her arm. "Thank you for your invaluable advice, Miss Kay."

Blushing at Edouard's effusive gratitude, she shrugged. "Of course. Although Elise would have said the same. Why didn't you talk to her?"

His gaze lowering, Edouard coughed. "I was too embarrassed to admit what I'd done."

Kit smiled and shook her head. Gentlemen were truly idiots sometimes. Although ladies weren't always any better.

CHAPTER 20

*A*s Mel and the others waited in the family dining room, Elise glanced at the door again and nibbled her lip. "*What* is taking Kay and Edouard so long? I hope he's not guzzling more spiritwine."

Mel smiled to reassure Elise. "I suspect she's quizzing him about what happened with Pippa." Yet again, Kit had rushed to help.

Elise sagged in her chair beside Farson. "I doubt Kay shall have much success. Edouard shan't even talk to *me* about it."

As Farson took Elise's hand, Mel chuckled and shook his head. "She'll persuade him to talk. She's quite stubborn." 'Twas being used well for once.

Arvan sighed while eyeing his empty plate. "I hope Miss Kay hurries. I'm famished."

Farson grinned at the young duke. "Don't fret; you shan't starve before they join us."

Striding into the family dining room with Kit, Edouard flashed a broad grin. "Even though it may feel like it."

His heart warm, Mel smiled as Kit sat beside him. He'd known she could help Edouard.

Gesturing for the servants to bring the first course, Elise

beamed at her twin. "Finally. You appear more cheerful than you have in weeks."

Still grinning, Edouard began his creamy rhubarb soup. "Miss Kay helped me see how to inspire Pippa to forgive me."

Mel squeezed Kit's hand beneath the table to thank her for helping his cousin, and a faint blush darkened her cheeks.

Elise leaned toward Edouard. "Why must Pippa forgive you?"

A grimace flitted across Edouard's face. "I'll tell you later. Now, I must concentrate on eating so I can get to Pippa."

While everyone ate luncheon, Elise and Farson asked Mel and Kit about life at the Great Temple, so they described visiting local temples and community programs. Edouard rushed out as they began discussing Goddess's Refuge. Mel shook his head. His cousin was definitely eager to see Pippa—he'd left without touching his shokolat hazelnut mousse Arvan had said was the cook's specialty. A shame.

When Mel and Kit rose to leave, Elise drew Kit into a fierce embrace. "Thank you so much for helping Edouard like you helped me at the duchess's luncheon."

Kit blushed again. "'Twas nothing. I just offered a female perspective and some sensible advice." She smiled at Elise. "And how are you? I didn't get to ask earlier."

Mel smiled at Kit again. She was always so embarrassed to acknowledge her tender heart.

Elise shrugged with a wistful smile. "I'm better, and I'm sure I'll be able to properly celebrate meeting little Isabel in three weeks."

Farson wrapped his arm about Elise. "And probably spend much of the luncheon holding her to practice for our own children."

Mel chuckled. "That's if you can get Mother to relinquish Isabel."

Kit coughed a laugh. "Or Lord Treyvan. From his besotted letter, he likely fusses over his daughter."

Unable to resist another chuckle, Mel took Kit's arm. "True."

Then he and Kit said farewell to Elise and Farson before striding back to the Great Temple. After being away for luncheon, he'd even more duties to handle this afternoon.

OVER THE FOLLOWING WEEK, Mel visited more local temples and community programs in Ormas with Kit. At each community program, especially the family refuges, she threw herself into helping, revealing the compassion she took such pains to conceal and refused to admit. Although his chest warmed at her caring, he knew better than to say anything—she'd just continue to deny 'twas special.

Yet every day Kit was more like the tender and devout girl he'd admired as a boy and less like the lady who'd hurt Hawke and Wren with a cruel lie. When word spread that Miss Winston, the warrior priest, and the elf lore master had finally neutralized the Magehaven ore—exactly like the veiled witch had foretold—Kit beamed and suggested they visit the Sun Chapel to give thanks to the Goddess. During their prayers, Mel couldn't help smiling at Kit. Surely she was becoming who she was meant to be and would soon break the Goddess's illusion.

The morning he and Kit were to visit a youth guild, a center for engaging youth through activities, Elder Priestess Agnes sent him a note requesting they meet. So he and Kit headed to Peaceful Minds instead, and she wandered about the prayer house while he visited the elder priestess's study.

The wizened priestess smiled as he sat before her orderly desk. "I know we last met a few days ago, but I realized we must begin discussing the court event the Great Temple shall host to solicit donations after the season officially starts on Plantfete." She grimaced. "Such fancy events take forever to plan."

Mel rubbed his chin. No doubt they did, especially for people who didn't enjoy planning them. He straightened. But Kit did and would doubtless help if he asked. He leapt upright. "Hold on a moment."

He strode through the prayer house looking for Kit. He finally found her in the counseling room beside Sarah's, talking to a teary woman. Once the woman left, no longer crying, he joined Kit and asked, "Could you accompany me to the elder priestess's study?"

Kit stiffened, paling slightly. "Did Elder Priestess Agnes find out about me?"

He squeezed Kit's arm to hearten her as he led her down the hall. "No, but I want to introduce you. There's something we need your help with."

Kit blinked at him. "What could *I* possibly help you with?"

Mel winked back. "Something you're even better at than Mother." He swept Kit into the study and escorted her to the other chair before the desk. "Elder Priestess Agnes, this is my old friend Kit. She's a talent for planning court events, so she can help with that event you mentioned."

Her brow furrowing, Kit glanced between him and the elder priestess. "What event?"

Elder Priestess Agnes pursed her lips. "The charity event the Great Temple hosts at court." She eyed Kit's plain dress. "Forgive me, but I'm not sure how you can help plan that. You appear a former maid who would possess no experience with court."

Kit lifted her chin. "Appearances can be deceiving." She waved at him. "I'm old friends with Mel, who's the son of a duke. Obviously I've experience with court."

He began to smile. 'Twas the first that Kit had hinted about being the fashionable Countess of Blaine to anyone else. "And as I said, Kit is renowned for her spectacular events. Even Mother praises them."

The elder priestess inclined her head. "Having help planning this shall be most welcome." She grimaced. "I'm the daughter of a road mason, so I've never really understood how to entertain court."

Kit quirked a wry smile. "Fortunately, 'tis the one thing I do well."

Mel almost frowned. Kit did more than that well if she could only see it.

Kit continued, "Although I can't give you a plan immediately. I'll need some time to decide the perfect charity event. Could I have pen and paper?"

Elder Priestess Agnes handed her some. "The Great Temple's event is a month and a half away, just two days after the royal ceremonies at the start of the season. Is that enough time?"

Kit smiled. "Of course. I only had two weeks for the last court event I planned, and 'twas on the day after Longnight, so no servants were working, which made arranging everything challenging."

His stomach tensing, he scrutinized Kit's smile. She'd not mentioned the Duke of Oakmoor since writing the letter formally ending their almost betrothal. Did she miss the duke? After a moment, Mel relaxed—no longing darkened Kit's smoky eyes, so she clearly didn't.

Tilting her head, Kit hummed. "From what I recall, the Great Temple's previous court events weren't well attended. They possess the reputation of being duller than the Landrys' events. We must make the Great Temple's events fashionable to get all of court to attend. Having a supporter, or supporters, from the fashionable at court should resolve that. We've quite a few charity-minded ones to approach, including Mel's family."

He beamed at Kit. His family wasn't the only charity-minded one. "I'm sure Mother would be delighted to help." He chuckled. "From what Aragon mentioned, she made Kiera's education initiative the most fashionable cause last autumn."

Nodding, Kit jotted some notes. "Approaching Lady Kiera might be good as well. She'll have just been crowned on Plantfete, so supporting a charity event early into her first season as queen shall set an excellent precedent. And she'll be especially eager to help if we feature charities involving children." She glanced up at the elder priestess. "Did you have any charities you wanted to focus on soliciting donations for?"

Elder Priestess Agnes blinked at her. "Not particularly. They're all worthy causes."

Kit nodded again then rose. "I'll consider our options then update you once I've decided more details."

As he stood to take Kit's arm, Elder Priestess Agnes rose too with a bright smile. "Thank you for all your help. I can see the Great Temple's court event shall be well handled this year."

Kit grinned at the elder priestess. "I'm glad to help. I've always enjoyed planning court events."

While they strode back to the Great Temple, Mel slanted Kit a warm smile. She was glowing with excitement. "Mother and Kiera aren't the only ones who could act as supporters. The fashionable Countess of Blaine could as well."

Her glow dimming, Kit stiffened. "Only if I can do so without being seen—or I break the Goddess's illusion. Attending family events as a hideous crone with you is one thing, but I'm not attending any actual court events."

He suppressed a frown. So much for her hinting she was Lady Blaine. "Not even the public royal wedding ceremony and Kiera's coronation on Plantfete? Her coronation might be the last one we ever experience."

Shuddering, Kit grimaced. "Maybe if I'd an invisibility cloak, which I don't. 'Twould ruin Lady Blaine if anyone at court discovered," she gestured at herself, "all this."

Mel sighed. Kit shouldn't miss the royal ceremonies because of the Goddess's illusion. He set his jaw. He'd just have to procure an invisibility cloak for her. When they got back, he'd write to Hawke and request a bolt of arachne silk. He'd take it to Celeste's, Kit's favorite dress shop, to be made into a cloak before taking it to Mirage to be enchanted. Then he could give it to her on her natalday a week before the royal ceremonies, although he'd not purchased a natalday gift in years since the adults in his family only exchanged small gifts on Longnight. He smiled. His invisibility cloak would be a fashionable faegift Kit would wear long after she returned to court.

THE FOLLOWING MORNING, Mel grinned when Sarah whisked Kit away to spend the day together. Although Kit had grumbled about needing to plan the Great Temple's court event, she'd enjoy a relaxing day with her friend. Unfortunately, he couldn't do the same. He still hadn't visited two-thirds of the places run by community priests in Ormas.

He was about to head to the youth guild he'd meant to visit yesterday when High Priest Theodag firmly knocked on his door. His gold trim glittering, the high priest strode inside. "I wanted to check how your training was proceeding."

Mel waved for the high priest to sit. "Well enough, your excellency. I still have quite a few local temples and community programs to visit, but I'm making progress."

Once they both sat, the high priest leaned forward, his austere face more intense than usual. "Agnes mentioned you brought an old friend to plan the Great Temple's court event. She was most impressed by the lady's expertise and readiness to help."

Mel tensed. He should have realized the high priest would soon hear about that. Kit wouldn't be pleased the high priest was so close to discovering her. "My friend enjoys planning court events."

High Priest Theodag hummed. "How long have you known your friend?"

Shifting in his seat, Mel smoothed his priest robes. "All my life. She'll do well by the Great Temple's court event. She's excellent at understanding people," other than herself, "and managing them. Plus, her devout and tender heart leads her to help others, although she rarely tells anyone that."

The high priest's face softened in a warm smile. "I'd enjoy meeting her sometime."

Mel swallowed. Kit wouldn't leave her bedroom if she heard that. He'd best not tell her about the high priest's visit today. "She's rather shy about meeting people right now."

His eyes crinkling, High Priest Theodag nodded. "I see." He rose. "I'm glad your training is still proceeding well, and I look forward to hearing about your friend's plans for the Great Temple's court event."

Once the high priest strode out, Mel sighed and rubbed his forehead. Although the high priest had discovered Kit, at least he didn't seem to realize she was staying here. He'd return to meet her if he did, and 'twould upset Kit. Grimacing, Mel rose and left to visit the youth guild.

CHAPTER 21

*A*s Sarah drew her into the sweltering and bustling Great Temple kitchen beneath the priest quarters, Kit sighed and shook her head. "I'm not certain me helping bake spice buns is a good idea. I've never cooked anything before." Despite Father drinking away their money, he'd believed no gentleman could live without household servants, so they'd always had a cook.

Sarah beamed at her. "You'll have fun baking. Plus, afterward you can enjoy eating those spice buns and giving some to Mel." She chuckled. "He's more appreciative of desserts than anyone I've ever met."

Kit warmed at Mel devouring desserts she'd prepared herself. He could use someone to take care of him sometimes. "Very well."

Still smiling, Sarah waved toward the approaching priestess wearing gray-trimmed priest robes who always directed the other kitchen priests during meals. "Morning, Esther. This is my friend Kit. We're going to bake some spice buns. Kit, Esther and I were novices along with Deacon, Mel, and Jemima. Esther is now the head kitchen priestess."

The other kitchen priests continuing to cook and chatter

behind them, Esther halted and eyed Kit. "Yes, we met briefly last month."

Kit almost blushed. When she'd refused to let Mel introduce her. "I'm glad to formally meet you. I was flustered by the Great Temple's glories before."

Esther inclined her head. "Understandable."

Sarah led Kit to an unoccupied corner of the kitchen then gathered all the ingredients they needed. While Kit stirred the flour and yeast, Sarah melted butter and asked, "So why did Mel take you to see Elder Priestess Agnes yesterday?"

Kit shrugged as she stirred. "He wanted my help planning the Great Temple's court event after Plantfete."

Her brows rising, Sarah mixed sugar, milk, and eggs into her butter. "The elder community priest of Calatini, or the high priest on occasion, always plans events of such significance."

Kit hummed while Sarah poured the liquid mixture into the dry ingredients then had her stir them together. "Mel knew I excel at planning court events." Since Mel was right that she should tell Sarah the truth, she glanced about to check no one was close enough to overhear before murmuring, "I'm actually the Countess of Blaine."

Sarah stared at her. "The lady who used to visit villagers with Mel when you two were young?"

Kit stared back, a faint blush warming her cheeks. Mel had told Sarah about that? "Yes, but please don't tell anyone I'm Lady Blaine, not even Deacon. 'Twould be a scandal if court discovered the Goddess made me appear a crone."

Blinking, Sarah nodded. "I suppose it would. Our dough appears thoroughly mixed now, so 'tis time to knead."

As they continued preparing the spice buns, Sarah didn't ask her about being Lady Blaine but instead asked about her recent visits to family refuges. Then while they waited for the dough to rise, Kit asked Sarah about Peaceful Minds. After the spice buns were done baking, Sarah let them cool for a few minutes before serving them each one.

Kit sighed as she ate her first bite. "How are these spice buns even better than the ones you brought before?"

Sarah giggled. "Spice buns are always best when hot from the oven."

Once they finished their spice buns, Kit took two for Mel then returned to his chambers. He'd not returned from the youth guild yet, although a note in Wren's handwriting lay inside the threshold. When Mel finally returned, she beamed at him. "A note from Wren arrived, and I brought you some spice buns Sarah and I baked together."

Mel flashed a grin. "I should refuse since 'tis nearly dinner, but I can't." He devoured his spice buns faster than a ravenous manticore. "Delicious—more so than usual. Thanks, Kit."

She blushed. His delight was even better than she'd imagined. She must get Sarah to teach her how to prepare more desserts.

Opening Wren's note, Mel said, "'Tis an invitation to an orphanage play in a few days. I'll have to skip visiting a community program, but I should attend to support Wren. You should join me."

Kit nodded. Although she'd always refused to admit it aloud, Wren's plays were entertaining and well worth attending. "I'd like that."

Two mornings later, Kit remained in the Sun Chapel while Mel left to organize the almskitchens. She wanted to enjoy the peace smelling the Goddess laurels gave her. As she bent to inhale their cinnaspice-apple fragrance, she hummed. Goddess laurels would make the perfect accent for the Great Temple's court event. They'd provide a unique air as well as reconnect people with the Goddess, which would make them more generous.

So when the distinguished priest joined her, she asked, "Can Goddess laurels be temporarily moved from Goddess-consecrated grounds without making them stop blossoming and bearing fruit?"

The priest blinked, his brows rising. "For a few hours, but the high priest of Calatini can bless them to last longer. Why?"

She straightened. Her idea was possible then, although she'd need to involve High Priest Theodag. Since she couldn't risk meeting him, she must have Mel or Elder Priestess Agnes request his help. "Goddess laurels would enhance something I was asked to plan."

A faint smile warmed the priest's austere face. "I see."

Before the priest could ask what something, she excused herself and left to join Mel on his visit to a prayer house.

Over the three days before Wren's orphanage play, Kit continued pondering the Great Temple's court event while she and Mel visited various local temples and community programs. The charity event was vital, so she must ensure 'twas perfect. Not that she minded taking time to plan it—using her expertise to craft a worthy event was much more fulfilling than using it to maintain Lady Blaine's fashionable reputation. But as soon as she decided the location for the event, she wrote out and sent the invitations to ensure everyone could attend.

Yet since she'd not finalized all her plans before she and Mel visited Waterstreet Orphanage, she couldn't ask Mel's mother and Queen Kiera about acting as supporters for the Great Temple's court event even though she'd see them at Wren's play. Everything must be ready before she asked for their help, and she could arrange meetings with them another time.

Kit chuckled as she and Mel entered the orphanage's rowdy dining hall. 'Twas fortunate she'd not wanted to talk with Queen Kiera this afternoon. Queen Kiera and King Devon were surrounded by orphans chattering and bouncing with excitement. Getting through that would be impossible.

Mel's mother sailed over with her husband and embraced Mel then Kit. "So wonderful to finally see you both again." She scrutinized her son. "You appear tired—how's training to become the next elder community priest of Calatini?"

Mel shrugged. "Busy, but going well."

The duchess hummed. "Just don't forget to rest because of all your new duties."

Nodding, the duke added, "Exhausting yourself shan't help anyone."

Kit suppressed a wry smile. At least she wasn't the only one to worry about Mel doing too much.

Sighing, Mel frowned at his parents. "I can handle my new duties fine."

The duchess hummed again before turning to Kit. "How's the prayer house? Which are you staying at? You've never mentioned it."

Kit tensed. Yes, Mel's mother definitely knew she wasn't his assistant. Otherwise the duchess wouldn't ask about the prayer house she assumed Kit was staying at. Since she couldn't admit she was actually staying with Mel, Kit merely replied, "The prayer houses are nice."

Mel smiled at his parents. "We should go greet the others before the play starts. Excuse us."

Kit exhaled as Mel escorted her across the dining hall to Elise, Lord Farson, and Arvan.

After everyone exchanged greetings, Mel grinned at Arvan. "Are you looking forward to the play? You didn't attend the one last summer, did you?"

Arvan shrugged. "'Tis a *children's* play."

Kit almost laughed. Arvan's youthful scorn was doubtless why Elise and Lord Farson hadn't brought him before.

Lord Farson shook his head at his ward. "You can still enjoy the play despite being the ancient age of fifteen."

Elise nodded. "Yes, Wren's plays are delightful." She grimaced. "Even when you've half the lines."

As Kit and the other adults chuckled at Elise's reference to performing in the fete play, Arvan merely sighed.

Edouard and Pippa swept over. From the glow about them, he'd explained everything, and she'd forgiven him. Good.

Pippa beamed. "I'm so excited to see another of Wren's marvelous plays." She turned to the young duke. "You're going to love it, Arvan."

Arvan sighed again with a frown.

As Edouard began to tease Arvan over that sigh, Pippa bounded to Kit and embraced her. Pippa murmured, "Thank you so, so much for the advice you gave Edouard. Without it, I might never have forgiven him and been miserable the rest of my life."

Kit blushed. "I'm sure you'd have resolved matters eventually." She glanced at Edouard and couldn't help asking, "So what dramatic act did Lord Blaine do to inspire your forgiveness?"

Pippa giggled, her brown eyes radiant. "He climbed in my bedroom window after midnight with a bouquet of melissa peach blossoms and refused to leave until we talked. I never dreamt he'd risk something so dangerously romantic." Fingering the gold chain around her neck, she beamed at Edouard, who was now talking with Dane and Xavier. "Although we're not officially betrothed thanks to Father's restrictions, I'm wearing his parents' wedding tokens as a promise we'll marry one day."

Her chest squeezing at their deep joy, Kit smiled at Pippa. "I'm so happy for you both."

Then Lord and Lady Ravenstone glided into the dining hall, and Kit froze. Why hadn't she realized Wren's other close friend would attend the orphanage play? She must hide before Lady Ravenstone spotted her and recognized her aura. 'Twas bad enough that Mel's mother knew who she was.

Glancing at Mel, who was chuckling with Lord Farson and Arvan, Kit muttered to Pippa, "Excuse me." Then she slipped behind the curtain before the stage, the only place to hide in the orphanage's dining hall.

Behind the curtain, excited children in colorful costumes darted about, with Wren preparing the children closest to Kit while Hawke prepared those on the other side of the stage.

Kit inhaled then weaved through the many children. She must find a quiet corner before the play started. But just as she passed Wren, Wren swayed and began to collapse.

Kit whirled and caught Wren then rasped, "Are you all right?"

Her skin flushed and hands swollen, Wren blinked and rubbed her brow. "Just lightheaded for a moment."

Tsking, Kit turned to the sober girl hovering beside them. "Please find a chair so Lady Beza Hawke can sit."

As the girl raced off, Wren attempted to stand unassisted. "'Tisn't necessary. I'm fine."

Kit snorted. If she released Wren, Wren would likely fall on her face. "No, you aren't. You're nearly seven months pregnant, and you almost fainted. You should be resting more."

Wren scowled and attempted to jerk free again. "I rest plenty."

Kit raised her eyes skyward. "Somehow I doubt that." She smiled at the sober girl as the girl dropped a chair behind Wren. She helped Wren sit. "You can direct the play just as well from a chair."

Exhaling, Wren sagged in her seat. "I suppose so." She rubbed her brow again and grimaced up at Kit. "Sorry to be so fractious. 'Tis simply that Hawke is forever nagging me to rest."

A pang darted through Kit at Hawke's loving care of Wren. No one would ever care for *her* like that. Yet she made herself smile. "He adores you and wants to look after you and your twins. Surely you can't begrudge him that."

Wren sighed and rubbed her vast stomach. "I don't. Except he'd never allow me to leave bed if he could. And that can be frustrating when I'm accustomed to remaining active."

Kit tilted her head. That *did* sound frustrating. "I can imagine, but you have a duty to remain healthy for your unborn children. Plus, Lord Beza would go mad with grief if anything ever happened to you."

Sighing again, Wren straightened. "I know. I'll attempt to rest more. Thanks for catching me."

Kit was nodding in reply when Hawke bolted over, his hands clenched about his violin and bow. "Wren, what's wrong?"

After slanting Kit a pleading glance, obviously asking Kit not to mention her almost faint, Wren smiled at Hawke. "I'm merely a bit tired. Kay arranged for me to sit."

Kit blushed when Hawke beamed at her and bowed then said, "My deepest thanks."

She lowered her gaze. Hawke wouldn't be so grateful if he knew who she truly was. "'Twas nothing. Any lady would have done the same." She began toward the corner. "I'll leave so you can start the orphanage play. The children might burst from excitement otherwise."

CHAPTER 22

When the orphans began performing Wren's play, Mel suppressed a frown as he glanced about the dining hall for Kit. Where had she hidden herself? Had whatever she'd been discussing with Pippa upset her? Or did she just not want to watch her childhood rival's play?

Like usual, the performing children were adorable as they romped about the stage, telling the tale of a clan of werefoxes cursed to remain in human form until they righted an ancestral wrong. Yet his gaze kept drifting from the stage to find Kit.

The play soon came to its happy conclusion with the werefoxes shifting to foxes for the first time, and the orphan players took their bows amid vigorous applause. Then all the orphans thundered to the refreshments table while the adults began to talk.

Mel strode straight to Hawke and Wren. Since they managed the orphanage, they should know where Kit could hide. He smiled at them. "A lovely play, as always." Once they thanked him, he asked, "Have you seen the lady acting as my assistant?"

Nodding, Hawke gestured toward the stage with his violin bow. "She's on the stage somewhere. I suspect the orphans' excitement overwhelmed her into hiding." He grinned down at Wren. "Although I'm grateful she did because she convinced Wren to sit for the entire play, rather than running about like usual."

As Wren wrinkled her nose at Hawke, Mel stared at them. Kit had *helped* Wren rather than needling her?

Wren turned toward him and tilted her head. "Why do you appear almost surprised that Kay helped me? She's your assistant, after all."

Tensing, Mel managed a shrug. Kit would be upset if Hawke and Wren discovered her identity due to his careless tongue. "I'm more surprised you actually agreed to rest." As Mother, Father, and the Keyes approached, he smiled at Hawke and Wren. "I'll leave you to your congratulations."

Flashing a crooked grin, Hawke nodded at him. "I've that bolt of arachne silk you requested. Make sure to collect it before you return to the Great Temple."

Mel smiled. He could take the arachne silk to Celeste's later this week to be made into Kit's soon-to-be invisibility cloak for the royal ceremonies on Plantfete. It should be ready well before Kit's natalday next month. "Thanks, Hawke."

Then he headed to the stage to find Kit. He finally found her tucked into the far corner, practically invisible as she restlessly twisted then smoothed her plain skirt. He arched his brows as he halted before her. "Why are you hiding back here?"

Kit shrugged and worried her lip. "I got concerned someone might recognize me."

He frowned at Kit. She'd not been concerned about that when talking to her stepchildren earlier. And hiding on the stage placed her near Hawke and Wren, who were almost as likely as Mother to recognize her since they'd all grown up together. Yet he only said, "No one besides Mother has recognized you so far. We should rejoin everyone."

Her jaw setting, Kit shook her head. "I don't wish to risk it. I'm remaining here until the other guests have left."

Mel sighed. Of course Kit was determined to be stubborn. "Hawke mentioned you convinced Wren to sit during the play."

Kit pursed her lips. "The fool was doing too much again. Just like you and the rest of your family always do."

Stiffening, he narrowed his eyes at Kit. He only did what was necessary. "I don't do too much."

Kit snorted. "High Priest Theodag, Elder Priestess Agnes, and your parents all believe you do."

Mel leaned toward Kit. She was only saying that to distract him from her helping Wren. "How did you convince Wren to sit? Not even Hawke has managed that."

Snorting again, Kit tossed her head. "I reasoned with, not ordered, Wren to sit. And she *had* to listen to the crone who'd caught her when she'd almost fainted."

He blinked. Kit had prevented her childhood rival from an embarrassing faint? Why? His chest warmed. Perhaps because she felt remorse for hurting Hawke and Wren, even though she stubbornly refused to admit it?

As he stared at her, Kit scowled and crossed her arms. "What?"

He leaned closer, smiling into her eyes. "I'm surprised—and pleased—you didn't let Wren collapse."

Her gaze dropping, Kit muttered, "I was right beside her, and any lady would have done the same."

Mel extracted her stiff hands from across her chest. Squeezing them, he drew her toward him, and his pulse quickened. "The fashionable Countess of Blaine wouldn't have. She was only concerned about enhancing her cachet at court."

Kit winced and attempted to free her hands.

Smiling, he caressed her palms with his thumbs and drew her closer still. He wasn't releasing her until she acknowledged her tender heart. "But you're so much more than Lady Blaine, Kit."

Wrenching her hands free, Kit croaked a laugh. "No, I'm not."

Mel captured her shoulders before she could flee. He bent

until their faces almost met so she'd listen to him. "Then why do you keep rushing to help whenever you see someone needs it?"

Kit's gaze flew to meet his. "I don't."

He leaned closer, tingling warmth surging through him. "You do."

Their gazes locked, Kit inhaled and licked her lips.

Her delectable cinnaspice scent filling his lungs, Mel shuddered and began lowering his head. Goddess, he needed—

"Mel, Kay, what are you doing in the corner?" Wren's voice called.

He jerked back and dropped Kit's shoulders. Had he almost *kissed* her? He fisted his hands in his priest robes. Even under the Goddess's illusion, Kit was much too tempting. He mustn't touch her again, including when escorting her. "She and I were simply talking." At first, anyway.

Leaning on Hawke's arm, Wren waddled over to them. "Don't you do enough of that during your duties every day? You've been back here for ages. All the other guests have left, even Kiera and Devon."

Mel swallowed, not glancing at Kit. Had they truly been back here so long? "We should return to the Great Temple."

Hawke tossed him the bolt of arachne silk wrapped in brown linen. "Don't forget this."

Nodding at Hawke, Mel tucked the bundle beneath his arm. Fortunately, his brother hadn't revealed what it was before Kit and spoiled his faegift. "Thanks again."

After Kit mumbled her farewells, he escorted her from the orphanage, but he didn't risk taking her arm. Halfway back to the Great Temple, he glanced at Kit. Her eyes were dark, and a faint frown furrowed her brow. His almost kiss had upset her. Rightly so—he was a priest and shouldn't be almost kissing anyone except his wife. And Kit would never be that. He muttered, "I'm sorry. I didn't mean..."

A blush darkening her cheeks, Kit snorted a laugh. "Of course you didn't." She inhaled then asked, "What did Hawke give you?"

Mel tensed. "Some fabric I requested last week. Kit, I—"

Lifting her chin, Kit blurted, "Where are you visiting tomorrow?"

Since Kit clearly wanted to discuss anything other than their almost kiss, he sighed and replied, "I'm visiting Elder Priestess Agnes in the morning then the youth guild closest to the Great Temple."

Almost relaxing at his reply, Kit hummed. "I should also meet with Elder Priestess Agnes so I can update you both about the Great Temple's court event."

Mel nodded, and they lapsed into silence for the remaining walk back to the Great Temple.

MEL AND KIT didn't talk much before heading to Peaceful Minds the following morning. And he refused to touch her as they attended services, ate meals, and walked together. He couldn't trust himself. Yet *why* had he almost kissed her? They weren't courting, and Kit would never become a priest's wife even if he asked. She wanted a wealthy and titled husband. Perhaps everyone was right that he was doing too much. Surely only exhaustion could be causing such erratic behavior.

When they sat before her orderly desk, Elder Priestess Agnes smiled at them. "I wasn't aware you were joining us, Kit."

Kit laced her fingers in her lap. "I wanted to update you on my initial plans for the Great Temple's court event before you and Mel meet." After the elder priestess waved for her to continue, she said, "I still haven't decided if we should focus on one charity or all the various charities the Great Temple runs, but I've decided the location for the event and how to make it unique. I want to use Goddess laurels as decorations—they're enthralling yet holy, so no one else could ever use them."

Mel blinked at Kit. Very clever, although he'd never have thought of it. No wonder her events were spectacular.

Kit glanced between him and the elder priestess. "Could either of you ask High Priest Theodag to bless four dozen to last a day away from Goddess-consecrated grounds?"

Elder Priestess Agnes hummed. "I'll ask him when I see him next. I'm sure he'll be eager to agree. Theodag was intrigued when I told him that you were planning the Great Temple's court event."

Stiffening, Kit paled. "You told the high priest about me?"

Mel almost winced. If only he could take Kit's hand to reassure her. Yet he couldn't risk touching her, and the elder priestess would be suspicious if he did.

Her brows arching, Elder Priestess Agnes scrutinized Kit. "Of course I told the high priest. We're typically the ones responsible for planning the Great Temple's court event."

A smile trembled on Kit's lips. "I see." She rose. "I'll leave you and Mel to your meeting."

Once Kit hurried from the study, the elder priestess frowned at him. "What was that about?"

Mel swallowed, resisting the urge to shift in his seat. "Kit's shy about meeting people right now, especially someone as eminent as High Priest Theodag."

Elder Priestess Agnes nodded, her frown fading. Then she asked, "How have your recent visits to the local temples and community programs gone?"

He relaxed. "Well. I've now visited nearly half of my list. I should finish in another month or so."

Sighing, the elder priestess pursed her lips. "You still have that many left? I thought you'd be further along by now."

Mel tensed again. Was she going to suggest once more that he quit handling the almskitchens? "I can only manage to visit one or so a day. They take too long to walk to since they're spread across Ormas."

Elder Priestess Agnes blinked at him. "Why didn't you request one of the Great Temple's carriages?"

His neck warming, he shrugged. "I'm well able to walk, and I figured the carriages were all being used for more important temple business."

The elder priestess shook her head. "You're too modest. Training the next elder community priest of Calatini *is* important temple business. Request a carriage in the future. I want to show you the other aspects of my position as soon as possible so you can assume my duties." She sighed. "Continuing to handle them has become a heavy burden. I no longer possess the energy I once did."

His stomach tightening, Mel nodded. He should have realized. "I'll begin visiting places faster then." He rose. "Excuse me. I should go prepare for that."

So over the following days, he redoubled his visits about Ormas. He requested a carriage each day, leaving straight after organizing the almskitchens and not returning until well after dinner. Then he spent his evenings reviewing his papers and planning for the following day. Yet everything seemed to take longer every day, so he kept staying awake later and later to finish it all.

Four days after his meeting with Elder Priestess Agnes, even he had to admit his hectic visits were exhausting. He couldn't wait until he finished. He could rarely attend services and had to devour quick meals in a carriage traveling to another local temple or community program. Plus, he didn't see Kit often since she'd quit joining him after the first day he'd taken a carriage. And he never had time to visit Celeste's about Kit's cloak—hopefully, he would before 'twas too late.

As he struggled to force his blurry eyes to focus on his notes for tomorrow, Kit tidied her papers and rose. She frowned at him. "You appear more exhausted than Wren at the orphanage play. Go to bed."

Rubbing his head, Mel blew a weary sigh. "I shall once I finish preparing for tomorrow."

Kit pursed her lips. "Exhausting yourself like this isn't healthy."

He sighed again. "I know, but I must finish visiting all of my list. Everything shall settle after that." Please, Goddess.

Tsking, Kit drifted to her bedroom. "Well, good night then." At her door, she turned and repeated, "*Go to bed.*"

Once Kit shut her door behind her, Mel stumbled toward the cabinets. Perhaps a cup of tea would help him remain awake until he finished preparing for tomorrow. He gulped that down without sweetening it, shuddering at the bitter taste, but the tea failed to help. His vision kept blurring, and his eyes kept drifting shut. Perhaps resting them for a moment would revive him enough to finish preparing. Exhaling, he succumbed to sleep's sweet embrace.

CHAPTER 23

After leaving Mel working at the table, Kit lay in bed unable to sleep. He was doubtless still preparing for tomorrow, which would soon be today. Then he'd rise at dawn like always to organize the almskitchens. The stubborn fool was going to make himself ill.

She sighed and tossed aside her covers. She'd better check that he'd gone to bed. Grumbling to herself, she yanked on her dressing gown before striding from her bedroom.

Kit scowled at Mel slumped on the table, sound asleep atop his papers. Sleeping like that, he'd ache in the morning. He definitely needed someone to take care of him tonight. Hopefully, she was strong enough to move him.

She managed to rouse Mel enough to steer him into his bedroom and drop him into bed, although he was too exhausted to truly wake. Panting, she removed his boots and wrenched his covers over top of him. Then she shut his curtains so that the dawn light wouldn't wake him. He needed the extra sleep, and she could use his notes to organize the almskitchens in the morning.

Mel taken care of, Kit fell into her bed and sank into sleep as well. She woke when her bedroom brightened with the dawn and flung on a dress. After checking Mel was still asleep, she strode to the chapter house with his notes then told the waiting priests and novices which almskitchen to visit. Mel's notes were nearly complete, so 'twasn't difficult.

Then she fetched breakfast from the dining hall before returning to Mel's chambers. She sweetened his tea with his usual three heaping spoons of honey before placing it and his breakfast on the fire plate to keep warm until he woke. While reviewing her notes for the Great Temple's court event, she drank her cinnaspice tea and ate her bacon and cinnaspice-seasoned porridge.

Nearly two hours later, Mel stumbled from his bedroom, unshaven and still wearing his creased clothes from yesterday. "How did I get to bed last night?"

Eyeing him, Kit set aside her notes. He looked a bit less exhausted than last night, but he still needed days of solid sleep before he recovered. "I helped you."

Blushing, Mel rubbed his face. "I see. What time is it?" He glanced at the clock on the mantel. "The almskitchens!"

She tsked then rose to fetch his breakfast. He needed food in addition to more sleep. "Don't fret; I handled those using your notes. Come eat."

Mel grimaced. "A carriage is waiting to take me to Serenity then Saplings then Mermaid Temple. I can eat on the ride."

Kit thumped his breakfast on the table before fisting her hands on her hips. He was planning to visit a prayer house, a youth guild, and a local temple all in one day? Would he ever learn? "No, you're eating here. Then you must change and shave before you leave your chambers. You appear like a vagrant."

Wincing, Mel rubbed his dark jaw and sank into his seat. "You're right, of course."

When Mel reached for the honey, she sat across from him and suppressed a smile despite herself. Even he'd find his tea undrinkable if he added more honey to it. "I already sweetened your tea for you."

Mel blinked at her. "You did? Thanks. And thanks for fetching breakfast for me and handling the almskitchens."

A blush warming her cheeks, Kit lowered her gaze. "Of course. You'd have done the same for me—and have during my megrims."

Mel hummed then devoured his breakfast before striding back to his bedroom to change and shave. Afterward, he thanked her again while rushing from his chambers to meet his carriage.

She frowned after Mel. He was going to exhaust himself again. She rose and drifted to the Sun Chapel, needing the peace she received from the Goddess laurels to help her decide how to convince Mel to rest when he returned tonight. She inhaled their heavenly fragrance, and her chest lightened like usual, yet she found no answers.

When the distinguished priest joined her, he narrowly eyed her. "You appear troubled today. What's wrong?"

Kit sighed and studied the priest's austere face beneath her lashes. He was a priest like Mel, so he might know how to convince Mel to rest. Yet could she risk revealing Mel's secrets? Surely 'twould be safe since the distinguished priest didn't know she was connected to Mel. She inhaled then told the priest that an old friend was doing too much and asked for his advice.

Smiling, the priest suggested she convince Mel he didn't need to do everything himself and that he couldn't help anyone if he made himself ill. Then he said to offer to share Mel's duties because he'd trust an old friend to help.

Kit swallowed a snort. Mel would never trust the fashionable Countess of Blaine who was only concerned about enhancing her cachet at court and had cruelly hurt Wren and his brother. Yet perhaps offering to share his duties would make him realize how worried she was and get him to see sense. She returned the priest's smile. "I'll try that. Thank you."

She swept a curtsy then headed to Goddess's Refuge. Mel would doubtless return well after dinner again, and she must keep busy to distract herself from their upcoming quarrel. And helping the abused women and children was a very worthwhile distraction.

That evening, she was too nervous to eat dinner with Sarah and Deacon like normal. Although she could use Sarah's cheer, Deacon's disapproval would worsen her nerves. Instead, she fetched dinner for herself and Mel, taking extra dessert for him, then ate alone in his chambers.

When Mel finally trudged through the door, Kit leapt and collected his dinner from the fire plate. "I fetched dinner for you."

Mel rubbed his face. "Thanks, but I ate some bread stuffed with meat and cheese on the carriage ride back."

She tsked while setting his food on the table. "'Tisn't dinner. Eat. I brought you two bread puddings."

Brightening, Mel sat and devoured his dinner, starting with his bread puddings. She made herself cinnaspice tea and sipped it across the table in silence while he ate. He must eat before she attempted to convince him to rest.

Once his dishes were empty, Mel leaned back with a sigh. "I didn't realize how much I needed a decent meal. Thanks, Kit."

She set Mel's dishes on the cabinets so neither of them would be tempted to throw them during their quarrel. Then she inhaled a bracing breath and turned to face him. "You need more than a decent meal—you need days of solid sleep as well. Not that you'll ever get that if you keep doing too much."

His eyes narrowing, Mel leapt upright. "I only do what is necessary to fulfill my calling to spread the Goddess's love through charity."

Kit strode toward him, burning to fist her hands on her hips but resisting to avoid riling him. "Exhausting yourself isn't *necessary*."

Mel grimaced and shook his head. "It is when Elder Priestess Agnes is desperate for me to assume her duties. I can rest once I finish visiting the local temples and community programs."

Snorting, she arched her brows at Mel. Except he never had previously. "Somehow I doubt that. You'd too many duties *before* you agreed to train as the next elder community priest of Calatini. Now, you've enough for two people. You can't keep doing it all. You *must* relinquish some of your duties—like organizing the almskitchens."

Mel glared at her. "People are relying on me. I can't forsake them."

Glaring back, Kit tsked. Stupid man. "You shall if you exhaust yourself into a coma. Who shall handle all of your duties then?"

Mel's jaw tightened. "I'm not exhausting myself into a coma."

She leaned toward him, fire flashing through her. "You fell asleep on *the table* last night. You must find someone to share your duties."

Mel raked a hand through his coal-brown hair. "I can't! Even if I wanted to quit organizing the almskitchens, there isn't another community priest to replace me. Very few of us have the inclination or skills to lead others."

Kit strode forward and poked Mel's chest. "Then let *me* organize them for you. Our visit to Lady's Way Almskitchen showed me how they run, and I've watched you organize the almskitchens enough to understand doing that. I've the time to devote to them, and you know I excel at organizing people and events."

Mel blinked at her. "Yes, you're nearly as skilled as Mother at that." He sighed. "But you can't take over organizing the almskitchens—you'll be returning to court once you break the Goddess's illusion."

Her lips twisting, she shrugged. Except she'd made no progress with that in the two months she'd been at the Great Temple. "I shan't break the Goddess's illusion for a while. And doubtless by then, we'll have unearthed a community priest to replace you."

Humming, Mel inclined his head. "I suppose." He sighed again. "Fine, you can organize the almskitchens for me. It shall be a relief, actually. I'll miss providing charity to the less fortunate, but like Elder Priestess Agnes and High Priest Theodag warned me, I no longer possess time to fulfill my duties there." He smiled at her. "Thank you, Kit."

Although warmed by Mel's smile, Kit made herself narrow her eyes at him. "*And* you slow your frantic visits. You eat all your meals here at the Great Temple as well as attend Lauds, Sext, and Vespers like you did before. Plus, you relax in the evening and quit staying up late."

Mel chuckled. "So peremptory."

She tossed her head. Her brusque commands were for his own good. "You're too stubborn to listen otherwise."

Smiling, Mel leaned toward her. "Not half as stubborn as you. I'm not the one under the Goddess's illusion until I become who I'm meant to be." When she frowned at him, he chuckled again. "Very well, I'll follow your sensible restrictions."

Her frown melting into a grin, Kit flung her arms about Mel. He'd actually listened to her. "Thank the Goddess."

Mel stiffened in her embrace. "'Tisn't appropriate for us to touch like this."

Although her heart quickened at their closeness, she blinked up at Mel and refused to release him. Holding him after their quarrel soothed her, and he'd never do anything improper. "Old friends often embrace."

Mel stiffened further. "Not gentleman-lady ones—it leads to kissing."

Kit inhaled, her lips parting. Surely he couldn't be implying he wanted to kiss *her*. As she stared up into Mel's deep-brown eyes, they darkened to almost black. Or perhaps he did. Tingling warmth flooding her, she licked her lips.

Mel shuddered and began lowering his head, and she lifted hers until their mouths met in a tender kiss, and she shuddered too. Breathless from the hunger flaring in her veins, she threaded her arms about his neck and deepened their kiss.

His rough jaw scratching her, Mel groaned and pulled her

tighter against him then devoured her mouth as if she were his favorite dessert, cinnaspice-honey burnt custard. Not that she protested—she was devouring him right back. They kissed and kissed until somehow they stumbled into the table.

Suddenly, Mel jerked free and bolted halfway across the room.

Wobbling without him, Kit sank into the table chair behind her. As she gaped at Mel, who was panting with his hands fisted in his priest robes, she pressed her fingers against her tingling, swollen lips. *What* had just happened?

Mel had *kissed* her—not decorously either. And she'd *enjoyed* it.

She inhaled. Unlike when she'd kissed Lord Blaine and the Duke of Oakmoor, she'd not frozen to stone. She'd kissed Mel back like a starving venus who'd been banned from entering men's dreams to seduce them. If he'd tumbled her to the floor and taken her virginity, she wouldn't have protested—she probably would have encouraged him. Apparently, she was more like her "whore of a mother" than she'd realized.

Lowering her hand, Kit snorted a giggle. Yet it had taken one of the Goddess's most diligent priests, instead of her dear husband or the greatest rakehell in Ormas, to make her enjoy kissing and burn to make love. Why? Was she so perverse that she could only desire a priest who must remain chaste?

Mel began stepping closer then halted, his hands clenching and unclenching in his priest robes. "Kit, I..."

She blinked at Mel, and her heart fluttered in her chest. Just like it always did whenever they met or she truly looked at him. No, she'd enjoyed their kisses because she'd been kissing *Mel*, not simply any priest. How could she have been so blind? Despite years of telling herself she no longer loved him, she adored Mel as much as she had as a girl. How could she not? He was the most compassionate, perceptive, and diligent gentleman she'd ever known.

Kit twisted her hands in her lap. No wonder she'd despised

kissing anyone else. She swallowed. Not that loving Mel did her any good. She wasn't worthy of marrying a priest, and he knew that, so he'd never ask her. And loving him like she did, she couldn't marry another.

She drooped in her seat. Had *that* been the truth the Goddess wanted her to learn? That she was meant to remain alone for the rest of her life?

Mel almost stepped toward her again before halting, his face pinched. He must be appalled by their wild kisses. He was too chivalrous to ever kiss a lady he didn't intend to marry. She should have released him when he'd asked. But she hadn't, and physical instincts had goaded him into kissing her.

Her throat tightening, Kit made herself stand and gritted a tremulous smile to comfort Mel. "Well, that was unexpected."

Mel shuddered. "Not really." He stepped closer then lurched back and began toward the door. "I have to go. Now."

As Mel bolted from his chambers, she collapsed in her chair again, and tears burned her eyes. Her thoughtless embrace and their resulting kisses had made him flee, so he'd not get any solid sleep tonight. Not what he needed when exhausted. She gulped a breath. And now that she knew she loved Mel, how was she to treat him like merely an old friend? Her unrequited love would make him uncomfortable, and he'd soon pity her—not something she could stand.

Straightening, Kit set her jaw. To escape Father, she'd enticed Lord Blaine into marriage then made herself a fashionable court lady at seventeen, so surely she could manage to conceal her love from Mel. She'd just pretend he was Hawke or Aragon since she'd never wanted to kiss either of his brothers.

CHAPTER 24

Kit's delectable cinnaspice scent still clinging to him, Mel fled his chambers to escape his hunger for her and almost collided with Deacon, who was heading back to his and Sarah's chambers.

Deacon frowned, his ascetic face tightening as he eyed Mel. "What happened to you?"

As kissing Kit echoed through Mel, his pulse throbbed, and a blush scorched his skin. He'd kissed her like a lusty satyr determined to ravish her. But Deacon would be aghast if he admitted that, so he swallowed and lied, "Nothing. I'm fine. Excuse me."

Then he rushed past Deacon before his friend could ask anything further. He must find a place to hide until he settled himself. If he returned to his chambers now, he might kiss Kit again, and he might not stop until he made love to her.

He shuddered. When he'd kissed Kit, hunger had consumed him, and his only thought had been to possess her. 'Twas fortunate they'd stumbled into the table—that had jolted his mind awake. He hurried faster. How could he have behaved like that? He was a *priest* and required to remain chaste before marriage. He and Kit weren't married, and they never would be. The fashionable Countess of Blaine would *never* marry a humble priest.

So he'd no right to kiss her like he had. No matter how much he burned for her.

Mel clenched his hands in his priest robes. Not only that, but Kit was staying with him, so she was under his protection. He should be ensuring no one preyed on her, not doing it himself. She needed a friend, not a seducer, while she struggled to break the Goddess's illusion. He was a horrible friend and must apologize as soon as he could be near Kit without kissing her.

Setting his jaw, he slipped into the Sun Chapel. Since 'twas normally empty and dark after sunset, no one would disturb him. He sat in the front pew then inhaled a deep breath. As the Goddess laurel's cinnaspice-apple fragrance, so like Kit's scent, washed over him, his body tightened anew. 'Twas wrong that a holy shrub could make him burn for Kit simply because it reminded him of her.

Mel ran a hand through his hair. He could *definitely* never touch Kit again. And he should probably stay across the room from her at all times to ensure he didn't. He snorted a laugh. Although he doubtless couldn't manage to stay away. Kit had always been too alluring, even when he'd been disappointed with her for hurting Hawke and Wren.

He bent his head and began to pray to the Goddess. After apologizing for his shameful hunger and kissing Kit, he begged the Goddess for the strength to resist Kit and treat her like nothing more than an old friend. Yet unlike when he usually prayed, no peace filled him, and he couldn't hear the Goddess's whisper in his heart.

When he began drifting to sleep in the pew, Mel made himself rise and return to his chambers. From the priests heading to the Moon Chapel for Nocturns, it must be almost midnight. Surely Kit would have retired by now. Fortunate since he wasn't strong enough to face her yet.

He exhaled as he slipped into his still and dark chambers. Barely breathing, he crept to his bedroom and shut the door. Then he opened his curtains so he'd wake on time before collapsing into bed. But although he was exhausted and fell asleep swiftly, his sleep was poor and suffused with sensual dreams of kissing Kit.

Because of that, he woke later than usual, despite the light brightening his bedroom. Groaning, he forced himself to rise then dress before emerging to face Kit. Please let him be strong enough to not pull her into his arms and kiss her good morning.

Kit was preparing to leave when he joined her. She nodded without truly glancing at him then swept toward the door.

His heart twisting, Mel swallowed. He must apologize for kissing her before she fled. "Where are you headed?"

Still not glancing at him, Kit murmured, "I must organize the almskitchens."

He almost winced. After kissing Kit, he'd forgotten all about his duties. "I'll join you."

Kit's shoulders stiffened. "No, thank you. I can handle them alone." Then she bolted.

Unable to resist, Mel strode after Kit but halted at his door and stared after her. His throat tightened. She couldn't bear to talk to him now. Another reason he should never have kissed her.

He was still staring after Kit when Deacon and Sarah stepped into the hall. Surprising since they rarely emerged until after breakfast. His married friends exchanged a frown, then Deacon asked, "*What* is wrong with you lately, Mel?"

His skin heating, Mel made himself turn toward Deacon and Sarah. "I told you, I'm fine."

Sarah pursed her lips. "You don't look it, and neither did Kit yesterday evening when Deacon and I checked on her after Deacon mentioned you'd fled. What happened between you two? Kit refused to say."

Blushing harder, Mel managed a shrug. "Kit and I quarreled."

Deacon and Sarah exchanged another frown, then Sarah said, "That must have been a fierce quarrel. Kit's lips were swollen from how she worried them afterward."

Mel stiffened. No, his ravenous kisses had done that when he'd practically ravished her on the table. He was such a cad. He gritted a smile at Deacon and Sarah. "Excuse me, I must fetch breakfast so I can apologize to Kit as soon as she returns."

Before his friends could quiz him further, Mel strode to the dining hall. He fetched breakfast for him and Kit then prepared cinnaspice tea for her. Waiting for her to return, he paced about his chambers. What could he say to apologize?

When Kit finally returned, he halted and stared at her like a sailor stared at a singing siren. Why must she be so tempting? Even the Goddess's illusion couldn't diminish Kit's allure. He swallowed. Finding the words to apologize would be near impossible while imagining kissing her again. He gestured toward their food on the fire plate. "Come eat breakfast. Then we must talk."

Her gaze averted, Kit licked her lips, and tingling warmth flooded him. She said, "I ate in the dining hall after organizing the almskitchens."

A pang darted through him. Kit clearly wanted nothing to do with him. "I see. You can drink the cinnaspice tea I prepared while I eat then."

Once Kit nodded, he collected his breakfast and handed her the mug of cinnaspice tea, ensuring their fingers didn't touch. Then he forced himself to eat, even though his eggs, bacon, and tubers tasted blander than unsweetened porridge.

When he lowered his fork, Kit arched her brows at him over her cinnaspice tea. "So what did you want to talk about?"

Mel shifted in his seat then muttered, "About how I practically ravished you last night."

Sighing, Kit lowered her gaze. "You didn't ravish me. You merely kissed me a few times."

He gaped at Kit. Was she jesting? "*Merely kissed you?*"

A blush darkening her cheeks, Kit shrugged. "But 'twas my fault—I should have released you when you asked." She set down her mug of cinnaspice tea with a clink. "We should just forget those kisses ever happened."

Mel swallowed, his heart squeezing. "I'm not certain I can."

Paling, Kit lifted her chin. "We have to, Mel. We're friends. Nothing more."

He winced. And he'd betrayed their friendship by kissing her like a seducing cad.

Kit sighed again. "You're too dear a friend for me to lose over a few trifling kisses." She flashed Lady Blaine's blinding smile. "'Tisn't as if I'd never been kissed before. I *am* a widow, after all."

Mel stiffened, his chest clenching. How could he have forgotten that although he'd never kissed anyone before, she was considerably more experienced? Doubtless his ravenous kisses had meant nothing to her after her late husband and the rakehell Duke of Oakmoor had made love to her. His stomach hardened as them kissing and caressing Kit flashed before his eyes.

He leaned toward Kit. "Except I'm a priest and shouldn't be kissing anyone other than my wife. I never should have kissed you. I'm sorry."

Kit nodded, an almost smile trembling on her lips. "I know you are. I'm sorry too. I never should have embraced you." After a moment, she coughed then said, "Now that we've both apologized, can we quit talking about this?"

Mel made himself nod and return her weak smile. To restore their friendship, they *should* quit talking about kissing. "How did organizing the almskitchens go this morning?"

Humming, Kit tilted her head. "Well, although some priests asked where you were."

He sighed. He should have realized that would happen. "I'll join you tomorrow to explain that you're an old friend acting as my assistant while I train as the next elder community priest of Calatini. Then the priests and novices serving at the almskitchens shan't question you."

Kit shrugged. "None of them were disrespectful, merely

concerned about your absence. They thought you might have fallen ill."

Mel suppressed a grimace. Even the almskitchen helpers had worried he'd been doing too much. He'd definitely overdone his duties in recent weeks.

Kit smiled at him. "So where are you visiting today?"

Suppressing another grimace, he rubbed his jaw. He'd not even considered that yet. "I've not decided, but I should visit somewhere since I've a carriage awaiting me."

Her gaze narrowing, Kit pursed her lips. "Promise you shan't do too much."

Mel shifted and almost blushed at her stern expression. He deserved that. "I promise." He inhaled then added, "Thanks for making me see sense yesterday." He shrugged. "I sometimes forget about myself in the midst of all my duties."

Leaning forward, Kit laid her hand atop his. "I know you do. 'Tis why you're such a worthy priest. But everyone shall miss you if you make yourself ill."

He swallowed as tingling ran up his arm at her touch. He should really move, but he couldn't. "Surely not *everyone*."

Kit sighed. "Everyone who knows you or is helped by the work you do."

Mel studied her without moving his tingling hand from beneath hers. "Including you?"

A blush darkened Kit's cheeks. "Especially me."

Warmth suffusing his chest, he flipped his hand to caress Kit's wrist with his thumb. So even though she didn't want his kisses, he was still important to her.

The silence began to hum as he and Kit stared at each other with their hands entwined.

Mel couldn't help rising and drawing Kit toward him. Her smoky eyes soft and dark like in his arms the evening before, she didn't protest. His pulse quickening, he bent his head while she lifted hers.

Then a firm knock shattered the humming silence, and they both froze.

Releasing Kit as if scorched, he jerked backward. How could he have been about to kiss her again? Especially after scolding himself for doing so since last night. He scrutinized Kit's dazed eyes and flushed cheeks. But at least he'd not been the only one to lapse. Despite all her talk of forgetting their trifling kisses, she'd glided into his arms like she belonged there and been about to kiss him again.

Another knock pounded on his door, so Mel whirled from Kit and strode to open it. He stiffened at High Priest Theodag standing there with a frown on his austere face. Mel said, "Good morning, your excellency."

High Priest Theodag inclined his head. "Good morning, Mel. Deacon just shared something I felt that I must discuss with you at once."

A faint chill prickling his skin, Mel swallowed then waved for the high priest to enter. "Of course. Please come in."

As the high priest strode inside, his gold trim glittering, Kit drew a sharp breath behind them.

Mel spun to face her, and his ribs tightened. Kit was white as she eyed the high priest like a moonrabbit eyed a hellhound. To hearten her, he strode beside her and captured her arm. If only he could embrace her without the high priest becoming suspicious.

When Kit didn't relax, he frowned. Perhaps introductions would help. "High Priest Theodag, this is my old friend Kit—the one planning the Great Temple's court event. She's also agreed to handle organizing the almskitchens for me." He squeezed Kit's arm. "Kit, this is High Priest Theodag."

Kit continued silently staring at the high priest without moving. Not at all like her. Why was she so upset?

Mel drew Kit closer despite High Priest Theodag watching. He'd better tell the high priest that he'd visit later to discuss whatever Deacon had shared. He must take care of Kit right now.

CHAPTER 25

*H*er pulse skittering, Kit eyed the gold trim on High Priest Theodag's priest robes and suppressed a shudder as Mel drew her closer then opened his mouth to speak.

But before he could, High Priest Theodag nodded at her and said, "Yes, Kit and I have met, although we didn't introduce ourselves."

She flinched and gulped a breath. Oh, Goddess, she'd never dreamt the distinguished priest from the Sun Chapel could be the *high priest of Calatini*. She never would have dared talk to him if she'd known. And she definitely wouldn't have revealed Mel's secrets to seek advice. She swallowed. Plus, now that the high priest knew she wasn't just a crone who loved Goddess laurels but was actually Mel's old friend, he'd soon realize she was the fashionable Countess of Blaine who'd suddenly disappeared. He'd not be pleased such an unworthy lady was hiding with one of his priests and might evict her from the Great Temple.

His brow furrowed, Mel glanced at her then the high priest. "You two have met? Where?"

Kit stiffened further. "At the Sun Chapel when I first examined the Goddess laurels."

Mel inhaled. "He was the priest who encouraged you to eat

your bestowed Goddess laurel apple." At her weak nod, he asked, "How did you not recognize him as the high priest?"

She glanced at the high priest and winced. She should have from his distinguished air. "We'd never met at court, and he was wearing plain robes with no trim."

A wry smile quirking his lips, High Priest Theodag nodded. "When reaffirming my relationship with the Goddess in the mornings, I prefer leaving my rank behind. 'Twas also why I never introduced myself. And I could tell you didn't want to either, so I didn't pry, although I did realize you were Mel's old friend when Elder Priestess Agnes told me about you planning the Great Temple's court event."

Flushing, Kit swallowed. So the high priest had *known* what she was planning when she'd asked him about moving the Goddess laurels. And known she was Mel's friend. Had he already realized she was Lady Blaine?

Mel hummed and released her arm. "Why don't we sit and talk? I'll make us some tea. I suspect this discussion shall be long." He fetched a chair from before his bookcase and set it at the table then encouraged her to sit.

She sank into the plush chair while Mel strode to the cabinets and the high priest sat across from her. As Mel prepared their tea, she studied her gnarled-looking hands tightly laced in her lap. Yet once she'd her cinnaspice tea while Mel and the high priest had regular tea, she forced herself to look up. 'Twas no sense not facing the high priest when he was already here. Then she froze.

High Priest Theodag was narrowly eyeing her and Mel as he sipped his tea. The opposite of the kindhearted smile that had often softened his austere face in the Sun Chapel. "Although I knew you two were old friends, what I didn't realize until Deacon told me was that Kit was staying *here*. 'Tis why I stopped by this morning."

When she clenched her teacup, Mel took her free hand beneath the table and squeezed it, likely to hearten her. He leaned toward the high priest and said, "She's an old friend in need with nowhere else to stay."

High Priest Theodag shook his head. "Yes, but 'tisn't appropriate for a young lady not related or married to you to be staying in your chambers. No matter how old of friends you are."

As Mel reddened and dropped her hand beneath the table as if burned, Kit blushed too, and tingling echoed through her. Doubtless he was also remembering their wild kisses last night and almost kiss this morning. The high priest was right that she shouldn't stay here. Yet where else could she go? Then she tensed. "Wait, how do you know I'm young?" He *must* know she was Lady Blaine.

The high priest's eyes crinkled. "Because you don't move or sound like the venerable lady you appear. Plus, you're under an illusion from the Goddess."

Mel inhaling sharply beside her, she shifted in her seat. Perhaps the high priest didn't realize her identity yet. A faint chill prickled her skin. Although somehow he knew about the Goddess's illusion. She muttered, "You can sense the Goddess's illusion?"

High Priest Theodag sipped his tea. "Of course. I'm a witch priest and could sense the air of holy magic about you, so I cast a probing spell while you ate your bestowed Goddess laurel apple."

Kit stared at the high priest. Not surprising she'd missed that while engrossed in devouring the impossibly delicious holy fruit. Then she glanced at the high priest's gold trim and almost frowned. Shouldn't he have two types if he was also a witch priest? "But you've no ivory trim on your priest robes."

Mel sighed and shook his head. "High priests only wear gold trim to avoid detracting from their rank."

The high priest chuckled. "I believe the custom was instituted by one of my predecessors who was insecure about possessing no special abilities."

She gulped some cinnaspice tea, almost burning her mouth. As the Goddess's chosen high priest of Calatini, he must be a powerful witch, especially about holy spells. "Can you see my true appearance?"

High Priest Theodag cocked his head. "No, I suspect only a very powerful seer could."

Kit traded a glance with Mel. Like the veiled witch.

The high priest leaned toward them, his mouth firming. "Now, you two must tell me *everything*."

As Mel smiled at her and nodded for her to start, Kit swallowed and scrutinized the high priest. Although he'd not realized she was Lady Blaine, he was too trenchant to miss if she concealed anything. And during their meetings at the Sun Chapel, he'd been kind despite knowing she wasn't who she appeared to be. Perhaps he'd remain so when she confessed the full truth. She inhaled then said, "I'm not just Mel's old friend. I'm also the Countess of Blaine."

Nodding, High Priest Theodag hummed. "The lady who disappeared at Longnight. I should have realized. You and Mel did grow up together."

When she stiffened and stared at the high priest, Mel frowned then asked, "How do you know that? I never told you about Kit."

The high priest chuckled. "The Duchess of Childes mentioned it. She said you two used to visit poor villagers together as children."

Kit twisted her free hand in her skirt. No doubt Mel's mother had been proud to share her son's childhood charitable visits. But why had the duchess mentioned *her*? And when had his mother discovered she'd joined Mel on his visits? The duchess had never referred to knowing that.

High Priest Theodag smiled at her. "I suppose the Goddess's illusion is why you disappeared from court so suddenly."

Lifting her chin, she sipped some cinnaspice tea to brace herself. Despite his apparent kindness, would the high priest react like Deacon had? "Yes. The Goddess's female avatars mani-fested in my chambers on Longnight morning and made me appear," she gestured toward her face, "like this. I couldn't allow anyone at court to see me."

Still smiling, the high priest leaned forward. "What exactly did the Goddess's avatars say when they cast the illusion?"

As Mel encouraged her again with a warm nod, Kit exhaled and relaxed her grip on her skirt then detailed her conversation with the Goddess's avatars, and the high priest's kindhearted smile never wavered.

When she finished, High Priest Theodag rubbed his chin. "Become who you were meant to be? Not much concrete advice there. But the Goddess and her avatars do love being cryptic." He chuckled. "Probably because we better appreciate lessons when we figure them out ourselves. Particularly those of us who are more stubborn."

As Mel pointedly arched his brows at her, she sipped her cinnaspice tea and resisted the urge to grimace back. She wasn't the only stubborn one.

Mel turned toward the high priest. "Fortunately, we did consult the veiled witch, a Rhiannon-descendant seer, who provided more concrete advice. She said Kit must participate in life here at the Great Temple to grow as the Goddess intends."

The high priest's smile grew. "I see." Then he set down his teacup. "I didn't realize any seers lived in Ormas, let alone a Rhiannon descendant."

Mel shrugged. "She owns Rhiannon's Veils on Mountainglass Lane near the docks. My family has consulted her on several matters since Wren discovered her. The veiled witch's magic is incredibly powerful, and her prophecies accurate—she gave Devon and Kiera one that helped neutralize the Magehaven ore."

High Priest Theodag nodded. "I'd heard about that prophecy, although not where they'd gotten it. Knowing such a powerful seer can be useful. I must visit the veiled witch one day soon."

Kit shifted in her seat as she finished her cinnaspice tea. "Be warned that meeting her can be eerie, and she's nearly as cryptic as the Goddess's avatars."

The high priest chuckled. "Somehow, I'm not surprised by that." He sobered and sternly eyed her and Mel again. "Now that I know everything about the Goddess's illusion, we must discuss your living arrangements. As I said, 'tisn't appropriate for you two to stay in the same chambers."

Another blush heating her cheeks, she kept her gaze firmly from Mel. 'Twould only make her blush harder. "But I've nowhere else to stay."

Mel shifted beside her. "And Kit mustn't leave the Great Temple."

High Priest Theodag leaned forward. "She doesn't need to." He smiled at her. "Deacon and Sarah are willing for you to stay with them."

Kit frowned. No doubt Sarah was, but not her dismissive husband. "I'm not certain 'tis wise. Deacon dislikes me."

The high priest arched his brows. "Deacon is the one who offered."

She blinked. He what? Why? She glanced at Mel, who was blushing into his teacup. She swallowed. Sarah and Deacon must suspect their wild kisses. No wonder Deacon had offered.

Leaning back in his chair, High Priest Theodag studied her. "As to participating in temple life... I've heard you've been joining Mel on his visits to local temples and community programs, so you've a good understanding of a community priest's life. Although two-thirds of priest are community priests, now you must understand other priests' lives."

Kit exchanged a frown with Mel then asked, "How shall I manage that?"

The high priest smiled. "I'll take you to visit the other types of priests."

While Mel's eyes widened, she gaped at High Priest Theodag. Surely the high priest of Calatini had more important matters to handle than an unworthy lady like her. She sputtered, "*You shall?*"

High Priest Theodag inclined his head. "You acting as a novice shan't do. Their lengthy training would take years for you to discover who you're meant to be. I doubt the Goddess wants that. Besides, a novice at your apparent age would lead to questions. But no one shall question it if I take you."

As she silently stared at the high priest, Mel grimaced and said, "The high priest taking an old lady to visit different types of priests shall lead to *more* questions."

Humming, High Priest Theodag shrugged. "Not if we tell everyone the truth."

Kit froze. "That I'm Lady Blaine?" Her chest tightened. Then court would soon discover her crone appearance.

The high priest scrutinized her, his gaze probing. "Not if you don't wish it. We can simply say you're a friend of Mel's under the Goddess's illusion."

Although Mel nodded, she suppressed a wince. 'Twas almost as bad as revealing she was Lady Blaine. "But spells sent by the Goddess are exceedingly rare, so shan't saying that engender gossip?"

High Priest Theodag shrugged again. "Such gossip is inevitable if you fully participate in temple life. Witch priests shall sense the air of holy magic about you as soon as they meet you."

Kit swallowed. So there would have been gossip already if she'd met more witch priests than Deacon and the high priest. 'Twas fortunate the other witch priests had been too busy to notice her when she'd visited Charmed Blessings with Mel.

The high priest continued, "And no one shall believe it odd that a high priest is shepherding a lady blessed by a spell from the Goddess."

She glanced at Mel, who gave her an encouraging smile. Albeit not worthy of it, the high priest's guidance might help her *finally* break the Goddess's illusion. Inhaling, she turned back to the high priest. "Very well, and thank you so much for your generous offer, although I doubt I deserve it." She leaned forward. "I'll shift my belongings today, but Mel and I have a family luncheon to attend tomorrow, so I'll begin visiting priests with you the day after."

Smiling, High Priest Theodag rose. "I look forward to meeting you in the Sun Chapel after breakfast in two days."

Once the high priest strode out the door, Kit exhaled and sagged in her chair. High Priest Theodag learning the truth had gone so much better than she'd feared. He'd not evicted her and was even prepared to help her break the Goddess's illusion. Her heart twisted. Yet she'd hardly see Mel after tomorrow. And although he could never return her love, she'd enjoyed spending their days together. Surrendering that would be hard.

CHAPTER 26

After High Priest Theodag left, Mel eyed Kit sagging in her chair beside him. She appeared relieved the high priest had accepted everything so calmly, except for them staying in the same chambers. Mel swallowed. How much had Deacon shared about last night with the high priest? Or had the high priest merely been opposed on principle? Hopefully, 'twas the latter.

He swallowed a sigh. Kit staying elsewhere was sensible, yet he'd rather she remain here. Even though not kissing her again would be trying. But he must forget his shameful hunger. He forced a bright smile. "That went well, I believe."

Lifting her head, Kit blinked at him. "Much better than I'd expected." She sighed and rose. "I'd better go gather my belongings."

Although he shouldn't risk entering her bedroom, to prolong their remaining time together, he leapt upright and said, "I'll help you."

Her hand on her doorknob, Kit stared at him over her shoulder. "I can manage. I've only one bag. Besides, don't you have local temples or community programs to visit?"

Mel stiffened. How could he have forgotten that—again? "So

I do." He glanced at the clock on the mantel and grimaced. 'Twas already late morning. "And thanks to High Priest Theodag's long visit, I'm extremely late. I don't believe I'll be back until Vespers, even though I promised I'd attend services and eat meals here."

Kit's eyes narrowed. "Understandable today. Just don't make it a habit."

He smiled, warmed by her stern caring. "I shan't. I'll see you tonight then."

Once Kit nodded and disappeared into her bedroom, he sighed and left. His visits to a family refuge and a nearby youth guild were uneventful, yet somehow they seemed more solitary than usual, even though Kit hadn't joined his hectic visits the past few days.

He returned to the Great Temple just as Vespers began and strode straight to Kit, who was sitting between Deacon and Sarah. He exchanged smiles with Kit and his friends, but since the service was starting, they couldn't talk until they headed to dinner afterward.

Over his shredded chicken stew, Mel made himself smile at Kit. "All settled in at Deacon and Sarah's?"

Kit nodded. "Of course. As I said, I've only one bag, and I didn't need to think about where to put everything because my new bedroom is identical to your spare room."

Sarah beamed at Kit. "I'm so excited you're staying with us. I've not enjoyed female friends staying overnight since Esther and I roomed together as novices."

A smile softening his ascetic face, Deacon shook his head. "No doubt you and Kit shall stay up half the night exchanging secrets like you and Esther used to."

Mel blinked at his friend. Deacon had spoken without any hint of disapproval toward Kit. Had her moving altered his opinion of her that much?

Kit pursed her lips. "I can't stay up too late. I've the almskitchens to organize in the morning."

Mel leaned toward Kit, his pulse stirring as he eyed her lips.

"Don't forget that I'll join you to explain why you're assuming my duties."

Kit nodded then asked about his visits today, and they discussed that for the rest of dinner. Afterward, Sarah captured Kit's arm and swept her back to her and Deacon's chambers, while Mel and Deacon followed at a more sedate pace.

Deacon slanted him a glance. "I hope you're not angry at me for telling High Priest Theodag that Kit was staying with you. But after your... quarrel last night, I felt I had to."

A blush heated Mel's neck. Deacon definitely suspected more than a quarrel had happened between him and Kit. "I understand, and you were right to do so. Thanks for offering to let Kit stay with you."

Deacon sighed but shrugged. "I knew 'twould please Sarah. Besides, I needed to atone for how I treated Kit before. The high priest scolded me about that, reminding me 'twasn't my place to judge how the Goddess chooses to bestow her magic."

Mel nodded. Well, *that* explained Deacon's altered opinion. And now Kit wouldn't have to endure his disapproval while she stayed with him and Sarah. Good.

At their doors, Mel and Deacon said good night, then Mel strode into his empty chambers. He sighed as he reviewed his list of local temples and community programs to select the one he'd visit tomorrow before the family luncheon. Without Kit, his chambers were too still and almost hollow. Odd that he'd never noticed that before she'd stayed with him.

Thanks to his promise to Kit to relax in the evenings, he made himself some tea and read after he'd decided to visit Merrick House, a family refuge, tomorrow. Then he headed to bed early to get extra sleep.

THE FOLLOWING MORNING, Mel rose before dawn then lingered in the hall for Kit to emerge to attend Lauds. When she did, he grinned at her, his chest loosening. "So how late did you stay up with Sarah?"

Kit chuckled and shook her head. "Not as late as she wanted. I didn't realize she enjoyed evenings so much. No wonder she and Deacon rarely attend Lauds or eat breakfast in the dining hall."

He hummed as they began down the hall, side by side but not touching. He still couldn't risk that. "Yes, Deacon fetches breakfast for them so she can sleep longer."

Kit smiled. "I suspect he also enjoys the time alone with his wife before their duties begin. I'll make sure to stay away in the mornings."

Mel swallowed. Kit could be sweeter than cinnaspice-honey burnt custard sometimes. He fisted his hands in his priest robes to avoid pulling her into his arms. "Deacon and Sarah shall both appreciate that."

After Lauds, he and Kit strode to the chapter house, and he explained about her assuming his duties to the waiting priests and novices. None of them seem surprised or upset. Once she'd organized the almskitchens, he and Kit swiftly ate breakfast before he left for Merrick House and she returned to Deacon and Sarah's chambers.

As soon as he returned to the Great Temple, he hurried straight to his friends' chambers to fetch Kit for the family luncheon. He brightened at her warm smile when she opened the door. "Ready to meet Isabel?"

Kit nodded, and they headed outside to the carriage Mother had sent. However, unlike on previous trips, he only touched Kit when helping her into the carriage and settled in the backward seat across from her. He'd be too tempted to kiss her if he sat beside her like before.

The hand he'd held curled in her lap, Kit blushed and leaned back in her seat.

Mel swallowed as tingling warmth flooded him. From her blush, Kit wouldn't protest if he spent the entire carriage ride kissing her. To distract them both, he asked, "What did you do this morning after breakfast?"

Kit tilted her head. "I talked with Sarah before she left for Peaceful Minds, then I returned to the Sun Chapel. Being near the Goddess laurels settles me and helps me think."

He smiled at Kit. "They do for me too." Until last time when their cinnaspice-apple fragrance had made him burn to kiss her again. Shoving that aside, he arched his brows at her. "What were you thinking about?"

Sighing, Kit smoothed her skirt. "Tomorrow. Although High Priest Theodag seemed confident about taking me to visit different types of priests, I suspect they shan't approve of me, and I'm worried about the gossip my visits shall engender."

His chest squeezed. If only he could risk wrapping her in his arms to comfort her. He gave her a warm smile instead. "High Priest Theodag shall ensure everything proceeds smoothly. Managing priests is his main duty."

Kit sighed again. "I suppose." Then she asked about his visit to Merrick House, and they discussed that for the rest of the ride.

Once the carriage halted, he helped Kit alight, dropping her arm immediately afterward. After Perkins ushered them inside, they joined everyone in the drawing room.

Mother swept over with Father then embraced him and Kit. "Finally. You two are the last to arrive except for Devon and Kiera." Tilting her head, she eyed him and tsked. "You still appear tired. You've not been resting enough, have you?"

As Kit slanted him a knowing look, Mel smiled at Mother and Father to reassure them then replied, "I have been doing too much recently, but I made sure to retire early last night."

Father chuckled with a crooked grin. "I believe 'tis the first you've ever admitted to doing too much. What happened? Did you exhaust yourself until you collapsed?"

His face warming, Mel straightened his priest robes. "Almost. I fell asleep at the table and was fiercely scolded for it."

Mother smiled at Kit. "I imagine you were the one to deliver that scolding. Thanks for taking such excellent care of Mel."

A faint blush darkening her cheeks, Kit muttered, "Of course."

Mel tensed. If they kept discussing this, Mother would soon realize that scolding had led to ravenous kisses. She was too perceptive not to notice the longing between him and Kit. To prevent that, he said, "Tell us about Isabel."

Mother beamed. "She's the sweetest infant. Always calm and adores everyone."

Grinning, Father added, "Fortunate considering she's been prodded and fussed over by the entire family today."

Shaking her head at Father, Mother captured Kit's arm. "Come, you must take a turn holding Isabel. She's wonderful practice."

Her eyes flaring, Kit stiffened beside Mel. "I don't require practice."

Mother chuckled. "Of course you do."

As Mother pulled Kit across the drawing room to the other ladies surrounding little Isabel, Mel suppressed a sigh. Hopefully, Mother's attitude toward Kit wouldn't make everyone realize her identity. 'Twould upset her.

Warmly smiling after Mother, Father hummed while Aragon and Hawke joined them. "Your mother has been so ecstatic about Isabel."

Aragon grinned at Father. "You're hardly any less so." He eyed his infant daughter across the room and sighed. "Although at times I wish Mother were slightly less ecstatic. I don't get to hold Isabel enough."

Mel almost laughed. Aragon was definitely as besotted as Kit had predicted from his letter.

Hawke nudged Aragon's arm. "You'd say that you didn't get to hold Isabel enough even if Mother wasn't always fussing over her. You still have to share her with Selena." He flashed a crooked grin. "Fortunately, Wren and I shall have one each."

Tsking, Mel murmured to tease Hawke, "But shall they be as sweet and easy to handle as Isabel?"

Father shook his head at Hawke. "Since they're your children, I suspect not. You were our most tempestuous infant—even then you were stubborn and hated being made to do anything you hadn't decided to do, like sleep on a schedule."

As Sir Alaric joined them, Hawke shrugged and said, "They're Wren's children too, so I'm sure they shan't be as tempestuous."

Waggling his brows at Hawke, Sir Alaric chuckled. "Considering the chase my daughter led you on, are you certain of that?"

Hawke stilled for a moment. Then he turned to Mel. "I'd expected you'd be wearing priest robes of arachne silk today."

When Father, Aragon, and Sir Alaric stared at him, Mel shifted his weight. Why had Hawke chosen Kit's arachne silk to distract his father-in-law? Mel made himself shrug. "The arachne silk wasn't for me." Although the bolt still remained under his bed since he'd not had time to take it to Celeste's yet. He really must do so—Kit's natalday was less than three weeks away.

As Aragon and Sir Alaric blinked while Father simply smiled, Hawke grinned and leaned toward him then drawled, "Ooo, a faegift? Who's the fortunate lady? The one you visited witch shops for? Mother shall begin planning your wedding ceremony as soon as she hears."

His neck heating, Mel shrugged again and refused to glance at Father. Since Father knew Kit was the old lady acting as his assistant, Father would realize the arachne silk and visiting the witch shops were both for her. Not that either was more than him helping an old friend in need.

Thankfully, before he'd devised a retort to Hawke's teasing, Devon and Kiera strode into the drawing room. As Aragon and Devon began discussing Isabel while Father asked Hawke about the orphanage, Mel slipped away to join Edouard and Farson as Arvan and Pippa's brothers left to plan their ride tomorrow.

Once they exchanged greetings, Farson nodded at Elise

cradling Isabel in her arms and cooing. "As I suspected, Elise has held little Isabel nearly the entire time we've been here."

Mel hummed. Somehow Kit must have dissuaded Mother from making her hold Isabel. "I'm surprised Mother and Selena let Elise be the only one to hold her."

Edouard chuckled. "Selena was too nice to protest, and your mother too distracted with greeting her guests. Although that appears about to change now that everyone is here."

Mel almost laughed as Mother spoke to Elise, who sighed but relinquished little Isabel to her loving grandmother. Then Mother turned to Kit with Isabel. Kit began to retreat but froze when Mother dropped Isabel into her arms. She relaxed when Isabel stared up at her without crying or flailing. Her face softening, she cradled Isabel against her chest and offered her finger.

He swallowed as warmth suffused him and hunger flared in his veins. With her deep strength and tender heart, Kit would make a wonderful mother one day.

Edouard slanted him a narrow glance. "Mel, are you all right?"

Mel wrenched his gaze free from Kit cradling his infant niece and gritted a smile. "I was just thinking I should meet my niece. Why let the ladies monopolize her? Excuse me." Then he strode across the drawing room.

CHAPTER 27

*W*armth filling her, Kit couldn't help smiling at little Isabel gazing up at her with such trusting, dark-gray eyes while squeezing her finger. She swallowed to ease her tight throat then rasped, "She's adorable, Lady Treyvan."

Her freckled face glowing, Selena dimpled. "I know." She was clearly just as besotted as Aragon with their daughter.

Never having held an infant before, Kit cooed at Isabel like Elise had moments ago and was rewarded with a sweet wriggle. 'Twas amazing how tiny and fragile yet precious infants were. She sighed. "Isabel is a lovely blend of you and your husband, with Lord Treyvan's hair and your eyes."

Between Selena and Kit, the duchess hummed while beaming at her granddaughter. "'Tis too early to truly tell that. Hair color takes years to settle, while eyes take at least a year. Aragon and Mel both had eyes that color at this age—Hawke's were navy, however."

Kit studied Isabel, and her chest squeezed. So if Mel ever found the perfect priestess to marry, their child could look exactly like Isabel.

Selena chuckled. "I'm hoping Isabel's eyes change, while Aragon is hoping they remain the same."

Warmly grinning at Selena, Mel strode between Kit and his mother. "Because Aragon wants a miniature you running about." He turned to Kit. "Could I hold Isabel?"

She nodded, and her heart fluttered as Mel gathered Isabel from her arms and cradled his infant niece against his chest. He was so compassionate and diligent and would be such an amazing father. The opposite of hers. His children—and his beloved wife—would be incredibly blessed.

Tears pricking her eyes, she forced herself to quit watching Mel. As she did, her gaze met his mother's, and the duchess smiled. Kit blushed. No doubt her love for Mel had been stamped on her face while watching him hold Isabel, especially to his perceptive mother. Not that the duchess had appeared to mind, probably because she knew they'd never be more than friends. Kit swallowed. But hopefully, no one besides the duchess had noticed her unrequited love.

Queen Kiera beside her, Wren waddled over to Mel and asked, "Do you mind if I hold Isabel now? 'Tis been years since an infant was left at the orphanage, and I sorely need the practice."

Mel nodded and handed over Isabel. After Wren and the others took a turn holding Isabel, Selena scooped her drooping daughter from Pippa's arms, saying, "Isabel is tired from meeting everyone. I'll take her up to the nursery."

Aragon joining her, Selena left the drawing room, and once they returned, everyone headed to luncheon. Afterward, Kit and Mel made their excuses so they could return to the Great Temple.

Mel's parents walked them to the door, and the duchess embraced them then said, "Make sure you don't do too much and get some rest."

The duke arched his brows. "Shall you be able to visit before the royal ceremonies on Plantfete?"

Mel sighed. "I'm not certain. I must finish my training, so I can start my new duties."

The duchess turned to Kit. "What about you?"

Kit lifted a shoulder. "I've some new duties as well." She blushed as Mel's parents traded a glance. "But I'll attempt to visit soon." She must ask the duchess about acting as a supporter for the Great Temple's court event.

She warmed when the duchess smiled at her and replied, "I'll look forward to it."

As soon as Kit returned to Sarah and Deacon's chambers, she wrote to Queen Kiera requesting a meeting about the Great Temple's court event. Once the queen replied, she could arrange her visit with the duchess.

THE FOLLOWING MORNING AFTER LAUDS, organizing the almskitchens, and breakfast, Kit smoothed her dress as she returned to the Sun Chapel to meet High Priest Theodag. Please let these visits to different types of priests go well and not engender gossip that reached court. To settle herself, she bent to inhale the Goddess laurel's heavenly fragrance.

As her chest lightened like always at that, the high priest strode beside her. Unlike their previous meetings here, he was wearing priest robes with gold trim. "Good morning, Kit."

She swept a curtsy. "Good morning, your excellency."

High Priest Theodag smiled at her. "You needn't be so formal. I'm still the same simple priest you met here last month."

Although warmed by the high priest's kindhearted attempt to reassure her, Kit shook her head at his delusion. "You're no more a simple priest than I'm a humble novice."

The high priest hummed while they left the Sun Chapel. "You sound as if you believe I'm some kind of paragon. I'm not perfect —no one is, other than the Goddess and the other gods, of course." His eyes crinkled. "I embroiled myself in quite a bit of trouble before I listened to the Goddess's call to serve as her priest."

She suppressed a snort. The high priest's trouble surely was nothing compared to her wickedness. Her own father had always despised her for being wicked and vulgar, she'd cruelly hurt the family of the gentleman she loved, and she'd blindly pursued wealth and status despite being in love with Mel.

High Priest Theodag shrugged as they entered the covered walkways connecting the buildings of the Great Temple. "But my youthful mistakes did help make me a better priest and leader. They provided me with compassion and understanding for those in trouble. I suspect I'd not have become the high priest without them."

Kit blinked. Except High Priest Theodag had doubtless always been worthy to become the high priest, no matter the minor mistakes he'd made. And the Goddess had probably never needed to curse *him* to become who he was meant to be. She arched her brows at him. "What priests are we visiting today?"

The high priest rubbed his jaw. "I thought we'd begin with temple priests since they're most similar to community priests—they simply serve the temple rather than the entire community. Here at the Great Temple, we've several types of temple priests. The general ones oversee the novices responsible for cleaning, and they act as porters, messengers, and the like. The special types are garden priests and kitchen priests, who tend to their respective areas."

She swallowed. She couldn't visit all those types of temple priests until well past Vespers and dinner. She'd not see Mel, and such hectic rounds would soon exhaust her like Mel had been after visiting all those local temples and community programs. "I'm visiting all the temple priests today?"

Chuckling, High Priest Theodag grinned at her. "No, just the kitchen priests. I thought you'd help them for a few days to understand their duties before continuing to the next type of temple priest."

Kit exhaled, her tension easing. That sounded more manageable. "I'm relieved to be starting there. Sarah introduced me to the head kitchen priestess Esther a couple weeks ago."

The high priest nodded. "I suspected she might have. Sarah loves getting people to bake with her." He smiled. "She's one of the few Esther allows to trespass in the temple kitchen with impunity. They roomed together until Sarah married Deacon."

When they strode into the sweltering and bustling temple kitchen, the busy priests and priestesses quieted while turning to stare, mostly at her. Not at all like the last time she'd visited.

She stiffened. Clearly, all the kitchen priests knew she was the lady under the Goddess's illusion. Titillating gossip traveled as quickly at the Great Temple as at court. Wonderful.

Esther hurried over, her bright gaze intent on Kit.

As the head kitchen priestess curtsied, High Priest Theodag nodded back. "Good morning, Esther. I've heard you already met Kit."

Esther beamed at Kit. "Yes, your excellency, although I didn't know she was blessed by a spell from the Goddess then."

A blush heated Kit's cheeks. "We were keeping that quiet."

High Priest Theodag smiled at them both. "Kit, I'll leave you with Esther, and I'll see you in the Sun Chapel at the same time tomorrow."

Once the high priest left, Kit smiled at Esther, who was still beaming. How embarrassing. "Where did you want me to start? I must warn you that the only time I cooked anything was those spice buns with Sarah."

Esther nodded. "Not surprising, given you're a lady and all."

Kit stiffened. Did Esther know she was Lady Blaine? If temple gossip already knew that, then court would soon hear of it too. "How did you know I'm a lady?"

Chuckling, Esther tilted her head. "Everyone knows you're an old friend of Mel's, so you must be a lady. Plus, you speak and carry yourself like one, despite your servant's dress."

Kit swallowed but made herself nod. So temple gossip didn't know her identity, but if anyone from court heard the temple rumors, they could easily realize she was the missing Lady Blaine. Great.

Esther beckoned her. "I'll have you begin with chopping vegetables for luncheon's ham and tuber stew. 'Tis simple enough as long as you watch your fingers."

Once the head kitchen priestess demonstrated how to properly clean then chop, Kit chopped all the vegetables before her. Then more were placed before her. The Great Temple kitchen had to feed almost two thousand priests, after all.

She was sweating from the kitchen's persistent heat with cramping hands when Esther hurried over and said, "Come along, 'tis time to attend Sext. Everything is prepared for luncheon, and only one of us remains to watch the food."

Kit exhaled as they headed outside and followed the covered walkways. She'd only been helping in the kitchen for a few hours, and she was already tired. "Preparing food is more demanding than I realized, and the kitchen is so hot. How do you stand it day after day?"

Esther chuckled. "I suppose I'm accustomed to it. Besides, I've always loved cooking. 'Tis nothing like preparing a delectable meal then watching people devour it."

Humming, Kit nodded. True, watching Mel devour the spice buns she'd made with Sarah had been delightful. She and Sarah must prepare more desserts for him soon. But she'd enjoyed feeding Mel because she loved him. She studied Esther. Cooking must be how kitchen priests showed their love.

In the nave of the main temple, Esther led her to the back row of chairs. "When the service is before a meal, we always sit here and leave directly afterward so we can return to the kitchen first to serve the meal."

Kit swallowed a sigh. So even though Mel was here too, she'd not get to join him and would be busy during luncheon. Doubtless 'twould be the same for Vespers and dinner. Her chest squeezed. After staying with him for two months, she missed being near Mel every day, and she'd barely left. But at least they'd attended Lauds together this morning.

After Sext, she headed to the dining hall with the kitchen

priests and helped serve. She and Mel could only exchange brief greetings while she handed him a pot of honey. Following luncheon, Esther had her wash dishes, a task that shriveled her hands and left her covered with soapy water. Once that was done, she helped stir the creamy fish chowder for dinner. Then like she'd expected, Vespers and dinner were a repeat of Sext and luncheon. When she returned to Sarah and Deacon's chambers, she talked with Sarah for a few moments and prepared for tomorrow before collapsing in bed.

Her days while helping in the Great Temple kitchen were all similar to her first, except after her second day when she met with High Priest Theodag, she began helping prepare breakfast too, so she didn't even get to attend Lauds or eat breakfast with Mel. Despite her duties with kitchen priests, once breakfast began, she still organized the almskitchens in the chapter house before returning to help serve breakfast.

While helping kitchen priests, she also received a note from Queen Kiera agreeing to meet for luncheon at the palace in a few days. She'd only a few details left to decide about the Great Temple's court event, but even with her new duties, she should manage to finalize her plans before her luncheon with the queen. Once she replied to Queen Kiera, she wrote to the duchess asking to visit Childes House a few days after her royal luncheon.

On her final day helping the kitchen priests, Kit woke with the most vicious megrim she'd suffered in months. Probably because she'd not had one for four whole weeks, something that hadn't happened since Lord Blaine had died. Yet she still forced herself to rise and head to the kitchen after gulping her megrim tonic. Esther and the other kitchen priests were expecting her.

When she trudged into the kitchen, Esther narrowly eyed her. "You look wretched."

Kit managed a tremulous smile as her head throbbed at the kitchen's heat and din. "I've a megrim today."

Esther tsked. "Then why are you here?"

Gripping a table to remain upright, Kit shrugged. "I couldn't not appear for my final day helping you."

Esther shooed her toward the door. "Go and rest. You're not well enough to help today, and you've helped plenty on your previous three days."

Kit exhaled and nodded before shuffling from the kitchen. She also wasn't well enough to organize the almskitchens. Perhaps Mel could handle that for her. So instead of returning straight to bed, she knocked on his door.

Mel opened it then stiffened with a fierce frown. "You appear about to collapse, Kit. Why aren't you resting?" He wrapped her in his arms then drew her inside.

CHAPTER 28

*H*is chest tight, Mel half-carried Kit to his small table and helped her sit. She was trembling and whiter than a banshee with pain pinching her face. "You're suffering a bad megrim, aren't you?"

Kit whimpered and covered her eyes. "Yes."

He hurried to the cabinets to prepare Kit's megrim tea and cold compress. Fortunately, she'd not taken them when she'd left. Once she'd wrapped her cold compress about her head and gulped her tea, he began massaging her shoulders to ease some of her pain.

Kit shivered then muttered, "I'm not sure we should touch like this."

Mel swallowed, his hands tingling like always at touching Kit, despite her suffering. Shameful. Burying his hunger, he couldn't resist pressing a tender kiss on her hair. "I can't leave you in pain."

He massaged Kit until she sagged against the table. He eyed her, his heart squeezing. She was clearly still suffering and not well enough to walk.

When he scooped her into his arms, Kit stiffened and began to wriggle. "Mel, what are you doing?"

He kissed Kit's hair again as he headed toward the door. She always seemed so shocked when he took care of her. "Carrying you to bed. Did you eat breakfast yet?"

Drooping against him, Kit shuddered. "No, but I doubt I could right now."

Mel hummed while carrying her into Deacon and Sarah's chambers. At his entrance, his friends quit eating their breakfast and gaped, but thankfully they didn't manage to speak before he strode into Kit's bedroom.

As he laid her in bed, Kit gripped his shoulders. "Wait, the almskitchens..."

He kissed Kit's brow and tucked the covers about her. Even suffering, she still remembered her duties. "I'll handle them. You rest."

After he closed Kit's door behind him, Deacon and Sarah frowned at him, then Sarah asked, "What was that about?"

Mel blushed and straightened his priest robes. "Kit is suffering a bad megrim. Could you ensure she eats later?" To prevent his friends from asking further questions, he left to organize the almskitchens for Kit.

That handled, he devoured breakfast then returned to his chambers to collect the wrapped bolt of arachne silk. He was visiting a prayer house in the fashionable areas of Ormas today, so he could finally take the arachne silk to Celeste's. Hopefully, just over two weeks would be enough time for Celeste's to make it into a cloak and Mirage to enchant it afterward.

Before he left, he checked on Kit. She was sleeping and didn't stir, but a tray of crackers, soup, and tea was beside her for when she woke. Sarah must have brought it prior to leaving for Peaceful Minds. Good.

Resisting the urge to kiss Kit's brow again, Mel hastened to the waiting carriage. He'd check on her again when he returned for Sext and luncheon. Perhaps she'd be well enough to attend services and eat by then.

His visit to the prayer house went smoothly, and he left the carriage there while heading to Celeste's a few streets over. He didn't want anyone to witness him entering a fashionable dress shop—a priest had no reason to shop there, so 'twould cause gossip.

Halting in front of the door with Celeste's painted above the door in elegant, blue letters, he glanced about the street, but no one was watching him, so he strode inside Kit's favorite dress shop. And luckily, the only person in the anteroom was the clerk. He joined her with a warm smile. "Good morning. I need you to make a cloak for me."

The clerk eyed him. "We don't make gentlemen's clothes, holy sir."

Mel shifted the bolt of arachne silk beneath his arm. Thanks to his unease about visiting Celeste's for the first time, he wasn't explaining well. "I know. 'Tis for a lady—a frequent patron of yours, actually."

Pursing her lips, the clerk shook her head. "We'd still need the lady here to take proper measurements."

He frowned. Wouldn't a dress shop keep those for their patrons? "'Tis a natalday gift, and taking measurements would spoil the surprise." Plus, Kit would refuse to show herself here while under the Goddess's illusion.

The clerk sighed. "I understand, but Mother insists on taking proper measurements. She says the fit isn't right without them."

Mel leaned forward. Somehow he must convince the clerk to help him. Kit needed this natalday gift to not miss the royal ceremonies. "Surely a simple cloak doesn't require such precise measurements, and you must have hers recorded somewhere. According to Mother, Lady Blaine purchases all her clothes here."

Inhaling, the clerk brightened. "'Tis a natalday gift for Lady Blaine?" She scrutinized him then blinked. "You're Priest Melchior Hawke. I recall you from when you visited her last summer. She agreed to see you even though she'd a terrible megrim, and she never allows anyone to see her like that."

He almost winced. Kit also had a bad megrim when he'd scolded her about hurting Hawke and Wren? Despite his angry disappointment, he should have noticed that and waited to confront her. He swallowed. "I suppose you were there for a dress fitting."

The clerk frowned. "No, I'm Lady Blaine's maid Willa." She gestured toward one of the fitting rooms. "Celeste is my mother. Lady Blaine sent me to stay with her while she attended her unexpected business." She leaned toward him. "If you're purchasing Lady Blaine a natalday gift, you must have seen her recently. How is she? I've not heard from her since she left, and I thought she'd be back by now."

Mel shifted the arachne silk beneath his arm. Willa appeared worried, but he couldn't reveal Kit's secrets, so he simply said, "She's well, although still busy handling her unexpected business. And I'm not certain when she'll be finished."

Willa sighed. "I'm glad Lady Blaine is well at least." She extended a hand. "Here, give me that bundle you're holding. I assume 'tis fabric for her cloak. I'll gladly make it for Lady Blaine without new measurements."

He smiled at Kit's maid and handed her the arachne silk and three gold coins. That should be enough to pay for the cloak here since a set of his evening clothes for court cost twice that. "Thank you, Willa. I'll let Lady Blaine know you asked after her once I give her the cloak. When shall it be ready?"

Willa unwrapped the bolt of arachne silk and hummed. "A week, most likely. It shall take longer to sew than normal since the arachne silk is still transparent. Too bad you couldn't have Lady Blaine bond to it and set the color without spoiling her natalday gift."

Mel exhaled. A week should give Mirage long enough to make Kit's cloak an invisibility cloak before her natalday. He nodded at Willa. "Thank you again. Send word to me at the Great Temple when 'tis ready."

He was about to leave when Mother glided from the dressing

room that Willa had gestured at earlier, followed by a regal woman who resembled Willa, surely Celeste.

Mother's brows rose. "Mel, what are you doing here?"

He stiffened but gritted a smile. Although Mother wouldn't gossip about his visit, she'd assume Kit's natalday gift meant more than it did, especially since adults in their family didn't exchange natalday gifts. "Ordering a cloak."

Mother glanced at the arachne silk in Willa's hand and smiled. "Ah yes, Eldridge mentioned Hawke had given you some arachne silk. A natalday faegift for Kit, I assume?"

A blush heating his neck, Mel nodded. Yes, Mother definitely assumed he felt more than friendship for Kit and would likely attempt to matchmake. A senseless endeavor since Kit wanted a wealthy and titled husband. He managed to smile at Mother again. "Excuse me, I must return to the Great Temple."

Then he escaped before Mother could quiz him further about Kit's natalday gift.

At the Great Temple, he first checked on Kit, who was still sleeping with her untouched tray of food beside her. He sighed then headed to Sext, but the singing didn't hearten him as much as it usually did. After a quick luncheon, he left to visit a family refuge in the afternoon.

When Mel returned for Vespers and dinner, Kit was awake at last, but she wasn't well enough to leave Deacon and Sarah's chambers. So he and his friends left her to rest, but he brought her dinner afterward. Her weak yet grateful smile made him ache to remain and talk, but he forced himself to leave before he succumbed to temptation and kissed her again. He shouldn't be hungering for that, especially when she was ill.

THE FOLLOWING MORNING, Mel grinned when Kit joined him for Lauds. She appeared her normal self once more, albeit under the Goddess's illusion. While they shared breakfast for the first time in three days, he asked, "What priests are you helping today? Not kitchen priests since you didn't serve breakfast."

Kit tilted her head. "Garden priests, I believe. Although first, I asked High Priest Theodag for an hour to sit in the Sun Chapel every morning after breakfast. I need that to settle my soul and prepare for the busy day ahead. Helping kitchen priests was draining."

He studied Kit. Yet she'd still thrown herself into helping like she had since she'd begun participating in temple life. Except for her devotion to remaining fashionable and determination to return to court, she acted much like him and the priests she was helping. But since she wanted her fashionable life at court, she didn't share their calling, so she'd never remain at the Great Temple once she broke the Goddess's illusion.

Kit smiled. "But the high priest readily agreed to my time in the Sun Chapel, saying he needed the same, which was why we'd met. He'll be taking me to the garden priests after my hour."

Mel swallowed a sigh. If only he could join Kit. Praying in the Sun Chapel would be wonderful. Yet given his hunger to kiss her during her megrim yesterday, he couldn't trust himself to remain alone with her, even in a chapel. "Sounds like an excellent idea."

That day and the next, he saw Kit for services and meals, unlike when she'd been helping kitchen priests. But they were never alone like they had been when she'd stayed with him, and he missed their private conversations. She understood things in a way no one else at the Great Temple did since they'd grown up together, and she was strong enough to share her thoughts even when she knew he'd not agree. Perhaps he could risk joining her in the Sun Chapel to enjoy their private conversations again.

So during breakfast the following morning, Mel glanced about the dining hall to make sure no one overheard then asked, "Do you mind if I join you in the Sun Chapel in the mornings?"

Kit beamed at him over her cinnaspice tea. "I'd like that."

He beamed back, his heart quickening. She'd missed him too. "Are you helping garden priests again today?"

Kit leaned toward him and lowered her voice, "I would be, but I'm meeting Queen Kiera for luncheon to discuss the Great Temple's court event."

Warmth expanding his chest, Mel nodded. To help the charities, Kit was willing to visit the palace where she'd encounter many from court. "I'm certain Kiera shall be excited to help. Do you mind if I tell Elder Priestess Agnes about your visit when I meet with her this morning?"

Straightening, Kit smiled and shook her head. "That's fine. You can also tell her I'm meeting with your mother in a few days to discuss the Great Temple's court event as well."

He winked at Kit to tease her. "You're approaching Mother second? She'll be upset when she learns that."

Kit chuckled while they returned their dishes. "Etiquette demands I do. She's only a duchess, after all."

Mel couldn't help chuckling too. "*Only* a duchess? I doubt anyone has called Mother *that* before. She's the most influential duchess in Calatini, despite never serving on the council."

Her mouth twitching, Kit nodded as they entered the covered walkways. "I know. 'Tis why I'm asking her to act as a supporter for the Great Temple's court event."

He sobered and slanted her a probing glance. "Do you want me to join you to deflect Mother's quizzing? If you meet her alone, she'll keep asking until you tell her everything."

Kit sighed. "I suspect she's already guessed most of it, so deflecting her questions would be futile." She smiled at him just before they entered the main temple. "But thanks for offering."

Falling silent, he and Kit strode through the main temple to the Sun Chapel then sank into the first pew on the side beside the wall. The nearest Goddess laurel was close enough to touch if they extended a hand, but neither did. Instead, they inhaled the holy shrub's cinnaspice-apple fragrance, and he, at least, began to pray.

Unlike after he'd prayed here following their ravenous kisses, peace filled him as the Goddess whispered in his heart. He was serving the Goddess as he was meant to do, and he was helping Kit discover her purpose as well. Exhaling, Mel reached out and threaded his fingers through Kit's then squeezed her hand to share the peace filling him. And although he tingled at touching her, somehow he couldn't make himself release her hand.

CHAPTER 29

When Mel squeezed her hand, Kit swallowed and resisted the urge to nestle against him. Even if he loved her like she loved him, 'twouldn't be appropriate in the Sun Chapel. She should really extract her hand, but she wasn't strong enough. Instead, she remained still and barely breathed to prevent him from realizing they were holding hands. Yet the longer they touched, the more she ached to kiss him again. The peace that usually filled her while praying among the Goddess laurels was nowhere to be found today—hunger for Mel consumed her.

She shuddered a breath when he drew her upright then released her at last. Fisting her hands in her skirt to avoid touching him, she eyed him as they left the Sun Chapel. From his serene expression, he'd suffered none of the love and desire that had tormented her. Doubtless because he saw her as nothing more than an old friend in need, despite how he'd kissed her nine days ago. Her heart twisting, she somehow managed to bid him farewell with a blinding smile when he helped her into the carriage waiting to carry her to the palace.

As she followed a maid's directions to the royal wing, Kit forced herself to walk purposely and ignore the curious glances of the servants, government clerks, and members of court she passed. Please let none of them notice she carried herself like a lady as everyone at the Great Temple had, but simply see a crone in a maid's dress.

At the private dining room in the royal wing, she lifted her chin and said to the female royal guards flanking the door, "I'm here for luncheon with Q—Lady Kiera." Once they waved her inside, she sank into a deep curtsy before Queen Kiera. "Your majesty. Thank you for agreeing to see me today."

Queen Kiera inclined her head with a warm smile. "Of course, Kay, is it?"

Clasping her hands before her, Kit shifted but nodded. She'd simply signed her note to the queen as "K" because everyone at the Great Temple knew Mel's old friend Kit was planning their court event while all of his family knew her as his assistant Kay.

The queen continued, "As Mel's assistant, you're almost family, and the Great Temple's court event is important. Please sit. I'm afraid I've not much time with the public wedding ceremony and my coronation only three weeks away."

Nodding again, Kit sat across from the queen, who appeared invigorated rather than worried about being so busy. Definitely a perfect match for the dutiful King Devon. "I can imagine, your majesty. I'll attempt to be brief."

As her maid served luncheon, Queen Kiera eyed Kit and fingered the gold bracelet about her left wrist that was a twin to her husband's powerful protection charm. Her wedding token, perhaps? "Mel told you about our ceremony on Longnight."

Kit coughed. "I *am* acting as his assistant. But no one else at the Great Temple knows." She exhaled when Queen Kiera released the gold bracelet. Thankfully, the queen didn't realize she was actually the fashionable Countess of Blaine who'd told all of court about Wren's scandalous pregnancy. Her reassurance wouldn't have comforted the queen then. And Queen Kiera might not trust her enough to hear her request for support.

The queen sighed as they began their creamy leek soup. "I'll be relieved when Devon and I can quit concealing our marriage." She arched her brows at Kit. "So what did you want to discuss about the Great Temple's court event?"

Kit leaned forward. "I need influential supporters to make it fashionable, and your support would ensure everyone at court attends." She flashed a wry smile. "Just consider how fashionable supporting orphanages and your education initiative are now."

When the queen chuckled, Kit straightened. "The charities the Great Temple runs are all worthy causes, so we'll feature different areas on each wall: prayer houses, almskitchens, family refuges, and youth endeavors." To help persuade the former orphanage matron, she added, "The youth wall shall show the youth guilds the Great Temple runs as well as the spiritual guidance the temple provides to orphanages and the temple's involvement with your education initiative."

Queen Kiera's navy eyes gleamed—clearly she recognized the reason behind the extra details. "I agree all those charities are worthy. But what support do you need from me? I'm not certain how much I can help since the Great Temple's court event is just two days after the royal ceremonies."

Kit nodded. She'd suspected as much. "Everything is already planned, so all I need is your visible support of the event. Tell people at court how excited you are to attend. Then at the event, donate more openly than you might otherwise would. I'll also be asking the Duchess of Childes to do the same."

Finishing her rhubarb pie, the queen smiled. "I suspect the duchess could get all of court to support your cause without me, but I'll gladly help as well." She paused then asked, "I know the invitations went out earlier, but would you like to move the Great Temple's court event to the palace's ballroom? 'Twould demonstrate my support even more."

Her pulse quickening, Kit beamed. No one at court would fail to attend then. "That would be amazing. I'll resend the invitations this week. Thank you."

Queen Kiera rose with a sigh. "Sadly, I must go. But after

Summerday, we should plan another event supporting charities run by the Great Temple. I'd love to be more involved."

Kit leapt upright. An excellent idea. Hopefully, if she managed to break the Goddess's illusion by then, the queen would still be interested in working with her. "One featuring the youth endeavors, perhaps? We could include your education initiative as well."

As Kit darted a curtsy, Queen Kiera grinned. "Sounds perfect."

Kit returned to the Great Temple and immediately began rewriting the invitations. Now that she was helping priests, 'twould take longer to prepare those. But having the Great Temple's court event at the palace would be worth it.

OVER THE FOLLOWING FEW DAYS, Kit finished helping garden priests then began helping general temple priests during the day. But every evening, she'd pen more invitations. Mel offered to write some, although she demurred since her handwriting was more ornate. Yet she still finished all the invitations the day before her luncheon with the duchess and asked some temple priests to deliver them.

Despite struggling to finish the invitations, she continued praying in the Sun Chapel every morning, and Mel still joined her, although he didn't hold her hand again. Yet she ached for his touch, so she began tucking her hands beneath her skirt to prevent herself from reaching for him. But even with her aching hunger for Mel, the mornings in the Sun Chapel settled her soul.

The day of her meeting with his mother, Mel arched his brows at her after they left the Sun Chapel. "Are you certain you don't want me to join you at luncheon today to deflect Mother?"

Warmed by Mel's tender concern, Kit couldn't resist squeezing his arm. If only she could do more. "No, I'll manage. But thanks for checking again."

Mel smiled at her and laid his hand over hers. "Of course."

Her pulse fluttering and breath stilling, she began leaning toward Mel as he began bending his head. Goddess, how she needed him.

But when their lips were about to meet, Mel stiffened and jerked backward. His hands fisting in his priest robes, he muttered, "Sorry, Kit." Then he fled.

She gazed after Mel, rubbing her chest above her heart. 'Twas almost as if he ached to kiss her too. Surely not. Her own longing must be confusing her. She whirled and retreated to the Sun Chapel then remained there until she must leave for luncheon. She required the peace she found there before meeting Mel's perceptive mother.

When Kit joined the duchess in the family dining room at Childes House, the duchess embraced her and kissed her cheek. "I'm so glad you could finally meet for luncheon, Kit."

Swallowing at the duchess's warm welcome even in private, Kit returned the duchess's embrace. Despite Father and her own unworthy behavior, Mel's mother was invariably gracious and almost as kind as her son.

The duchess gestured toward the tea table already laden with two courses and dessert, probably so the servants wouldn't over-hear her quizzing. Fortunate since gossip among the servants that Mel's crone assistant was Lady Blaine would soon spread to court. The duchess grinned. "Sit and tell me about those new duties of yours." Once Kit sat, the duchess poured them spiced cider then handed her a mug. "I suppose one of your new duties is planning the Great Temple's court event."

Kit sipped her delicious spiced cider, her throat tightening. Although most quit drinking spiced cider after the Longnight season, the duchess must have requested it knowing how she adored it. Definitely like Mel. Swallowing again, Kit set down her mug. "How did you know I'm planning the Great Temple's court event?"

Her pale-blue eyes shimmering with laughter, the duchess smiled. "I recognized the handwriting on the invitations."

Kit sighed. Of course the duchess had. Hopefully, she was the only one. "Yes, the Great Temple's court event is one of my new duties, and 'tis why I asked to meet for luncheon. I'd like you to publicly support the event to encourage court to attend and donate more. Queen Kiera agreed to do the same earlier this week."

The duchess tilted her head. "That explains the change in location." She beamed over her roasted cauliflower soup. "I'll happily support your event. Not only is the cause worthy, but your events are always spectacular. You're precisely the right person to revitalize events known as the dullest of the season. Too bad court doesn't know the fashionable Countess of Blaine is planning it."

Shuddering, Kit clenched her spoon. If they did, everyone would soon know she appeared a hideous crone. "You mustn't reveal that to anyone. Please."

The duchess tsked but nodded. "As you like. Tell me about your other new duties."

Kit exhaled as she sipped her spiced cider. Thank the Goddess the duchess hadn't argued. "I began organizing the almskitchens for Mel after he fell asleep at the table."

A smile hovering about her mouth, the duchess began her mussels in garlic-wine broth. "'Tis good Mel trusts you enough to let you assume some of his duties."

Kit blushed and shifted in her seat. "He'd little choice. There's not a community priest to replace him, and he finally accepted he couldn't handle everything."

The duchess chuckled. "I imagine your scolding was what helped Mel accept that at last. When it comes to his duties, he can be almost as stubborn as Hawke."

Her chest squeezing, Kit studied her half-finished mussels. "Mel's diligence is why he's such an excellent priest." And part of why she loved him. Burying that, she lifted her gaze. "In addition to organizing the almskitchens for Mel, High Priest Theodag began having me help different types of priests once he discovered I was staying at the Great Temple."

The duchess blinked, her brows rising. "You're staying at the Great Temple? No wonder you'd not tell me which prayer house you were staying at."

Another blush heated Kit's cheeks. Since she couldn't tell Mel's mother about staying with him at first, she said, "Yes, I'm staying with Mel's married friends Sarah and Deacon."

Humming, the duchess began her lymon trifle. "I assume High Priest Theodag having you help priests involves the illusion you're under."

Kit swallowed. Not surprising Mel's mother had immediately guessed that. "Yes, I need to experience temple life to become who I'm meant to be and break the Goddess's illusion." She shifted in her seat. "Then I can return to court where I belong."

The duchess smiled. "How intriguing. Any success so far?"

Sighing, Kit poked her untouched lymon trifle as her stomach twisted. "Not yet."

Mel's mother patted her hand across the tea table. "I'm certain you shall succeed soon."

Kit suppressed a grimace. Not likely given her current progress. Saying farewell to the duchess, she returned to the Sun Chapel. Perhaps further prayer would help.

CHAPTER 30

*A*fter almost kissing Kit outside the Sun Chapel, Mel made himself visit the final family refuge in Ormas. Yet despite helping the families escaping abuse, Kit leaning forward to receive his kiss with her delectable cinnaspice scent weaving about him kept echoing through him, and his body would stir. Every time, he'd bury that shameful hunger to focus on his duties, but soon almost kissing Kit would torment him again.

He frowned as he left the family refuge after several hours. Why could he never resist Kit, even in his thoughts? Because of his weakness, he should quit joining her in the Sun Chapel. He sighed. But praying in the Sun Chapel every morning had made his duties during the day so much lighter. And he'd miss his time alone with Kit if he quit joining her.

Shaking his head at himself, he took the carriage to Celeste's rather than returning to the Great Temple for Sext. Willa had sent word yesterday that Kit's cloak would be ready. When he reached the fashionable dress shop, he checked no one was watching again before entering, and no one was, although three ladies he vaguely recognized from court events were lingering inside the anteroom.

His neck heating, Mel nodded at the court ladies from the

opposite wall, and they began whispering to each other. Even though they'd never been introduced, the ladies doubtless recognized him—he resembled Father and his brothers too much for them not to, and his priest robes made him distinct. Please let gossip about him visiting Celeste's not spread. Although Mother already knew and she'd likely told Father, he'd rather the rest of his family didn't know, especially Hawke, who'd tease him about his faegift again.

The ladies' prying gazes following her, Willa bustled toward him then curtsied and handed him the wrapped bundle containing Kit's arachne silk cloak. "Here you are, holy sir." Not glancing at the ladies, she lowered her voice to a whisper, "Is my lady still well?"

As the ladies craned to hear, he murmured back to prevent that, "She is."

Willa nodded. "Good. When you give this to her, please tell her I'll happily serve her wherever she is." She sighed. "I don't like not working while still receiving my wages."

Despite the watching ladies, Mel smiled at Willa. Of course Kit had ensured her maid was well taken care of even amidst her own troubles. Thanks to her unfortunate childhood, she understood how distressing the lack of money could be. "If she arranged for you to receive your wages, I'm certain she wants you to have them. Although if you truly aren't comfortable receiving them, you could donate them to charities."

Smiling back, Willa hummed. "My lady *would* approve of that, given how she spends her excess allowance."

He shifted Kit's wrapped cloak beneath his arm. Not surprising her maid was aware of her secret donations—servants always knew such things, although loyal ones never revealed them. And given her concerned interest, Willa appeared extremely loyal to Kit. He nodded at Willa, his smile warming. "Thank you for making this for her, and as I said, I'll pass on your regards once I give it to her."

Then Mel strode from Celeste's with the court ladies' eyes

following him as they surged toward Willa. Not that they'd pry anything from her.

He headed to Mirage next. With Kit's natalday so close, he couldn't delay having them enchant her cloak. When he entered the sleek and bright illusion witch shop, the exotic young witch who'd helped him and Kit before glided toward him.

The girl smiled at him. "A pleasure to see you again, holy sir. Did the old woman ever find help with her invisible illusion?"

Mel inclined his head. "She did, thank you." Before the clerk could ask further questions about Kit, he offered her the bundle beneath his arm. "I'd like this enchanted into an invisibility cloak, please."

Unwrapping the brown linen, the girl fingered the transparent arachne silk inside. "What type of fabric is this?"

He blinked at the young witch. Didn't she recognize it? "Arachne silk."

The clerk inhaled. "The magical fabric woven by arachne that can transform to any color? I'd heard rumors about it, but I didn't think I'd ever see some this close. Only the affluent can afford it, and they've it made into ballgowns, not dresses they wear here."

Mel tensed. He'd not considered how unusual arachne silk would be outside of court or a fashionable dress shop. Hawke and his merchant friend Buford had just begun selling the magical fabric last year, and they were the only ones to trade with Mist Isle where the arachne lived. Hopefully, the arachne silk wouldn't allow the clerk to guess his identity. Although him visiting a fashionable witch shop wasn't as odd as him visiting Celeste's, he still didn't want gossip spreading about it.

Fingering the arachne silk, the girl hummed. "I must check with the owner about if we can enchant this. Since 'tis already magical, our spells mightn't work."

He frowned as he followed the clerk across the witch shop. He'd wanted a fashionable faegift Kit would wear long after she'd left him, but perhaps he should have selected ordinary fabric instead.

Once the girl explained and handed the owner Kit's cloak, the older, more exotic witch peered at the arachne silk. Then she flicked her fingers and muttered a probing spell like she had on Kit during his and Kit's previous visit. After a lengthy moment, the owner glanced at him. "We should be able to make this an invisibility cloak without interacting with the arachne silk's residual magic. However, doing so shall be somewhat complicated since we must cast the spell differently than we normally would."

Mel exhaled, his frown fading. His natalday faegift for Kit was possible, after all. He handed the owner six gold coins since the spell would be a complicated one. "When shall the invisibility cloak be ready?"

The owner pursed her lips. "Next week, most likely."

He nodded. "I must collect it no later than eight days from now." The following day was Kit's natalday.

Rewrapping the bundle, the exotic witch handed it to the clerk and smiled at him. "We'll ensure 'tis ready the day before that. Stop by then to collect it."

Mel returned the owner's smile. Perfect. If he continued visiting two local temples or community programs a day, his final visit should be that morning, and he could collect Kit's cloak afterward. "Thank you, madam witch."

He smiled as he returned to the Great Temple, even though he'd missed Sext and had to eat luncheon alone since Kit was with Mother. How was that going? Please let Mother's quizzing not be upsetting Kit. She'd enough to handle attempting to break the Goddess's illusion without having to withstand Mother as well. He must check about how their meeting went when he finally saw Kit at dinner tonight.

• • •

So once he and Kit began eating with Deacon and Sarah that evening, Mel smiled at her over his stewed beefsteak. "How was your luncheon with Mother?"

Kit's lips quirked. "Well. Your mother agreed to support the Great Temple's court event at once. She'd already guessed I was planning it from the handwriting on the invitations."

As Deacon and Sarah traded an amused glance, Mel nodded. That sounded like Mother. Eyeing Kit, he leaned toward her. "Was Mother's quizzing too terrible?"

Kit lifted a shoulder as she sipped her tea. "No, although she managed to discover nearly all of the details about the Goddess's illusion and my life here."

Mel shifted in his seat. Hopefully, nearly meant Kit hadn't told Mother that she'd stayed with him or about their ravenous kisses. He eyed Kit. Doubtless she'd be blushing if she'd revealed either.

Stirring her stewed beefsteak, Kit hummed. "When are you visiting Elder Priestess Agnes next? I should join you to update her about the plans for the Great Temple's court event."

He smiled at Kit. 'Twould be nice to have her join him on his duties again. "Three mornings from now. Shall you be able to skip helping priests that day?"

Sighing, Kit grimaced. "I already arranged that with High Priest Theodag—as well as Elder Priest Archibald since I'll still be helping general temple priests then. But unfortunately, I can't join you that day."

Sarah grinned at Mel and Deacon. "I'm not serving at Peaceful Minds, so Kit and I were going to spend the day together." She tilted her head. "Although we can rearrange if you like, Kit."

Kit slanted Mel a glance beneath her lashes. "No, we've not spent the day together in ages."

He smiled. From that glance, whatever Kit and Sarah were planning involved him. Another of Sarah's delicious desserts, perhaps?

Kit turned to Mel. "I'll write a note for you to give Elder Priestess Agnes instead. I hope she shan't be irritated I'm not updating her in person."

He squeezed Kit's hand beneath the table to hearten her. "I'm certain she'll understand. Everyone deserves a day's respite now and then."

His ascetic face crinkling, Deacon snorted a laugh. "I'm surprised to hear you say that, Mel. When's the last time *you've* taken a day's respite?"

Almost wincing, Mel began his cream cake. "Just because I never remember to take one doesn't mean I don't deserve to. Besides, I enjoy remaining busy."

Not extracting her hand from his, Kit narrowed her eyes at him. "So much so that you almost exhausted yourself into a coma. You should heed your own advice."

Warmth flooding him at her concern, he squeezed her hand again. "How about I promise to not work after my meeting with Elder Priestess Agnes?"

Although Deacon and Sarah stared at him, Kit simply nodded with a faint smile. "An acceptable compromise, I suppose."

Over the following few days, Mel continued visiting the remaining local temples and community programs in Ormas. He'd definitely finish the day he collected Kit's invisibility cloak. He also continued praying with Kit in the Sun Chapel before his visits, and kissing her pervaded his dreams at night. So he prayed to the Goddess every morning for strength to resist Kit and made sure to remain several steps apart to avoid pulling her into his arms.

The closest they came to touching was when Kit handed him her note for Elder Priestess Agnes while he and Kit left the Sun Chapel on the day of his meeting with the elder community priestess. As he tucked Kit's note into his pocket above his heart, he eased away with a smile. "I'll give this to Elder Priestess Agnes first thing. Have fun with Sarah today."

Kit leaned toward him. "I shall. Remember your promise to not work after your meeting." She pursed her lips. "I'll visit you this afternoon to check that you did."

His pulse quickening, Mel nodded, even though he should be dissuading Kit instead. Or telling her to have Sarah join them. "I'll enjoy devouring whatever delicious dessert you and Sarah bake together."

Kit sighed. "You guessed we're making a dessert together, did you? 'Twas *supposed* to be a surprise."

He winked at Kit. "It still is—I don't know what dessert you're bringing."

Chuckling, Kit shook her head. "'Tis something at least. Until this afternoon."

Mel smiled after Kit as she headed toward the priest quarters. He couldn't wait until this afternoon. Then he sighed and strode the other direction to meet Elder Priestess Agnes. He was anticipating time with Kit much more than he should. And not because she'd be bringing delicious desserts.

He suppressed a grimace. His daily prayers to the Goddess weren't dampening his desire for Kit. But 'twas just because they were often together and would surely fade once she finally broke the Goddess's illusion and returned to court. He could manage to remain strong until then and not kiss her again. Please, Goddess.

CHAPTER 31

When Kit entered Sarah and Deacon's chambers, her chest twisted at the warm and doting affection between them while they finished breakfast. She swallowed. She'd never enjoyed that, and never would. Although she loved Mel like Sarah loved Deacon, Mel didn't love her in return. One day, he'd find the perfect priestess to marry and treat her like Deacon did Sarah, but that fortunate lady wouldn't ever be her.

She shoved aside her hopeless longing as Sarah beamed at her then leapt upright and asked, "Ready to go?"

While Kit nodded in reply, Deacon rose as well and drawled, "What are you two baking today?"

Sarah laughed. "Nothing. We're making shokolat mousse."

Deacon grinned at Kit. "How did you convince Sarah to forgo her usual baking?"

Kit couldn't help returning Deacon's grin. 'Twas remarkable how differently Deacon had treated her in recent weeks. He was no longer distrustful but accepting and kind. Despite their offer for her to stay with them, he and Sarah mustn't suspect her wild kisses with Mel. Deacon surely wouldn't approve if he knew. Still grinning, she shrugged. "I asked to make shokolat mousse, and she happily agreed."

Deacon chuckled. "Why am I not surprised?" He kissed Sarah. "Have fun."

Sarah threaded her arm through Kit's. "We shall." Once they began toward the Great Temple's kitchen, Sarah squeezed Kit's arm. "How have you been? You're so busy I feel as if I hardly see you—even less than before you began staying with us."

Kit blinked. She and Sarah saw each other more now. "You see me at Vespers and dinner every evening, if not more frequently."

Sarah waved a hand. "Yes, but Deacon and Mel are with us then, so we can't truly talk."

Kit inclined her head. Even though Deacon no longer disapproved of her, she couldn't share secrets with him there. Plus, she and Mel often talked during meals. "I've been well. Helping different types of priests has been fascinating, and everyone has been welcoming."

She and Sarah entered the kitchen and greeted Esther before heading to the unoccupied corner they'd used before. As they both began melting shokolat pieces in cream, Sarah slanted her a glance then asked, "Do you miss staying with Mel?"

Her cheeks heating, Kit shrugged and kept her gaze on her pot. If she admitted that, Sarah would doubtless realize she loved Mel and pity her.

Sarah hummed. "The two of you can't seem to resist each other's company. Whatever quarrel you had on your final day together appears mended."

Kit shifted as her blush scorched her skin at hungrily kissing Mel that day. "Not really, just buried." Except whenever they touched or drew close.

While they set aside their shokolat mixtures to cool, Sarah tsked and shook her head at Kit. "'Tisn't healthy to leave a quarrel fester."

As they began whisking cream with powder sugar and vahnila, Kit muttered to make Sarah quit discussing Mel, "'Twasn't just a quarrel."

Sarah smiled. "Yes, but you shouldn't let kisses fester either."

Kit froze, her entire body flushing. So Sarah and Deacon *did* know about her kisses with Mel. Why hadn't Sarah said anything until now? And why wasn't Deacon disapproving? She gulped a breath. "When did you know?"

Grinning now, Sarah chuckled. "As soon as Deacon and I saw your lips after your quarrel. 'Twas obvious you'd been well-kissed." She pointed her whisk at Kit. "You'll never make mousse if you remain still."

Swallowing, Kit forced herself to resume whisking.

Sarah shook her head. "Not that you and Mel kissing surprised me or Deacon. Kisses are inevitable between a couple as in love as you two."

Kit froze again, her chest twisting like earlier. "Mel doesn't love me."

Smiling, Sarah tsked. "No? He does an excellent impression of it. He's forever taking care of you and always wants to be near you. Plus, he kissed you—passionately from the state of your lips after that quarrel."

Another blush swamping her, Kit began whisking once more. "Those kisses were my fault. And Mel takes care of everyone and only spends time with me because we're old friends." When Sarah frowned and began to reply, Kit interjected, "Could we discuss something else, please?"

Sarah sighed but nodded. "Very well. But remember I'm here if you need to talk." She arched her brows. "So what made you ask to make shokolat mousse?"

Still blushing, Kit shrugged. "I thought 'twould be good practice for making Mel's favorite dessert, cinnaspice-honey burnt custard, for his natalday on Plantfete." Even though adults in his family didn't exchange natalday gifts and she never received them herself, she had to give the gentleman she loved *something*. She made herself flash a wry smile. "Although since the royal ceremonies are on Plantfete too, we must prepare Mel's dessert the day before."

Sarah grinned. "I'll ensure I'm not serving at Peaceful Minds that day." She scrutinized their cream mixture, which had formed stiff peaks. "We can fold in our shokolat mixtures now. But save half the cream mixture for topping."

Once they finished preparing the shokolat mousse, they stored the glasses of the dessert in the cold pantry, and Kit fetched two after luncheon and brought them to Mel's chambers. She'd rather give him his dessert in private since Sarah and Deacon knew about their kisses. When she entered, she smiled at Mel reading in a chair before his bookcase. "I see you took your promise to not work seriously."

Mel winked at her as he joined her at his small table. "I knew you'd scold if I didn't." He ate a spoonful of his dessert then sighed. "Your shokolat mousse is delicious, Kit."

Warmed by his delight, she ate a spoonful as well. It *was* delicious—silky, rich, and very shokolaty. "I'm glad you like it. I've two more glasses for us to eat after dinner."

Mel grinned. "I suppose I can manage such a hardship." He devoured his mousse then scraped the glass clean. "So good."

She smiled and handed Mel her half-eaten mousse. Watching him devour it would be better than eating it herself. "Here, finish mine."

Chuckling, Mel began her mousse. "Wren would faint if she heard you offer that."

Kit giggled. So Wren would. Wren adored shokolat almost as much as she adored Hawke. "Now that I know how, I should make Wren shokolat mousse sometime."

Mel smiled and leaned toward her. "That's quite a change toward your childhood rival."

Blushing, she glanced down and shrugged. If only she'd changed *before* she'd hurt Wren and Hawke years ago. "'Tis nothing. Shokolat mousse is remarkably easy to make."

She inhaled and tingling flooded her when Mel reached beneath the table to squeeze her hand. She met his gaze, and her heart fluttered at the warmth darkening his deep-brown eyes.

Dear Goddess, she burned to kiss him again. Before she could succumb to temptation, she extracted her hand and asked, "How was your meeting with Elder Priestess Agnes?"

Mel sighed and finished her shokolat mousse. "Fine. She was excited to hear your updates about the Great Temple's court event as well as that I'll finish visiting local temples and community programs in a few days." He arched a brow. "But should we be discussing that? According to you, I'm supposed to be *not* working."

Kit blushed again. True, but she'd had to distract them somehow. She collected the empty glasses and rose. "I'm going to return these to the kitchen then spend the afternoon in the Sun Chapel." More prayer would be good for her, and kissing wasn't possible there. Although she should go alone, she couldn't resist asking, "Care to join me?"

Mel nodded, and they silently headed to the Sun Chapel.

THE FOLLOWING MORNING, Kit and Mel were praying in the Sun Chapel again when High Priest Theodag joined them. A kindhearted smile softened his ascetic face as he sat beside them in the first pew. "I apologize for disturbing your time with the Goddess, but I must talk with you both."

She and Mel traded a glance, and her stomach quivered. Why would the high priest need to talk with them together? Could he have discovered their kisses?

High Priest Theodag smiled at her. "How was yesterday?"

She relaxed, inhaling the Goddess laurels' heavenly fragrance. The high priest just wanted to check on her. "Very relaxing. Sarah and I made shokolat mousse together, then Mel and I spent the afternoon here. I'm eager to resume helping temple priests today."

Humming, the high priest nodded. "I'm glad. When you require another day's respite, please let me know."

Kit smiled and returned the high priest's nod. She must ask

for another the day before Plantfete but not with Mel beside her. 'Twould spoil his natalday gift.

High Priest Theodag turned to Mel. "Agnes tells me you'll finish your visits in a few days. She seems relieved she can finally begin the rest of your training."

Mel inclined his head. "Elder Priestess Agnes is eager to relinquish her duties. They drain her now."

Lacing her hands in her lap, Kit studied Mel. Once he began acting as the elder community priest of Calatini, she must ensure he didn't allow those duties to drain him as well.

The high priest sighed. "We waited longer than we should have to train you as Agnes's successor." He shook his head. "However, I did warn Agnes that you can't assume her duties until after Plantfete. I require your assistance with the royal wedding ceremony and Queen Kiera's coronation."

Kit and Mel glanced at each other again. Traditionally, just the high priest performed those. Then Mel smiled at the high priest and replied, "I'll gladly assist you, but why?"

High Priest Theodag quirked a wry smile. "The priest who performed King Devon and Queen Kiera's secret wedding ceremony should assist with their public one."

As Mel stiffened, Kit laced her hands tighter to avoid squeezing his to reassure him.

The high priest chuckled. "Not that I was surprised when King Devon admitted their romantic elopement on Longnight so I could properly perform their public ceremony. Everyone knows how mad he's been for Queen Kiera since they met. And you performing their secret ceremony wasn't surprising either, given how close they both are to your family. We can even use that closeness to explain why you're assisting me."

Mel relaxed. "I'm relieved you're not upset—or convinced I should be your successor, after all."

High Priest Theodag's eyes crinkled. "No, my successor lies elsewhere." He turned to Kit. "You must accompany us to the ceremony. Perhaps you could perform a reading."

Although Mel smiled and nodded, she shuddered. She couldn't possibly expose herself to court like that. "'Tis better if I avoid court events right now."

The high priest arched a brow. "Even the one you're planning?" At her fierce nod, he and Mel exchanged a glance. Then the high priest rose. "I'll let you two attend to your duties."

Once High Priest Theodag left, Kit asked to prevent Mel from urging her to attend the royal ceremonies, "Do you think the high priest knows about King Devon and Queen Kiera's bloodbinding?"

Mel hummed and shook his head. "He'd have mentioned it if he knew. I doubt Devon and Kiera shall tell anyone about their bloodbinding. Although romantic, 'twould make many in Calatini too nervous that only Kiera can bear our next king and that she and Devon shall likely die together."

She nodded. Their death before Kiera bore a son or before their son was old enough to rule would devastate Calatini. Devon's family had ruled since the kingdom's founding a millennium ago, so no one could imagine anyone other than a Vireni being king. And regencies were often fraught with intrigue and unrest.

Kit rose as Mel narrowly eyed her and opened his mouth to speak. She blurted, "I must go find Dirk. I'm helping him act as porter today. Until tonight." Then she swept from the Sun Chapel without awaiting his reply.

CHAPTER 32

After visiting the final local temple, Mel headed to Mirage to collect Kit's invisibility cloak instead of returning to the Great Temple for Sext and luncheon.

As soon as he entered the illusion witch shop, the owner smiled at him. "Just a moment, holy sir. Let me fetch your purchase from the back room." She glided out then soon returned with the bundle containing Kit's invisibility cloak. As she handed it to him, she murmured soft enough the other two patrons couldn't overhear, "Enchanting this was more complicated than I'd expected, but we managed it—with an interesting side effect."

He eyed the wrapped invisibility cloak as he tucked it beneath his arm. Was that good or bad? "Side effect?"

The exotic witch hummed. "We couldn't entirely prevent our enchantment from interacting with the arachne silk's residual magic. The invisibility spell seems active, although it appears it shall only work for whomever bonds to the arachne silk. And since this cloak is unbonded, we weren't able to test it. But I'm fairly certain it should work fine. However, if it doesn't, just have the recipient bring it back, and we'll adjust the enchantment."

Mel frowned. Hopefully, the invisibility cloak would work.

Kit likely wouldn't want to return here while under the Goddess's illusion. And with her helping different types of priests every day, she might not have time before the royal ceremonies either.

The witch leaned toward him. "Inside the bundle, I've included detailed instructions for using the invisibility cloak as well as recharging it and renewing it. However, I would suggest bringing the cloak back here to renew it because the spell is complicated."

Nodding, he smiled at Mirage's owner. "Thank you, madam witch. Do you have any paper I could purchase to wrap this in?" Although the arachne silk was wrapped with brown linen, proper gifts should be wrapped in decorative paper as well.

The exotic witch beckoned him across the room. "We do. We've several types enchanted to show moving scenes. Or we can enchant a custom scene for you."

Mel inspected the different types of paper, selecting the crimson one that sparkled like an unending cascade of rubies. 'Twas Kit's favorite color, after all.

Then he returned to the Great Temple and went straight to his chambers to wrap Kit's natalday faegift before concealing it beneath his bed. That finished, he grabbed a quick luncheon from the dining hall before returning to his chambers to prepare for tomorrow's meeting with Elder Priestess Agnes.

At dinner that evening after Vespers, Kit frowned at him as soon as they began eating. "Why weren't you at Sext and luncheon today?"

Almost tensing, Mel made himself continue eating his spicy bean stew. "I'd an errand after visiting the final local temple."

As Deacon and Sarah exchanged an amused glance, Kit drawled, "What kind of errand was more important than worshipping the Goddess and eating a decent meal?"

He forced a shrug. "Shopping." To distract Kit, he asked, "How was your last day with general temple priests?"

Her eyes narrowing, Kit replied, "Fine. I begin helping

worship priests tomorrow—High Priest Theodag said starting with pulpit priests."

Mel glanced at Deacon and Sarah, and they all began to chuckle. Of course the high priest would start with pulpit priests out of the three types of worship priests. One garrulous one in particular.

Kit blinked and leaned toward him. "What?"

Still chuckling, he shook his head. "High Priest Theodag's great-nephew Fitzwilliam is a pulpit priest. The high priest shall probably have you start with him."

Kit lowered her laden spoon. "Isn't Fitzwilliam the pulpit priest that rambles whenever he gives a sermon?" When he and their friends nodded, she winced. "He's going to talk at me for *days*."

Unable to resist comforting Kit, Mel patted her hand even though tingling flooded him when he touched her. "I'm certain you'll find a way to silence him. You're almost as good at managing people as Mother."

Her gaze flickering, Kit sighed and shifted her hand away, and his chest tightened. She murmured, "I'll need to be." Then she turned to Deacon and Sarah with a smile. "How were your days?"

As their friends replied, Mel clenched his spoon. He really must quit touching Kit, even to help her. It only tempted him to kiss her again. Yet for some reason, her sensible withdrawals always made him ache and burn to recapture her. So far, he'd managed not to, but how long would that last?

AFTER PRAYING with Kit in the Sun Chapel the following morning, Mel wished her good luck with Fitzwilliam then strode to Peaceful Minds to meet Elder Priestess Agnes.

When he entered her study, the wizened elder priestess beamed at him like a cheery sun nymph from behind her orderly desk. "How did your final visits go?"

He smiled back as he sat before the elder community priestess, who was clearly still eager to start the rest of his training. So was he. "My final visits went well, although I'd begun to think I'd never finish them—there are many more local temples and community programs than I remembered."

Elder Priestess Agnes nodded. "What else did you learn from your visits?"

Mel rubbed his jaw. "That once I assume your duties, I should continue visiting places run by community priests. I'd forgotten some of the details about our charities even though I'd taught novices about them for years. Frequent visits shall keep me familiar with our charities as well as the community priests." He flashed a wry smile. "Although I'd met many before, I mostly know well the ones who serve in the almskitchens. And there are *many* community priests to remember since we make up two-thirds of priests."

The elder priestess smiled at him. "I used to do the same before such frequent visits exhausted me. Knowing your priests and their concerns makes managing them much easier."

He shifted in his chair. Yet unless he spent years traveling across Calatini, he could only meet local community priests. "How do we get to know the community priests we'll never meet? Only a tenth of Calatini's priests serve in Ormas."

Elder Priestess Agnes waved to the communication mirror hanging beside her desk. "Witch priests enchant this powerful communication mirror for me, and all community priests who serve outside of Ormas have its call signature." She sighed. "Although many of the smaller temples don't have a communication mirror, so they must find someone who does to contact me that way."

Mel stared at the elder priestess. With the amount of community priests in Calatini, she must be on the communication mirror forever. "How many mirror calls do you have a day?"

The elder priestess shrugged. "Around five to ten." She grimaced. "It takes around five years to call all the community priests in Calatini, so I don't know them as well as I'd like. However, they send monthly updates and write if they require assistance. I attempt to reply as frequently as possible."

He almost shuddered. No wonder she'd said he'd not have time to organize the almskitchens as the elder community priest of Calatini. "You read all their correspondence yourself?"

Her eyes crinkling, Elder Priestess Agnes snorted a laugh. "Of course not. Community priests typically send their correspondence to the elder community priest that works with the bishop for their duchy. I have weekly meetings with those elder community priests to review matters. Plus, like the high priest, I've a team of assistants who handle reading any correspondences sent to me as well as scheduling my mirror calls and visits. They provide daily summaries, ensure I see the most pressing ones, and write reports on priests I'm meeting with that day."

Mel exhaled. That sounded more manageable, although still a lot.

The elder priestess leaned toward him. "Since you can't act as the elder community priest of Calatini until after the royal ceremonies, I'll use this week to show you the scope of your new duties. That should also allow you time to set up your study at the Great Temple. Although my assistants work there, that study hasn't been used since I became elder community priestess. I already had this one set up like I wanted, and I prefer the tranquil air of the prayer house."

He nodded. 'Twas fortunate he'd have his own study since he'd never be as tidy as the elder priestess, which would doubtless bother her if they worked in the same room. "How often did you want to meet now?"

Elder Priestess Agnes tilted her head. "Every day from midmorning until dinner, although we'll pause for Sext and luncheon. That should be long enough for me to show you everything. After the royal ceremonies, you'll begin acting as the elder community priest from your study, but I'll be beside you for the first few weeks. Once you seem prepared, I'll return here but be available as needed to advise you."

Mel swallowed but nodded again. Just over a week wasn't long for the elder priestess to show him everything. Hopefully, he could learn quickly. But him beginning his new duties after Plantfete would give him nine months of acting as the elder community priest of Calatini before his investiture on Longnight—three months longer than she'd originally wanted.

The elder priestess handed him a sheaf of papers. "Speaking of reports, here's the latest one from the elder community priest of Valcrest. I've a mirror call with him after luncheon to discuss it."

Once they reviewed that report, Elder Priestess Agnes showed him the reports her assistants had prepared for her other mirror calls. Then after Sext and luncheon, he and the elder priestess spent the afternoon on mirror calls, but he remained silent once she introduced him. Yet although he'd done little more than watch, he was still tired when he joined Kit, Deacon, and Sarah for Vespers and dinner.

Kit eyed him once they sat in the dining hall. "How was your first day training with Elder Priestess Agnes?"

Mel shrugged and began his vahnila pudding first since he deserved a treat after today. "Busy and full of meetings, even though we barely left her study. Elder Priestess Agnes is determined to have me assume her duties straight after the royal ceremonies. How was *your* day?"

Kit quirked a wry smile. "As expected, High Priest Theodag began my visits to pulpit priests by taking me to Fitzwilliam, who thankfully didn't talk at me the entire time. He showed me the resources pulpit priests use to write their sermons."

Deacon chuckled. "I'm surprised Fitzwilliam knows how to use those, given how he rambles."

As Sarah tsked at her husband, Kit shrugged and sipped her bacon tuber chowder. "He did admit to becoming so excited when giving sermons that he forgets to reference his notes."

Mel hummed while he finished his vahnila pudding. "That explains the rambling. But 'tis good Fitzwilliam enjoys his duties so much—every priest should."

Her gaze lowering, Kit stirred her chowder. "All the priests I've met so far seem to. Their peace and confidence in how they've been called to serve the Goddess is amazing."

His chest squeezed. No doubt Kit yearned to feel the same. But thanks to the Goddess's illusion and participating in temple life, she would one day, and she'd become who she was meant to be—whatever that was. He swallowed. And then she'd return to court. He managed a shrug. "Our rigorous training as novices and the Goddess's approval at our ordination examinations help develop that certainty in our purpose."

Sarah smiled at Kit. "Although finding that isn't always easy. As a novice, I couldn't decide whether to become a kitchen priestess, teach novices, or serve in a prayer house. Eventually, the Goddess helped me see the prayer house was my deepest calling, so I serve there, and I do the others when I've time."

Raising her gaze, Kit weakly returned Sarah's smile.

To cheer Kit, Mel nudged her with a grin and asked, "Did you request to not help pulpit priests tomorrow?"

Kit blinked at him, her spoon halfway to her mouth. "No, why would I?"

He suppressed a wince. Had he misremembered? "Tomorrow is your nataldgay, isn't it?"

Shrugging, Kit ate her bacon tuber chowder. "Yes. So?"

Sarah gaped at Kit. "Why didn't you mention that? I'd have baked you something special."

Kit shifted in her seat. "I forgot. I've never made a fuss about my nataldgay."

Fire flared through Mel. Because her vile father had never cared enough about Kit to celebrate it. She'd always been so grateful for the nataldgay trinkets he'd given her when they were children despite never having a celebration. But surely her husband had celebrated her natalday. "Not even with Lord Blaine?"

A blush darkened Kit's cheeks. "No. I think my natalday reminded Lord Blaine I was several months younger than Elise and Edouard, and he preferred to forget that. But I didn't mind not celebrating."

As Deacon and Sarah exchanged frowns, Mel set his jaw while finishing his bacon tuber chowder. If he'd known, he'd have continued giving Kit trinkets to celebrate, even though giving her gifts wouldn't have been entirely appropriate since she'd been married and wasn't his sister or cousin. Hopefully, her invisibility cloak would make up for all of her neglected nataldays.

Sarah leaned toward Kit. "After Lauds tomorrow, return to our chambers for breakfast so we can at least enjoy that together before we head to our duties. Although 'tisn't much of a celebration."

While Deacon nodded to echo his wife, Kit smiled at them. "'Tis plenty. Thanks."

Mel swallowed. He'd meant to give Kit her invisibility cloak at breakfast, but he couldn't do that before their friends. They'd remark on him giving her a faegift, and she might be overwhelmed by her first natalday gift in years. Please let him resist kissing her when she thanked him.

So after Lauds the following morning, he glanced at Kit as they returned to the priest quarters and asked, "Could we stop by my chambers before heading to Deacon and Sarah's? I forgot something."

Her brows arching, Kit nevertheless nodded. "Of course."

He ushered Kit inside his chambers then strode into his bedroom while she waited by the table. He fetched her natalday gift from beneath his bed then rejoined her with a grin. His heart quickening, he extended the crimson-wrapped gift toward her. "Happy natalday, Kit."

She stared at him then licked her lips. "You got me a gift?"

Wrenching his gaze from Kit's tempting lips, he pressed her natalday gift into her hands. "Of course. Open it."

Tingling warmth flooded Mel when Kit smiled up at him while blinking rapidly and hugging his gift to her chest. Her delight was even more enthralling than he'd expected. How was he ever to resist kissing her?

CHAPTER 33

Blinking to restrain the tears pricking her eyes, Kit smiled up at Mel and embraced his natalday gift. Although he'd mentioned her natalday yesterday, she'd never dreamt he'd gotten her a gift—he'd not gotten her one since before her marriage.

Mel swallowed then rasped, "You should open your gift before Deacon and Sarah fetch us for breakfast."

She wobbled a nod and opened Mel's gift without tearing its enchanted crimson paper that sparkled like a river of the richest rubies in the sunlight. He'd taken time to find enchanted paper in her favorite color, so she must save it to treasure later. Then she opened the brown linen beneath the paper and gasped at the radiantly transparent arachne silk inside. He'd gotten her a *faegift*? Gentlemen only purchased magical gifts for family, wives, or ladies they were courting, and she wasn't any of those to Mel.

Her heart fluttering, she glanced at him through her lashes. "Oh, Mel, 'tis lovely."

Mel swallowed again, his hands clenching in his priest robes. "You should check it fits. Your maid was concerned about making it without new measurements."

She set the paper and linen on the table then unfurled the arachne silk. A note fluttered to the floor as she eyed the elegant cloak. "You met Willa?"

Mel nodded. "At Celeste's. Willa asked after you and said she'd happily serve you wherever you are. She was relieved to hear you were well since she'd not heard from you since you left court."

Kit winced while fastening the arachne silk cloak about her shoulders. She should have written her loyal maid when she'd first written the duchess and Elise. "I'll write Willa tonight to reassure and thank her." She smoothed the perfect-fitting cloak, her chest warming. 'Twas the best natalday gift she'd ever received. Not that she'd many to compare it to—only Mel's small gifts when they were children. Tears pricking her eyes again, she smiled at him. "I can't believe you got me an arachne silk cloak from my favorite dress shop. I love it. Thank you."

His gaze on her lips, Mel leaned toward her. "'Tis more than just an arachne silk cloak. I also had Mirage enchant it into an invisibility cloak so you can attend the royal ceremonies and the Great Temple's court event without anyone from court seeing you."

Breathless and blinking back her tears, she stared at Mel. He'd visited Mirage for her cloak as well? With all his duties, he barely had time to rest. But somehow he'd visited two fashionable shops that were far from his duties to purchase a natalday faegift for her. A faegift she truly needed. And one chosen with her tastes in mind. Goddess, Mel was the most wonderful and considerate gentleman.

She blinked harder. If she'd not already loved him, his exquisite natalday faegift would have made her fall. As it was, she ached to kiss him to express her love. Yet she mustn't. He didn't love her as anything more than an old friend and never would. Giving her the perfect natalday gift was just Mel being his usual compassionate and perceptive self. Although the effort he'd taken could almost make her believe Sarah's conviction that he loved her. If only he did. The tears she'd been restraining spilled down her cheeks like hot rain.

Inhaling, Mel strode forward and wrapped her in his arms. "Why are you upset?"

Kit buried her face against his chest and inhaled his scent. Her tears falling faster, she couldn't help sliding her arms about his waist. "I'm not. These are tears of joy." And unrequited love. "I've never received such a perfect gift."

Mel captured her face in his hands then tilted it until their gazes met.

Her tears slowing, she barely breathed as they stared at each other, nestled together like mated griffins. Dear Goddess, she loved him.

Wiping away her tears with his thumbs, Mel shuddered, and his eyes darkened to match his coal-brown hair. Then he lowered his head and feathered a kiss against her lips.

Kit sighed into Mel's tender kiss. So sweet. Her pulse quickened as she pressed closer and kissed him back.

Mel began deepening their kiss until they both froze at the spritely knock on his door.

Sarah called, "Kit, Mel, are you there? Breakfast is getting cold."

Kit shivered when Mel lifted his head and stared into her eyes without releasing her. He appeared as if he didn't want to stop kissing either. Surely not. He rasped, "We'll be there in a moment." Then he murmured, "I'm sorry, Kit."

She forced a tremulous smile. "Why? 'Twas just a natalday kiss."

Mel released her. "It still wasn't appropriate."

To ease his guilt for kissing a lady he didn't intend to marry, she lifted her chin and lied, "Nonsense. A natalday kiss is nothing between old friends."

Mel snorted then bent to collect the note at her feet. "You should wrap up your invisibility cloak to avoid questions from Deacon and Sarah. Here are the instructions for using it."

Kit nodded as she accepted the note that had fallen when she'd unfurled the cloak. Questions about Mel's natalday faegift would be distressing—their friends would only believe it further proof he loved her. She wrapped her invisibility cloak and note inside the brown linen and enchanted crimson paper then tucked it beneath her arm.

When she and Mel joined Sarah and Deacon, she beamed at them. Hopefully, they'd not realize Mel had kissed her like they had last time. "Sorry we're late. Mel was giving me a natalday gift."

Deacon smiling beside her, Sarah chuckled and asked, "What kind of gift?"

Not glancing at Mel, Kit lifted a shoulder. "A cloak. Let me put it in my bedroom."

Sarah grinned and stepped closer. "Show it to me first."

A blush heated Kit's cheeks. "Not now. I'm famished." Before Sarah could protest, she darted into her bedroom and slid Mel's wrapped gift beneath her pillow.

Once she returned, Sarah beamed at her. "I've a natalday gift for you as well." Sarah lifted the lid on the covered plate with a flourish. "Spice buns. I baked them last night, and Deacon cast a preservation spell so they'd remain hot from the oven until now. But I wish we could have managed something better."

Warmth suffusing her chest, Kit smiled at Sarah and Deacon. "These are fabulous." The second best natalday gift she'd ever received. "Thank you." As everyone sat to eat breakfast, she slanted Mel a teasing smile to feign mere friendship. "I just hope I get a spice bun before Mel eats them all."

Eyeing her mouth like before, Mel drew the plate of spice buns toward them. "I'll serve you one first to avoid that."

Kit swallowed as tingling flooded her at Mel's stare. Was he thinking about their kisses and wishing for more? She gripped her hands together in her lap to resist leaning toward him and making those kisses more than wishes. Then she turned to Sarah and Deacon with a blinding grin. "I'd better eat quickly so I'm not late for my visit with Fitzwilliam. I'm helping him write his sermon for Vespers tonight."

OVER THE WEEK before Mel's natalday, Kit continued helping the different types of worship priests, and he continued training with Elder Priestess Agnes, so they only met for services and meals. He no longer joined her in the Sun Chapel after breakfast every morning—probably just as well. Goddess knew if she'd resist kissing him if he did.

She also bonded to Mel's natalday faegift with a drop of blood and turned the arachne silk a sober black. Although the fabric still possessed a magical luster, black was much less noticeable than transparent. Then she read all the instructions and practiced using the invisibility cloak to be prepared for the royal ceremonies. She even had Mel try using the invisibility cloak once to test if she was truly the only one who could use it, and he couldn't, so Mirage's owner had been right about that.

The day before Mel's natalday, High Priest Theodag joined her in the Sun Chapel. "How was helping the different types of worship priests? Did you prefer pulpit priests, liturgy priests, or bard priests?"

Inhaling the Goddess laurels' cinnaspice-apple fragrance, Kit tilted her head. "They were all fascinating, but I believe I preferred pulpit priests. They craft words to touch their listeners' hearts." Liturgy priests only chose readings, and although she enjoyed music, she hadn't the talent to perform or write songs like bard priests.

The high priest smiled at her. "I'll have you begin helping healer priests once you finish handling the Great Temple's court event."

She nodded and laced her hands together. After healer priests, she'd only scholar priests and witch priests left since no warrior priests were in Ormas. The one who'd helped handle the Magehaven ore had continued on his journeys without visiting the Great Temple after the dangerous ore had been neutralized over a month ago. She suppressed a sigh. Even though she'd helped half of the different types of priests in Ormas, she was still no closer to discovering who she was meant to be and breaking the Goddess's illusion.

High Priest Theodag arched his brows. "Are you certain you shan't attend the royal ceremonies tomorrow?"

Kit swallowed and shifted in her seat. Thanks to Mel she would be, but she'd rather no one but him knew, not even the high priest. He'd simply chide her for wearing an invisibility cloak. "I can't risk anyone from court seeing me." She rose. "Excuse me, I must find Sarah."

The high priest rose as well. "What are you baking together?"

She shook her head. She couldn't tell the high priest they were making a natalday gift for Mel. He mightn't approve since gifts between unmarried ladies and gentlemen were often considered acts of courtship. And she couldn't reveal what dessert in case the high priest saw Mel today—he might mention something and spoil Mel's natalday gift. "'Tis a surprise."

Then she hurried from the Sun Chapel before High Priest Theodag could probe further. She met Sarah at Sarah and Deacon's chambers, and they headed to the Great Temple's kitchen to make Mel's cinnaspice-honey burnt custard.

When they arrived, Kit gaped. The kitchen was even hotter and busier than normal as the kitchen priests prepared for Plant-fete tomorrow. She and Sarah nodded at Esther across the kitchen before darting to their unoccupied corner, which was smaller than before.

While they brought their cream and cinnaspice mixture to a simmer, Sarah glanced at the nearby kitchen priests then quietly said, "Mel shall be thrilled when you give this to him tomorrow. Although we make custards at the Great Temple, we rarely bother with burnt custards since the karamelized topping is too much bother. 'Tis likely been ages since he enjoyed it."

Removing the simmering mixture from the heat to steep, Kit

shrugged then murmured so no one could overhear, "I'm certain the duchess ensures 'tis a frequent dessert when Mel visits."

Sarah winked. "But *she* doesn't prepare it with her own hands, so that makes yours extra special. Even if 'twasn't from the lady he loves."

Blushing, Kit narrowed her eyes at Sarah. "Nonsense. Shall we help with tomorrow's feast while our mixture steeps?"

Sarah nodded, and they chopped vegetables for Plantfete's many hare pies with some kitchen priests for the next hour. Once they were alone in their corner again, they began simmering their mixture once more, and Sarah asked, "When shall you give these to Mel?"

Kit hummed while whisking honey and sugar into the mixture. Even though she and Mel were missing most of the Plantfete festivities, tomorrow would be hectic with Plantfete Lauds here at dawn then the royal wedding ceremony and coronation at the palace later. "After breakfast. Mel must leave for the palace soon after."

Once Kit set aside the cream mixture, Sarah handed her whisked egg yolks. "Are you joining him?"

Whisking as Sarah added the cream mixture into the yolks one ladle at a time, Kit swallowed and kept her gaze on their work. If only she could tell Sarah the truth without revealing Mel's faegift. "I don't want anyone from court seeing me."

Sarah tsked. "Then you must join Deacon and me at the Plantfete festivities. The egg games, creation songs, and planting rituals are such fun."

Kit almost winced as she ladled the custard mixture into four baking dishes submerged in boiling water. "Thanks, but after my many visits to priests lately, I require a quiet day alone."

Sarah slanted her a concerned frown but didn't protest as they rejoined the kitchen priests to chop vegetables while the custards baked. After they'd set the baked custards in the cold pantry, Sarah said, "I'll help you prepare the karamelized topping tomorrow just before you give the custards to Mel."

Kit smiled at her friend as they left the busy kitchen. "Thanks, Sarah. You're the best."

The following morning, Kit immediately changed into her arachne silk gown and turned it to a muted gray before donning her inactive invisibility cloak. She'd not have time to change later, and she couldn't wear her maid's dress to the royal ceremonies, even if no one could see her. She concealed a grin when Sarah and Deacon joined her and Mel for Plantfete Lauds. Sarah didn't appear awake at all.

They all headed outside for Plantfete Lauds, rather than the Sun Chapel like usual. The festival service began with watching the dawn since it celebrated the Goddess's gift of the upcoming day and growing season. Yet the morning air was frigid despite the beauty of the festival service and the vivid dawn. Thankfully, her invisibility cloak kept Kit warm.

After the four of them devoured a quick breakfast, Kit and Sarah hurried to the kitchen to finish preparing Mel's cinnaspice-honey burnt custard. They sprinkled sugar and cinnaspice on the custards before taking a salamander, a long-handled iron paddle heated in the stove, to make the karamelized topping.

Then Kit set the four burnt custards on a covered tray and strode to Mel's chambers. He was waiting for her to accompany him to the palace, although he didn't know she was arriving with a natalday gift. She inhaled as she knocked on his door. Please let him love his natalday gift as much as she'd loved hers.

CHAPTER 34

At the brief knock, Mel straightened his formal priest robes over the evening clothes he was wearing for the royal ceremonies despite the early hour. That must be Kit knocking. Inhaling, he strode to his door to let her in. This was the first they'd been truly alone since their last kiss on her natalday. Please let him be more restrained on his own natalday.

He blinked when Kit swept into his chambers with a covered tray. "What's that?"

Smiling at him, Kit set the tray on the table then beckoned him to sit. "A natalday gift. I hope you don't mind I didn't wrap it."

His chest warmed as he sat. He'd not received a natalday gift in years. And from the tray, 'twas likely a dessert rather than an embroidered pocketcloth like she'd given him every year as children because she couldn't afford anything else. He lifted the cover and almost drooled. Four cinnaspice-honey burnt custards!

Kit hummed and sat across from him. "Since burnt custard doesn't keep, you'll need to eat them now. I know 'tis early for dessert, but with the royal ceremonies today, I wasn't sure when I'd have a chance to give them to you otherwise."

Mel laughed. Eating her gift now would be no hardship. "You know I can always eat dessert—especially my favorite one. Thanks, Kit." He set a custard before her. "Have one."

Pursing her lips, Kit attempted to return her custard. "I made them for *you*."

He smiled at Kit. Sweet, stubborn lady. "And I want you to have one. I *could* devour them all, but I'd feel a glutton if I did."

When she tsked but accepted her custard, he grinned then began his remaining three. He sighed at his first spoonful. Rich, creamy, and decadent, the custard contained the perfect blend of honey and cinnaspice with the karamelized topping adding a contrasting crunch and a subtle hint of bitterness. "This is the most delicious cinnaspice-honey burnt custard I've ever eaten."

Kit blushed. "Nonsense. I'm certain your mother's cook prepares better. She's an expert."

Mel shrugged as he finished his first custard. "Yours are still more delicious." He stilled when Kit blushed harder and licked her lips then mumbled her thanks. She was as tempting as her burnt custards. He forced himself to devour his other two custards while she ate hers.

Then he rose and pulled Kit upright. Unable to release her, he squeezed her hands, and his pulse quickened. "Thanks again for the perfect natalday gift."

Kit smiled up at him, her smoky eyes lambent. "Yours was the perfect one, but I'm glad you enjoyed your gift."

He swallowed as Kit's delectable cinnaspice scent surrounded him. He needed to quit touching her and step back. Yet instead, he drew her closer and kissed her. As she returned his kiss, he dropped her hands to yank her against him. Sweet with a hint of spice, she tasted even *better* than her delicious burnt custards. He could kiss her forever. As he devoured her lips, hunger surged through him, and his body tightened.

A firm knock on his door made him still with a groan. Why did everyone keep interrupting when he was kissing Kit? Then he wrenched himself free from Kit, who swayed and blinked at him. He should be *grateful*, not annoyed by the interruption. He mightn't have stopped without it. His shameful hunger for Kit had become nearly impossible to control. What was *wrong* with him?

Another firm knock sounded, and High Priest Theodag called through the door, "Mel, are you ready yet? The carriage is waiting to take us to the palace."

As Kit paled whiter than a banshee, Mel swallowed and replied, "Almost ready, your excellency." He turned to Kit, and his chest constricted. If only he'd time to beg her forgiveness again, but the high priest might burst in if they took much longer. "You should activate your invisibility cloak."

Kit jerked her cloak closed and over her head before muttering, "Kelare." She vanished, and a moment later, her hand rested on his sleeve. "I'll hold on to you while I'm invisible, so you know where I am and don't step on me."

His arm tingling at her touch, Mel nodded then joined the high priest in the hall.

High Priest Theodag eyed him while they strode from the priest quarters. "Everything all right? You appear... unsettled."

Forcing himself not to glance at Kit beside him, Mel gritted a smile. 'Twas fortunate she was invisible—otherwise the high priest might guess he was unsettled due to their ravenous kisses. "'Tis nothing."

The high priest hummed as they reached the carriage. "Were you delayed because you were attempting to persuade Kit to join us?"

Mel almost winced while waiting for Kit to climb into the carriage. Was it so obvious he was unsettled because of her? He slid onto the backward carriage seat as close to the center as he could with her beside him. The high priest might wonder otherwise. "Kit can't bear for anyone from court to see her."

High Priest Theodag sighed. "I know."

On the ride to the palace, Mel stared out the window and attempted to review his part of the upcoming ceremonies. Yet the invisible Kit nestled against him made that futile. Kissing her kept echoing through him instead. If the high priest hadn't been sitting across from them, he doubtless would have yanked Kit onto his lap and spent the entire carriage ride kissing her. Not appropriate behavior for a priest toward any lady other than his wife, and Kit could never be his.

Eventually, the torturous carriage ride ended, but Kit's hand on his arm kept tormenting him as they headed to the throne room. When they entered the vast chamber teeming with extravagantly dressed guests, the high priest strode straight to the dais containing the two thrones, but Mel was waylaid by Mother and Father, who were with Hawke, Selena, and the Keyes. Aragon and Wren were acting as witnesses for the royal wedding ceremony, so they must be in the royal anteroom with Devon and Kiera.

Mother embraced Mel. "Happy natalday, Mel." Once Father and the others wished him the same, she asked, "Where's Kit?"

He stiffened, his back prickling at Kit standing behind him with her invisibility cloak brushing his priest robes due to the crowd. "She refuses to let anyone from court see her."

As Mother tsked, Father flashed a crooked grin and said, "Kit is the most strong-willed lady I've ever met—and I've been married to your mother for thirty years."

While Mother frowned at Father, Mel turned to Hawke and Selena, who both appeared tense despite their smiles when wishing him happy natalday earlier. Selena was cuddling little Isabel against her chest while eyeing the crowd jostling them, doubtless praying they wouldn't upset her tiny daughter. A frown between his brows, Hawke kept glancing toward the royal anteroom—he must be worried with his heavily pregnant wife out of sight.

Mel smiled at Hawke and Selena. "How are you?"

Rocking the wide-eyed Isabel, Selena sighed. "Ready for the ceremonies to be over. Having Isabel among all these strangers is overwhelming, but I didn't want to leave her with her nursemaid for so long, and I couldn't skip attending to support Devon and Kiera."

Hawke grimaced, continuing to watch the royal anteroom. "Same. Wren was ill this morning and still has a terrible headache. I need to get her home so she can rest. She's been increasingly unwell lately."

As Kit shifted against his back, Mel squeezed Hawke's arm to reassure him. "Fortunately, Devon and Kiera requested their wedding ceremony and Kiera's coronation remain as simple as possible." He glanced toward the dais, where the high priest was beckoning him. "I should go so we can get the ceremonies started."

Mel thrust through the crowd with Kit close behind. When they reached the dais, she murmured in his ear, her delectable scent swamping him, "I'll stand between the thrones before the Mirror of Wisdom so I'm not underfoot."

Once Mel stood beside High Priest Theodag on the dais, the crowd began to settle in their places for the ceremonies. His immediate family was in the front near where Devon and Kiera would stand, with Lord and Lady Ravenstone beside Hawke, and Lady Moonbud and her mate beside them. Just beyond that were his Hawke cousins as well as Lady Juliet and the councilors with their spouses and children. Then sonorous music filled the throne room, and the crowd turned toward the royal anteroom.

Resplendent and regal in their white arachne silk attire with elaborate green and gold designs that matched the throne room's furnishings, Devon and Kiera glided down the aisle, followed by Aragon and Wren. For once, Devon was wearing his crown—a heavy gold circlet studded with emerald firegems created for Calator's coronation shortly after the founding of Calatini. Kiera's matching crown created for Calator's wife Annalise was sitting atop her throne awaiting her coronation.

Mel almost frowned as his gaze drifted to Aragon and Wren behind Devon and Kiera. Hawke was right about Wren being ill. Her skin flushed, she leaned heavily against Aragon as they processed down the aisle. Hopefully, Wren could manage to remain upright for both the royal wedding ceremony and Kiera's coronation.

Once Devon and Kiera reached the dais with Aragon and Wren flanking them, High Priest Theodag welcomed everyone then led the opening prayer before gesturing for Mel to begin the wedding ceremony.

Smiling at Devon and Kiera, Mel read the sacred words about marriage then crowned them with tied myrtle garlands and led them through their vows. Devon and Kiera exchanged the detachable contraceptive strand from their protection charms as wedding tokens because their true wedding tokens from before were fused to the rest of their protection charms.

After Mel announced them as husband and wife, Devon drew Kiera close for a decorous kiss—much more restrained than the passionate one at their first ceremony—as befitted a public royal wedding. While Devon released Kiera and sat on his throne, Mel, Aragon, and Wren stepped off the dais and rejoined their family. Mel eyed Devon. Please let him not realize Kit was directly beside him.

High Priest Theodag led another prayer then asked Kiera to kneel. He anointed her brow with oil infused with the Goddess laurel apple bestowed on her and led Kiera through her vows to serve the kingdom of Calatini for the rest of her days. The high priest placed the queen's crown on Kiera's head and waved for her to rise. "Arise, your majesty, and ascend to your throne."

Kiera gracefully rose and climbed the dais then sank onto her throne to the left of Devon, who reached and took her hand with a proud smile.

Mel swallowed. Kit must have moved at some point, but where? The white velvet curtain concealing the Mirror of Wisdom wafted like it always did, so she couldn't be directly before it. Yet the floor beyond the dais was packed, so she must have remained there. Perhaps she'd moved throughout the ceremonies. Hopefully, she'd find him once the crowd began leaving—he couldn't return to the Great Temple without her.

High Priest Theodag faced the crowd and gestured toward Kiera, a beam illuminating his austere face. "People of Calatini, I present to you our new and gracious queen, Queen Kiera Waterstreet Vireni I. By the grace of the Goddess, may she reign with her husband and our noble king, King Devon Calator Vireni IV, for many glorious and prosperous years."

Applause and cheers swept through the throne room. Once the tumult faded, sonorous music filled the throne room again. Devon and Kiera rose and glided to the royal anteroom. Then the music quieted, and the crowd began to disperse, starting with the guests in front like Mel and his family.

As he began down the aisle, Kit's hand rested on his shoulder again, and he exhaled a silent sigh. Thank the Goddess she'd found him. He and his family plus Lord and Lady Ravenstone and the two nightmara joined Devon and Kiera, who'd already removed their antique crowns, in the royal anteroom. Since the anteroom was more crowded than the throne room had been, he retreated to a corner with Kit sheltered behind him.

After a round of congratulations, Hawke guided the wobbly Wren to a chair while Mother smiled about the anteroom and said, "Everyone must visit our townhouse to celebrate today's ceremonies and Mel's natalday."

Mel tensed. Although he'd enjoy celebrating with his family, Kit would need to remain invisible to avoid questions. But how could he refuse without hurting his family and rousing their suspicions?

Frowning, Hawke shook his head. "I wish we could, but Wren must return home to rest."

Kiera and Lady Ravenstone exchanged worried frowns, then Kiera murmured, "Perhaps Annalise should accompany you, Wren."

As Kit inhaled sharply behind him, Mel blinked. Why would

Kiera suggest that?

Wren straightened in her chair. "I'm fine. I simply require some rest."

Still frowning, Lady Ravenstone shook her head. "I really should accompany you."

Wren wrinkled her nose. "No, stay and celebrate with everyone." She turned to Hawke. "Help me stand."

While Hawke led Wren from the royal anteroom, Kit whispered in Mel's ear, "Go celebrate with your family. I'll be fine walking back to the Great Temple alone."

He fisted his hands in his priest robes. Perhaps, but he didn't *want* Kit returning alone. Yet he couldn't argue with her without revealing her presence.

Frowning after Hawke and Wren, Mother sighed then turned back to Mel and the others with a smile. "Shall the rest of us head to Childes House?" Once everyone murmured agreement, she grinned. "Wonderful. I'll go invite the rest of the family." She arched her brows at Mel. "You return to the Great Temple and fetch that assistant of yours. She must celebrate your natalday with us."

He smiled and nodded, his tension easing. That would allow Kit to become visible without any questions. "Of course, Mother. I'll fetch her straightaway."

CHAPTER 35

$\mathcal{A}$s Mel strode from the royal anteroom, Kit hurried beside him with her hand resting on his arm. Although still teeming, the crowd in the palace had thinned enough that she no longer needed to walk behind him. Fortunate because pressing against his back had made her ache to wrap her arms about his waist and press closer. When they finally reached a near empty hall, she muttered, "We're not returning to the Great Temple, are we?"

Mel immediately murmured back, "No. We'll walk toward my family's townhouse, find a hidden spot for you to reappear, then wait for a while before continuing."

She squeezed Mel's arm, her throat tightening. Since she'd sought his help breaking the Goddess's illusion, he'd become adept at deceiving his family without telling any lies. She was horrible for corrupting a priest so. "A sensible plan."

Halfway to his parents', Mel slipped into an alley. "You can deactivate your invisibility cloak here."

Sheltering behind Mel, Kit inhaled and glanced toward the street to check no one was watching then whispered, "Osvelare." Like when she'd activated her invisibility cloak, heat flickered through the arachne silk before she reappeared. She lowered her hood then studied her old-looking hands. 'Twas almost odd to see herself again—or herself as she appeared under the Goddess's illusion, at least.

Mel eyed her. "Where did you stand during the royal ceremonies? From how Devon held Kiera's hand, you couldn't have been between their thrones."

She grimaced. "When I saw how close Lady Moonbud and her mate were," along with Lady Ravenstone, "I was concerned they might sense my aura, so I hid behind Queen Kiera's throne. 'Twas cramped, but I could still see most of the royal ceremonies." She smiled at Mel. "Thanks for giving me the invisibility cloak so I could attend."

His gaze jerking toward the street, Mel inclined his head, and they lapsed into silence. Eventually, he said, "I believe we've waited long enough."

Kit nodded, and they continued to Childes House. As they ascended the steps, she smoothed her arachne silk gown. Please let no one notice that 'twasn't a maid's dress and that the cut was too flattering for a crone. Everyone but Mel's parents would wonder why.

When she and Mel joined everyone in the drawing room, she glanced about for Lady Ravenstone and the nightmara to ensure she avoided them. Then she exhaled—they weren't among the guests. They mustn't have wanted to intrude on a family event.

The duchess sailed over with her husband and embraced Kit. "Finally. You two are the last to arrive. We couldn't start celebrating Mel's natalday without him." She narrowed her eyes at Kit. "Why weren't you at the royal ceremonies today?"

A blush warmed Kit's cheeks, but she shrugged. "I was concerned the presence of an unknown crone would engender questions at court."

As the duke's mouth quirked, the duchess tsked then said, "Nonsense. No one would have been surprised to see the lady acting as Mel's assistant join him." She shooed them toward the others. "Go talk. We'll proceed to luncheon shortly."

Since King Devon and Queen Kiera were laughing with Edouard and Pippa, Kit and Mel didn't congratulate them first as protocol would demand, but instead joined Aragon and Selena, whose arms appeared empty without their infant daughter. Mel asked them, "Where's Isabel?"

Selena flashed a wry smile. "Upstairs sleeping after I fed her."

Aragon shook his head. "Yes, Isabel endured enough people at court today. Thank the Goddess she remained quiet during the ceremonies."

Beaming, Elise bustled over with Lord Farson and said, "Your daughter is truly the sweetest infant I've ever seen. I hope we're as fortunate."

Kit scrutinized Elise. Her stepdaughter had said that with joy rather than longing. Could she be pregnant at last? So as Mel and the others began discussing Isabel, she drew Elise aside with a warm smile and whispered, "Do you have happy news to share?"

Elise's pale-blue eyes glowed. "I've found a way to conceive." She glanced at her husband. "Although I must decide how to convince Seanian to attempt it."

Kit hummed. "A fertility spell of some kind?" Those could have a high magical cost, and Lord Farson might not want his beloved wife risking that.

Lifting a shoulder, Elise smiled. "No, the veiled witch said I didn't need a fertility spell."

Before Kit could probe further, Arvan bounded over to Elise and Lord Farson. "Hurry, the duchess says we can proceed to luncheon now. And I'm *famished*."

Lord Farson slapped the gangly duke's shoulder as they began toward the family dining room. "You always are."

Luncheon was the traditional Plantfete feast of roast lamb, hare pie, early rhubarb, spring greens, and white wine. Everyone ate heartily amid lively discussion and frequent toasts to King Devon and Queen Kiera as well as Mel. When the servants brought the dessert course, the duchess beamed at her middle son. "Mel's favorite in honor of his nataldny."

Mel returned the duchess's smile. "Thanks, Mother." He ate a spoonful of cinnaspice-honey burnt custard. "'Tis delicious as always." After another spoonful, he glanced at Kit beside him and murmured, his lips barely moving, "The second best I've ever eaten."

Blushing, Kit glanced at Arvan beside her and Edouard beside Mel. Fortunately, neither had overheard. Arvan was too intent on devouring his burnt custard, while Edouard was flirting with Pippa under the watchful eyes of her brothers and her father Sir Julian, who was attending an event for once. Kit ate a spoonful of her burnt custard then blinked. It tasted little different from the one she'd prepared. Mel was just saying hers was better to be kind.

After dessert, everyone returned to the drawing room, then Kit and Mel joined King Devon and Queen Kiera, and Mel said, "Congratulations on your ceremonies today."

Queen Kiera smiled. "I'm relieved they're finally over."

Squeezing her arm, King Devon chuckled. "And that we can quit concealing our marriage."

As Queen Kiera and King Devon shared a heated glance, Kit swallowed a sigh. If only she could be so open about her hunger and love for Mel and have it returned.

Then Queen Kiera turned to Kit. "I'm looking forward to the Great Temple's court event the day after tomorrow. As promised, I've been telling everyone how excited I am to attend. Do you have everything you require for the event?"

Kit nodded. She'd all the entertainments planned, the charity-themed decorations were ready, and the temple kitchen would begin preparing the refreshments tomorrow since Plantfete would be done. "Yes, your majesty. We'll be setting up the palace's ballroom tomorrow."

Queen Kiera grinned. "Wonderful. If you require anything, please let me know. With the wedding ceremony and coronation over, I should have time to help after Devon and I bid farewell to Moonbud and the other nightmara in the morning."

Kit smiled at their kind and dedicated queen. She should enjoy an afternoon free with the husband who adored her instead. "Thank you for the offer, but several community priests are helping me set up."

Mel slanted her a probing glance, then they began their good-byes. As they were about to leave, Perkins arrived with a note for the duchess.

The duchess frowned as she read. "'Tis from Hawke. He writes that Wren fainted when they got home."

Kit and the others tensed. She swallowed to ease her tight throat. Please let nothing serious be wrong.

The duchess continued, "Hawke fetched Healer Althea, and she ordered Wren to remain in bed until the twins are born. Kiera, Wren enclosed notes for you and Lady Ravenstone."

As Queen Kiera snatched the notes, Kit shuddered. Poor Wren would hate the enforced bedrest, but Healer Althea was the best witch healer in Ormas and would take excellent care of her.

Sober after hearing about Wren, Kit and Mel finished their goodbyes and walked back to the Great Temple without speaking. It had been a busy and dramatic natalday for him—too bad it had ended with worrying news.

THE FOLLOWING DAY, Kit and the community priests helping her carried everything to set up the palace's ballroom, except the refreshments, outside to the carriages set aside for them. They needed two to fit her and the helpers, the Goddess laurels High Priest Theodag had blessed, the four massive illusion curtains enchanted by witch priests, and the other charity-themed deco-rations she'd gathered.

As the carriages were about to leave, Mel strode outside. "Do you have space for another helper?"

Kit blinked at Mel. Wasn't he supposed to begin acting as the elder community priest of Calatini today? Yet she simply nodded because she couldn't refuse spending time with him. Her pulse quickened when he slid into the second carriage beside her, but she feigned indifference with a calm smile since they weren't alone.

Mel flashed a wry grin. "Sorry I'm late. It took longer than I'd planned to convince Elder Priestess Agnes to agree I could wait until after the Great Temple's court event to assume her duties."

In the palace's ballroom, she, Mel, and the others placed the charity-themed decorations about youth endeavors on the wall with the doors, prayer houses on the garden wall, almskitchens on the interior wall, and family refuges on the wall with the musicians' balcony.

While they set up the blank illusion curtain for the family refuges that covered most of the wall, Mel arched his brows at her. "What are these massive curtains for?"

Kit panted as she stretched the curtain taut. "Witch priests enchanted them to show scenes from our charities once I activate them tomorrow. And when people approach, the illusions shall even begin a speech about the charities."

Mel's eyes widened. "Even at court, such massive and elaborate illusions are rare."

She grinned. "I know. And the Goddess laurels shall further impress court."

Mel chuckled while they set up tables with donation pledge books and donation boxes as the others placed the Goddess laurels about the ballroom. "You're hoping to awe them into donating."

Her grin turning wry, Kit shrugged. "Plus, Queen Kiera and your mother have promised to donate openly, which shall make donating *very* fashionable. And I've games planned where the winner can select which charity they donate their winnings to, as well as auctions for retreats to a prayer house of the winner's choice."

Humming, Mel frowned at her. "How are you planning on managing all that if you're invisible and can't direct anyone?"

She worried her lip. That *was* a problem, yet she couldn't let anyone from court see her. "I'll provide my helpers with lists beforehand."

Mel sighed while they finished the final donation table. "That shall only work if everything goes according to plan. How about we have Deacon enchant a pair of communication crystals for us, and you can tell me what to do?"

Kit beamed. "That shall be perfect. Thanks, Mel." She scrutinized the decorated ballroom. Everything was ready for tomorrow. Court was going to be amazed and hopefully donate more than they ever had.

When they returned to the Great Temple, they met High Priest Theodag and Elder Priestess Agnes in the high priest's study on the top floor above the chapter house. After Kit updated them, the high priest smiled and asked, "How soon before the event should we meet to head to the palace?"

While Kit struggled to decide how to reply, Elder Priestess Agnes shook her head and said, "I shan't be attending this year. You know I've never enjoyed court events, and Mel can attend in my stead as the future elder community priest of Calatini." She pursed her lips at Mel. "'Twas the only reason I agreed to delay Mel assuming my duties."

As Mel inclined his head in acknowledgment of his superior's annoyance, Kit swallowed and made herself smile at the high priest. "Mel and I must head to the palace after luncheon to manage the preparations, but you're much too busy for that, so you should arrive in the evening for the event itself."

High Priest Theodag studied her. "Very well. You *are* attending tomorrow, unlike the royal ceremonies, aren't you?"

Not glancing at Mel, she shifted in her seat. "Yes, although I doubt you or anyone from court shall see me. Mel shall be directing matters for me while I remain behind the scenes."

High Priest Theodag's eyes narrowed. "I see."

Before the high priest could ask more questions, Kit excused herself, and Mel joined her with a faint frown. He clearly didn't like misleading the high priest. But then, neither did she. Yet she couldn't risk the high priest ordering her not to use her invisibility cloak tomorrow. Court might realize she was Lady Blaine if they saw her, especially while hosting a fashionable event.

CHAPTER 36

$\mathcal{A}$ half hour before the Great Temple's court event, Mel grinned as he and Kit studied the palace's ballroom. All the refreshments were laid out, and the charity-themed decorations were still perfect, even though the illusion curtains hadn't been activated yet. Tonight was going to be Kit's most spectacular event ever—she'd thrown herself into planning it like she'd thrown herself into helping when they'd visited the community programs together.

Kit smiled at the community priests helping with the event. "Go eat some refreshments before the guests arrive. None of us shall have time later, and we don't want anyone fainting because they skipped dinner."

Her helpers laughed then surged toward the refreshments. Everyone was starving after spending all afternoon adjusting the decorations and carrying the delicious refreshments kitchen priests had prepared.

As Kit began inspecting the decorations again, Mel tsked then fetched heaping plates for them both. She'd be the one who fainted otherwise. He handed her a plate. "You should heed your own advice."

Kit shrugged and began devouring her refreshments. "I was about to, but thanks for fetching me a plate."

He smiled at Kit. "Of course." As they ate, her eyes kept scrutinizing the palace's ballroom, so to reassure her, he said, "Tonight shall be spectacular."

Kit grinned while they returned their empty plates to the refreshments table. "I believe it shall."

Mel arched his brows at Kit as she bustled about the ballroom with him following. She was going to exhaust herself before the Great Temple's court event began. "If you're so confident, then why are you fussing?"

Kit tossed her head, her arachne silk gown shimmering like an inky waterfall while she hurried from the family refuge wall to the almskitchen wall. "I'm not fussing. I simply dislike remaining idle while awaiting guests."

Wrapping an arm about Kit, he tugged her into the nearest alcove then sat and pulled her into his lap to ensure she remained still. "You should rest."

Kit stiffened, barely breathing. "Mel, what are you doing?"

He swallowed, his gaze on her lips. They were so close that he could capture them if he bent his head. "Ensuring you rest."

Swallowing, Kit shifted in his lap and braced her hands on his chest. "This isn't restful."

Mel shuddered as his body hardened. "No, it isn't." Unable to resist, he drew Kit closer and kissed her.

Kissing him back, Kit slid her hands about his neck and pressed against him.

As Kit's delectable cinnaspice scent flooded him, he devoured her lips and began caressing her skin beneath the edge of her bodice. More, he needed *more*.

"Kit, Mel, where are you? The guests are about to arrive, and the illusion curtains still must be activated," one of the community priests called.

Mel and Kit wrenched their lips apart, panting and staring at each other. He swallowed. Her eyes were black, her skin flushed, and her lips swollen. An obviously well-kissed lady. And the community priests they were leading were just steps away with all of court about to join them.

He jerked his treacherous hands from Kit's skin. *Why* did he keep touching her when he knew that only made him burn to kiss her? And what madness had deluded him into believing he could hold her in his lap? Gentlemen didn't manhandle friends so. Damn his shameful hunger for her turning him into a seducing cad. He must apologize—again. "Kit, I—"

She clapped a hand on his mouth then scrambled from his lap. "We've no time for apologies. I must activate the illusion curtains."

As Kit bolted from the alcove, Mel leapt after her while straightening his plain priest robes. Hopefully, his unruly body would settle before the other priests noticed or the guests arrived.

Him close behind, Kit darted about the palace's ballroom, touching each of the illusion curtains then muttering the words to activate them. Once they all began displaying their scenes, she snatched her invisibility cloak from beside the refreshments table. She smiled at the community priests. "We're all set for the guests. Mel shall greet them while I ensure everything proceeds smoothly. Remember, if you've any questions, find Mel since I'll be hard to locate."

When Kit hurried into the nearest anteroom, Mel joined her and grasped her elbow. "I'm sorry for upsetting you before your court event. You were already nervous enough."

Kit pursed her lips while freeing her elbow. "I'm fine."

He swallowed, eyeing Kit's lips. How he ached for another kiss. Not that he'd take one—he'd still no right to kiss her. "You don't appear fine."

Flashing a blinding smile, Kit donned her invisibility cloak. "Then 'tis fortunate no one shall see me."

Before Kit could activate her cloak, Mel captured her shoulders and pulled her closer to comfort her. "Tonight shall be perfect. I promise."

Kit stared up at him, her gaze soft. "Thanks for agreeing to help."

He smiled as warmth suffused his chest. Although Elder Priestess Agnes was annoyed with him, he'd been right to delay acting as the elder community priest of Calatini to help Kit. "How could I not help with such a vital event? The donations your event shall raise shall support the Great Temple's charities for months. I'm so proud you threw yourself into planning tonight's event."

Kit blinked and caressed his cheek. "Oh, Mel."

His heart surging, he began bending his head to give her a tender kiss.

But before their lips met, Mother said from the door behind him, "Mel, what are you doing hiding in an anteroom? I thought you were supposed to be helping. And where's Kit?"

Mel froze, as did Kit. How could he have been about to kiss her again moments after scolding himself for doing so?

Pale as parchment, Kit breathed, "Kelare," and vanished. Please let his greater height and priest robes have concealed her before she'd activated her invisibility cloak.

Forcing a smile, he turned to face Mother. "I was just taking a moment before the guests arrive." He waved about the anteroom. "And Kit's around somewhere."

Mother hummed and eyed him. "Everything all right?"

Mel fought not to blush. Everything except Kit kept making him forget he was a priest who should only kiss his wife. "Why wouldn't it be?"

Humming again, Mother stepped toward him. "Because you've seemed unsettled since Kit began staying at the Great Temple."

His neck heating, he suppressed a wince. He couldn't discuss that with Mother—especially with the invisible Kit nearby. "I should go greet the guests. Excuse me."

He strode from the anteroom, extracting the communication crystal Deacon had enchanted yesterday from his pocket. He secured the communication crystal inside his ear before tapping it so he and Kit could hear each other, although not what people said in reply. He murmured, "Kit, are you there?"

Clear as if she stood beside him, Kit whispered through the communication crystal, "Yes. I'm heading to the musicians' balcony to watch the event from above to better direct you. The musicians shouldn't notice me over their playing if I mutter into my invisibility cloak."

When Mel joined High Priest Theodag by the door, the high priest sighed and shook his head then said, "I'd hoped Kit would change her mind and greet the guests too."

Mel almost snorted. Kit rarely changed her mind once she'd decided something. He tapped before the ear holding his communication crystal. "No, but she's directing me through this."

The high priest eyed him. "All the witches here tonight shall see the glow of magic about your ear and know someone is directing you."

Mel stilled. Would they notice the magic from Kit's invisibility cloak as well? Surely not—otherwise 'twouldn't be very invisible. And no one had noticed her at the royal ceremonies. "The mystery shall only make the event more intriguing."

High Priest Theodag chuckled as Devon and Kiera approached. "True."

While Mel and the high priest greeted the guests with Kit advising in Mel's ear where to send them, all the members of court who were acknowledged witches scrutinized his ear, like the royal witch Lady Juliet and the Minister of Magic Lord Islaye. But so did several others who weren't, including the Ravenstones, Greysnowes, and the Duke of Oakmoor.

After narrowly eyeing the communication crystal, the Duke of Oakmoor glanced about the palace's ballroom. "A most unique and diverting event, Priest Melchior. Nothing like the previous

Great Temple court events. Did you plan it? Or your mother, perhaps?"

Mel gritted a polite smile at Kit's former suitor, who was just the type of husband she wanted—wealthy, titled, and influential—nothing like a humble priest. "No, the lady acting as my assistant did."

The Duke of Oakmoor hummed, his brows quirking. "For a priestess, she possesses remarkable insight into how to fascinate court. This event reminds me of one of Lady Blaine's."

Mel stiffened. What precisely had Kit written in her letter to the duke months ago? Why would she trust that *rakehell* when she refused to trust anyone else at court, including his family? She'd only told Mother after Mother had guessed the truth. He made himself nod at the duke. "High praise indeed. I must relay it to my assistant."

As the duke left, Kit whispered in Mel's ear, "What are you relaying?"

He rubbed his face to hide his mouth. "The Duke of Oakmoor said this event reminds him of one of Lady Blaine's."

Kit gasped. "He *what*? I never wrote anything about the Great Temple when I formally ended our almost betrothal. Please let the duke not have realized the truth somehow. All of court shall know by next week."

Mel exhaled, still hiding his mouth. So Kit *didn't* trust the duke. To soothe her alarm, he murmured, "I doubt he's guessed anything. He was simply complimenting the event."

Kit shuddered a sigh. "Even so, thank the Goddess I'm wearing an invisibility cloak so no one can see me and suspect the truth."

Once the guests slowed, Kit asked Mel to draw everyone's attention to the walls featuring the charities. Then they allowed people time to donate, which many rushed to do after seeing Mother and Kiera place their generous donations—exactly like Kit had intended. After that, Mel led the games and auctions she'd planned interspersed with dancing.

When Edouard collected his prize from the final auction, Mel grinned at his cousin while handing him the voucher for a three-night retreat at a prayer house of his choosing. "Quite an extravagant bid. I wasn't aware you were so desperate for spiritual growth."

Edouard chuckled as he tucked the voucher in his pocket. "The donations are for worthy causes, and I thought Pippa would enjoy the prize as a gift for her natalday next month. She's never stayed at one before."

Mel arched his brows. Such a gift between an unmarried couple was almost scandalous. "Sir Julian shall allow that?"

Grinning, Edouard shrugged. "Pippa and I shall be officially betrothed on her natalday, so hopefully he shall. But if not, she can save it until we're wed." He sobered and leaned toward Mel. "Can you still contact Kit?"

Mel stiffened and eyed his cousin. "Yes, why?"

Edouard grimaced. "I've a matter she must know, but we can't discuss it here. Could I visit you at the Great Temple tomorrow?"

Mel inclined his head. "Stop by for luncheon." He and Kit would be free then. She should hear Edouard's news directly, and Edouard wouldn't object to "Kay" overhearing since she'd helped both him and his twin.

Kit whispered through the communication crystal, "Why is Edouard visiting for luncheon tomorrow? Surely not to discuss his and Pippa's wedding ceremony. Sir Julian shan't allow them to marry until next year."

Mel hid his mouth behind a flute of sparkling wine. "No, Edouard has a matter he wants you to know. You'd better join us tomorrow."

Kit sighed. "No doubt 'tis about my frivolous spending, but very well."

Not long after that, Devon and Kiera left, and the rest of court soon followed. When nearly everyone had departed, Mother slid her arm through Mel's. "Could you escort me home?"

He blinked at Mother. "Where's Father?" He never left Mother behind.

Mother flashed a bright smile. "He went home earlier with Diana and Alaric."

Mel almost winced. Mother had likely sent Father home so she could resume quizzing him. Not good. Plus, he couldn't leave Kit behind. "I'm afraid I can't escort you home. I must stay and help disassemble the ballroom."

Mother pursed her lips. "Nonsense. 'Tis almost midnight."

Kit said in his ear, "Escort your mother home, Mel. We'll disassemble in the morning."

He frowned at the musicians' balcony where Kit must be still, although he couldn't protest aloud with Mother beside him.

Kit replied to his silent protest, "High Priest Theodag can escort me back to the Great Temple, which shall also prove I attended even though he didn't see me during the event."

Mel sighed. With both Kit and Mother determined, he couldn't avoid escorting Mother home. He made himself smile at Mother. "Very well."

Before Mother could ask any questions, he tapped his communication crystal to deactivate it and slipped it into his pocket. Mother's quizzing would be bad enough without Kit overhearing his replies.

However, Mother remained quiet until they'd settled inside the carriage. Then she studied him, her pale gaze probing in the lantern light. "Tell me what's been unsettling you lately. I imagine it involves Kit. You two could always rouse one another, and she's been staying at the Great Temple for months."

He swallowed as the carriage rumbled forward. Please let a half-truth satisfy Mother. "I don't like deceiving everyone about Kit's identity."

Mother tsked. "Although true, I doubt that's what's unsettling you. If it was, you'd be stern with Kit, but instead you're taking care of her like always." Mother smiled. "Your behavior toward Kay was how I realized she was Kit."

Wincing, Mel shifted in his seat. Not surprising. "We're old friends. Of course I take care of her."

Mother's lips quirked. "You don't take care of Kit like an old friend."

A blush flared across his skin, and he studied his fists. True, old friends didn't kiss whenever they were alone.

As the carriage halted before the family townhouse, Mother laid her hands on his fists. "If you don't open up, I can't help you. Please tell me what's the matter."

Mel exhaled. Perhaps he *should* tell Mother. She was perceptive, so surely she could help him solve how to quit kissing Kit. He raised his gaze. "Since Kit began staying at the Great Temple, we've been spending a lot of time together, and we became close again." He swallowed and shifted in his seat. "Then last month, I kissed her, and now I can't quit kissing her whenever we're alone. I even kissed her tonight before the guests arrived."

Smiling, Mother released his hands and leaned back in her seat. "Well, finally."

He gaped at Mother. Finally?! "But I'm a *priest* and shouldn't be succumbing to my shameful hunger to kiss Kit."

Mother's brows rose. "Shameful? Do you consider Aragon's and Hawke's desire for Selena and Wren shameful then?"

Mel frowned. His hunger for Kit wasn't at all the same—they weren't married and never would be. "No, but Aragon and Hawke are married and adore their wives."

Mother tilted her head. "True, you and Kit aren't married yet, but desiring the lady you love isn't shameful."

Breathless as if a nightmara had kicked his chest, he stared at Mother. "I don't love Kit."

Mother laughed. "Don't you? Any time you're in the same room, you two gravitate together. You never tire of the other's company and always rouse one another's emotions. And you're forever taking care of each other like devoted griffins. Plus, why else can't you resist kissing whenever alone?"

Mel shook his head. Mother's description seemed true, but he couldn't love Kit. Despite Kit's unacknowledged tender heart and her behavior since staying at the Great Temple, Kit was devoted to court and being fashionable. As soon as she broke the Goddess's illusion, she'd return there. Plus, she wanted to marry an influential court gentleman like the Duke of Oakmoor.

Tsking, Mother raised her eyes skyward. "How could I have birthed such idiot sons? Both you and Hawke have been in love forever yet determined not to see it. Even Aragon shared that tendency, although he realized his love in months rather than decades. I blame your father."

Mel frowned at Mother. She was ignoring the obvious. "Love between myself and Kit is impossible."

Mother hummed. "Because you believe the Goddess would refuse to approve your marriage?"

He snorted and frowned harder. If Kit loved him and truly wished to marry him, the Goddess would approve. Besides, the Goddess had blessed Kit with an illusion, so she took special interest in Kit and would accept Kit marrying one of her priests. He fisted his hands in his priest robes. "No, because Kit wants a wealthy and titled husband—she's the Countess of Blaine's fashionable reputation to maintain, after all."

Leaning forward with a warm smile, Mother squeezed his hands. "Does she? Since leaving court, Kit has been happier than I've ever seen her. Perhaps you should ask her to marry you and see what she says."

His heart wrenching, Mel jerked his hands free. He couldn't possibly. "I must return to the Great Temple. Good night, Mother." He leapt from the carriage before Mother could torment him further. Despite her usual insight, she must be wrong this time thanks to her matchmaking fervor.

CHAPTER 37

As Kit and Mel rolled up the illusion curtain for the family refuge wall in the palace's ballroom the following morning, she eyed Mel yet again and hummed. He'd been tense and quiet all day, and he'd barely looked at her. *What had his mother said to make him so troubled?* She must soothe him until he was himself again.

Once they set the illusion curtain with the others, she glanced at the community priests helping them. Fortunately, they were all busy disassembling the rest of the ballroom and were out of earshot. She risked laying a hand on Mel's arm and murmured, "What's wrong?"

Still not looking at her, Mel jerked away from her touch. "I'm fine."

Her chest squeezed. Why was Mel so uneasy with her? Had the duchess revealed the love she knew Kit felt for him? Or was he ashamed about the hungry kisses they'd exchanged here last night? She swallowed. Hopefully, she could distract him. "Thanks for all your help managing the Great Temple's court event yesterday."

Mel shrugged as they gathered some Goddess laurels from the family refuge wall. "I simply followed your directions. You're why last night was a success." He finally glanced at her. "Everyone kept complimenting me on your event. You must have missed hearing court's adulation directly."

Kit echoed Mel's shrug. She'd not missed that at all, and watching from afar had emphasized how little she missed court's shallow games. Visiting priests and helping others was much more fulfilling. Perhaps she shouldn't return to court when she broke the Goddess's illusion. Her heart quickened. Maybe High Priest Theodag would allow her to stay at the Great Temple without being a priestess if she promised to plan further court events. Then she could remain near Mel.

She grinned at Mel while gathering more Goddess laurels. "I could sense court's adulation through their excitement and generous donations. On the carriage ride back, High Priest Theodag said we'd received the most funds ever at one court event."

His mouth tightening, Mel looked away and nodded. "How wonderful."

Then the other community priests joined them to finish disassembling the family refuge wall, and they loaded the two carriages before returning to the Great Temple. During the ride, Mel lapsed back into his earlier silence, and Kit sighed as she eyed him. If only she knew why he was so troubled.

After they alighted, Mel smiled in her direction without truly looking at her. "Do you mind fetching luncheon from the dining hall and bringing it to my chambers? I'll wait here for Edouard so he doesn't get lost in the priest quarters."

She made herself nod and bustle to the dining room. Please let Edouard's visit distract Mel from whatever was troubling him. Even if Edouard was only visiting to grumble about her frivolous spending.

In Mel's chambers, she activated the fire plate to keep their luncheon warm and prepare tea, regular for the gentlemen and cinnaspice for her. Then she sat and waited for Mel and Edouard.

A few moments later, Mel opened his door and waved a grave Edouard inside. "I hope you don't mind if the lady acting as my assistant joins us for luncheon."

Edouard nodded at her, a smile briefly warming his face. "Of course not. Kay's wisdom is always welcome."

Her lips quirking, Kit returned Edouard's nod before fetching their luncheon. Especially when the matter involved herself.

Once they sat and began luncheon, Edouard sighed and stirred his beefsteak barley soup with a frown. "Thanks for agreeing to contact Kit for me. What I've to discuss isn't pleasant, and you can tell her with better tact than I could ever manage."

She and Mel exchanged a glance. From his gravity, Edouard couldn't be here simply to discuss her spending. He'd appear annoyed not worried about that.

Edouard sighed again. "Plus, I'm somewhat ashamed to face Kit after how I've behaved toward her over the years." He winced. "You were forever reproving me for calling her brazen and grasping, Mel, but I couldn't truly understand her desperation to escape. Not until I met *him*."

As Edouard sighed again, Kit froze with her spoon halfway to her mouth. *Him*? Surely, Edouard couldn't mean...

His brow furrowed, Mel sipped his tea. "Him who, Edouard?"

Edouard grimaced. "Kit's father—Sir Jason Sutton."

Her stomach seizing, she set down her laden spoon before she dropped it. Why was Father in Ormas? Not only could he not afford the journey, but he also despised court since 'twas comprised of people like Mel's family—the neighbors he'd always detested for outranking him, possessing more wealth, and enjoying their lives. Because of his hatred for them, he'd rarely socialized back in Childes, hence why Edouard had never met him before.

Scowling at Edouard, Mel squeezed her hand beneath the table. "What is that degenerate drunkard doing here?"

Edouard frowned and tapped his fingers on the table. "He

says to see Kit. But I'm not certain 'tis wise. Sir Jason is the most repugnant man I've ever met. He arrived the morning after the royal ceremonies, reeking of drink and decay while spewing filth and cruel insults. No lady should be subjected to that. I've not even mentioned his arrival to Elise or Pippa."

Kit swallowed and gripped Mel's hand. Why did Father want to see her? The morning she'd left to marry Lord Blaine, Father had spat on her and said he was well rid of his whore of a daughter. She'd fled Sutton Manor determined to never return and endure his drunken cruelty again. No matter the price she'd have to pay for that.

Mel caressed her palm with his thumb until she turned toward him. Then he arched his brows, clearly asking what she wanted to do about Father.

She sighed. Although she didn't want to see Father, Edouard shouldn't be responsible for caring for him. And thanks to the Goddess's illusion, Father would never recognize her. She almost snorted. Father's arrival had turned that curse into a blessing. Firming her jaw, she turned to Edouard. "Could you transport Sir Jason here? He can stay in Mel's spare room so we can unearth why he wants to see his daughter. Then we can relay to her whatever she should know."

As Mel glowered beside her, Edouard sagged in his seat and said, "I'll be relieved to relinquish responsibility for that repugnant man." Frowning, he leaned toward them. "You'll protect Kit from him, shan't you?"

Kit blinked at Edouard. He was actually concerned for the stepmother he'd always disliked?

Squeezing her hand again, Mel flashed a tight smile. "Of course."

Edouard sighed. "Good. I never cared for Kit, especially after she married Father, but now I can't help but admire her fortitude and grace considering her malicious father." He smiled. "I should have trusted your opinion of her, Mel. When we were young, you said she was a tender, devoted, and insightful girl."

She blushed as Mel dropped her hand and shifted beside her. He'd said that about *her*? She swallowed. But doubtless he'd quit believing she was tender, devoted, or insightful after he'd learned how she'd hurt Wren and Hawke, even though he'd since forgiven her for that.

To distract everyone, she smiled at Edouard and asked, "Any romantic plans for Pippa's natalday next month?"

Grinning, Edouard nodded but refused to disclose his plans, so she and Mel spent the rest of luncheon teasing him.

As soon as Edouard left, Mel turned to her with a frown. "Are you certain you want your father staying here?"

Kit grimaced and rubbed her brow. "Not particularly, but he can't remain at Blaine House. However, I've no intention of telling Father who I truly am. We can simply tell him we'll relay what he says."

Mel stiffly nodded. "Good. But even so, you avoid him as much as possible and let me tend to him."

Warmth filling her chest at Mel's protectiveness, Kit smiled and laid her hand on his. "I shall. Thanks."

WHEN EDOUARD'S carriage brought Father to the Great Temple several hours later, Kit paced about Mel's chambers. Mel had insisted she remain behind while he and some temple priests fetched Father. She whirled toward the door as it slammed open.

Mel and Paul staggered inside, carrying Father between them with Dirk behind them bearing Father's belongings.

She gasped at Father's ghastly appearance. His once handsome face was yellow with spiderlike veins marring his skin, his now grizzled hair lifeless, and his body emaciated and trembling, yet with swollen limbs. His clothes were similarly decrepit, and his drunken stench swept before him. Goddess, Father had deteriorated in the seven years since she'd seen him.

Father's bloodshot smoky eyes met hers, and he sneered, slurring, "Who's the hideous hag?"

Father's past cruelty echoing through her, Kit winced and lowered her gaze. Had he seen that her eyes matched his and recognized her? Please let him not be so perceptive.

His voice hard, Mel snapped, "This kind lady is acting as my assistant. You will treat her with respect."

Glancing up, Kit gaped at Mel as he and Paul hauled Father toward the spare room. Mel's jaw was clenched, his body stiff, and his eyes black. He appeared ready to throttle Father—she'd never seen Mel so furious. But then, he'd always disliked Father, and Father was obviously worse than ever.

Once Mel and Paul dropped Father onto the narrow bed, Paul scurried toward the door, almost tripping on Dirk setting down Father's belongings. The rabbity temple priest muttered while fleeing, "I'll fetch a healer."

She shivered. Father did seem in desperate need of one. Her gaze fell to the large red chest and bulging satchel Dirk had set beside the bed. The red chest had fascinated her since a merchant had brought it to Sutton Manor on her eighth natalday. The merchant had been striding toward her with the chest, doubtless to locate Father, when Father had staggered outside. After a muttered argument, Father had wrested the chest from the merchant and carried it to his study. She'd followed as if lured by a singing siren, and Father had slapped her so hard her nose bled when he'd found her outside the door. Locking his study, he'd ordered her to never touch the chest. Yet until she'd left Sutton Manor, she'd attempted to find it every few months, but Father had kept his study locked, so she'd never seen the red chest again until now.

She swallowed, her fingers tingling to open it at last. Knowing Father, it probably held nothing more than half-empty bottles of spirits, but somehow she burned to see for herself.

She was about to step toward the red chest when Mel grasped her elbow with a frown. "Are you all right?"

As Mel drew her from the bedroom and shut the door, Kit

shoved aside her fascination and managed to smile. "Yes." When Mel narrowly eyed her, she brightened her smile. "Promise."

Gazing into her eyes, Mel took her hands. "Please tell me if that vile man ever distresses you too much. I'll handle him."

Her heart warming, Kit let her smile become genuine. Mel was the dearest gentleman. So protective and sweet. If only he returned her love.

They were still staring at each other when a sharp knock sounded on his door. Sighing, Mel released her hands and strode across the room. He inhaled as he opened the door. "Elder Priestess Letitia. I wasn't expecting Paul to fetch *you*."

A brisk priestess swept into Mel's chambers. From the green, ivory, and white trim on her priest robes and her gold torc with melissae terminals, the elder healer priestess was also a witch healer. "When Paul described the man's symptoms, I thought it best if I visited myself."

Mel waved for Elder Priestess Letitia to follow him, and Kit hovered outside the bedroom door while the elder healer priestess cast the spell to invoke her healing sight and examine Father.

After a moment, Elder Priestess Letitia flicked her fingers to drop her healing sight. She shook her head. "Sadly, I can do nothing. All that's keeping him alive is a powerful geas, but it shall fade once he fulfills it."

Kit blinked. So the geas on Father must be a magical obligation rather than a magical injunction. But who had cast a geas on him? And why?

A sneer still twisting his lips, Father cackled and glared at the red chest. "I've resisted fulfilling that damned geas for sixteen years, and even though it forced me to Ormas, I'll continue resisting forever, so I'll *never* die."

The elder healer priestess pursed her lips. "Even so, your body shall continue to deteriorate, and you'll be in excruciating pain. You should fulfill your obligation so you can return to the Goddess."

While Father crudely jeered at that, Mel escorted the elder healer priestess from the bedroom then shut the door again. Mel said, "Thank you for examining him, holy lady."

Elder Priestess Letitia sighed. "I wish I could have helped, but only a soul healer could heal someone that far gone. Not that any live in Calatini."

Kit swallowed as Mel ushered the elder healer priestess out. Except a soul healer *did* live in Calatini. Should she ask Lady Ravenstone to soul-heal Father? A good daughter would. But Father was a cruel, revolting man, and even if Lady Ravenstone soul-healed him, he'd likely drink himself to death again within a few years. She set her jaw. She'd not bother Lady Ravenstone to waste her rare and extraordinary magic on him.

She hummed. Although perhaps she could discover Father's geas and fulfill it, so he wouldn't remain alive in excruciating pain. Not that Father would thank her for doing so. But at least he'd finally be at peace. Her pulse quickened. From Father's earlier glare, his geas must involve the red chest. She'd inspect it tomorrow when Mel wasn't around. She couldn't explain without revealing her lack of filial feeling and her peculiar fascination with that chest.

That evening, Kit had difficulty succumbing to slumber because she kept considering the red chest. Doubtless 'twas why she woke with a megrim throbbing behind her left eye the following morning. However, she simply gulped a megrim tonic before attending Lauds then organizing the almskitchens like normal.

Afterward, she headed to Mel's chambers instead of breakfast, her megrim pounding despite her earlier tonic. She slipped inside his spare room and eyed Father, who was barely breathing but still reeked of drink, as if he'd spent all night downing spirits even though Mel had none. If she was quiet, Father shouldn't wake from his deathlike sleep.

Kit crept to the red chest and knelt before it. Although her fingers ached to touch it, she simply studied it at first. No words or patterns adorned the wood to provide guidance, and the chest appeared sealed shut but had no locks.

Eventually, she laid her hands on the top of the chest. She gasped as the wood warmed and her hands tingled before the seal vanished and the chest clicked open. What the—?

Then Father flailed in the bed and snarled, "What are you doing, hag?"

Her megrim flaring inside her skull, she winced and turned to face him.

Father inhaled. "You opened the chest." A vicious smirk twisted his lips. "Well, daughter, whatever spell happened to *you*? Did you provoke a witch by seducing her husband? How shall you survive if you can't use your looks to entrap men like the whore you are?"

While Father continued ranting, Kit skittered across the floor beyond his reach to avoid a blow, although he was much too weak to manage one. Yet as his cruel words pelted her like stones and melded with his unceasing derision from her childhood, she couldn't make herself flee or retort because he was right. She was wicked and vulgar, and thanks to the Goddess's illusion, she no longer had her youth and sultry beauty to conceal that.

Her megrim began throbbing fiercer than ever as tears burned her eyes. Why was she even bothering to participate in temple life to discover who she was meant to be? Clearly, 'twouldn't be anything involving Mel or the other priests. She wasn't near worthy enough. They'd been called by the Goddess to serve, while she'd been cursed by her.

CHAPTER 38

When Kit didn't join him for breakfast after a quarter of an hour, Mel frowned at the dining hall entrance. Where was she? She'd appeared somewhat pale and pinched at Lauds—doubtless suffering a megrim, although it hadn't appeared a vicious one. Had it worsened while she was organizing the almskitchens, so she'd retreated to Sarah and Deacon's chambers to rest? He'd best go check.

He fetched breakfast for them then hurried back to the priest quarters. But as he neared his and his friends' chambers, he frowned at the shouting penetrating his door. The dying ravings of Kit's vile father would make it impossible for her to rest.

Mel strode inside his chambers then halted, his chest clenching. Just inside his spare room, Kit was crouched on the floor, white and frozen as she stared at the bed containing her ranting father. What was that degenerate *doing* to her?

Fire erupting in his veins, he slammed the breakfast trays on the table then burst into the spare room. As Sir Jason kept raging about his "whore of a daughter", Mel pulled Kit into his arms. How dare her father treat her so? From what little Kit had mentioned when they were children, he'd known her father had constantly insulted and belittled her, but he'd never realized how brutal her father's abuse truly was. If Sir Jason wasn't dying, he'd strangle the vicious cad.

He glared down at the shouting man. "Enough!" When Sir Jason silenced at last, Mel drew Kit closer and continued, "You're a vile and vicious drunkard who doesn't deserve a daughter as sweet and wonderful as Kit. Don't you *ever* speak to her so again."

As Sir Jason's cackle echoed in the tiny bedroom, Kit shuddered in Mel's arms, and he pressed a kiss against her brow.

Sir Jason sneered at them. "Sweet and wonderful? Clearly, my daughter's let you beneath her skirt. Surprised she bothered with a priest—but you *are* the son of a wealthy duke, and hag that she is now, she can't entrap a titled lord."

Burning to punch the supine man, Mel gritted a glacial smile instead. "You're a venal cretin with no understanding of decency or kindness. I almost pity you." He swept Kit from the room and slammed the door behind them.

His fury crumbling to ash, he halted beside the table to eye Kit. She was still white and unusually quiet with her gaze lowered and face pinched. No doubt she was reeling from her father's abuse, and her megrim was likely worse too. His jaw clenched. He must remove her from here to tend and comfort her. He placed her megrim tea and cold compress on their breakfast trays then ushered her from his chambers.

When they entered the hall, Deacon and Sarah were emerging from their chambers. Sarah frowned at them and asked, "What was that shouting?"

As Kit winced, Mel scowled and replied, "Kit's father." A dying man who'd been depleting strength he no longer had. "Could you two check on him while I tend to Kit?"

Deacon and Sarah nodded, and they bustled into his chambers while he ushered Kit into theirs. Setting the breakfast trays on the table, he frowned at the still silent Kit. "How's your head?"

Kit shrugged then muttered, "Throbbing."

Aching to kiss her brow again, he sighed. His poor Kit. "I'll make you some megrim tea while you eat."

Kit shuddered. "I'm not hungry. Excuse me." She slipped inside her bedroom and shut the door.

Mel repeated his earlier sigh. Kit needed rest, but she needed food too. She also couldn't manage her duties today, and he must remain with her. So while devouring his breakfast, he brewed her megrim tea and wrote notes to High Priest Theodag and Elder Priestess Agnes explaining their absences.

Leaving the notes on the table for Deacon and Sarah to deliver, he gathered Kit's breakfast, megrim tea, and cold compress then strode inside her bedroom. His chest clenched at her curled on her side facing the wall like a wounded child. "You must drink this and eat your porridge. Then you can rest."

Rubbing her eyes, Kit exhaled then rolled upright. "Very well."

Mel hovered as Kit donned the cold compress, drank her megrim tonic, and ate her breakfast without another word. Then he set her dishes outside her bedroom door before shutting it so they could talk without Deacon or Sarah overhearing later. He must get Kit to share her distress with him. That should help lighten it.

He sat beside Kit on the bed and began massaging her shoulders to ease her megrim, and as always, his body quickened, but he didn't spin her around to kiss her. Kit needed tenderness, not passion right now. "What happened earlier?"

Kit shuddered. "I was inspecting the red chest to discover Father's geas, and somehow he recognized me and began ranting."

Fire flared through Mel again at Sir Jason's insults as he massaged Kit's neck. "I suppose your father was always that derisive and vulgar toward you."

Her shoulders sagging, Kit sighed and nodded.

He swallowed a growl. That degenerate. How had Kit endured such rants as a tender, vulnerable girl? Brushing a kiss against her neck, he slid his fingers into her hair and massaged her scalp. "I wanted to strangle him for insulting you like that. Your father is fortunate that I'm a priest and he's dying. Otherwise, I would have."

Kit snorted a weak laugh. "At most you'd have punched him. You're too noble to ever kill anyone."

Humming, Mel massaged Kit's face. Her faith was misplaced considering the almost uncontrollable fury that had filled him earlier. Returning his hands to her shoulders, he kissed her neck again. "I would to protect you."

Kit inhaled. "You'd break your vows to the Goddess for me?"

Mel stilled, his heart wrenching. He'd do anything to protect her. Because Mother was right that he loved Kit. 'Twas why his fury at her father had been so uncontrollable, why he ached for her when they were apart, and why he always burned to kiss her. He loved Kit even though love between them was impossible because the fashionable Countess of Blaine would never marry a priest.

Shoving all that aside, he squeezed Kit's shoulders. "How's your head now?"

Kit turned around and mumbled, "Better. Mel, I'm not worth such a sacrifice."

His chest aching at her lowered gaze, he cupped her face in his hands and brushed a featherlight kiss against her lips. "Yes, you are."

Kit jerked free. "No, I'm not."

Mel frowned and recaptured her chin as his pulse flared. Damn her vile father. "Don't accept your father's venom as truth, Kit. He's a malevolent drunkard, and his cruel insults are a reflection of him, not you."

Tears shimmering in her eyes, Kit swallowed and finally raised her gaze. "But his blood runs through my veins."

Mel smiled at Kit with all the love he felt for her. Not that he could ever confess it aloud—if she even believed him, his love would only make her uncomfortable since she wanted a wealthy and titled husband.

He rubbed away the tears trembling on Kit's lashes with his thumbs. "You're so much more than his daughter or what he calls you. When you let your genuine self show, you're tender and thoughtful and throw yourself into helping others. You adore attending services worshipping the Goddess and praying in the Sun Chapel among the Goddess laurels. And you're insightful with a gift for managing anyone, from humble priests to the most influential at court."

A blush darkening her cheeks, Kit stared at him and breathed, "Oh, Mel." Then she leaned forward and kissed him.

Despite the tingling warmth flooding him, he only returned Kit's kiss for a moment before withdrawing. Although he loved her, it still wasn't appropriate since they'd never marry. Besides, she was too fragile after her father's insults and while recovering from a megrim. He released her face and rose. "Rest now. I'll fetch a chair and sit beside you."

Kit nodded then curled on her bed and soon drifted into slumber.

As she slept, Mel watched Kit rather than reading Sarah's book about prayer he'd fetched along with the chair. Dear Goddess, how he loved Kit. He'd probably loved her since he'd been transfixed by her glowing smile during her first Sext as a girl, and his love had only deepened when they'd visited poor villagers together. How could he have refused to see he loved Kit until now? He sighed. When they were children, he'd refused to think of it because they were too young. And later, because loving her was impossible—she'd been married, and once widowed, she didn't want him.

When Kit woke, he fetched luncheon for them and ensured Kit ate. Then they headed to the Sun Chapel and spent the after-noon in prayer. As they left for the dining hall for dinner, which was now before Vespers since 'twas after Plantfete, she was relaxed and almost smiling. He exhaled. Good, she'd mostly recovered from her father's cruelty this morning.

While they began their chicken chowder, Sarah eyed Kit. "How are you?"

Kit lifted a shoulder. "Better, thanks to Mel. He always takes such excellent care of me."

He almost blushed. Hopefully, Deacon and Sarah wouldn't realize why. Sarah would surely tell Kit.

Sarah nodded. "Good." She exchanged a narrow glance with Deacon. "About your father..."

His jaw tightening, Mel took Kit's hand beneath the table to support her. What had that degenerate done now?

As Sarah frowned but didn't continue, Deacon leaned toward Kit and said, "He was seizing when we arrived. We got him to the Center for Healing, but Elder Priestess Letitia said 'twas nothing they could do except house him. Your father fell into a coma, and she doubts he'll wake. I'm sorry, Kit."

Mel and Kit glanced at each other. Had her father fulfilled his geas somehow? Or was it no longer powerful enough to keep him alive?

Kit smiled at Deacon and Sarah. "'Tis fine. We knew Father was dying, and he wasn't a... good man. Thanks for getting him to the Center for Healing."

Mel scrutinized Kit, whose smile revealed nothing. Was she truly fine? So once the two of them left for Vespers, he asked, "How do you truly feel about your father?"

Grimacing, Kit shrugged. "I'm not certain yet, but perhaps I'll know when I begin helping healer priests tomorrow."

He frowned, his throat tight. But what if her father woke and raged at her again? "Maybe you should ask High Priest Theodag to help scholar or witch priests instead."

Kit hummed. "No, 'tis best if I help healer priests as planned. Despite how you found me this morning, I can usually handle Father—not that he's likely to wake."

• • •

THE FOLLOWING MORNING, Mel narrowly eyed Kit as they attended Lauds and ate breakfast, but she still appeared relaxed and insisted she was fine when he asked. He watched her for a moment when they separated, his stomach clenching. Please let seeing her despicable father again not distress her too much. Then he sighed and headed to his new study on the top floor above the chapter house to begin acting as the elder community priest of Calatini.

When he arrived, Elder Priestess Agnes pursed her lips. "At last. I half expected *another* note delaying your duties yet again."

He winced and fisted his hands in his priest robes. "I apologize. I'd a crisis to handle yesterday."

The elder priestess arched a brow. "What kind of crisis? Your note didn't explain."

Swallowing, Mel dropped into his seat behind the desk. "I'm afraid 'tis private, so I can't." Kit would hate it if he discussed her unfortunate childhood and drunkard father with anyone.

Her eyes narrowing, Elder Priestess Agnes frowned at him. "Being the elder community priest of Calatini isn't a lark you can do when you feel like it. 'Tis a vital, consuming duty."

He winced again. But Kit had needed him, and she was more important to him than his duties.

Shaking her head, the elder priestess continued, "I know you were reluctant to assume my position, but you agreed to do so, and you must see it through. As the second most influential priest in Calatini, many people are relying on you, and you can't forsake them."

Mel flushed and shifted in his seat. The Goddess *had* called him to serve, but yesterday he'd allowed his love for Kit to eclipse that calling. And he'd burned to kill her father, which violated one of the Goddess's most basic tenets. Plus, he constantly hungered to make love to Kit despite not being married, and that also violated the Goddess's rules for her priests.

He swallowed again. Loving Kit had become a distraction—

nothing should be more important to a priest than the Goddess. Not even the lady he loved. He must focus first on his duties before allowing himself to care for Kit. Perhaps he should stop joining her at services and meals to wean himself from seeing her every day. After all, once she broke the Goddess's illusion, she'd return to court, and he must prepare himself for that.

His chest hollow, Mel clenched his hands in his priest robes again. Surely if he focused first on his duties, he'd not need to quit seeing Kit. And now that he knew he loved her, he'd be better able to control his hunger for her. Spending more time in prayer would help him do both as well as reaffirm his relationship with the Goddess. However, he should pray alone rather than joining Kit in the Sun Chapel every morning. 'Twould be much too tempting.

He made himself smile at the elder priestess. "I do understand that people are relying on me, and I'll do better focusing first on my duties in the future."

Elder Priestess Agnes hummed. "I hope so. There have been so many delays regarding you assuming my duties that I'd begun to fear Theodag and I had chosen the wrong priest to become the next elder community priest of Calatini."

Mel winced once again. For the elder priestess to fear that, he'd definitely been neglecting his duties. "You haven't, I promise. Shall we review the reports our assistants prepared for today?"

The elder priestess nodded, and they began to work. Yet even though he'd vowed to focus first on his duties, he kept worrying about Kit being at the Center for Healing with her father. But he managed to bury that whenever he did, so it didn't impede him acting as the elder community priest for the first time. However, after saying farewell to Elder Priestess Agnes, he bolted to the dining hall to see Kit.

CHAPTER 39

*J*ust before she left the Center for Healing, Kit allowed herself to approach the bed where Father lay comatose. She swallowed. Except for the faint movement of his chest, he appeared dead already. Yet no tears burned her eyes or clogged her throat. Instead, she could truly breathe for the first time since learning Father was in Ormas. She was a horrible daughter.

Elder Priestess Letitia joined her and rubbed her back. "Sarah mentioned he's your father. I'd have been less blunt yesterday if I'd known."

Kit almost winced. "'Tis fine. We're not close, and I appreciated your candor. How long do you think he'll survive?"

The elder healer priestess sighed. "A day or two. The geas keeping him alive is gone, and his liver quit functioning some time ago, leading to swelling inside his brain which caused his coma. Once that happens, death isn't far behind. I'm sorry."

Humming, Kit nodded. So Father had fulfilled his geas somehow, but what was it? Doubtless she'd never know for certain. She smiled at Elder Priestess Letitia. "Thank you. I know Father shall enjoy the best possible care here, and I'm grateful for that.

I'll return midmorning tomorrow to continue visiting healer priests."

Then she headed to the dining hall, and as soon as she arrived, Mel grasped her hands and asked, "How are you?"

She shrugged. Better than she should be, considering her father was dying. "All right. Helping healer priests was interesting. I started with the ones without magic."

Mel frowned and leaned toward her. "Did you see your father?"

Kit nodded and coolly told Mel what Elder Priestess Letitia had said.

His deep-brown eyes dark with concern, Mel squeezed her hands. "That must be distressing."

She sighed. Not particularly. The distressing part had been Father's final derisive rant, but Mel had halted him and defended her then helped her recover afterward. Mel's solicitude yesterday made her ache to hold him and never let go. But they were in public, and he didn't love her like she loved him. So instead, she flashed a wry smile and slid her hands free. "Hearing about my father's imminent death isn't the same for me as 'twould be for you. Your father is actually a decent gentleman, and he loves you. Now, shall we eat? Sarah and Deacon are waiting for us."

Mel's jaw tightened, but he nodded, and they joined their friends. Thankfully, no one mentioned Father as they ate their mushroom spinach soup and creamy egg custard, although Mel studied her with a worried frown throughout dinner.

THE FOLLOWING DAY, Kit returned to the Center for Healing and helped healer priests without magic again then checked on Father before she left, but he appeared unchanged. Her third day at the Center for Healing began the same as her first two until the elder healer priestess joined her midmorning.

Elder Priestess Letitia embraced her. "I'm afraid your father just returned to the Goddess. My condolences."

Kit briefly embraced the elder healer priestess back before striding to Father's bed. Her chest hollow but eyes dry, she stared at his wasted lifeless body for several lengthy moments. 'Twas appalling how little grief she felt for him. She murmured to the elder healer priestess beside her, "Do you mind if I leave for the rest of the day? I must arrange the funeral."

Elder Priestess Letitia embraced her again. "Of course not. If you require more time to grieve, please let me know."

Kit managed a faint smile. "I'll return tomorrow morning, unless the funeral is then."

She left the Center for Healing and headed to the Sun Chapel. Inhaling the cinnaspice-apple fragrance of the Goddess's laurels, she knelt and prayed for Father until her knees hurt, but hollowness still suffused her rather than the peace she usually felt here. She rose and drifted to Mel's new study on the top floor above the chapter house, not far from High Priest Theodag's study. Inhaling, she tapped on the door then slipped inside when Mel called to enter.

Behind a desk strewn with papers, Mel leapt upright. "Kit, what is it?"

Her gaze darting toward Elder Priestess Agnes, who was eyeing her with a frown, Kit swallowed and replied, "Father died."

Mel hurried around the desk and pulled her into his arms. "Oh, Kit."

Although she ached to bury her face in Mel's chest, she made herself step back since the elder community priestess was watching.

Mel turned toward the wizened priestess. "I must take an early luncheon to help Kit."

Elder Priestess Agnes inclined her head. "Just remember you've a mirror call with the elder community priestess of Mage-haven late this afternoon—the one we rescheduled from the last time you skipped your duties." Her face softening, the elder community priestess turned to Kit and murmured, "My sympathies for your loss."

Once they nodded at Elder Priestess Agnes, Mel swept Kit from his study. He squeezed her arm as they headed downstairs. "We must find Oliver to finalize arrangements. I hope you don't mind, but I spoke to him about performing your father's funeral after you told me his death was imminent."

Exhaling, she almost smiled. Mel was always so thoughtful. "Thanks for arranging that."

They found Oliver, and the venerable death priest gently asked her if she wanted a body funeral or an ash funeral, where she wished the funeral held, and if they must wait for additional guests. She chose an ash funeral held in the Sun Chapel with just her and Mel since Father had no one besides her. After Oliver said he'd arrange everything and meet them in the Sun Chapel, Mel escorted her there.

Once they settled in the first pew, Mel wrapped an arm about her. "How are you feeling?"

Kit sighed and laid her head on Mel's shoulder. He knew what Father had been and was too compassionate to judge her for admitting the truth. "Numb, mostly. But also relieved."

Mel brushed a kiss on her brow. "Understandable given how he hurt you over the years. Now he can't."

She swallowed, her throat tightening. Exactly. "But I'm ashamed how little genuine grief I feel for Father."

Mel kissed her brow again. "You shouldn't be. Anyone in your situation would have trouble grieving." He squeezed her shoulders. "*I'd* probably feel angry at all he done to hurt me and how he never felt remorse over any of it."

Kit blinked, but before she could reply, Oliver strode in with a white urn painted with verdant vines. She sat upright but didn't separate from Mel as the death priest opened the funeral with a prayer.

While Oliver read the sacred words about the Goddess's love

for her children and returning to her arms in death, Kit studied the urn containing Father's ashes and inhaled the Goddess laurels' fragrance. Witch priests must have incinerated Father for his ashes to be ready so quickly. She needed to thank Deacon and the other witch priests later. Having Father's funeral today was a relief.

Then without the usual uplifting hymn, Oliver began an eloquent sermon about death and grief and joyful remembrance. Unlike when he'd performed Lord Blaine's funeral almost two years ago, this sermon wasn't interspersed with anecdotes about the deceased gathered from the family. She almost snorted. Not that 'twere any happy anecdotes the death priest could include.

For the first time, tears burned her eyes, and her throat closed. Why couldn't Father have been a different man? True, the servants had whispered of some tragedy in his youth that he blamed his father for and had precipitated his drinking and cruelty. But why hadn't he released his bitterness so he could forgive the past and enjoy life again? With such bitterness filling his heart, Father had been unable to love those left to him, including his only daughter who'd no one else.

Her tears scorched her cheeks. If Father had let her, she'd have loved him the way she ached to be loved. They could have cared for each other and spent time together and been happy. Father wouldn't have drowned himself in drink, so he'd not have died in such lingering pain before becoming old. He'd still be alive, and she'd not be an orphan with no family at twenty-four.

When Oliver ended the funeral without the hymn of peace or asking if she wished to speak like family members often did, Kit wiped her face then accepted Father's urn from the death priest. Father had made his choice to cling to his bitterness, but she'd not make the same mistake. Although she'd come perilously close with her blind pursuit of wealth and status despite her heart lying elsewhere as well as with her struggle to break the Goddess's illusion. She stiffened her spine. She must focus on the joy and love in her life and becoming who she was meant to be.

Staying at the Great Temple and participating in temple life had helped, but she still had more learning to do since the Goddess's illusion hadn't ended.

Staring at Father's urn in her lap, she let his scathing derision and drunken cruelty echo through her until none was left. Then she whispered, "I forgive you, Father. I hope you're happier in death than you were in life."

Mel squeezed her shoulders. "What's that?"

Warmth filling her at Mel's tender concern, Kit smiled and shook her head. "Simply saying farewell."

Helping her rise, Mel scrutinized her then relaxed and nodded. He sighed as he ushered her from the Sun Chapel. "Sadly, I must return to my duties, although I hate to leave you."

She let herself kiss Mel's cheek. "I understand. Thanks for staying with me. Enduring all this without your support would have been much harder."

Her heart fluttered in her chest when Mel cupped her face and began leaning toward her. But just before he kissed her, he shook himself and released her. "Of course."

Once Mel left, Kit devoured a late luncheon before finding Paul and asking the temple priest to find someone she could hire to travel to Childes to spread Father's ashes at Sutton Manor. Then she wrote her bookkeeper informing him her father had died and asking him to inquire about Father's will.

She frowned. If she'd inherited Sutton Manor as expected, she'd need to quit supporting her charities to repair the estate. Although Lord Blaine's generous allowance likely wouldn't be enough. But she must do what she could—even though she'd no love for Sutton Manor after her childhood there with Father, she'd a duty to the people the manor supported.

THE FOLLOWING morning when Kit was about to leave the Sun Chapel to join the healer priests, High Priest Theodag sat beside her with a frown creasing his austere face. "I was sorry to hear about your father yesterday. How are you doing?"

She smiled at the high priest, warmed by his concern. "I'm fine."

High Priest Theodag slanted her a narrow glance. "The day Mel wrote me about your megrim was when your father arrived, wasn't it? You should have told me. I could have delayed your visits to healer priests so you could have time with your father."

Kit suppressed a shudder at that. "Father actually arrived the evening before, and I'd already had enough time with him—he's what inflamed my megrim."

The high priest leaned toward her. "I see. Do you require some days away from helping priests?"

Swallowing, she shook her head and rose. "Thanks to Mel, I could handle everything yesterday, and I grieved enough at the funeral."

His gaze probing, High Priest Theodag nodded and rose too. "Very well. Then you'll finish helping healer priests tomorrow and begin helping scholar priests the day after. But if you decide you need time later, please let me know."

After thanking the high priest, Kit headed to the Center for Healing and helped healer priests with magic until she joined Mel, Sarah, and Deacon for dinner.

During dessert, Mel arched his brows at her over his karamel cinnaspice pudding. "I forgot to ask earlier, but what did you want to do with your father's belongings? They're still in my spare room."

Kit inhaled, her fingers tingling. She could finally open the red chest and discover its secrets. "Bring them to my bedroom so I can go through everything."

After Vespers, Mel deposited the large chest and bulging satchel beside her bed. "Do you want me to stay while you go through your father's belongings?"

Her gaze fixed on the red chest, she almost blushed. Mel

would notice her peculiar fascination with the chest if he stayed. "Thanks, but I can manage alone."

Eyeing her, Mel hummed but nodded then left.

Once he did, Kit forced herself to empty the satchel first, which only contained a set of decrepit clothes and several empty flasks. No items worth saving or donating.

Then she knelt before the red chest and laid her hands on top of the wood, her pulse quickening. Unlike before, nothing unusual happened. She flipped open the lid and inhaled.

Rather than bottles of spirits, the chest was stuffed with a vibrant, rolled carpet and dozens of letters. She extracted the carpet and unfurled it. The carpet was just large enough for two people to sit on, but 'twas exquisite and filled her tiny bedroom with rich color. From the Tsarkan Empire given the gold, ivory, and navy arabesques woven into the mostly crimson carpet. How had Father afforded such a luxury? And why hadn't he sold it to fund his drinking?

Kit turned back to the many letters inside the chest. Written in a delicate hand, each of the letters bore her name and a date on the front. She rifled through them—the oldest was dated her eighth natalday when the red chest had arrived, while the newest was dated her most recent natalday two weeks ago. But there were many more letters than for just her nataldays.

She gaped at the many letters, Tsarkan carpet, and red chest. Clearly, 'twere all hers. When the merchant had brought the chest, he'd not been striding toward her to locate Father, but to give her the chest. Yet Father had kept it from her for all these years, even though the chest had been sealed until she'd touched it. Her heart twisted. Another instance of Father's cruelty.

With trembling hands, Kit opened the oldest letter. 'Twas merely a page, but the delicate hand was smeared by tears throughout. She gasped as she began to read.

My dear daughter—

Happy eighth natalday, dearest Kit. 'Tis been nearly seven years since I last saw you, and I've grieved every day we've spent apart. How I love you, my darling daughter! Please don't hate me for leaving you behind. 'Twas never my intention, and I'd have returned if I could.

I'm sorry for not writing until now, but it took us years to discover how to circumvent the ward spell about you, and even longer to afford the magical items necessary. I'll explain more of our unfortunate tale once you're old enough to understand, but please forgive me for all that you've suffered since I was forced to leave without you.

I ache to get to know the wonderful girl you've become in the years we've been apart. If you feel the same, please write back and place your letter inside the red chest. Not only is it spelled so only you can open it, but it also acts as a transport box for us to magically send items to each other. I eagerly await your first letter.

All my love,

Mother

Kit dropped the letter as if burnt by a fire witch's mirror. Mother was *alive*?! Father had always said she was dead. Kit shuddered. But invariably with such a savage sneer. She'd assumed because he despised Mother, but his sneer had been because he'd been *lying*. How could even Father have been so cruel as to keep a mother from her daughter?

She swallowed as burning tears blurred her vision. She still had some family left after all—a mother who seemed to love and want her more than Father ever had. So why had Mother abandoned her? She snatched the next letter and tore it open. She spent the rest of the evening devouring Mother's many letters, finally discovering the truth about her parents as well as the Tsarkan carpet.

When she finished, 'twas later than she typically went to bed, but she couldn't have slept not knowing everything. Hopefully, rising to attend Lauds at dawn wouldn't be too difficult. She smiled into her pillow. And hopefully, she could resist showing Mel her letters until tomorrow evening after their duties.

CHAPTER 40

When he and Kit met outside his chambers to attend Lauds, Mel blinked at her. Although shadows lingered beneath her eyes, a bright smile curved her lips. She must have stayed up late going through her father's satchel and chest, but whatever she'd found had pleased her. "What was in your father's belongings?"

Kit beamed, making his pulse surge, and he almost leaned forward to kiss her and taste her joy. Why had he ever assumed he could control his hunger for her better now that he knew 'twas because he loved her?

Then Kit replied, "Letters from my mother mostly. I'll show you tonight after Vespers."

He grinned and squeezed her hand. No wonder Kit was excited—she'd known nearly nothing about the lady who'd died before she could talk. "You can show me now."

Shaking her head, Kit tugged him down the hall. "'Twould take too long, and we've duties to attend to."

Mel nodded. True, and they must focus first on those, no matter their own needs. He couldn't neglect his duties again.

So after he'd spent the day acting as the elder community

priest while she helped healer priests, they ate dinner and attended Vespers with Deacon and Sarah, but Kit tugged him to leave as soon as the service ended rather than remaining with their friends to talk to people. She was definitely eager to show him her mother's letters.

In her bedroom, Kit knelt before the large red chest and flipped open the lid, revealing a Tsarkan carpet covered with stacks of letters. "Mother sent me all this, but Father cruelly hid it from me."

Blinking, Mel sat beside Kit. The countless letters each had her name and a date on the front. "Your mother wrote that many letters to you before she died?" Her death couldn't have been sudden then—perhaps she'd suffered a wasting disease of some kind.

Kit laughed. "No, Mother isn't dead. The red chest is a transport box that she ensured a merchant acquaintance brought on my eighth natalday, and she's been sending me letters with it ever since."

He gaped at Kit. "Your mother is still *alive*?" When Kit bobbed a nod, fire flashed through him. "And she abandoned you as an infant to your degenerate father's 'tender' care?"

Sighing, Kit grimaced. "She didn't intend to, and Father made it impossible for her to take me with her." Kit sifted through the letters then handed him one. "Here, this one explains everything."

Mel frowned but accepted the letter dated shortly after Kit's marriage to Lord Blaine and began to read. Her parents had been forced to wed when they were teenagers despite loving others, and when that caused the village girl her father loved to kill herself and their unborn child, he became a cruel, bitter drunkard. A year after Kit's birth, her mother had been planning to take Kit and flee with her childhood love, who'd become a smuggler in Dracwyn to support them. But Kit's father had discovered their plans, so he'd purchased a ward spell on Kit from a Rhiannon-descendant witch that prevented her mother or anyone working for her from coming within a mile of Kit or delivering anything for her. No matter Kit's mother's pleas and promises to remain, Kit's father swore that mother and daughter would never see each other again, so eventually Kit's mother and her beloved left in despair. However, Kit's mother remained in contact with Sutton Manor's cook to know how Kit fared, and when her beloved built his fortune, she indirectly sent an enchanted chest that could circumvent the ward spell because 'twas a transport box with a geas obliging whomever possessed it to give it to Kit. But Kit's father had foiled that by hiding the chest for years even with its geas. Yet Kit's mother had continued to write, hoping one day Kit would get the chest.

Mel's ribs squeezed as he returned the letter to Kit, who'd suffered the most from her parents' disastrous marriage. But with her father dead and knowing the truth at last, she could finally get to know the mother who loved her. And Kit deserved to enjoy such love. He smiled at her. "Have you written your mother yet?"

Kit shook her head. "'Twas too late when I finished all her letters last night. Besides, I hardly know what to write."

He swallowed. Doubtless because Kit had no experience with parental love. Damn her cruel father. Taking her hand, he kissed her palm. "Whatever you write shall be fine as long as 'tis the truth. Your mother already loves you, and she'll love you even more when she gets to know you."

Sighing, Kit curved her fingers against his cheek. "But what truth do I write her? Revealing my childhood with Father shall only distress her, and explaining I'm hiding at the Great Temple because of the Goddess's illusion sounds odd."

Mel kissed her palm again. "Start with small truths. Remember, you've time to share more once you're better acquainted." When Kit grimaced and lowered her hand, he nodded at the rolled carpet to distract her. "Why did your mother send you a Tsarkan carpet?"

Kit smiled. "'Tis a flying carpet that Mother had enchanted to only work for me. She sent it for my fifteenth natalday, hoping we could circumvent the ward spell if *I* came to her."

He hummed and eyed the flying carpet. Such a faegift was beyond any but the most affluent—Kit's mother's beloved must have done *very* well as a smuggler. "Depends on how the ward spell was cast, I suppose. A thorough witch would have prevented that."

Pursing her lips, Kit sighed. "I fear the witch who created my ward spell was quite thorough. Mother wrote they visited every few years to test if the ward spell had weakened, but it never did. Not even when they visited Ormas after Lord Blaine's death." She tilted her head. "I'm surprised the veiled witch didn't mention the ward spell when we visited her. I'd like to visit again tomorrow evening to ask about it."

Mel nodded. Plus, the veiled witch could easily break the spell that had kept Kit and her mother apart for over two decades. But even appearing an old lady, Kit shouldn't visit that part of Ormas alone. "I'll join you."

Kit smiled at him. "Thanks." She tidied her mother's letters then closed the red chest. "I'd better begin my first letter to Mother."

When he and Kit left her bedroom, Deacon and Sarah glanced up from their chairs by their bookcase. Sarah asked, "Why did you leave Vespers so abruptly?"

Kit explained about her mother's letters, although not the details of her parents' disastrous marriage or about the magic involved except the transport box. Then she said, "I'm going to write back to Mother now."

As Deacon grinned, Sarah leapt up and embraced Kit. "How exciting!"

While Kit wrote at the table, Mel sat beside her and read the book of Sarah's he'd started during Kit's last megrim.

Once Kit finished her letter, she murmured, "Would you mind reading this before I send it?"

He swiftly shut his book to read Kit's letter.

Dear Mother—

When I received the red chest after Father's recent death, I was so excited to learn you were still alive. I devoured all your letters—thank you for sending them for years without any reply. I'm moved you learned how I fared through Cook Ruth since you left. (Although your association *does* explain why she asked to join me when I left Sutton Manor even though that cost her position as head cook. I always believed 'twas because Father could no longer pay her.)

You probably haven't received any updates about me recently—I hope you weren't too worried. On Longnight, I decided to leave court to reflect on my life. The Duchess of Childes's middle son Priest Melchior, a childhood friend, helped me stay at the Great Temple so I could do so. I've been very happy during the months I've stayed here.

Like you, I ache to get to know you and would love to exchange letters. I can't wait to learn more about your life in Dracwyn with Christopher and my younger siblings. Perhaps if we can figure out how to break the ward spell, we can do more than write to each other one day.

Love,

Kit

Mel smiled at Kit as he returned her letter. "An excellent start. Your mother shall be ecstatic to receive it."

Licking her lips, Kit sighed and rose. "I hope so. I'd best send this before my nerves force me to rewrite it."

He rose as well, his gaze on Kit's lips. If Deacon and Sarah weren't nearby, he'd have kissed her until she forgot her nerves. Not appropriate between them, but he loved her too much to resist.

. . .

As they walked to Rhiannon's Veils after Vespers the following evening, Mel arched his brows at Kit, who'd been increasingly tense all day. "Any response from your mother yet?"

Kit swallowed, her face tightening. "No."

He threaded his fingers through Kit's to hearten her. "She's been writing for sixteen years without a reply, so she probably doesn't check her transport box every day. She'll write you as soon as she does."

Kit eked a tremulous smile. "Thanks, Mel."

To distract Kit, he asked her about her final day helping healer priests, and they discussed that until they reached the witch shop. He inhaled when he ushered her inside. Lit by a few dim witchlights, the veiled witch's mostly empty shop was even more eerie in the darkness of evening.

The veiled witch sashayed through her glass beads then stilled, her exotically lined eyes scrutinizing Kit. "Are you here for further advice about the Goddess's illusion? I doubt I can provide any."

Gripping his hand, Kit shook her head. "I wanted to ask about the ward spell cast on me as an infant to keep my mother and I apart. You didn't mention it when we visited before."

The veiled witch's brows rose. "Because there isn't a ward spell about you."

As Kit stiffened, Mel frowned at the veiled witch and said, "There must be. Kit's mother attempted to visit her after Lord Blaine died, but the ward spell prevented it."

Her bracelets and tiny bells jingling, the veiled witch flicked her fingers. "Doubtless there was one *then*." A chuckle undulated her black veils. "But a holy spell like the Goddess's illusion would have overpowered and broken a spell created by a human witch, even a powerful one that had lasted for decades."

Kit straightened, her face alight. "Truly?" When the veiled witch nodded, Kit swept a curtsy. "Thank you again for your wisdom, madam witch."

Smiling, Mel handed the veiled witch three gold coins before escorting Kit from Rhiannon's Veils. He grinned at Kit as they returned to the Great Temple. "What exciting news. You can meet your mother whenever you wish."

Kit beamed. "I know. I'll write Mother another letter tonight informing her the ward spell is gone." Her face dimmed. "Although perhaps we should wait to meet until after the Goddess's illusion is broken too. I don't want Mother's first view of me to be as a crone or have to explain why the Goddess felt compelled to make me appear one."

Even though they were in public, he halted and captured Kit's face in his palms. "Your mother shan't care about that. No one who loves you would."

Kit's lips parted as she gazed up at him. "Do you believe so?"

His heart twisting, Mel swallowed. "I know so."

Unable to resist any longer, he kissed Kit. When she threaded her arms about his neck and her delectable cinnaspice scent swamped him, he shuddered and kissed her harder. How he needed her. Not that she appeared to mind.

A slamming carriage door jolted him to their surroundings. He was kissing Kit on a public street. Even if they'd been married, 'twouldn't be appropriate. His body aching, he forced himself to release her and step back. Panting, they stared at each other.

Then Kit lifted her chin. "You needn't kiss me to prove the Goddess's illusion doesn't matter."

Mel winced. Except he hadn't. But explaining that he'd kissed her because he loved her was impossible. Thankfully, she'd not realized his love from his revealing words before he'd kissed her. He waved for her to proceed him. "We should continue back to the Great Temple. We've an early morning tomorrow."

Kit's mouth tightened. "We always do." Then they walked the rest of the way back in silence.

The following morning, he and Kit were still quiet when they attended Lauds together, but at dinner she was glowing with excitement again. And surely not because she'd begun helping scholar priests. So while they walked to Vespers behind Deacon and Sarah, Mel asked Kit, "Did you receive a response from your mother?"

Kit grinned. "Yes, and she was effusively elated—much more than my short letters deserved." Her grin fading, Kit smoothed her dress. "Since the ward spell is gone, she asked if I'd access to a communication mirror for a mirror call."

He gripped his priest robes to avoid touching Kit to ease her nerves. He'd surely kiss her again if he did. "I've a communication mirror in my study. You can use it to call your mother whenever you like."

Glancing at him, Kit gulped a breath. "You genuinely believe Mother shan't care about the Goddess's illusion?" At his firm nod, she exhaled. "Then I'll write her after Vespers to explain about that and ask if she can meet around luncheon the day after tomorrow. I'd rather our first call have constraints in case it goes poorly."

Mel hummed. It wouldn't, but Kit wouldn't believe that until it happened. "I'll fetch food from the dining hall for you so you've more time to talk, and I'll be there afterward to discuss how it went."

Kit smiled at him. "Thanks, I appreciate that."

But after Vespers, Paul scurried over to Mel with a note from Father. Mel frowned as he read the brief note requesting they meet for luncheon the day after tomorrow. He must refuse to be here to support Kit.

Kit eyed him. "What is it?"

He sighed. "Father wants to meet for luncheon when you have your mirror call with your mother. I must see if we can meet another day."

Kit shook her head. "Your father rarely requests you join him for luncheon. 'Tis probably important—you should go." When he began to protest, she frowned at him. "I'll be fine. We can talk after you return."

Mel sighed again. From Kit's fierce frown, she was determined to be stubborn about this. Hopefully, he could keep luncheon with Father brief. He'd even take a carriage to ensure he'd return quicker. "Very well, I'll accept his invitation."

CHAPTER 41

Kit gulped a bracing breath as she left the Center of Learning for her first mirror call with Mother. Oh, Goddess, what if Mother decided she couldn't love a strange daughter after all these years apart or was disgusted by her crone appearance?

When Kit slipped inside Mel's study, Elder Priestess Agnes gave her a warm nod before saying to Mel, "Since your luncheon with the Duke of Childes might run long, I'll wait to return until your mirror call with the elder community priestess of Golddell late this afternoon. And I'll handle your earlier mirror calls from Peaceful Minds."

Mel nodded at Elder Priestess Agnes. "Thank you." Once the elder community priestess bustled out, he grasped Kit's hands with a concerned frown. "Are you certain I shouldn't stay to support you? I can meet Father for luncheon another day."

Her tension easing at Mel's solicitude, she smiled and squeezed his hands. "I promise I'll be fine. Go enjoy luncheon with your father."

Mel sighed but released her. He gestured toward the curtain to the right of his desk. "My communication mirror is there behind the curtain. I'll ask a temple priest to bring you luncheon on my way out."

Kit swallowed, her stomach quivering anew. Doubtless she'd be unable to eat, but Mel wouldn't leave if she shared that. So instead, she brightened her smile and nodded.

After a final penetrating glance, Mel strode from his study.

She exhaled and sank into his chair, letting her shoulders sag now that she was alone. Should she call Mother straightaway, or should she attempt to eat first? She studied her gnarled-looking hands that almost trembled. She might faint if she didn't eat first.

Unable to remain still, she leapt upright and paced as she waited. She practiced what she'd say to Mother when she finally managed to call. Then Paul brought her luncheon, and she made herself eat her bean soup, although her stomach roiled with every spoonful.

Afterward, she inhaled to steady herself and drew the curtain covering Mel's communication mirror. Extracting Mother's last letter to check her mirror's call signature, Kit chanted a brief spell and waved to activate Mel's mirror. She gripped her hands in her lap as the mirror glowed white then cleared to reveal a lady with a face achingly like hers before the Goddess's illusion, except for the older lady's ash-brown hair, clear-blue eyes, and the faint lines about those eyes. Definitely her mother, although her coloring was all Father's.

Kit swallowed with a tremulous smile. "Hello, Mother."

Mother blinked several times then began to sob.

Her heart squeezing, Kit frowned and leaned forward. Her poor mother appeared overwrought.

Then Mother wiped her face and flashed a sweet smile despite the tears still trickling down her cheeks. "Hello, Kit. 'Tis wonderful to finally see you again. You were so tiny the last time —but you're all grown now."

As Mother's tears resurged, Kit quirked a wry smile and drawled to cheer her, "Rather more grown than I should be, thanks to the Goddess's illusion. Anyone looking at us would think I'm *your* mother."

Mother burbled a laugh as her tears subsided and wiped her face again. "True, I suppose. So why did the Goddess bless you with that illusion? Even with your explanation, I was somewhat confused about why appearing old would help you become who you were meant to be."

Almost grimacing, Kit shifted in her seat. Then she confessed, "Because I was using my youth and sultry beauty to pursue all the wrong things. My fashionable life at court was empty, and I was unhappy even though my stubborn pride wouldn't let me admit it. I needed to stay at the Great Temple," and be close to Mel again, "to see that."

Tilting her head, Mother beamed. "Somehow I'm not surprised you much prefer your life at the Great Temple. Ruth always wrote how you adored attending services worshipping the Goddess as a girl. She was convinced you were going to become a priestess one day, especially after you began visiting poor villagers."

Kit lowered her gaze, her chest aching as Father's scathing derision when she was twelve echoed through her. "I do enjoy worshipping the Goddess, but I'm not someone she'd call to serve as a priestess."

Mother hummed. "I don't see why she wouldn't. You're devoted to the Goddess, and you've quietly donated much of your allowance to charities for years."

Her gaze jerking upward, Kit stared at Mother in the communication mirror. She knew about that?

A gentle smile curving her lips, Mother continued, "So you're devoted to helping the Goddess's children as well. But I suppose you'd know better than I if the Goddess called you to serve as a priestess."

Kit stilled. "Did Ruth tell you about those donations? How did she find out? I thought no one knew."

Mother shook her head. "No, when we visited Ormas after

Lord Blaine's death, Christopher," her voice warmed and eyes glowed at her beloved's name, "hired a former magic marshal to investigate you so we could discover a new way to circumvent the ward spell."

Kit exhaled a sigh. Someone who'd once policed magical crimes for the Ministry of Magic could have easily discovered her anonymous donations. But others wouldn't have.

Smiling brighter but with tears shimmering in her eyes, Mother held up a small moving portrait of Kit dancing in a crimson ballgown with Lord Blaine. "The former magic marshal even acquired this likeness of you from your first season then enchanted it. Seeing you so joyful and vibrant has been a great comfort to me."

Scrutinizing the moving portrait, Kit inclined her head. She'd worn that ballgown at the first ball she'd hosted for court. She'd rented a tenth-century assembly room and decorated it with magical facsimiles of Lord Blaine's art collection because her husband disliked entertaining and had refused to host a ball at Blaine House. Her unique setting and decorations had impressed court and started her reputation for hosting exceptional court events. But during her first ball's opening waltz, she'd not known that yet and had been practically ill with nerves, although she'd feigned joy remarkably well. She almost smiled. However, 'twas good her false joy had comforted Mother.

As Mother set aside the moving portrait, Kit swallowed and asked, "After I married Lord Blaine, why didn't you send another transport box with a geas to circumvent the ward spell? Father couldn't have foiled it then."

Her smile fading as her tears burgeoned, Mother winced. "The Rhiannon-descendant witch who enchanted your chest said that we couldn't ever risk another. Christopher and I had to give our blood for the spell to enchant it, and she said that a second one might kill us. We couldn't leave your brothers and sister orphans."

Aching to reach through the communication mirror to

squeeze Mother's hands, Kit smiled at her instead. "Of course not. And in the end, the first one did succeed—Father was just stubborn enough to resist the geas until he was dying."

Mother's tears cascaded down her cheeks. "Because he was so terribly bitter. I hurt your father dreadfully during our unfortunate marriage."

Kit pursed her lips. And Father had been determined to return that hurt tenfold. "He clung to his bitterness until it poisoned his life as well as the lives of everyone around him. Although difficult and scandalous, he should have agreed to dissolving your marriage once you both reached the age of majority. Considering you and Father were underage when forced to marry, the priests likely would have granted a marriage dissolution if you both requested it. Then you could have married again and found happiness with others."

Continuing to cry, Mother shook her head. "Your father didn't wish to marry again. He didn't believe he could love anyone after what happened with his beloved Sally. And if he could never be happy, he didn't want me to be either. After all, I betrayed him by never forgetting my first love and planning to flee with you."

Kit grimaced. A compassionate gentleman would have released such a miserable wife. Although if Father had been compassionate, Mother probably wouldn't have planned to flee. She frowned at Mother, whose tears hadn't slowed. Surely 'twasn't healthy to cry so much.

Before she could ease Mother's tears, a gentleman's voice rumbled, "Elinor, are you all right?"

Her tears drying at last, Mother beamed at him over the communication mirror. "You know I can't help crying whether I'm happy or sad."

The gentleman, who must be Mother's Christopher, offered her a pocketcloth from behind the mirror. His tone loving, he replied, "Or when you sense others are, my darling watering pot."

Still beaming, Mother dried her face. "'Tis fortunate you like getting wet then." She returned her radiant gaze to Kit. "Would you care to meet Christopher?"

Kit smiled, warmth filling her at Mother's obvious love for Christopher. He clearly made her much happier than Father ever had. "I'd enjoy that."

A sturdy gentleman with faded blond hair and warm brown eyes, Christopher sat beside Mother and wrapped his arm about her shoulders. As Mother nestled against him, he smiled at Kit. His smile was almost as kind as Mel's, although a hint of daring gleamed in his eyes as befitted a successful smuggler. A perfect match and protector for a lady as sweet and gentle as Mother.

Christopher leaned toward Kit. "I'm pleased to meet you at last." His smile fading, he sighed. "Although I must apologize for stealing your mother away from you."

Kit returned Christopher's earlier smile. Definitely a decent and thoughtful gentleman like Mel. "You and Mother couldn't have known how Father would pursue revenge above all else."

Christopher grimaced. "We should have guessed, given how he'd already treated your mother."

Humming, Kit shook her head. Except Father's stubborn bitterness was doubtless unfathomable to both Mother and Christopher. Letting her smile warm, she leaned toward them. "I'm simply glad you two could build a happy life together. And provided me with the siblings I always wished I had."

More tears flooding her eyes, Mother drooped in Christopher's arms. "If only we'd fled at once rather than meeting to arrange the final details, you'd have grown up with them."

Kit stiffened. But then she'd not have grown up with Mel. She wouldn't have met the most compassionate, perceptive, and diligent gentleman she'd ever known. She never would have shared the joy of attending services or visiting poor villagers with him. And she never would have loved him.

As Christopher squeezed Mother's shoulders, Kit swallowed to ease her clenched throat. Knowing and loving Mel was one of the bedrocks of her life, along with her childhood with Father and worshipping the Goddess. Because of Mel, she knew how to love and how to serve others. Because of her childhood, she was strong and understood suffering. And because of the Goddess, she could see the glory of life and feel peace. Who would she be without two of those bedrocks? Would she be happily married to a Dracwyn smuggler with a passel of children? Her stomach tightened. Children who weren't Mel's. She swallowed again. She'd be a stranger if Mother and Christopher had taken her from Childes as an infant.

She flashed a bright grin to hearten Mother. "We mustn't mourn the past, but instead take joy in what we have now. The Goddess had reasons for allowing everything to happen as it did."

Brushing away her tears as Christopher smiled, Mother chuckled and straightened her shoulders then said, "Not surprising someone who enjoys staying at the Goddess's Great Temple would say that. Are you certain you shouldn't be a priestess?"

Her heart twisting, Kit clung to her grin. "Quite certain." She glanced at the clock in Mel's study. "Unfortunately, I must go. I've duties at the Center of Learning to attend to this afternoon."

Mother sighed and leaned forward. "Before you go, we must arrange our next mirror call."

Kit shifted in her seat. Except her duties at the Great Temple would make that challenging. "I'm not certain when we can. The communication mirror belongs to my friend Mel, who's acting as the elder community priest of Calatini. I must check with him about when 'tis free."

Mother and Christopher traded a glance, then Mother asked, "Mel as in Melchior? Your childhood friend who helped you stay at the Great Temple?" At Kit's nod, Mother smiled. "We'd very much like to meet him next time."

Suppressing a blush, Kit nodded again. Was her love for Mel so obvious that her long-lost mother could already see it? "He'd like to meet you too. But before our next mirror call, we can exchange letters with the red chest."

Mother grinned. "I'll write tomorrow, and you can reply the day after."

Kit returned Mother's grin, light suffusing her. "Sounds good."

Still grinning, Mother blinked back the tears shimmering in her eyes again. "I love you, Kit."

Kit swallowed as tears pricked her eyes as well. No one had told her that before, especially not Father. She beamed. "I love you too, Mother."

After exchanging farewells with Mother and Christopher, she waved her hand to deactivate the communication mirror, which glowed white before clearing to reflect Mel's study. She glanced at the clock again then sighed. If only she could remain to tell Mel how her first mirror call with Mother had gone, but the scholar priests were expecting her. She rose. She'd just have to wait until tonight to tell him.

CHAPTER 42

Over his first spoonful of salmon bisque in the family dining room, Mel arched his brows at Father. "What prompted your invitation for luncheon today? I can't stay long—I've duties at the Great Temple this afternoon." And he must return to Kit to check how her first mirror call with her mother had gone.

Sipping his wine, Father sighed. "Your mother and I have been concerned about you recently. And after your unproductive conversation with your mother the other week, we decided you required a gentleman's perspective instead."

Mel tensed. He never should have told Mother about kissing Kit. Although she'd helped him see he loved Kit, she'd persuaded Father to lecture him. "I've been adjusting to my new duties as the elder community priest of Calatini. I'll be fine once I become accustomed to everything."

Father narrowed his eyes at Mel over his nearly empty bowl. "Your new duties aren't concerning us—your relationship with Kit is."

His fingers clenching his spoon, Mel set his jaw. Somehow, he must get Father to quit discussing Kit. Admitting his love would only inflame Mother's futile matchmaking attempts once she heard. "Kit is an old friend who required my help breaking a spell from the Goddess."

Snorting, Father began his creamy chicken and spinach. "You're too serious to ever kiss a lady you considered merely an old friend. And you'd never *keep* kissing her whenever you two are alone."

A blush burned Mel's neck. Yes, he definitely should have never told Mother about kissing Kit.

Father shook his head. "Not that 'twas surprising. Kit was always special to you." He chuckled. "Otherwise, a boy of ten wouldn't have begged his father to teach him every possible megrim remedy when he discovered she suffered them. Your mother and I knew then you'd marry Kit one day."

Mel blushed harder. Of course his perceptive parents had realized his love for Kit so long ago. He should have too.

Father sobered. "Which is why your refusal to admit your love for Kit after the Great Temple's court event concerned us."

His blush cooling, Mel stiffened. He must end this torturous discussion. "Discussing love between myself and Kit is senseless."

Father frowned as he served himself some roast pork with cauliflower mash. "Refusing to admit or discuss your love doesn't make it disappear."

Mel forced a shrug. True, but doing either made him ache for what he could never have. "There's no sense in considering the impossible."

Arching a brow, Father leaned toward him. "Is love between yourself and Kit truly impossible? Or does it simply require effort? Pursuing love isn't always easy."

Mel glared at Father. He could have remained an idle second son of a wealthy duke if he wanted easy, rather than following his calling to become a priest. "I don't need easy. But I'll never be the influential court gentleman Kit wants. I can't forsake my duties to the Goddess."

Father hummed. "Duties Kit has happily shared since she joined you at the Great Temple months ago."

His heart twisting, Mel fisted his hands in his priest robes. "Only because she's too embarrassed to let anyone from court see the fashionable Lady Blaine as a 'hideous crone.'"

Shaking his head, Father began his cinnaspice custard. "I doubt 'tis the only reason Kit fled to you. But you'll never know for certain until you ask her. Unless you confess your love first, I doubt Kit shall share her true feelings. She's been too hurt by that horrible father of hers."

Mel glowered at his cinnaspice custard. Damn that degenerate for his vicious cruelty toward Kit.

Father smiled and leaned forward. "Although you must speak first, you owe it to you both to do so. Pursuing love is always a risk, but 'tis worth it because life without love is empty. Remember, the Goddess wouldn't let us feel such love if we're meant to spend our lives alone. And that includes her priests."

Swallowing, Mel sighed and poked his cinnaspice custard. Except despite his parents' loving delusion, Kit didn't want to marry a priest. So he only replied, "I know."

Flashing a crooked grin, Father nodded at Mel's untasted dessert. "Aren't you going to eat that?"

His stomach tightening, Mel rose. "No, I must return to the Great Temple. I've already remained longer than I should have."

He hurried back to the Great Temple in the carriage he'd taken to save time, but when he reached his study, Kit had already left. Should he go find her at the Center of Learning? Frowning, he dropped into the chair behind his desk. No, Kit wouldn't appreciate him asking her about her mother while among others. He'd need to wait until they were alone after dinner and Vespers.

So as they left the main temple after Vespers, Mel arched his brows at Kit beside him. "Shall we talk in the Sun Chapel?"

Kit beamed. "Yes, I've so much to tell you, and no doubt you do too."

He almost winced. Except he couldn't tell Kit that Father's important matter was his love for her. "Actually, I don't."

Kit eyed him as they settled in the first pew of the Sun Chapel. "Why did your father request you join him for luncheon then?"

Resisting the urge to shift in the pew, Mel eyed the many Goddess laurels before the windows. "Mother persuaded him to." He turned back to Kit with a tight smile. "Enough about that. Tell me how your mirror call with *your mother* went."

Her face glowing, Kit sighed. "So wonderful. Mother was overjoyed to meet me at last, and you were right that she didn't care about the Goddess's illusion. She even told me she loved me."

Warmth suffusing him at Kit's joy, he grinned at her. Finally, Kit was receiving the love she deserved. "How could she not?"

Kit blushed. "I also met Mother's Christopher, and he was welcoming as well. He seems a kind and thoughtful gentleman —he reminded me of you. I'm glad Mother had him to protect her."

Mel's heart fluttered. Although some might have, his tender Kit didn't resent the gentleman who'd stolen her mother, but instead she warmly accepted him. "Did you meet your three siblings too?"

Sighing, Kit tilted her head. "Not yet, which was probably just as well. Even though I'm eager to meet them, I doubt any of us could have handled that today—particularly Mother."

He blinked. What did Kit mean by that?

Before he could ask, Kit grinned and said, "But we've time to meet later. Mother wants to arrange another mirror call soon." She glanced at him. "I told her I must check with you first about when your communication mirror is free."

Mel rubbed his jaw. "Unfortunately, I don't think it shall be for at least a week, but I can have a date for you tomorrow."

Kit beamed. "'Tis fine. Mother and I shall exchange letters until then." She studied him beneath her lashes. "Do you mind being there for our next mirror call? Mother said she'd like to meet you."

He smiled and threaded his fingers through Kit's to reassure her. "If you want me to, I'll be there."

Her smoky eyes soft, Kit caressed his face with her free hand. "Thanks, Mel, for supporting me through all this."

Holding Kit's gaze, he pressed a tender kiss against her palm. He'd support her forever if she let him. "Of course."

For a timeless moment, he and Kit stared at each other without moving, and his pulse surged. He could kiss her again by just leaning forward.

Then Kit swallowed and withdrew until they were no longer touching. She flashed a wry smile. "In addition to being wonderful, my mirror call with Mother was most illuminating."

Aching to pull Kit into his arms, Mel gripped his priest robes to remain still. Even if she returned his love, ravenous kisses weren't appropriate in the Sun Chapel. "Illuminating how?"

Kit sighed. "After meeting Mother, I've realized I'm very much Father's daughter."

He stiffened and eyed Kit. Not that again. "You're *nothing* like that cruel drunkard."

Shaking her head, Kit lifted the shoulder closest to him. "I'm more like him than Mother. Mother is... sweet and gentle."

He frowned at Kit. Why did she never acknowledge her tender heart? "So are you. Look at how you throw yourself into helping others."

Kit waved a hand. "That's not what I mean. Mother cried for most of our mirror call and needs protection from everyone's distress because she feels it as her own. I can't imagine how she survived even three years of marriage to Father."

His chest clenching, Mel took Kit's hand and kissed her palm. "Being raised by him *forced* you to learn how to protect yourself."

Kit shrugged but curled her hand about his. "Although without my stubbornness that you're forever grumbling about, I couldn't have managed to do so. And that stubbornness is *all* Father. He clung to his bitterness for most of his life and resisted a powerful geas for most of mine just to spite Mother."

Mel squeezed Kit's hand. She'd never be that cruel. "Just because your father was stubborn too doesn't mean you're *like* him."

Sighing, Kit grimaced. "Except I could see myself stubbornly clinging to my bitterness like Father did—if not for your influence on my life."

He stared at Kit. She considered *him* that important to her? "My influence? What did I do?"

Kit studied their entwined hands. "You taught me what compassion and love were."

Mel inhaled, his heart quickening. Could his parents be right that Kit returned his love? Was that why *she* kept kissing *him* whenever they were alone? But he'd never be the wealthy and titled husband she'd said she wanted. He tilted her chin until their eyes met. "Love?"

Freeing her chin, Kit hummed. "Through how you treated your family and helped others and worshipped the Goddess."

His heart and breath stilled. That wasn't how he loved Kit. Her kisses must be nothing more than the habitual flirtation the fashionable Countess of Blaine practiced with other gentlemen.

Kit turned toward the nearest Goddess laurel. "Your loving compassion showed me another way to live besides Father's cruel bitterness." She sighed. "And even with that, I still might have echoed him if the Goddess's illusion hadn't woken me up."

Breathing again, Mel caressed Kit's palm with his thumb. She almost sounded as if she'd been unhappy at court. Perhaps she'd not return there, after all. "Woke you up how?"

Kit shrugged. "By making it impossible for me to continue as I had been and forcing me to seek your help. Being close to you again reminded me of everything I'd let myself forget about life." Her lips quirked. "Which was doubtless one of the reasons the Goddess blessed me with her illusion."

He leaned toward Kit. Her rueful gratitude about the Goddess's illusion was nothing like her initial resentment. Surely she was close to breaking the holy spell. "Any inkling on becoming who you were meant to be yet?"

Kit exhaled, her shoulders sagging. "No, not really."

To hearten her, Mel squeezed her hand as he drew her upright. "You shall one day soon. And until then, you've a place here at the Great Temple. Tell me how helping scholar priests went."

Kit coughed a laugh. "I fear they found me incredibly slow. I was so distracted by meeting Mother I could hardly follow their obscure theological discourse."

He winked at Kit. "I'll lend you one of my theological tomes to read tonight so you can impress the scholar priests tomorrow."

Kit laughed again. "Thanks, but don't bother. I probably already read it when still hiding in your chambers."

When he reluctantly released Kit at Sarah and Deacon's chambers, Sarah grasped Kit's arm with a grin and said, "Finally. You and Mel disappeared for ages. How did your mirror call with your mother go?"

Deacon chuckled as Kit and Sarah began to chatter faster than excited sprites. He drawled, "I hope they go to bed before midnight, especially since Kit rises early to attend Lauds with you."

Mel grinned at Deacon then jested, "Perhaps you should consider casting a sleep spell on them to ensure they do."

Chuckling again, Deacon smoothed his ivory-trimmed priest robes. "Except if I did, I'd also require a ward spell on myself when Sarah found out."

Mel laughed, then he and Deacon talked for a while, but Kit and Sarah were still chattering when he left. He shook his head as he strode across the hall. Hopefully, Kit would get some sleep tonight. When he entered his chambers, inside his threshold was a note from Elise inviting him, Kit, and Kay to a family dinner next week. He'd show it to Kit tomorrow—she'd not welcome him interrupting her and Sarah now.

CHAPTER 43

At breakfast the following morning, Kit blinked when Mel handed her a note from Elise. Dinner next week? Did Elise have news concerning her plans to conceive? Kit returned the note to Mel. "I'll write back accepting Elise's invitation." She sighed. "Even though I still can't attend as myself. I hope Elise shan't be too upset by my continued avoidance."

Mel finished his heavily sweetened tea. "Perhaps you should finally tell Elise about the Goddess's illusion."

Kit shifted in her seat. Perhaps she should. Like Mel had said, Mother hadn't cared about the Goddess's illusion. And neither had he, the duchess, nor anyone at the Great Temple. Maybe Elise wouldn't either. And if she explained, she could quit devising ways to avoid Elise without slighting her.

She grimaced as they returned their dishes. Except when she told Elise, Edouard would know too. Hopefully, he'd not be angry about the confidences he'd shared with his disliked stepmother without knowing it. Although Pippa might be able to sweeten his temper. The bubbly lady was deft at that and grateful for Kit's advice about their relationship.

After separating from Mel, Kit headed to the Sun Chapel like usual. She was midway through her prayers when the high priest strode into the chapel.

High Priest Theodag smiled while settling beside her. "How are you doing?"

She warmly returned his smile. Not surprising the kind-hearted high priest was checking on her again. "Quite well."

His brow furrowing, High Priest Theodag eyed her. "Agnes mentioned you'd a mirror call yesterday. Was it because of your father?"

Kit grinned. "In a way." She told the high priest about Mother and Father's unhappy marriage then her first mirror call with Mother.

Once she finished, High Priest Theodag kept studying her for several moments then asked, "Are you angry at all you missed with your mother?"

She blew a sigh. "Not really. I'm excited I can get to know Mother now, along with Christopher and my younger siblings." She swallowed then admitted, "But I realized I'd not be who I am now if I'd lived a different life."

The high priest nodded. "And the Goddess always has reasons for allowing the experiences that shape us."

Kit chuckled. "I said almost exactly that to Mother when she mourned the past."

High Priest Theodag smiled at her. "Anyone devoted to the Goddess would, especially one blessed with a Goddess laurel apple." As a blush heated her cheeks, he leaned toward her and said, "Without our experiences—whether happy or sad, peaceful or painful, mistakes or triumphs—we can never become who we're meant to be."

Her blush cooling, she swallowed and studied her hands turned ancient by the Goddess's illusion. Except determining that seemed almost impossible for stubborn fools like her. She'd been pursuing the wrong things for too long.

When she remained silent, the high priest hummed. "Do you

need time away from helping priests to get to know your mother?"

Kit raised her gaze. She'd be bored if she did. "No, we're exchanging letters mostly, and I can write those in the evenings."

High Priest Theodag nodded, his eyes crinkling. "Then you'll finish helping scholar priests this week before continuing to the final type of priest in Ormas—witch priests. Because of your friendship, Deacon requested that he introduce you to Elder Priest Sidney. Do you mind?"

She smiled, warmed that the once-dismissive priest had called her his friend. "Of course not."

THAT EVENING, Kit received a long letter from Mother inside the red chest. She chuckled as she read it—'twas full of amusing anecdotes about her younger siblings and life in Dracwyn. She really must meet her two brothers and little sister soon. Since she hadn't such happy tales to share, she wrote back the following evening about life at court and the Great Temple. However, to avoid upsetting Mother, she didn't include anything distressing, like court's shallow games or the suffering she'd seen at family refuges and almskitchens. She also shared that Mel's communication mirror was free next week, two days after Elise's family dinner. The evening after finishing her visits to scholar priests, she received Mother's tearstained reply, which included more family stories.

After breakfast with Mel the following morning, Kit returned to Sarah and Deacon's chambers to meet Deacon so he could introduce her to Elder Priest Sidney. When she entered, Deacon kissed Sarah then rose, and he and Kit began to Charmed Blessings.

Halfway there, Deacon coughed and glanced at her, his ascetic face tight. "I should have said this ages ago, but usually Sarah and Mel are with us, and I'd rather say this without an audience."

She waved for Deacon to continue. Whatever he wanted to say must be why he'd requested that he introduce her to the elder witch priest.

Deacon sighed. "I must apologize for how rude I was to you when we met and while you stayed with Mel. I was jealous that the Goddess had blessed a spoiled court lady with an illusion, rather than a devoted priest like me."

Kit flashed a wry grin. She could understand that. "My blasphemous determination to break the Goddess's illusion didn't help either."

Deacon sighed again. "No, and neither did Mel's obvious love and desire for you. All that made me assume you were no better than you should be, so I felt I had to tell High Priest Theodag about you."

She smiled at Deacon to ease his guilt. "'Twas good you did. Not only was Mel and I staying together imprudent, but meeting the high priest allowed me to participate more in temple life."

Deacon grimaced. "Even so, I misjudged you, and I'm sorry. You're diligent with a tender heart and devoted to the Goddess —a great deal like Mel, actually. 'Tis little wonder he adores you."

Blushing, Kit waved a hand. If only Mel did. "We're simply old friends."

His brows quirking, Deacon snorted. But he only said, "Although 'tisn't my place to judge, now that I know you, I can see the Goddess chose wisely when she bestowed her magic upon you. And I hope you can forgive me for my earlier behavior toward you."

She leaned toward Deacon with a grin to evince her forgiveness. "Of course—Sarah would be upset with me if I didn't. Besides, you've been a very good friend to me since you offered me your spare room, and what's a little forgiveness between friends?"

Deacon smiled back as they entered Charmed Blessings. "Thanks, Kit." He led her to a tall witch priest with a powerful presence. "Elder Priest Sidney, this is Kit, the lady blessed with an illusion from the Goddess."

His eyes flicking over her, Elder Priest Sidney nodded. "A pleasure to meet you at last. Everyone speaks highly of you." He glanced at Deacon. "Especially your friend here." As Deacon bowed and strode away, the elder witch priest beckoned her. "Allow me to show you around."

While Elder Priest Sidney showed her Charmed Blessings and described the various relics, shrines, holy blessings, and other magic they provided for parishioners as well as the Great Temple, Kit's skin prickled at the weight of the witch priests' stares—they watched her like bewitched sailors watched a siren. Not since gossip had first spread about the Goddess's illusion had anyone stared at her so.

When the elder witch priest paused, Kit swallowed and asked, "Why are all the witch priests staring?"

Elder Priest Sidney smiled. "We can sense the air of holy magic about you, and 'tis alluring to behold. Spells cast by the Goddess are extremely rare, and most of us haven't seen one before."

She tilted her head. "So the Goddess's illusion appears different from other magic?" That must be why only priests and seers could sense it.

The elder witch priest nodded. "It still glows white like other magic, but it shimmers and hums with some of the Goddess's aura—reminiscent of Goddess laurels, but not as strong. 'Tis how we can tell your illusion was cast by the Goddess rather than another god."

Kit hummed. Seeing that *would* be alluring. "Can witch priests who serve other gods sense all that as well?"

Elder Priest Sidney chuckled. "Perhaps. They'd definitely sense your illusion is a holy spell, but not one cast by their god. However, some might not recognize the Goddess's aura, although many would." He glanced at his fellow witch priests and said, his soft voice resonating through the holy witch shop, "Enough staring. You're making our guest uncomfortable."

As the witch priests abruptly turned away while the dozen or so patrons continued shopping without pause, she stilled and eyed the elder witch priest. He must have used a spell allowing only the other witch priests to hear him. A useful trick.

Smiling at her, Elder Priest Sidney waved her toward a nearby door. "Let me show you the workroom where we enchant most of our spells."

Kit nodded and eagerly followed the elder witch priest. Touring Charmed Blessings was fascinating even though she was no witch. Although helping witch priests would be challenging since she'd no magical powers. But doubtless Elder Priest Sidney would figure out something.

OVER THE FOLLOWING FEW DAYS, Kit helped at Charmed Blessings by assisting patrons find spells and cleaning the holy witch shop. She also talked with witch priests about magic and the different spells they created—fortunately, their stares were much easier to handle one at a time.

Her second to last day helping witch priests, she and Mel walked to Golddell House as soon as they finished their duties so they could attend Elise's family dinner.

As they walked across Ormas, she kept glancing at Mel. He'd been quiet the past week, and although his gaze wandered to her often, he'd turn away whenever she looked at him. Something was clearly troubling him and had since his luncheon with his father. Yet every time she asked him, he'd deflect her question then inquire about Mother or her duties instead. But maybe he'd answer if she asked once again.

She gripped Mel's arm with a warm smile. "Mel, *what* has been troubling you recently?"

Mel sighed. "I've simply much on my mind right now."

Kit drew Mel to a stop and made him turn toward her. If he could finally admit that, surely he'd admit the rest. "Tell me what exactly."

His jaw tightening, Mel withdrew his arm. "Discussing it is senseless."

She grasped Mel's face before he could step back. Her pulse quickened at his skin beneath her palms. Goddess, how she loved him. "Please tell me. I'm your friend and want to help."

Motionless, Mel stared down at her, his deep-brown eyes dull and black.

Her heart clenched at the melancholy darkening his gaze. Although she shouldn't, she pulled down his head and kissed him to erase his sadness with her unspoken love.

Mel returned her kiss for a moment then jerked free. "I'm not one of your court flirts, Kit. You can't use kisses to manipulate me into doing as you wish."

Kit winced. Mel truly believed she'd do that to him? "I didn't."

Mel glared at her. "Then why did you kiss me?"

Looking away, she swallowed. She couldn't possibly admit that she'd kissed him because she loved him. Instead, she murmured, "We must get to Golddell House. We're already late."

Gripping his priest robes, Mel nodded, and they strode the rest of the way in silence. When they arrived at Golddell House, Elise was chattering with Pippa on a sofa, while Lord Farson, Edouard, and Arvan were talking across the drawing room.

Elise turned toward Kit and Mel then frowned. "No Kit again?"

As Mel slanted Kit a narrow glance, she stiffened and studied her ancient-looking hands. He was right—her continued deception was bothering Elise. She needed to explain about the Goddess's illusion, even if Elise and Edouard were upset afterward. Her stomach tensing, she sank into the sofa opposite of Elise and Pippa. "I must confess something, but please don't share it with anyone, not even the rest of the family."

While Mel inhaled and sat beside Kit, Elise and Pippa exchanged frowns, as did Edouard and Lord Farson. Yet everyone except Mel nodded.

Swallowing, Kit lifted her chin. "I'm Kit. I just appear a crone because of an illusion from the Goddess. I'm sorry to have deceived everyone, but I was ashamed to reveal the truth until now."

Silence hummed in the drawing room as everyone besides Mel stared at her.

Then Elise laughed. "No wonder you disappeared and weren't 'up to seeing anyone' as yourself. I should have realized the connection when Mel began bringing his 'assistant' to family events—he's never done that before. And you planning the Great Temple's court event explains why 'twas so spectacular."

Kit exhaled and smoothed the plain skirt of her maid's dress. At least Elise appeared amused rather than upset about her lying for months.

Rubbing his chin, Edouard narrowly eyed Kit on the sofa before arching his brows at Mel. "I'm surprised you agreed to Kit's deception."

As Kit tensed, Mel frowned at his cousin and took her hand then said, "Kit needed my help, and she wasn't ready to tell anyone yet."

To defend Mel, Kit added, "And Mel always encouraged me to tell the family the truth, but I stubbornly refused."

Edouard almost chuckled. "Somehow, *that* doesn't surprise me." He flashed a wry smile. "Although I'm grateful that I didn't know the truth—I likely wouldn't have listened to your advice about Pippa if I'd known."

Kit echoed Edouard's smile. Thankfully, he wasn't upset either. "I know."

While Edouard snorted a laugh, Pippa leaned forward and said, "I'm grateful too, but I don't understand why the Goddess would make you appear old."

Sighing, Kit studied her hand still entwined with Mel's. "I

don't know why the Goddess chose to bless me with her magic, but her illusion shall end when I become who I'm meant to be." She raised her gaze. "And making me appear old forced me to abandon my fashionable life at court."

Elise glanced at Lord Farson then winced before turning back to Kit. "That must have been distressing, especially since the Duke of Oakmoor was close to proposing."

As Mel stiffened and released her hand, Kit made herself smile and reply, "Somewhat, but leaving court made me acknowledge how unhappy I was there. I'm not certain who I'm meant to be, although I doubt it involves court."

She blushed when another silence descended as everyone, including Mel this time, stared at her again. That confession had shocked them more than the Goddess's illusion.

Arvan coughed. "Could we continue this discussion over dinner? I'm famished."

Everyone laughed, and they proceeded to dinner so the young duke wouldn't starve.

CHAPTER 44

*D*uring the lively dinner at Golddell House, Mel said almost nothing and only ate half his shokolat trifle. Instead, he kept glancing at Kit. Had she truly been unhappy at court? If so, she'd not wish to return there after breaking the Goddess's illusion. But what about that wealthy and titled husband she'd said she wanted? She'd only find him at court.

He gripped his priest robes beneath the table. Unless that aspiration was as false as her enjoyment of life at court had been. Could she secretly prefer a humble priest instead? She did seem to seek and enjoy his kisses. If she'd been unhappy being the sultry Countess of Blaine, surely her desire wasn't just habitual flirtation.

So once they said farewell and began walking back to the Great Temple, Mel took Kit's arm and asked, "If who you're meant to be doesn't involve court, what do you intend to do after you break the Goddess's illusion?"

Kit sighed. "That depends on who I'm meant to be, I suppose."

He drew Kit into an alley between two elegant townhouses so he could face her to read her expression. "But what would you like that to involve?"

Kit stared up at him then exhaled and lowered her gaze. "I'd like to stay at the Great Temple if possible, but I'm not certain I belong there."

His heart quickening, Mel squeezed Kit's hands. If she wanted to remain there, she'd not resent a priest's life. Like Mother had hinted, Kit might accept if he asked her to marry him. "You belong at the Great Temple as if you were meant to be there all along."

Inhaling, Kit glanced up at him through her lashes. "Really?"

He smiled. "Really." He captured Kit's face in his palms like she had his earlier. He asked her, his voice soft unlike last time, "Why did you kiss me today, Kit?"

Her lips trembling, Kit swallowed but held his gaze. "I... I..."

Warmth flooded Mel at the emotion softening her face. His tender Kit was too chary to confess her love first, just like Father had said. He brushed a gentle kiss against her trembling lips. "I think you kiss me for the same reason that I kiss you."

Kit blushed and blinked up at him.

He was about to tell Kit he loved her when a lady's shrill giggle from the street recalled him to where they were. An alley in the fashionable area of Ormas was no place for confessions of love and a marriage proposal.

So he stepped back and took Kit's hand. Caressing her palm with his thumb, he pulled her from the alley. "Let's go home."

Her gaze soft, Kit smiled and threaded her fingers through his. She breathed, "Yes. Home."

But when they reached the priest quarters, Sarah darted into the hall and swept Kit into her and Deacon's chambers, asking how dinner had gone.

Mel sighed as he eyed the door Kit had disappeared behind. He could wait until tomorrow after Vespers to confess his love and ask her to marry him. At least 'twould allow him time to plan a romantic evening. They should go somewhere alone so they'd not be interrupted. Tomorrow needed to be special—

confessions of love and marriage proposals didn't happen every day.

THE FOLLOWING DAY, Mel's mind kept drifting to their upcoming romantic evening despite his duties as the acting elder community priest of Calatini. They could use Kit's flying carpet to leave Ormas, but where should they go? Neither of them had anywhere special outside of the Great Temple.

While discussing beach services midway through his mirror call with the elder community priestess of Dracwyn, he stilled and began to smile. He and Kit could visit the royal bay—even though not special to them, the ocean was romantic, especially at sunset. And although Devon wouldn't object to a cousin visiting, he'd call Devon before leaving his study to request permission.

When he cut short his call with the elder community priestess of Dracwyn, Elder Priestess Agnes frowned and scrutinized him. She asked, "What has been distracting you today? 'Tis even worse than your distraction the past week."

A blush warmed his neck. He'd rather not tell Elder Priestess Agnes about his proposal until after Kit had accepted. So he only replied, "I'm planning an outing with Kit this evening. She and I have that mirror call tomorrow morning."

Elder Priestess Agnes's lips tightened. "I know you're old friends, but Kit is too much of a distraction and temptation for you. You forget your duties whenever she's around, and she inspires you to act inappropriately for a priest."

Mel blushed harder. The elder community priestess somehow knew about his and Kit's ravenous kisses. Doubtless someone had seen them kissing, and gossip had spread throughout the Great Temple. But 'twould quiet once they announced their betrothal.

Shaking her head, Elder Priestess Agnes continued, "You must always put your duties first. As the elder community priest of Calatini, you've no time for distractions."

He stiffened as the elder community priestess strode from his study. Although he'd been performing his duties, he *had* been brooding over his love for Kit since his luncheon with Father. But surely that hadn't hindered his duties. Sagging in his chair, he rubbed his face. Yet Elder Priest Agnes had been the elder community priestess of Calatini for nearly four decades and knew what was required to fulfill that. However, other priests married, even elder priests, so 'twas possible to balance duties and love. He just needed to determine what that looked like for him and Kit.

Sighing, Mel left his study without calling Devon. Until he determined balancing duties and love, he must wait to propose to Kit. He sighed again when she barely glanced at him during dinner while describing her final day visiting Charmed Blessings. Besides, Kit had endured multiple upheavals recently—she'd been under the Goddess's illusion for months while attempting to discover who she was meant to be with little guidance; her father had burst back into her life, cruelly insulted her, then died; and she'd discovered her dead mother was alive and was getting to know her as well as her newfound family. Another life change might be too much right now, so perhaps 'twas better for Kit too if he waited to propose.

After breakfast the following morning, Mel smiled at Kit as they headed to his study for her mirror call with her mother. But he didn't risk taking her hand. 'Twould only make him ache to kiss her, and kisses must wait until he could confess his love and propose. "Excited for your mirror call?"

Kit grinned. "Very." Her grin twisted. "'Tis also an excellent distraction from my meeting with High Priest Theodag this afternoon. He wants to discuss my visits to the different types of priests, but those visits didn't help me discover who I'm meant to be, so I don't know what to tell him."

To hearten her, Mel squeezed her hand even though that

made hunger surge through him. "High Priest Theodag shall understand."

Kit sighed as they entered his study. "I hope so."

Once they sat, Kit activated the communication mirror, which glowed white before clearing to reveal a mature lady with tears shimmering in her eyes. Kit flashed a grin. "Good morning, Mother." She gestured toward him. "This is my old friend Mel."

He smiled at Kit's mother, who strongly resembled Kit, other than her age, coloring, and tears. "A pleasure, my lady."

Kit's mother smiled back. "Mrs. Poole, please. I quit using my title from marrying Kit's father when I fled, so I've been called Christopher's wife for years, although we couldn't marry until yesterday."

Beaming, Kit leaned toward the mirror. "Congratulations! I wish I could have attended."

Mrs. Poole's eyes shimmered brighter. "Thanks, but the wedding ceremony was just me, Christopher, Priest Humphry, and his wife. We didn't have other witnesses to avoid gossip." She turned to Mel, her tears trembling on her lashes. "Thank you so much for taking such excellent care of Kit over the years."

Letting his smile warm, he hummed. Kit hadn't been exaggerating about her mother's crying. "Truthfully, we take care of each other." He glanced at Kit. "I hope we always continue to do so."

As Kit blushed but nodded, Mrs. Poole's tears cascaded down her cheeks, and she said, "Oh, how lovely!"

Kit grinned at her mother. "Tell me how everyone's been since your letter the other day."

Mel almost smiled at Kit's blatant attempt to dry her mother's tears.

Mrs. Poole wiped her face. "We've been well. After our wedding yesterday, Christopher and I told Thom, Chase, and Lizzie that we finally contacted their elder sister. They were all terribly excited—especially when we said we'd pause their schooling so we can travel to Ormas to meet in person. We'll sail on Christopher's fastest ship and be there within a week."

Kit stilled and worried her lip. "I can't wait to meet you all, but I think you'd better wait to visit until I break the Goddess's illusion. Between attempting to do that and my duties at the Great Temple, I shan't have much time to see you."

Eyeing Kit, Mel swallowed a sigh. That doubtless wasn't her sole reason for delaying her family's visit. She was probably embarrassed to meet her much younger siblings while still appearing ancient.

Mrs. Poole sagged, her eyes shimmering again. "I should have realized that, but I was so desperate to see you again at last."

To cheer Kit's mother, he smiled and said, "It shan't be long until you do. Kit is close to breaking the Goddess's illusion."

Mrs. Poole brightened. "Truly?"

Kicking his ankle, Kit nevertheless smiled at her mother. "Truly. Now tell me more about Thom's first smuggling run last week."

They spent the rest of the morning talking with Mrs. Poole. Every time her mother cried, Kit soothed her and made her smile again. Like Kit had alluded, she was definitely stronger than her mother. And she adored her mother even though they barely knew each other.

Once her mother bid them a teary farewell, Kit deactivated the communication mirror then spun toward him with a frown. "How could you tell Mother I was close to breaking the Goddess's illusion?"

He arched his brows. "Because you are." When Kit frowned harder, he took her hand with a warm smile. "Although you don't know precisely who you're meant to be yet, you're more like the devout and tender girl you once were than you've been in years. Except now you also possess a lady's insight and strength."

Kit blushed and licked her lips.

His body tightening, Mel pressed a kiss against her palm instead of her tempting lips. "I'm impressed how you've handled your recent life changes—the Goddess's illusion, your father, your mother."

Kit shook her head. "I don't think I handled the Goddess's illusion well. I was resentful and ashamed about it, and I still haven't learned whatever the Goddess wants to teach me. And with Father, I only did what was necessary." She grinned. "Plus, discovering a loving mother and family was no hardship. I could use more such life changes."

He inhaled. Like a loving husband, perhaps? Then he needn't wait to propose to Kit—except he still hadn't determined balancing duties and love. Yet he couldn't resist pulling her into his lap. "I could use a life change too."

Studying him beneath her lashes, Kit wrapped her arms about his neck, and her delectable cinnaspice scent weaved about him. "Maybe we could use the same one."

Groaning, Mel captured Kit's mouth in a deep kiss. His pulse surged and pounded in his veins when she moaned and pressed closer. She clearly needed him the way he needed her. As they kissed without stopping to breathe, he gripped her hips to keep his hands away from the laces of her dress.

Then a cough rippled through his study.

He and Kit wrenched their mouths apart and whirled to face his door.

Her wizened face blank, Elder Priestess Agnes stood there eyeing them. "Your afternoon meetings shall begin shortly."

Her skin red, Kit bolted without even a goodbye.

Blushing too, Mel straightened his priest robes but held the elder community priestess's gaze. "I intend to marry Kit."

Elder Priestess Agnes sighed. "I know." She settled in the chair before his desk. "I must apologize for my censure yesterday. 'Tis apparent to anyone who's seen you together that you're both very much in love, and Kit's a worthy lady who shall make a fine wife for you once the Goddess approves your marriage. I shouldn't have called her a distraction and temptation."

He stared at the elder community priestess. What had brought about that reversal? "Why did you?"

Grimacing, Elder Priestess Agnes sighed again. "Because I sometimes forget that others called to serve the Goddess aren't natural spinsters like me. I never wanted a husband or children, which made putting my duties first easy. You, however, long for a family, so your duties alone shall leave you unfulfilled. And unfulfilled priests can't serve the Goddess the way they should."

Mel exhaled. Yes, he'd always longed for a family as much as he'd longed for Kit. "I agree, but as you've said, being the elder community priest of Calatini is a consuming duty. How can I balance that and a family?"

Elder Priestess Agnes shifted in her seat. "As High Priest Theodag reminded me last night when I complained about your distraction, priests of higher rank do marry—including him, although his wife returned to the Goddess some years ago. You simply can't perform your duties the way I would. You need to have additional assistants and delegate more to make time for your family."

He hummed. So the high priest had brought about the elder community priestess's reversal. Then he quirked a wry smile. "Delegation isn't something I'm skilled at."

Elder Priestess Agnes humphed. "Well, you'll need to learn if you want to balance your duties and a family." She softened. "Although I suspect that shall be easier once you've a family to focus on in addition to your duties." She arched her brows. "Now shall we review your notes before your first mirror call?"

Mel nodded and fetched his notes from an assistant. While he did, he asked if the young priest could fetch him luncheon since he and Kit had neglected to eat. Then he returned to his study. Hopefully, he could finish his mirror calls early so he could call

Devon about visiting the royal bay tonight before arranging his romantic evening with Kit.

CHAPTER 45

Fleeing Mel's study, Kit bolted to the Sun Chapel even though she should be meeting High Priest Theodag in his study not far from Mel's. But she couldn't meet the high priest until she'd settled. Her body flushed and trembling, she sank into the first pew and laced her hands together. How embarrassing that Elder Priestess Agnes had caught her and Mel kissing so wildly, in his study no less.

She inhaled the Goddess laurels' heavenly fragrance to help settle herself. Oh, but that look filling Mel's eyes before he'd kissed her—the same as in the alley after Elise's family dinner. The tender yet ardent look that she'd always longed to see but never believed she would. A look that, along with his affectionate words, made her hope that he loved her the way she loved him. Which was why she'd dared hint at her feelings. She touched her still tingling lips. And her hint had inspired Mel to kiss her as if he needed her to breathe. Her pulse leapt. He'd not kiss her so unless he wanted to marry her.

Kit lowered her hand, her gaze catching on its gnarled and spotted appearance, and her heart stilled. But how could she possibly marry Mel while under the Goddess's illusion? The Goddess must approve his marriage, and why would the

Goddess approve one of her most diligent priests marrying an unworthy lady who still hadn't grasped whatever she was meant to learn? And even if the Goddess approved, people would snicker to see a handsome gentleman marry a crone.

She swallowed and closed her burning eyes. So although she loved Mel and ached to marry him, she must refuse him if he proposed before she broke the Goddess's illusion. Yet refusing would surely hurt him and devastate her. And would she even be strong enough to refuse the gentleman she'd always loved? Somehow she must. She worried her lip. She never should have hinted at her feelings this morning. If she hadn't, she'd not need to fret about Mel proposing—he was too chivalrous to ever propose to a lady he believed uninterested.

Kit exhaled then gulped another calming breath. She needed to quit brooding over Mel. Such brooding wasn't settling her, and she was now long overdue for her meeting with the high priest.

But before she made herself rise, High Priest Theodag strode into the Sun Chapel, his priest robes' gold trim glittering. "Sorry I'm late. I thought we were meeting in my study."

She winced as the high priest sat beside her. "We were. I visited here to reflect first and forgot the hour."

Eyeing her, High Priest Theodag hummed. "Something must be troubling you then. Tell me about it."

A blush heating her cheeks, Kit lowered her gaze. Since she couldn't reveal her love for Mel, she only replied, "I finished helping the different types of priests, but I still haven't discovered who I'm meant to be. I feel as if I'll never break the Goddess's illusion."

The high priest patted her hand. "You shall, never fear. But don't worry about that now. Let's discuss what you learned from helping at the Great Temple." When she nodded, he asked, "What are your overall thoughts about the different types of priests?"

Still unable to face the high priest, she studied the numerous

Goddess laurels before the windows instead. "The Goddess has as many ways to serve her as she has children. Even among the same type of priests, there are different ways to serve. Yet somehow, all the priests here have found the best way for them, one that fills them with peace, confidence, and joy." If only she could feel that too.

Nodding, High Priest Theodag smiled. "More than most, priests strive to listen to the Goddess's call in their hearts, and our rigorous training helps develop that as well as our diligence. However, even priests don't feel peace, confidence, and joy about our purpose all the time." He shook his head. "Sometimes, we fight against the call, like I did as an angry youth. Or deciding what calling best suits us can be difficult, like for Sarah. Or we become weary, like Agnes has. Or how the Goddess wants us to grow can be hard for us to accept, like with Mel."

Kit tilted her head. Mel *had* almost exhausted himself into a coma when taking on his new duties. And the high priest's other examples were surely true too. But none of *them* were Father's daughter.

High Priest Theodag chuckled. "You must also remember that the priests you visited wanted to impress the lady blessed with an illusion from the Goddess, so they did their best to appear perfectly fulfilled." His smile deepened. "Did the life of one of the different types of priests call to you?"

She stared at the high priest. Call to *her*? "I enjoyed helping and meeting everyone, but none of their lives *called* to me. I'm no priestess."

His gaze probing, High Priest Theodag studied her. "But which did you most enjoy and excel at?"

Kit shrugged. "Probably the life of a community priest. I enjoy and excel at organizing the almskitchens for Mel and arranging court events for the Great Temple. And I've insight to aid parishioners at the family refuges, although I don't think I could work at those without pause—too heartrending." She shook her head. "But I could have told you all that before I helped the different types of priests."

The high priest nodded. "True, but now you're certain of that, and you got to know priests throughout the Great Temple."

Swallowing, she shifted in the pew. "Could I continue helping like that even though I'm not a priestess? Assuming who I'm meant to be can remain here, of course. I much prefer my life at the Great Temple to that at court."

A kindhearted smile softening his austere face, High Priest Theodag squeezed her hand. "You definitely should. Managing others and handling court aren't duties many priests enjoy, so we could use your help there. And the family refuges could always use more volunteers. Plus, helping in ways that call you shall enable you to discover who you're meant to be."

Kit exhaled, her tension easing. Thank the Goddess the high priest would let her stay. "I hope so."

High Priest Theodag rubbed his jaw. "Several times you've said you're no priestess, including the day we met. Why do you say that?"

She stilled, Father's scathing derision echoing through her. Then she jerked another shrug. "I'm not the type of lady who can be a priestess."

The high priest arched his brows. "And why not? Priests and priestesses are simply people devoted to the Goddess and willing to dedicate their lives to serving her." He leaned toward Kit. "From what I've seen since you've stayed at the Great Temple, you're clearly that."

Kit wrenched back as her chest clenched. "I might long to be, but I can't. My heart is wicked and resentful—I destroyed a shy and selfless girl's love because I was jealous of her, and until the Goddess's illusion, I used my sultry beauty and empty flirtation to manipulate others. Plus, I'm stubborn and always pursue all the wrong things—I married an elderly count for his title and wealth even though my heart lay elsewhere, and until the

Goddess's illusion, I was determined to repeat that mistake with an influential duke."

High Priest Theodag frowned and shook his head. "You're too exacting on yourself. None of us are perfect—we all make mistakes and have flaws. Yet our mistakes help us grow, and we've virtues that balance our flaws." He smiled at her again. "You love the Goddess with your entire being. You're a kind-hearted lady who's happiest when helping others, and you're strong as well as diligent. You understand people, so you excel at managing, pleasing, and advising them. You're fierce when defending those you love, even from themselves, and you readily forgive everyone other than yourself. As for stubborn..." He chuckled. "'Tisn't a flaw if directed properly. I'm rather stubborn myself, and so are many of the priests who manage others, including Mel."

She blinked at the high priest, almost lightheaded at his approbation.

High Priest Theodag rose, the gold trim on his priest robes glittering like before. "While pondering who you're meant to be, you should also consider why the Goddess blessed you with that illusion to help you grow. Although she speaks to everyone in their hearts, she only bestows her magic, or even her Goddess laurel apples, on those special to her." He squeezed Kit's shoulder. "I'll leave you to your thoughts."

Once the high priest left, she gazed at the Goddess laurels and breathed in their soothing fragrance. Could he be right? Then her stomach rumbled louder than a manticore's. She glanced at the sunlight streaming through the windows. And no wonder—from the angle of the light, 'twas well into the afternoon, and she'd not eaten since breakfast. Her mind still whirling, she drifted to the dining hall, devoured some food, then returned to the Sun Chapel.

She studied her old-looking hands as she settled in the first pew again. If the high priest was right, perhaps her becoming a priestess wasn't impossible, even though Father had always sneered that it was. But Father had been a deeply bitter man who'd been determined to destroy everyone's happiness—hers, Mother's, even his own.

Kit grimaced. Was it any surprise that she'd done the same to Wren after seeing that as her example her entire childhood? Yet she'd repented her cruel lie as soon as she'd blurted it, and she'd never attempted to hurt anyone like that again. Even telling court about Wren's pregnancy hadn't been to hurt Wren, but to prove Kit wasn't the only lady who erred, although she'd repented that too and not gossiped so again. Perhaps she *had* grown from her mistakes like the high priest had said.

Drifting to the Goddess laurels, she risked caressing the edge of a leathery dark-green leaf, and the holy shrub quivered. And thanks to the Goddess's illusion, she'd learned that stubbornly pursuing wealth and status at court was also a mistake and would leave her unhappy. But to devote herself to serving others and the Goddess after spending so long serving only herself would be a profound life change. Could she actually sustain it?

As she bent to sniff a large white flower, Mel strode into the Sun Chapel with a warm smile and said, "High Priest Theodag thought you might still be here."

Shoving aside her introspection, Kit returned Mel's smile. "He left me with much to ponder."

Mel took her arm and began escorting her from the Sun Chapel. "You deserve a break after pondering all afternoon. I thought we could enjoy a picnic at the royal bay instead of joining everyone else tonight. Devon was fine with us visiting, and getting outside of Ormas shall be a nice change."

She hummed. So it would, and she'd not visited the royal bay since her water party months ago. A relaxing evening there would be perfect to settle her whirling thoughts about who she was meant to be. Mel was wonderful to think of that. She smiled at him. "I'd love to visit the royal bay. Are we riding or taking a carriage there?"

Mel grinned back. "Neither. I thought we could take your

flying carpet. You've not had a chance to use it yet, so 'twould be good practice, and a flying carpet shall get us there faster."

Kit suppressed a wince. She'd not practiced because flying carpets weren't common, and she'd not wanted the attention, especially while under the Goddess's illusion. She could have worn her invisibility cloak, but a flying carpet without a passenger would engender just as much gossip. "A flying carpet shall draw too much notice."

His grin turning almost impish, Mel chuckled and patted his pocket above his heart. "I suspected 'twould bother you, so I had Deacon create two invisibility charms large enough to cover us and your flying carpet—one for each carpet ride. Why don't you fetch your flying carpet while I fetch our picnic from Esther? We can meet in the Harvest Garden and leave from there."

Relaxing, she returned his grin and nodded. Mel had clearly thought through everything. "Very well."

She fetched her flying carpet and the letter Mother had sent along with it then met Mel in the Harvest Garden. Unfurling the vibrant Tsarkan carpet, she sat toward the front and reread Mother's instructions. Tingling flooded her as Mel settled behind her so close that their bodies touched.

Mel murmured in her ear, "I'll invoke the first invisibility charm once you get the flying carpet aloft."

Kit gulped a breath while sliding Mother's letter in her pocket. 'Twould be so tempting to nestle against Mel during the carpet ride, but she couldn't risk encouraging him. To activate the flying carpet, she murmured, "Sursum."

The carpet rippled beneath them before smoothly rising from the ground. As she gripped the front of the carpet to steer, Mel muttered something, and they vanished. She tilted the carpet upward until they were well above the buildings of Ormas, then she leaned forward, and the carpet sped toward the royal bay. The brisk breeze as they flew tangled her upswept hair, stung her cheeks, and roared in her ears, but they arrived at the royal bay in a quarter of the time it usually took.

As they started to descend, Mel muttered something again, and they reappeared. She exhaled and directed the carpet onto the golden sand. Then she said, "Deorsum," and the deactivated carpet quivered then stilled. So the flying carpet would gather energy from the nature around them for the return ride, she said, "Revis."

Mel chuckled while he began unpacking their picnic. "A thrilling ride. I don't think even nightmara can travel so fast."

Kit nodded as she accepted a plate, smiling at the food Mel set out between them. He'd obviously requested dishes he knew she'd enjoy—like spiced rhubarb spinach salad, cinnaspice pork with rolls, and spice buns.

During their picnic, Mel took care of her with even more than his usual solicitude, which warmed her yet made her chest tighten. He was taking care of her as if she were his beloved wife. He encouraged her to eat until she was bursting while entertaining her with amusing anecdotes. Yet despite his light-hearted words, his gaze focused on her with loving intensity.

Once Mel began packing their remaining food, she flopped on the flying carpet to bask in the early evening sun. When he finished, she sighed without moving. "We should return to the Great Temple."

Smiling down at her, Mel took her hand. "I thought we could remain until sunset. 'Tis only an hour or so, and the sun setting into the ocean is both beautiful and romantic."

Kit jerked upright, her heart clenching. She should have realized a romantic visit to the royal bay couldn't be to simply help her relax. But she mustn't let him propose yet—not until she broke the Goddess's illusion. Although the Goddess *might* approve their marriage if she was special to the Goddess as the high priest claimed, people still wouldn't understand Mel marrying a crone. And what if who she was meant to be wasn't a priestess and took her away from the Great Temple? She gritted a blinding smile. "No, we should return now. I don't want to fly a carpet in the dark."

CHAPTER 46

Mel captured Kit's face in his hands, his chest squeezing at her tight expression. She appeared almost panicked about flying in the dark. "If that concerns you, we can return well before dark, but we must talk first."

Her face tightening further, Kit jerked away from him. "No, not now. Please."

He frowned and eyed Kit. She'd been quiet during their picnic, doubtless pondering her meeting with the high priest, but why didn't she want to talk with him? Surely she suspected he meant to confess his love and propose, and given she loved him too, she'd not object to that. He took her hand again. "Why not?"

Kit swallowed as she extracted her hand. "My mind is still whirling after my talk with High Priest Theodag."

Aching to pull Kit into his arms to comfort her, Mel recaptured her hand and pressed a kiss against her palm instead. "What did you two discuss?"

Withdrawing once more, Kit shrugged. "What I learned from helping the different types of priests."

He hummed as his stomach tensed. Why did Kit keep withdrawing from him? Had his romantic picnic upset her for some reason? If so, would his confession of love and proposal upset her further? Gritting a calm smile, he asked, "Why did discussing what you learned make your mind whirl?"

Her gaze on the ocean beyond him, Kit repeated her shrug. "High Priest Theodag also suggested some startling things about who I'm meant to be."

Mel leaned toward Kit. Yet High Priest Theodag's suggestions couldn't have been harsh—although austere, the high priest was too kindhearted for that. "Like what?"

Kit stiffened, her gaze remaining averted. "I don't wish to discuss it."

He sighed. Kit was withdrawing from him more than physically. Please let confessing his love and proposing put an end to that. "Very well." He turned her chin until she faced him. "Then we should discuss what I brought you to the royal bay to talk about." He flashed a warm smile. "I promise it shan't startle you like whatever the high priest suggested."

Kit stared at him, her smoky eyes darkening. "Please don't, Mel. I can't bear it right now. I must discover who I'm meant to be first."

Unable to resist, he brushed a tender kiss against Kit's lips. She looked so vulnerable, her usual determination shorn from her. She'd endured so many upheavals recently, but his love would support her. And she'd hinted she needed that in his study this morning. He murmured, "Perhaps this shall help you discover who you're meant to be."

Kit shivered. "No, it shall only complicate that."

Mel lifted his head but pulled Kit into his arms. He swallowed as his body tightened at her curves pressing against him. Thankfully, once they were betrothed, ravenous kisses would no longer be inappropriate, and once they were married, they could quit resisting each other entirely. "In some ways, perhaps. But it shall simplify them in others."

Blushing and breathless in his arms, Kit silently shook her head, but she didn't withdraw this time.

His pulse surging, he kissed Kit again, but he forced himself to stop before hunger overwhelmed them. They must talk. He smiled into her eyes. "I love you, Kit. Although I refused to admit it, I've loved you since your first Sext when your glowing smile transfixed me, and your devotion to the Goddess, tender heart, wise insight, deep strength, even your sometimes maddening stubbornness all made me fall deeper in love with you over the years."

Kit stared at him, tears shimmering in her gaze and her lips trembling.

Mel shuddered. Dear Goddess, he burned to devour Kit's trembling lips. Instead, he continued, "I'm so grateful you sought my help and began staying at the Great Temple—without you, my duties had begun to consume me, and I ached for the love I believed impossible. But your presence reawakened me and made me admit how I loved you." He let himself feather a kiss against Kit's lips. "I can't imagine not having you beside me. For the rest of our lives, I want to enjoy your company, take care of you while you take care of me, kiss you—and more—until we can't move, raise a family together, even argue when we disagree. Will you marry me?"

Her tears now trickling down her cheeks, Kit shoved his chest. "I can't. Not now."

He froze, his heart wrenching. Kit had *refused*? Had he been mistaken about her love? Or did she still want that wealthy and titled husband, after all? "Why not?"

Still crying, Kit shook her head and pushed his chest again. "Marriage between us is impossible right now."

Mel hardened his arms about Kit. He couldn't release her until he'd answers. "I can't see why—unless you don't return my love."

Kit winced then slashed him a teary glance. "Of course I love you, Mel. I always have. Why else did I flirt with you as a girl and can't quit kissing you now despite knowing we shouldn't because you're a priest? Not loving you isn't the problem."

He exhaled as his aching heart began to ease. "Then what is?"

Her tears drying, Kit wiped her face then glowered at him. "The Goddess's illusion, obviously. You can't marry someone who appears like your grandmother."

Mel almost snorted. He should have realized that was the problem. He brushed another gentle kiss against her lips. "I don't care about your appearance. I love *you*, not your sultry beauty."

Kit's eyes shimmered anew. "I know, but no one shall understand. They'll snicker when they see us together as a couple."

He blew a sigh. Yes, people, other than their family and friends, probably would. "Those who love us shan't snicker." He snorted. "Both Mother and Father have lectured me to marry you for the past month, and they know about your appearance."

Kit blinked, her face softening. "Your parents want *me* as a daughter-in-law? Despite my drunkard father, everything I've done to their family, and appearing a hideous crone?"

A pang darted through Mel. Although Kit now knew her mother loved her, his parents' wholehearted acceptance no doubt surprised her after enduring her cruel father's abuse for years. He smiled at Kit. "Of course they do. They know we love each other. Father said they've expected our marriage since I was ten, and Mother called me an idiot when I refused to admit I loved you."

Her lips parting, Kit blinked again. "Oh." Then she stiffened and tossed her head. "Well, perhaps our friends and family shall understand. But the rest of the world shall assume you're a greedy fortune hunter and I'm a foolishly desperate crone. Not a good reputation for the next elder priest of Calatini, and I'd despise everyone regarding me with such disgusted pity."

He tensed. When Kit spoke like that, she sounded like the fashionable Countess of Blaine who lusted for wealth and status. "Even after all these months away from court, you still care too much about appearances." He arched his brows at her. "And how can you become who you're meant to be if you deny the love in your heart?"

Kit attempted to escape his arms once more. "I'm not denying it. We just need to wait awhile."

Mel gripped Kit's shoulders to prevent her escape. "I know our marriage shall engender gossip while you're under the Goddess's illusion." 'Twould regardless, given his family and position as well as her erstwhile influence at court and mysterious disappearance at Longnight. "But I love you too much to care about any of that."

Kit sagged. "I just can't. I'm sorry."

Swallowing to relieve his constricted throat, he squeezed Kit's shoulders. "The Goddess's illusion shan't last forever. We shouldn't delay our lives together because of a holy spell you're close to breaking."

Stiffening, Kit snorted. "How do you know that? Nothing has helped so far." She poked his chest. "And what if who I'm meant to be takes me away from the Great Temple?"

Mel sighed and tenderly kissed Kit's brow. Why was she fretting about that? "Then we'll devise a way to remain together. All couples must compromise at times."

Kit set her jaw. "No, 'tis better to wait."

His heart seizing, he eyed Kit. If she *truly* loved him, she'd be willing to risk that their lives mightn't be perfect. He dropped her shoulders. "We should return to the Great Temple to get back before dark."

Pale and pinched, Kit stared at him. Her voice trembling, she said, "Mel, I—"

He leapt upright before Kit could finish. He couldn't bear further excuses for her refusal. "I think we've talked enough for tonight. Let's go."

Hunching, Kit nodded and muttered the word to activate her flying carpet. As the carpet rippled, he sat behind her, making sure their bodies didn't touch this time. Once they were aloft, he extracted the second invisibility charm from his pocket and activated it. Then they sped back to Ormas—fortunately, the roaring wind made talking impossible.

As they neared the Harvest Garden, Mel inactivated the invisibility charm so Kit could see them to land. He leapt from the carpet as soon as they landed, and she deactivated then rolled the flying carpet. Without a word, he plucked the rolled carpet from her hands and draped it on his shoulder, and they began to return the priest quarters.

Kit kept glancing at him and worrying her lip as they walked, but she remained silent too, until he handed her the flying carpet at Deacon and Sarah's door. Then she whispered, "Good night, Mel."

His chest tight, he managed a polite nod. "Good night, Kit." He spun and strode into his chambers.

THE FOLLOWING MORNING, Mel and Kit attended Lauds then ate breakfast together like usual, but they both barely spoke or looked at each other. Yet whenever he glanced at Kit, his aching heart would twist anew. How could she have denied their love simply because of appearances? Apparently, she'd learned little from participating in temple life while appearing an elderly lady. Perhaps she wasn't close to breaking the Goddess's illusion, after all. And if she cared more about appearances than truth, she wasn't suited to a priest's life, so she'd doubtless return to court once she appeared young and gorgeous again.

Despite his brooding, he made himself ask as they left the dining hall, "Now that you're finished helping the different types of priests, what are you doing today?"

Kit twisted her hands in the plain skirt of her maid's dress. "I'm helping at Goddess's Refuge." She sighed. "Although tomorrow I must speak with High Priest Theodag about my future days here. I'd prefer having assigned duties."

Mel nodded. At least Kit's dislike of being idle was entirely genuine. If only she could learn to ignore appearances and listen to her tender heart, she'd be a significant boon to the Great Temple. "Have a good day. I'll see you at dinner."

Without waiting for Kit's reply, he strode to his study. Thankfully, his duties as the acting elder community priest gave him something to think about besides Kit and his refused proposal. However, some of his melancholy must have shown because Elder Priestess Agnes eyed him throughout the day. Yet he prevented her questions by asking her about his duties.

At dinner that evening, he and Kit could still barely talk to each other. Deacon and Sarah exchanged frowns whenever awkward silences descended because he and Kit failed to speak. And their friends frowned harder when he only ate two bites of his vahnila cake.

Once they began back toward their chambers, Sarah grasped his arm and pulled him several steps behind her husband and Kit. She murmured, "*What* happened at your picnic yesterday? All Kit would say was that 'twas romantic. Yet she's been close to tears since you returned. Did you quarrel, for real this time?"

Mel winced, eyeing Kit like a smitten griffin eyed his unwon mate. "Yes, but I don't wish to talk about it."

Sarah tsked. "You don't need to with me, but you and Kit had better talk before too long. You'll both be miserable until you do. And you two love each other too much to not resolve whatever quarrel you had."

He swallowed a bitter laugh. 'Twasn't likely when Kit was determined to deny their love. He walked faster until he and Sarah rejoined Deacon and Kit.

They'd just reached their doors when Hawke burst into the hall. "Mel, there you are!"

Mel stiffened when they turned to face Hawke. His normally assured younger brother was pale and shaking. He surged toward Hawke. "What's wrong?"

Hawke halted and clenched his hands, clearly to avoid pacing. "Wren. Healer Althea induced her this afternoon. But she'd barely the strength to push, and then—" He swallowed as tears slid down his cheeks. "She began seizing. Healer Althea performed a healing spell, but I could tell her magic was barely keeping Wren alive. I came to see if a healer priest could help."

Kit stepped forward, her brow furrowed. "Why didn't Wren just—"

While Mel frowned at Kit blaming Wren for falling ill, Hawke whirled to face Kit, his tears surging as he rasped, "Just what, Kay? Complain sooner? Take better care of herself? Never become pregnant?"

Kit stiffened. "No. Didn't Wren—"

At Kit continuing to needle a gravely ill Wren, fire flared through Mel. Glaring, he snapped, "Must you pursue your spite toward Wren *now*, Kit?"

He fisted his hands in his priest robes. Considering Kit's cruel needling, the devout and tender lady he loved was more of an illusion than the Goddess's. Kit was *still* the fashionable Countess of Blaine who lusted for wealth and status, spread malicious gossip, and only cared about herself. No wonder she'd refused to marry a humble priest. His love for the girl she'd been had blinded him.

Shoving that aside, he turned to Hawke and gripped Hawke's shoulder. "We'll head to the Center for Healing and fetch Elder Priestess Letitia. She's the best healer priest here. I'm certain she can help."

Hawke wiped his face and jerked a nod, then he and Mel hurtled down the hall.

CHAPTER 47

$\mathcal{A}$s Mel and Hawke ran from the priest quarters, Kit gaped after them without breathing. How could Mel have been so curt and scathing with her? All she'd been about to ask was why Wren hadn't requested Lady Ravenstone's help. As a soul healer, Lady Ravenstone could heal even fatal wounds or ailments, and Wren must know about her close friend's rare powers. Yet Hawke obviously didn't, which was odd. Usually everything Wren knew, Hawke knew as well.

Kit quit gaping when Sarah coughed behind her and asked, "Why did Mel snap at you like that?"

A flush scorching her skin, Kit turned to face Sarah and Deacon. How embarrassing that they'd witnessed Mel's scathing yet needless rebuke. "Mel is simply upset about Wren."

Sarah and Deacon glanced at each other, then Sarah replied, "Yes, but what did he mean by 'your spite toward Wren'?"

Tensing, Kit forced a shrug. "Wren and I have never gotten along. She was always so perfect," with such a perfect life, "that I couldn't resist needling her. Not that I was about to do so *now*." Even as a jealous girl of fifteen when she'd cruelly lied about Hawke, she wouldn't have stooped to needling Wren when she was close to dying.

Deacon hummed, a frown creasing his ascetic face. "I can't understand why Mel would believe that you'd behave with such cruelty."

Kit almost winced. Her past behavior toward Wren *could* lead someone to believe that she might. But Mel knew her better than anyone, and he loved her. Despite their quarrel over her refusal to accept his proposal right now, he'd called her devout, tender, insightful, and strong on several occasions. And he'd praised her when she'd helped Wren sit at the orphanage. He *must* know she'd never attack a gravely ill Wren.

Sarah squeezed Kit's hand. "I suspect Mel reacted harshly because he's also upset after whatever quarrel you two had during your romantic picnic yesterday."

Her heart twisting, Kit stilled. Surely not. She swallowed. But Mel had been so devastated that he'd barely looked at her since he'd accepted her refusal. And when he *had* looked at her, he'd addressed her with rigid politeness. Tears burned her eyes. "Perhaps it *was* our quarrel. Excuse me."

Before her tears could escape, she bolted into Sarah and Deacon's chambers then into her bedroom, firmly shutting the door behind her. Once alone, she allowed her tears to fall as she paced about the tiny room. Until Sarah had said that Mel's upset over their quarrel had inspired his scathing reaction, she'd assumed that their quarrel could be easily mended as soon as she'd determined who she was meant to be and broke the Goddess's illusion. But for him to be so wrongly harsh, when he was always so compassionate and perceptive, must mean he was furious with her as well as devastated.

She pressed her hands against her mouth. Had she turned Mel's love to hate by clinging to her fear of everyone's derision? *He'd* been willing to face the gossip their marriage would engender because he loved her. Yet she'd been too scared to listen to her heart—and not just about Mel. She wiped her face. He was right that she'd never become who she was meant to be if she continued denying her genuine self and the love she felt.

Kit stiffened her spine. So from this moment onward, she was going to say and do what she knew was right and live the way she'd always wanted, no matter the opinions of people she didn't love, respect, or share the same values. And that began with helping save Wren, her childhood rival. Because, as talented as Elder Priestess Letitia was, she was no soul healer, and Wren needed Lady Ravenstone now.

Kit snatched her flying carpet from where she'd abandoned it after her disastrous picnic with Mel. Then she burst from her bedroom and asked Deacon, "Does this have enough power to fly me around Ormas? I didn't recharge it last night." She'd been too upset.

As Sarah blinked at her, Deacon flicked his fingers and muttered a probing spell then replied, "Doubtful. But I could recharge it if you like."

Kit nodded. "Do it, but swiftly please. Wren mightn't have long." Please, Goddess, let her not be too late.

While Deacon took the flying carpet then muttered and gestured over it, Sarah eyed Kit. "Mel and his brother should be enroute now with Elder Priestess Letitia. What do you intend to do?"

Kit lifted her chin. "I must fetch someone who can better save Wren." When Sarah's brows rose, she added, "But I can't say whom." Lady Ravenstone's secret wasn't hers to share.

Fortunately, once she finished speaking, Deacon handed her the recharged carpet. "Here you are. Its power should last for several trips around Ormas now." He arched a brow. "Did you want some invisibility charms as well?"

Kit smiled at Deacon. "No, I've no time for that." And drawing too much attention wasn't important compared to Wren dying. "Thanks for recharging the carpet."

As Kit dashed toward the door, Sarah called after her, "Good luck, Kit. We'll be praying for you and Wren."

Kit raced through the priest quarters and past Dirk by the

door. Then she flung the flying carpet on the street and dropped atop it, muttering, "Sursum."

As the flying carpet rippled then rose, the people in the street gasped and pointed at her, but she ignored their stares as she tilted the carpet upward. Once above the buildings, she leaned forward, and the carpet sped toward Ravenstone House. Thank the Goddess she'd practice from flying to the royal bay yesterday.

At Ravenstone House, she pounded on the door while hovering above the front steps on the flying carpet. Remaining ready to whisk Lady Ravenstone to Wren and Hawke's town-house would get them there quicker.

The butler jerked open the door and gaped at her.

Kit snapped, "I require Lady Ravenstone at once."

Straightening, the butler quit gaping and frowned. "Do you have a card, madam?"

She gripped the front of the flying carpet. The butler clearly thought she was shifty and not to be trusted. "No, but I've an urgent message from Lady Beza Hawke."

The butler's mouth tightened, but then he sighed and replied, "Lord and Lady Ravenstone are out."

Kit clenched her jaw. This was taking forever. "Out *where*?"

His face stiff, the butler eyed her. "At Oakmoor House for the duke's soiree celebrating the arrival of the Orandian ambassador."

She swallowed a groan. Of course the Ravenstones were attending a court event hosted by her former suitor. She nodded at the butler. "Thanks." Then she spun the flying carpet and tore toward Oakmoor House.

As she approached, her stomach tightened. All of court would be at the Duke of Oakmoor's soiree. Not only had the social season started three weeks ago on Plantfete with the royal ceremonies, but councilors' events were always well attended, and the arrival of the first Orandian ambassador in a decade was momentous.

Although most wouldn't recognize her as Lady Blaine, letting all of court see her as a crone dressed as a maid would be wrenching, despite her new determination to ignore the opinions of those not important to her. Yet with Wren's life in danger, she couldn't falter.

Since she'd need to enter the soiree to find Lady Ravenstone, Kit sprang from the flying carpet at Oakmoor House. She draped the carpet on her shoulder without deactivating it to save time then pounded on the door.

The butler smoothly opened the door and stared down at her. "Yes?"

She flashed her blinding court smile and said in her most imperious voice, "I'm here to attend the Duke of Oakmoor's soiree." Please let her court demeanor convince the duke's butler to disregard her poor and old appearance.

The butler sniffed. "Do you possess an invitation?"

Kit brightened her smile. Too bad she'd not broken the Goddess's illusion yet. If she appeared herself, the butler would have let her enter without question. "I'm afraid I forgot my invitation. But find the Duke and Duchess of Childes or Lord Blaine or Lady Farson; one of them shall vouch for me."

His lips twisting, the butler snorted. "I think not." Then he slammed the door in her face.

She fisted her hands at her sides. She *had* to find Lady Ravenstone, but the duke's butler clearly wouldn't let her enter. She'd simply needed to find another way into the soiree. The garden would do. She should have started there rather than attempting the front door.

Flinging the flying carpet to the ground, she dove on and jerked it toward the sky. The carpet shot straight up, and she steered it into Oakmoor House's garden. Then she jumped off and wedged the still activated carpet beneath a stone bench rather than bringing it inside. The soiree would be packed, so carrying a carpet through the crowd would be impossible.

Kit ran toward the doors to the drawing room then swept

inside. She climbed atop the closest chair to hunt for Lady Ravenstone, her skin prickling at the whispers and sidelong glances from the surrounding guests. She grimaced when she spotted Lady Ravenstone across the drawing room beside her husband, Queen Kiera, King Devon, and a mature lady in an indigo tunic and white overcoat—surely the Orandian ambassador. Naturally, Lady Ravenstone would be as far away as possible.

She leapt from the chair and began shoving through the crowd to reach Lady Ravenstone when the Duke of Oakmoor strode before her. Doubtless the protesting guests around her had attracted his attention.

The duke scrutinized her, his usual suave smile missing. "Who are you? And why are you assaulting my guests?"

Blushing as more guests turned to stare, Kit lifted her chin and gritted a blinding grin. "I've an urgent message for Lady Ravenstone that must be delivered in person."

The Duke of Oakmoor frowned. "That doesn't answer who you are and how you got past my butler. I doubt you possess an invitation."

She glowered back, her blush fading. Must the duke keep delaying her? Wren's situation was dire. "Actually, I likely do possess an invitation—'tis simply at Blaine House." When the duke humphed, she set her jaw and said, "I'm Lady Blaine under a crone illusion."

While scandalized whispers rippled through the nearby guests, the Duke of Oakmoor snorted. "Since Lady Blaine disappeared months ago, 'tis easy enough to claim, but harder to prove."

Flushing again as all the surrounding guests peered at her, Kit fluttered her lashes at the duke with a coy moue like she had when they'd courted. "I promise you I am Lady Blaine. Just ask the Duke and Duchess of Childes or Lord Blaine or Lady Farson."

The duke grasped her wrist. "I'd prefer the opinion of the

royal witch instead. You might have deceived the others with some spell since they aren't witches and can't protect themselves against magic." He pulled her through the staring crowd.

Her flush cooling, she almost screamed. Not another delay. And unless Lady Juliet was a seer or could read auras, she'd not recognize her as Lady Blaine. But Lady Ravenstone should. "Let me speak with Lady Ravenstone. *Please*. 'Tis deadly urgent."

Ignoring her, the Duke of Oakmoor halted before the royal witch. "This crone here claims to be Lady Blaine under an illusion."

Slashing the duke a narrow glance, Lady Juliet pursed her lips. "I suppose you wish me to check for you."

The furiously gossiping guests becoming meaningless noise, Kit glowered at the duke and the royal witch. They must quit delaying her. Wren could be dying *right now*. She was opening her mouth to protest when Lady Juliet sighed and said, "Very well, I'll perform a probing spell."

Lady Juliet squinted at Kit as the feeling of magic flared about her—the royal witch must be performing her spell through will alone. Impressive. Then she tsked. "There's something peculiar about the lady, but I can't sense an illusion spell glowing about her."

As the duke humphed and clenched her wrist, Kit nearly winced but explained, "'Tis a spell from the Goddess, so only priests or seers can sense it. However, if you can read my aura, you'd recognize me as Lady Blaine."

The Duke of Oakmoor glared at her. "Spin your lies for someone more gullible."

Lady Juliet raised her eyes skyward. "If the lady *is* under a holy spell, she's correct that I'd be unable to sense it." She hummed and studied Kit. "I could read your aura if I wished, but 'twouldn't help since I don't know Lady Blaine's. Only seers, soul healers, and most magical creatures instinctively read auras. For the rest of us, 'tis difficult and considered an intrusion, so we rarely do so."

Kit sagged. Would these delays ever end? "Please, just let me speak with Lady Ravenstone."

The Duke of Oakmoor narrowed his eyes at her. "Why do you need to see *her*?"

Straightening, Kit tugged on her captured wrist and fiercely held the duke's suspicious gaze. She *must* convince him somehow. "I can't explain, but someone direly needs Lady Ravenstone's help."

Lady Juliet inhaled a sharp breath. "I think you'd better release the lady, Oakmoor."

The duke whirled to scowl at the royal witch, his grip remaining firm on Kit's wrist.

But before he could speak, Lady Ravenstone's serene voice interrupted them, "Lady Blaine? What happened to you?"

As the duke gaped and Lady Juliet relaxed, Kit wrenched her wrist free and faced Lady Ravenstone, who was on her husband's arm with Queen Kiera and King Devon beside them. Thankfully, the Orandian ambassador was elsewhere. Kit leaned forward. "Never mind what happened to me. Wren needs you. She's in childbirth and likely dying."

Both Lady Ravenstone and Queen Kiera turned white, and Queen Kiera gasped, "What?!"

Lady Ravenstone surged forward with little of her usual grace. "I'll go at once. I hope the carriage is fast enough."

Gulping a breath, Kit grabbed Lady Ravenstone's arm. "I've a flying carpet in the garden that shall get us there faster."

As Lady Ravenstone nodded and they bolted through the still gawking crowd, Queen Kiera called, "We'll fetch Wren and Hawke's families then follow you in our carriages."

In the garden, Kit yanked the flying carpet from beneath the stone bench. "Sit behind me and hold on. I'm going to fly as fast as this carpet can manage." Hopefully, 'twould counteract the many delays.

Once Lady Ravenstone grasped her waist, Kit jerked the

flying carpet upward, and they finally hurtled toward Wren. Please let them arrive in time.

CHAPTER 48

hile Elder Priestess Letitia, Healer Althea, and Healer Althea's apprentice bustled about a pale and still Wren, Mel prayed as he kept glancing between the healers and Hawke, who was pacing along the wall they'd been banished to when they'd arrived. In the ages they'd been here, little had changed—Wren remained unconscious, and the twins hadn't been born yet. And the longer they waited, the more his stomach tightened. But his fear was surely nothing compared to Hawke's.

He frowned at his pacing brother as Hawke muttered another curse and raked a hand through his tousled hair again. Somehow, he must calm Hawke and convince him to rest so he'd be fit to handle the twins when they arrived. Wren would likely be too weak to help much at first. Mel gripped Hawke's arm. "You should sit."

Hawke shuddered and shook off his hand. "I can't."

Before Mel could shove Hawke into a chair despite his protests, a sudden wail reverberated through Hawke and Wren's chambers, and both Mel and Hawke whirled toward the bed.

Her smile tight, Healer Althea's apprentice hurried over to them and shoved a whimpering bundle into Hawke's arms.

"Your daughter, my lord. Healthy and strong. I've washed her with a cleansing spell. You hold her while we deliver her twin."

As the apprentice healer strode away, Hawke cuddled his tiny daughter against his chest with a dazed expression.

Mel smiled. No doubt Hawke would be as besotted with his daughter as Aragon was with little Isabel. "She's lovely. Have you decided on a name?"

Hawke ran a gentle finger along his daughter's ruddy face. "Not yet. Wren and I were still debating." Then his head jerked toward the bed as another wail echoed through the room.

Healer Althea's apprentice hastened toward them with another whimpering bundle. "A fine and strapping son."

When Hawke gazed at his two squirming children without moving, Mel reached toward his brother and said, "Let me hold my niece so you can welcome your son."

Hawke nodded and relinquished his daughter then accepted his tiny son from the apprentice healer, who rushed back to the other healers.

Warmth filling him, Mel cradled his new niece against his chest. She was so much smaller and more fragile than Isabel when he'd first held his other niece, and she weighed almost nothing. He glanced at Hawke holding her brother—the other infant appeared just as tiny. "They're so small."

Hawke caressed his son's furrowed brow. "Healer Althea said twins usually are." He beamed down at his son. "Wren shall be ecstatic that we've one of each."

Mel chuckled and nudged Hawke. "Plus, you can tease Aragon that *you* had the first grandson, despite being the youngest."

Hawke flashed a crooked grin. "Oh, I shall. Although I suspect Wren shall tsk whenever I do." He sighed. "I hope she wakes soon to see what perfect children we made together."

Mel and Hawke both glanced toward the bed and stilled. The three healers continued bustling about an even more pale and still Wren while muttering healing spells. Mel's stomach clenched. For Wren to remain unconscious so long wasn't good. He began to pray again.

As Hawke drew a strangled gasp, Mel shifted his niece to one arm and squeezed his brother's shoulder, but he couldn't manage any comforting words that might be lies.

Eventually, Elder Priestess Letitia and Healer Althea quit casting their spells and trod across the room while the apprentice healer straightened the blankets about Wren.

Mel swallowed as Hawke stiffened beside him. Oh, Goddess, the healers' grave frowns didn't bode well.

Once the healers halted before them, Healer Althea murmured, "I'm so sorry, Lord Beza, but we shan't be able to save your wife. Our healing spells barely sustained her enough to deliver your children. If not for your bloodbond and Elder Priestess Letitia's assistance, I doubt I could have even managed that."

All the color leaving his face, Hawke froze. Clutching his son, he collapsed into the chair behind him and stared up at the healers, his gaze blank and wide. "No, no. Wren can't *die*."

Mel gripped Hawke's shoulder, his eyes burning with unshed tears. Hawke and Wren had always been inseparable—how was his brother to live without her? Plus, bloodbound couples often died within months of each other because their life forces were bound together. Would their twins give Hawke enough will to continue living?

Elder Priestess Letitia sighed. "Our magic shall continue keeping your wife alive long enough for you to say goodbye, my lord."

Hawke lurched upright and turned to Mel. "Could you..." His voice broke.

Gritting a soft smile, Mel took his little nephew from Hawke. Fortunately, the twins were so tiny that holding one in each arm wasn't difficult.

Hawke staggered across the room and collapsed beside Wren. Burying his face against her chest, he began to sob.

At his brother's grief, Mel's tears flowed as well. Cradling his niece and nephew, he pressed kisses against their foreheads. Please let Hawke recover so these precious infants weren't left orphans. Mother and Father would willingly raise them along with Aragon and Selena, but never knowing their parents would be hard.

Then footsteps thundered toward Hawke and Wren's chambers, and the door burst open, slamming against the wall. Mel and the three healers spun to face Kit and Lady Ravenstone bolting into the room. What was *Kit* doing here? And why with Lady Ravenstone?

When Elder Priestess Letitia, Healer Althea, and Healer Althea's apprentice surged forward, Kit blocked them, saying, "Lady Ravenstone must get to Wren."

Mel stared. What good would that do?

While the healers also gaped at Kit, Lady Ravenstone shoved aside Hawke and cupped Wren's face. A heartbeat later, color filled Wren's cheeks, and she gasped a shuddering breath then opened her eyes. She grinned at Lady Ravenstone while her friend sank onto the foot of the bed. "Thanks for saving me, Annalise."

As Lady Ravenstone grinned back, Hawke drew Wren into his arms, his eyes still bright with tears. He rasped, "Dear Goddess, Wren, I almost lost you."

When Wren caressed Hawke's face then kissed him, Mel beamed and hugged their twins against his chest. His niece and nephew wouldn't need to worry about becoming orphans now, thanks in part to Kit. Light suffused him as he glanced at Kit, who was watching Hawke and Wren with a teary smile. Somehow she'd known Lady Ravenstone could save Wren and had fetched the other countess, even though Wren was her childhood rival and facing the most beautiful lady in Calatini would remind Kit of her lost beauty. Perhaps he'd been wrong that Kit hadn't changed from the fashionable Countess of Blaine.

Their eyes wide, the three healers swept toward Lady Ravenstone, and Elder Priestess Letitia whispered, "You're a soul healer."

Mel inhaled. That explained how Lady Ravenstone could save Wren. As Lady Ravenstone nodded and rose to join the other healers, he strode to Kit and asked, "How did you discover Lady Ravenstone's powers?"

Not glancing at him, Kit shrugged. "While pursuing Lord Ravenstone, I overheard him and Lady Ravenstone discussing their secret soulbond." She frowned. "Wren obviously knew as well, although Hawke didn't. I assumed she would have told him."

His chest clenching, Mel gazed at Kit then shifted the twins as they began to fuss. "When Hawke arrived for a healer priest, you were attempting to suggest fetching Lady Ravenstone instead, weren't you?" And he'd snapped at her, wrongly believing she was needling Wren.

Kit inclined her head, eyeing the twins. "You should bring Wren her children. She'll be overjoyed to meet them, and they're probably hungry. I'll go handle arranging refreshments as well as the frantic family and friends about to arrive." She grimaced. "Besides, I doubt Wren—or Hawke—want me here right now."

As Kit swept from Hawke and Wren's chambers, Mel stared after her, his chest clenching further. How could he have been so wrong about her? Doubtless his lack of faith had hurt her—as much as her refusing his proposal had hurt him. He must apologize once they were alone.

He swallowed then, like Kit had suggested, approached Hawke and Wren, who were still kissing. "Would you like to meet your twins, Wren?"

Beaming, Wren quit kissing Hawke and reached for her children. "Yes, please." She cooed when Mel laid the tiny infants in her arms. "They're adorable."

Staring at Wren and the twins, Hawke stiffened. "And deadly."

Mel almost winced. Hawke must still be reeling from nearly

losing Wren for his earlier delight in their children to be so absent.

While he gripped Hawke's shoulder to comfort him, Wren narrowed her eyes at her husband and said, "Don't you dare blame the twins for that. I'm fine—thanks to Annalise. How did you know to fetch her?"

Hawke swallowed. "I didn't. But thank the Goddess someone did."

When Wren blinked, Mel opened his mouth to explain about Kit, but before he could decide how to, Wren called, "Annalise, come back so I can thank you properly for saving me."

Abandoning her hushed conversation with the other healers, Lady Ravenstone glided over to the bed with a warm smile. "You thanked me properly already. I'm just glad I arrived in time." She shuddered. "And that after Kiera's coronation, the veiled witch requested as her boon for helping Dare and I that we remain in Ormas through Summerday at least. If we were back in Wilde-wall like we'd planned, I never could have returned fast enough to save you."

As Hawke whitened, Mel squeezed his brother's shoulder again. His family owed the veiled witch deep thanks for that boon.

Wren hummed. "Kiera and I wondered why you altered your plans." She smiled down at the twins. "Hawke and I must thank the veiled witch for that. Did she tell you I needed you tonight as well?"

Lady Ravenstone tilted her head, her white-blonde hair shimmering. "No, Lady Blaine fetched me from the Duke of Oakmoor's soiree."

Mel inhaled. Kit had braved facing court while under the Goddess's illusion to fetch Lady Ravenstone to save Wren? He'd definitely been wrong that Kit hadn't changed.

Hawke and Wren traded a wide glance, then Wren muttered, "*Kit* did?"

Lady Ravenstone nodded. "Lady Blaine's appearance as an elderly lady shall be the gossip at court for months."

His throat tightening, Mel swallowed. So Kit's worst fear had been realized when she'd risked facing court to save Wren. She must be upset, although she'd concealed it well earlier, focusing instead on how else she could help. Exactly like she had at the Great Temple during the past few months. Kit *was* the devout and tender lady he'd believed her to be until he'd let his hurt blind him.

Blinking, Wren shifted the twins in her arms and asked, "Elderly lady? What—"

Before Wren could finish, her parents and Kiera hurtled inside with Kiera bearing a laden tray.

Tears shimmering in her eyes, Lady Keyes blurted, "Wren, are you all right?"

Wren smiled at her mother. "Perfectly. Come meet your grandchildren."

Mel and the others chuckled when Lady Keyes scooped both twins into her arms like a proud mama roc swooping up her chicks. Mother would likely do the same when she arrived. 'Twas amazing that she wasn't here already.

As Kiera set the tray of food on Wren's lap, Sir Alaric tickled the infants in his wife's arms. "Everyone else is downstairs. Kit insisted on only two guests at a time to avoid overwhelming you. I swear she's become more managing than your mother-in-law. Just like a proper elderly lady."

Kiera grinned at Wren while she handed one of the bowls of spiced apples with honey and cream to Lady Ravenstone. "Lady Blaine even refused to let me visit with your parents unless I brought food for you and Annalise."

Lady Ravenstone beamed. "Bless Lady Blaine for realizing we'd desperately need food after that soul-healing."

Mel stared as Lady Ravenstone devoured her spiced apples. He'd never imagined anyone could eat that fast, let alone a lady renowned for her ice-perfect reputation.

While Wren began her spiced apples too, Elder Priestess Letitia joined them with Healer Althea. "Kit did help at the Center for Healing for almost a week, so she saw how much powerful healing spells tired us and our patients. She had a maid bring us a tray as well."

Healer Althea nodded. "A most insightful lady." She smiled at Wren. "Your guests should keep their visits brief so you can rest, Lady Beza. Plus, the twins shall need their first feeding soon."

As Wren blushed but nodded, Mel smiled at her and Hawke then said, "I'll go fetch Mother and Father." No doubt they were desperate for their turn to visit Wren and their grandchildren.

Lady Ravenstone rose. "I'll join you." She embraced Wren. "Write when you're up for a visit." Once she took his arm and they left, she murmured, "Lady Blaine has everyone gathered in the drawing room."

He eyed Lady Ravenstone. Odd that she knew that, although the drawing room *was* a logical guess. However, he simply nodded and escorted her downstairs.

When they joined the others, Lady Ravenstone glided to her husband, and his parents mobbed Mel.

Father hovering beside her, Mother gripped Mel's arm. "How are Wren and the twins?"

Mel patted Mother's hand with a grin. "Well. They're waiting for you and Father to visit them." He laughed when his parents flew from the drawing room like djinns seeking freedom. Lady Keyes wouldn't get to monopolize the twins for long.

He glanced about the drawing room for Kit. His heart fluttered at her smile while speaking to Lord and Lady Ravenstone. He was about to join her when Aragon, Selena, and Devon waylaid him.

Aragon grinned. "Kit assured us that everyone was well, but Mother and Father were too worried to actually believe her."

Selena leaned toward Mel. "Wren and the twins *are* well, aren't they?"

Mel grinned to reassure Selena. "Yes, thanks to Lady Ravenstone's extraordinary powers. 'Twas remarkable to witness."

Devon glanced at the Ravenstones still speaking with Kit. "Although Kiera didn't admit Lady Ravenstone was a soul healer until the carriage ride over, I'd suspected as much once Lord and Lady Ravenstone became betrothed. Only a soulbond would have convinced the Greysnowes to accept their daughter marrying a Ravenstone. And Lady Ravenstone *was* at the nearly fatal duel between Lord Ravenstone and her brother."

His brows rising, Mel hummed. Lady Ravenstone must have soul-healed Lord Ravenstone's fatal wound and formed their soulbond then. "Kiera never told you that Lady Ravenstone was a soul healer before?" Although Wren clearly hadn't told Hawke, Devon was the *king*.

Devon shrugged. "Kiera said she and Wren were concerned that too many people knowing Lady Ravenstone's secret powers would lead to everyone discovering them. Being an acknowledged soul healer can be a heavy burden since they're rare and coveted."

Aragon inclined his head. "Kiera made all of us swear not to discuss Lady Ravenstone's powers with anyone else—not even the rest of the family."

Selena nodded as well. "Which we were all happy to swear. But 'tis fortunate Lady Blaine somehow knew that Lady Ravenstone was a soul healer. Although I'm surprised she didn't tell all of court when she discovered that."

Kit smiled while she and the Ravenstones joined them. "I decided to quit gossiping after telling court about Wren's pregnancy went painfully wrong for me." As a blush darkened Selena's freckled cheeks, Kit grinned at her. "But I can understand why you'd suspect I would. I was desperate to be influential at court back then."

As Aragon, Selena, and Devon blinked at Kit, Mel couldn't hide his grin. Kit had changed so much since last summer. He'd been a hurt and blind fool for believing she hadn't. His heartfelt apology couldn't come soon enough.

Then Mother, Father, and the Keyes rejoined Mel and the others, so Aragon, Selena, and Devon headed upstairs. They weren't there long before they and Kiera returned to the drawing room because the healers insisted 'twas time to feed the twins. After that, everyone left.

Carrying Kit's drained flying carpet as they walked back to the Great Temple, Mel kept glancing at Kit, but he didn't speak, and neither did she. It had been an intense evening and 'twas late. Plus, although they were alone at last, he must apologize somewhere he could kiss her afterward and renew his marriage proposal—like his chambers.

Yet when they reached their doors, Deacon and Sarah swept into the hall. Sarah asked, "How's Wren?"

Kit grinned. "Perfectly recovered and the proud mother of healthy twins."

Sarah grasped Kit's arm. "How wonderful! Tell me everything—or at least as much as you're free to."

Mel sighed as Sarah pulled Kit into her and Deacon's chambers. Apparently, his apology to Kit must wait until tomorrow. At least 'twould allow him time to think about what he must say to earn her forgiveness for misjudging her. He spoke to Deacon for a few moments then handed his friend Kit's flying carpet before retreating to his own chambers.

CHAPTER 49

*A*fter Lauds and organizing the almskitchens the following morning, Kit slanted glances at Mel while they fetched breakfast. They must discuss everything that had happened in the past few days. And from how he kept glancing at her too, doubtless he felt the same. Fortunate because she must apologize and make amends for hurting him. After thinking about it since leaving Wren and Hawke's yesterday, she knew precisely what she needed to say.

She sighed as they sat. But the dining hall wasn't private enough for an emotional discussion that would hopefully end in wild kisses. Plus, Mel mightn't have time before his duties. Perhaps they should wait until this evening instead. She could arrange a romantic dinner for the two of them, although not to the royal bay since her flying carpet hadn't recharged yet. She'd ask him once they finished eating.

His gaze on his tea as he added his three spoons of honey, Mel coughed then asked, "Would you mind not praying at the Sun Chapel this morning so we can talk privately before my duties?"

She beamed and leaned toward Mel. How wonderful that

they needn't wait to reconcile. Their romantic dinner could be to celebrate instead. "I'd like that. Very much."

Mel looked at her and grinned back, then they devoured their breakfast without speaking. She couldn't help smiling at how eager they both were to talk privately. Wild kisses would definitely be involved.

However, when they were leaving the dining hall, Paul scurried over and handed her a note from Wren. Her smile fading, Kit sighed while she read Wren's request that she visit this morning. Although Wren should be well after her soul-healing, a lady who'd given birth should need more time to rest. Plus, Wren had never invited *her* to visit before. Such an unwonted request shouldn't be postponed.

Studying her as they strode toward his chambers, Mel arched his brows. "What is it?"

Halting, she gritted a tight smile. "Wren wants me to visit this morning, so I'm afraid I must delay our talk. She'd not invite me unless 'twas serious."

Mel sighed as well but took her hand. "Do you want me to join you?"

Her smile warming, Kit squeezed his hand. "You've your duties to attend to, but thanks. As for our talk, perhaps we could have dinner in your chambers tonight instead?"

Mel tenderly kissed her palm. "I'll look forward to it."

As tingling flooded her, she almost pulled Mel closer for a true kiss. But she made herself free her hand instead. Kisses must wait until after they'd discussed everything and she'd made amends for hurting him. She grinned at Mel. "I'll handle the food tonight since you arranged our delectable picnic to the royal bay."

Mel inclined his head. "Very well." He grinned back. "Until tonight."

Then they separated—he to his study, and she to visit Wren. On her way, she stopped by the Great Temple kitchen to arrange dinner with Esther.

Quartering a chicken with a sharp knife, Esther smiled as she approached. "Morning, Kit. What brings you by?"

Kit returned the head kitchen priestess's smile. "Could you have some dinner set aside for me and Mel tonight? And could I make some cinnaspice-honey burnt custard this afternoon as well?" Bringing Mel's favorite dessert would make their dinner special and be part of her apology.

Her eyes gleaming, Esther chuckled. "*Another* private dinner for you two? Mel just arranged your picnic the other day. Shall there be an announcement soon?"

Kit blushed. "I hope so. Now about tonight?"

Esther chuckled again. "Setting aside dinner shall be fine, and I'll have everything for your burnt custard ready for you this afternoon in the corner Sarah uses."

After thanking Esther, Kit left and walked to Wren and Hawke's townhouse. When she arrived, their butler Hobb opened the door with a broad grin. "Good morning, Lady Blaine. Lord and Lady Beza are in the nursery with the twins. They said you should join them as soon as you arrived." Then he described the way to the nursery.

Nodding her thanks, she headed upstairs then quietly knocked on the nursery door before entering. Wren was nursing one of the twins on the sofa along the far wall, while Hawke was pacing with the other cuddled against his chest, although a nursemaid was sitting between the cradles.

Both Wren and Hawke smiled at her, and Wren nodded toward the seat beside her then said, "Kit, come sit so we can talk."

Kit smiled back and settled on the sofa beside Wren, who was lively again. Whatever she wanted to discuss clearly wasn't ill health. Good. "I was surprised you were up for a visit already."

Wren shrugged, her lips wry. "Annalise's soul-healing restored me to perfect health, as if I'd not given birth yesterday— except we've newborn twins to care for. I hope you don't mind that I'm nursing right now."

Kit smiled. She'd become accustomed to seeing women nurse at the Goddess's Refuge, although Wren being so comfortable with her was unexpected. "I don't mind."

Still pacing, Hawke flashed his usual crooked grin—nothing like the glares he'd given her in the months before the Goddess's illusion. "We were trying to ensure the twins were sleeping before you arrived so that you and Wren could talk easier, but neither of them seem to sleep without nursing and a lot of walking first."

Wren chuckled, beaming at the tiny twin she was nursing. "Your parents *did* warn us you hated sleeping on a schedule as an infant too."

Kit swallowed a laugh. Somehow that wasn't surprising.

Hawke hummed. "Yes, but I hoped your sweeter nature would triumph. Thank the Goddess for nursemaids." He peered at the twin in his arms then whispered, "She's finally asleep." He handed his infant daughter to the nursemaid who'd risen to join him.

As the nursemaid carefully settled the sleeping infant in her cradle, Wren smiled at her husband and said, "I'll see you later."

Kit's brows rose. Hawke was willingly leaving Wren and the twins?

Hawke bent to kiss Wren then straightened and studied Kit. "Before I go, Wren and I must thank you for fetching Lady Ravenstone yesterday. If you hadn't, Wren would have died." His voice roughened, "And I doubt I could live without her."

Kit inclined her head. It *was* impossible to imagine Wren or Hawke without the other. "I'm glad I could help." Glancing between them, she inhaled then said what she should have said years ago, "And I'm sorry for lying about kissing Hawke. 'Twas cruel and wrong of me."

Wren and Hawke blinked, then Hawke murmured, "True, although something I never expected you to admit." He sighed. "But as Wren has said, you weren't entirely to blame for our foolishness. She and I were both too young and scared to fight for our love."

Handing her infant son to the nursemaid, Wren smiled at Kit. "Plus, your help yesterday more than offset your long-ago lie." She shooed Hawke toward the door. "Go on then."

Once Hawke sighed again and left, Kit eyed Wren and murmured, "Hawke could have stayed. I'm certain he hates leaving you and the twins right now."

Wren smiled at the nursemaid pacing the nursery to settle her son. "Yes, but I wanted to talk with you alone. Besides, Hawke has business correspondence he's been neglecting." She turned to Kit. After a long moment, she said, "You seem different."

Shrugging, Kit quirked a wry smile. "Yes, I appear six decades older than I should." Although she was more her genuine self than when she appeared herself.

Wren wrinkled her nose. "'Tisn't what I meant. When you were at court, or even when I met you as Mel's elderly assistant at Annalise's wedding, you always seemed prickly and unsatisfied. But now, you've an air of serenity about you, as if you've discovered where you belong."

Kit chuckled. "Thanks to the Goddess's illusion, I believe I might have, although the details aren't quite settled." She still must reconcile with Mel then talk with High Priest Theodag. And the Goddess's illusion hadn't broken yet.

Wren beamed at her. "I'm glad."

Kit coughed a laugh. "Of course you are. You're a sweet, selfless paragon." She shook her head. "That, along with your adoring parents and Hawke's deep love, always made me terribly jealous. 'Tis why I could never resist needling you. And why I blurted that cruel lie about Hawke. I truly am sorry about that."

Wren squeezed her hand. "We were all so young. If I'd trusted Hawke's love like I should have, I'd never have believed you. And you suffered such a wretched childhood thanks to your horrible father. But we've all matured a lot since then. Now, I'd confront Hawke rather than burying my upset, and you'd let all of court see you as an elderly lady to save someone you'd once hurt." She arched a brow. "How did you discover Annalise's powers, anyway?"

Her chest lightening, Kit shrugged. "I overheard her and Lord Ravenstone together. I believe I did so that I was able to help save you yesterday. The Goddess always has reasons for our experiences."

Wren scrutinized her then smiled. "So it seems."

Kit glanced across the nursery as the nursemaid finally settled Wren's sleeping son in his cradle. "What did you and Hawke name the twins?"

Wren beamed at the two cradles. "Our daughter Kestrel, and our son Peregrine."

Kit giggled. How the duchess must have sighed at her newest grandchildren's unusual names. "Only you and Hawke would name your children after *birds*."

Wren flashed a grin remarkably like Hawke's. "Falcons, actually. They're basically halfway between wrens and hawks."

Laughing again, Kit rose. "I should go. Hawke is doubtless desperate to rejoin you."

Wren rose as well and embraced her. "Visit again soon, and bring Mel next time."

A blush warming her cheeks, Kit nodded. Hopefully, she and Mel would be betrothed before they visited together. "Of course."

After leaving Wren and Hawke's, Kit helped at the Goddess's Refuge until mid-afternoon rather than finding High Priest Theodag to discuss her future. She must reconcile with Mel first.

Then she returned to the Great Temple to prepare the cinnaspice-honey burnt custard. After making the karamelized topping, she sprinkled more sugar and cinnaspice on Mel's in the shape of a heart. 'Twould be a perfect prelude to what she needed to say to make amends for hurting him.

Dessert prepared, she collected the dinner Esther had set aside for them and arranged everything on the small table in

Mel's chambers. She placed their covered burnt custards on their plates so they could begin their discussion with her apology. As she waited for Mel to arrive, she perched on a chair before his bookcase, smoothing her maid's skirt and practicing what she would say again.

Fortunately, Mel soon strode through his door and grinned at the laden table. "Everything appears wonderful."

Her heart quickening, Kit rose and joined him then waved for him to sit. "I can't accept praise for most of it—I only prepared the dessert, which I thought we could begin with tonight."

Mel chuckled and sat across from her. "You know how I adore beginning with dessert."

As Mel began lifting the cover, she placed a hand on his to stop him. She inhaled. "But before you do, I've words to say."

Smiling at her, Mel released the cover and brushed a kiss against her palm. "I've words to say as well."

Tingling flooding her, Kit cupped his jaw. "Please let me go first." She inhaled another bracing breath. "I'm sorry that I was so scared of everyone's derision that I denied the love in my heart. Being fake to gain admiration was wrong, and my stubborn refusal hurt you—the gentleman I love. Can you forgive me?"

Mel kissed her palm again. "Of course. Can you forgive me for not trusting that you'd changed and wrongly accusing you of needling Wren when you were attempting to save her because I was hurt that you refused my proposal?"

Tears pricked her eyes, but she managed a tremulous smile as she echoed Mel, "Of course." She swallowed. "Shall we begin dessert now?"

Sighing, Mel released her hand and lifted the cover on his cinnaspice-honey burnt custard. Then he stilled. "My favorite— adorned with a heart, no less."

Her pulse pounding in her throat, Kit leaned toward Mel. "Because without you I don't have one. Mel, will you marry me?"

Mel stared at her, his deep-brown eyes warm and intense.

"But what about the Goddess's illusion and the gossip our marriage shall engender?"

She shifted in her seat. "I was a fool to care about the opinions of people I don't love, respect, or share the same values. Plus, I love you too much to live without you. Please marry me."

Grinning, Mel leapt upright. "Yes!" He pulled her into his arms and captured her mouth in a hungry kiss.

Tingling heat sparkling in her veins, Kit sighed and fisted her hands in Mel's hair as she deepened their kiss. She was breathless and flushed and giddy when he eventually lifted his head.

Mel smiled down at her. "Besides marrying me, have you decided what else you'll do here?"

She smiled back and smoothed the coal-brown hair she'd mussed. Unlike Father had, Mel would never scathingly deride her for confessing the calling in her heart. "I'm going to become a priestess."

A blinding flash flared about her as faint humming echoed and the cinnaspice-apple fragrance of Goddess laurels filled the room.

When the light vanished, Kit gasped and gaped at her hands, which no longer appeared gnarled and spotted with age. The Goddess's illusion had broken at last. Because her calling to serve the Goddess was who she was meant to be and always had been. She'd just been too scared and ashamed to believe it after suffering Father's bitter derision her entire childhood.

Warmth suffused her chest. But the Goddess had loved her enough to bestow an illusion that had taught her to see past her blindness and bring her home to the Great Temple where she belonged. And her calling was even shared by the gentleman she loved who loved her, so they could build a happy and fulfilled life together. She was so blessed.

CHAPTER 50

His eyes dazzled from the blinding flash, Mel stared down at Kit, whose hair was once more a vivid sable and her face smooth and gorgeous again. The Goddess's illusion had finally broken. He smiled. "You'll make a wonderful priestess." He kissed her nose. "Clearly the Goddess believes that too."

Kit laughed with a glowing grin. "I'm thankful she made her approbation so obvious."

Warmed by her joy, he arched his brows. "You've been successfully and happily acting like a priestess since you've begun participating in temple life. Why would you doubt your calling?" He'd only doubted it because he'd believed she wanted a fashionable life at court.

Kit sighed, her grin dimming. "Because throughout my childhood, Father always sneered about how wicked and vulgar I was." She shivered. "His scathing derision when I was twelve and told him about my calling to become a priestess convinced me 'twas impossible."

Fire flared through Mel. That despicable degenerate. Too bad Sir Jason wasn't still alive so he could strangle him. "After that abusive rant I interrupted, I should have realized your vile father's venom was responsible."

Kit caressed his clenched jaw. "But your steadfast love and support began to help me see past Father's bitter sneers, as did my contentment while participating in temple life. And my talk with High Priest Theodag the other day made me realize I didn't need to be perfect to become a priestess. I knew then I could be who I always longed to be."

His anger at her father easing, he kissed Kit's palm. No wonder her mind had been whirling afterward. "If you knew that then, why didn't the Goddess's illusion break?"

Kit tilted her head. "Probably because I didn't admit my decision aloud. Until I possessed the strength to do that, I wasn't ready to become who I was meant to be. And I didn't possess the strength for that until I realized how clinging to my fear had devastated you. Facing court as a crone to save Wren helped too. Not only did I discover that I could survive without the admiration of shallow people who care more about appearances than genuine decency or kindness, but I also atoned for how I'd hurt Wren and Hawke, which had shamed me from the moment I'd done it."

Mel squeezed Kit with a warm smile. "I knew your tender heart felt remorse about that when you didn't let Wren collapse at the orphanage." He narrowed his eyes at her. "Despite your refusal to admit it when I first confronted you about that."

Blushing, Kit shifted in his arms. "I was determined not to admit such vulnerability to anyone, not even you."

His chest tightening, he swallowed. "'Twas how you'd learned to protect yourself from your vile father's cruelty." He brushed a kiss against Kit's lips. "But why *did* you lie to Wren about kissing Hawke? Jealousy?"

Kit lowered her gaze. "In part. But mostly because I'd overheard you tell your brothers about your calling to become a priest."

Mel blinked at Kit. If she'd overheard that, she'd also overheard Hawke's plans to kiss Wren, which explained how she'd known to lie about kissing Hawke and ruin his and Wren's Longnight kiss.

Kit sighed. "I was devastated by your plans and blurted out my cruel lie when next talking to Wren." She grimaced. "Exactly like Father would have done."

He studied Kit with a faint frown. Then he tilted her chin until their gazes met. "Why did my calling to become a priest devastate you?"

Swallowing, Kit licked her lips. "Because I loved and planned to marry you as soon as I convinced you we were old enough. But I didn't believe I was worthy of marrying a priest. And to escape Father, I knew I must marry."

His heart wrenching, Mel softly kissed Kit again. Believing he wasn't worthy of anything he wanted would have devastated him too. "If only I'd realized back then how cruelly you'd suffered because of your father's abuse."

Kit smiled and captured his face in her palms. "As I told Mother when she mourned the past, we must take joy in what we have now. The Goddess has reasons for allowing the experiences that shape us." She kissed him. "If Father hadn't raised me, I wouldn't have known and loved *you*, and I'd not sacrifice that. Plus, I wouldn't be *me* if I'd lived differently, and I'll doubtless make a better priestess because of my childhood."

He smiled back at Kit despite the lingering ache in his chest at her childhood suffering. "You'll make one of the best priestesses ever then." Grinning to cheer them both, he asked, "Shall we eat? Your wonderful dinner is getting cold."

Kit nodded, and they returned to the table.

Mel sighed as he ate his first spoonful of his cinnaspice-honey burnt custard adorned with a heart. Delicious. "This burnt custard is even better than the ones you made for my natalday."

Kit tilted her head. "I used the recipe Sarah taught me before, so I can't imagine why."

He grinned at Kit. "The heart adorning it, I think. Or perhaps 'twas the proposal accompanying it." He leaned forward with a teasing frown. "Although that proposal spoiled the one I'd planned to make after my apology."

Giggling, Kit finished her burnt custard. "You're just jealous my tongue was faster." She sobered. "But I knew I needed to propose to make amends for hurting you with my stubborn refusal."

His heart warmed. And Kit had asked while still under the Goddess's illusion, proving that she no longer cared about engendering gossip and that she was willing to risk they might need to work to remain together if her place hadn't been at the Great Temple. He reached across the table to take her hand. "I love you, Kit."

Kit threaded her fingers through his with a radiant smile. "I love you too, Mel."

They smiled at each other, the joyous silence humming about them. Burning to kiss Kit until they were breathless, Mel sighed and released her hand. Although no longer inappropriate, their ravenous kisses could easily lead to more, and they weren't married yet.

So as he and Kit resumed eating, he said they should write their families as well as arrange a meeting with High Priest Theodag and Elder Priestess Agnes. Kit agreed, and they discussed that over dinner. Then they wrote their notes before he returned her to Sarah and Deacon's chambers.

When they reached their friends' door, it flew open, and Sarah beamed at them with Deacon grinning behind her. She said, "You broke the Goddess's illusion at last!"

Returning their grins, Kit squeezed Mel's hand. "Plus, Mel and I are betrothed."

As Deacon clapped Mel's shoulder, Sarah bounced and beamed brighter. "I knew you would be when Esther told me you'd arranged another private dinner." She pulled Kit inside. "Now, tell me all about who you're meant to be and Mel's proposal."

Kit laughed. "Actually, 'twas *my* proposal."

Smiling as she and Sarah began talking and giggling together, Mel left to send his and Kit's notes. He'd see Kit tomorrow.

AFTER BREAKFAST THE FOLLOWING MORNING, Mel and Kit headed to High Priest Theodag's study to meet with the high priest and Elder Priestess Agnes.

Once they sat in the chairs before the desk, the high priest smiled at Kit. "I see you've discovered who you're meant to be."

Mel took Kit's hand as she swallowed then lifted her chin and said, "I'm going to become a priestess."

High Priest Theodag's eyes crinkled. "I suspected you might."

Mel squeezed Kit's hand when she blushed at Elder Priestess Agnes's calm nod. Obviously neither of their superiors were surprised by Kit's calling. Not surprising. He leaned forward and added, "Kit and I also intend to marry as soon as the Goddess approves our marriage."

High Priest Theodag and Elder Priestess Agnes traded a smile. Then the elder priestess murmured, "We suspected that as well. Even before the gossip about your betrothal spread through the Great Temple."

The high priest chuckled. "Although you must wait until Summerday to seek approval from the Goddess."

Kit sighing beside him, Mel suppressed a grimace. He'd forgotten 'twas tradition for priests to wait until holy days to seek approval for their marriages because their god's presence was strongest on those days. Two months was a long time.

High Priest Theodag grinned at Kit. "But we'll endeavor to keep you busy until Summerday. You must begin your novitiate —an accelerated one that only takes two years since you're older than most novices. We do the same for warrior priests who enter the novitiate after becoming warriors. We'll discuss further details once Agnes and Mel leave to handle their duties."

Mel leaned forward. "Before Elder Priestess Agnes and I

leave, Kit and I require luncheon and the afternoon free. We wrote to our families about our betrothal last night, and Mother arranged a family luncheon to celebrate."

Elder Priestess Agnes smiled. "Of course she did. I'll handle your duties this afternoon, although we must choose some additional assistants for you soon. You no longer require my advice with your duties."

As Kit squeezed his hand, Mel grinned. So except for his investiture on Longnight, he wasn't just the acting elder community priest of Calatini anymore.

Then he and Elder Priestess Agnes left to handle his duties, but he returned to fetch Kit several hours later for luncheon. Although they took the carriage Mother sent, he and Kit were still the last to arrive at his parents' townhouse. Even Hawke and Wren were there despite her giving birth two days ago. When he and Kit entered the drawing room, everyone stared at them.

After a moment, his parents separated from Wren's parents, and Mother embraced him then embraced Kit while Father clapped his shoulder. As Father kissed Kit's cheek, Mother said, "I'm glad you two admitted your love at last." She tilted her head and tsked. "Although you didn't write that the Goddess's illusion had broken as well."

Between Farson and Arvan on a sofa across the room, Elise leaned toward Kit. "I suppose the Goddess's illusion broke when you accepted Mel's proposal because you were meant to be his wife."

Mel and Kit smiled at each other. Explaining that he'd accepted her proposal would simply confuse matters. Kit replied instead, "No, when I declared I was going to become a priestess."

Everyone except Mother and Father blinked at Kit. Then Edouard laughed from his chair beside Pippa and her brothers before drawling, "I shouldn't be surprised, considering how you *frivolously* spent most of your allowance on charities for years. I finally tracked down that bookkeeper of yours yesterday."

As Kit blushed, Pippa giggled and added, "Edouard was stunned when he did."

Mel grinned at Kit, light suffusing his chest. "He wouldn't have been if he'd known that Kit used to visit poor villagers with me when we were children."

Everyone but his parents blinked at Kit again. His arm about Selena, Aragon exchanged a glance with Hawke and Devon then asked, "How did the rest of us never know about that growing up?"

As Mel sighed, Kit grimaced and replied, "I kept my visits secret to prevent Father from discovering them. Although somehow your mother and mine knew."

This time, everyone—including Mother and Father—stared at Kit. From between Hawke and Kiera, Wren murmured, "I thought your mother was dead."

Mel smiled when Kit grinned and said, "No, just living in Dracwyn with her second husband and my siblings. Father magically prevented her from approaching me, so I didn't know she was alive until he died two weeks ago."

Everyone stared at Kit again, but no one bothered to mourn her vile father's death. Good.

After a lengthy moment, Mother waved toward the door. "Shall we continue discussing all these fascinating revelations over luncheon?" Following that lively discussion and several toasts during their delectable meal, Mother grinned at Mel and Kit. "Now that everything is settled, we'll host a fete here celebrating your betrothal in a month."

Mel almost sighed. He should have known Mother couldn't resist hosting a court event. "Kit and I can't request the Goddess's approval for our marriage until Summerday. Perhaps we should wait until after that for a celebration."

Mother pursed her lips. "Nonsense." She turned to Kit. "And if you stay away from court until the fete, no one shall realize you appear yourself again. *Everyone* shall attend to see you two together."

Mel and Kit traded a wry glance. So they would.

Then Kit shrugged. "As you like. I shan't have time for court events with my duties and novitiate, anyway." She hummed. "Although at this fete, I think the entertainment besides dancing should be charity themed rather than one of Wren's lovely plays."

Mel grinned when Wren sagged with relief and Kit winked back. Kit's request had clearly been to prevent Mother from forcing the shy Wren to pen a play for court like she had for her fete celebrating Isabel's future birth.

Mother inclined her head. "I'll let you handle the special entertainment. No doubt it shall be as spectacular as the Great Temple's court event."

Soon after, they finished luncheon with delicious cinnaspice-honey burnt custards with extra cinnaspice, although Kit's yesterday was still better.

As everyone began leaving, Mel turned to Father and asked, "Could Kit and I use your communication mirror to call her family? Mine at the Great Temple is busy." Elder Priestess Agnes was probably midway through the call with the elder community priest of Blackham right now.

Father smiled. "Of course. And tell Kit's family that they can stay at Childes House when they visit Ormas. I imagine they plan to do so soon."

Mel nodded, warmed by Father's offer. "Just to warn you, Kit's mother could only marry her second husband after Kit's father died, and he's a wealthy smuggler. They'll be somewhat scandalous."

Father flashed a crooked grin. "I suspected they would be. But Caro shall shape the gossip to their advantage—she always does."

Mel nearly snorted. Mother adored doing so too. Then he and Kit strode to Father's study, and she activated Father's communication mirror.

Once the mirror cleared to reveal Mrs. Poole and a sturdy

gentleman who must be her husband, Mrs. Poole's eyes immediately overflowed. "The Goddess's illusion broke. Oh, how lovely."

As his wife's tears silenced her, Mr. Poole wrapped an arm about her and smiled at Kit while asking, "Who are you meant to be then?"

Her lips wry, Kit chuckled. "A priestess—just like Mother suggested during our first mirror call."

Mel swallowed his laugh. So even Kit's long-lost mother had seen her calling at once.

Beaming, Mrs. Poole wiped her face. "I'm so happy that you've found your place at last and that we can visit now that the Goddess's illusion is broken."

Mr. Poole nodded. "I'll begin preparing my fastest ship. We'll be there in under a week."

Kit leaned forward with a warm smile. "I look forward to meeting you and my siblings in person. Although I shall be rather busy with my duties and my novitiate."

Mel squeezed Kit's hand. She adored being busy as much as he did. "But we should have most evenings free." He grinned at her mother and stepfather. "And my parents have offered for you to stay with them while you're in Ormas."

As her husband blinked, Mrs. Poole gaped at Mel then muttered, "The Duke and Duchess of Childes invited *us*?"

Still grinning, Mel shrugged. "You're family now—Kit and I intend to marry as soon as the Goddess approves on Summerday."

Mrs. Poole beamed and began crying again. "How wonderful."

While a smiling Mr. Poole offered his wife a pocketcloth, Kit grinned and said, "And since you'll be in Ormas, you can attend the betrothal fete the duchess is hosting for us."

Kit's mother exclaimed at that, then she and Kit spent the rest of the mirror call chattering about the betrothal fete and the upcoming visit while Mel and Kit's stepfather mostly looked on with indulgent smiles.

After ending the mirror call, Mel and Kit found his parents to say farewell before returning to the Great Temple. As he thanked Father for letting them use the communication mirror, Kit and Mother began to murmur together like conspiring imps.

So once they climbed into the carriage, he wrapped an arm about Kit and asked, "What was that conversation with Mother about?"

Kit nestled against his chest, her delectable cinnaspice scent surrounding him. "I was telling her about Willa. She'll require another position since a priestess doesn't need a lady's maid. Besides, Willa adores dressing a fashionable mistress. Your mother assured me she'd find one for Willa."

Warmth flooding him, Mel pulled Kit onto his lap. Of course she'd ensure her loyal maid was well taken care of still. He smiled and captured her face in his hands. "My sweet, tender Kit."

Then he kissed her. He groaned and his body tightened when Kit flung her arms about his neck and yanked him closer. They devoured each other's mouths until the carriage jolted over a deep rut.

Wrenching his head up, he panted as he stared at Kit's swollen lips, flushed skin, and smoky eyes turned black with passion. Why was Summerday so *far away*? He shuddered. "I burn for you—I can't wait until we're married."

Kit shivered against him. "Me too."

Mel forced himself to deposit Kit on the seat and quit touching her. "Although I hope you shan't be disappointed on our wedding night. I've never made love to anyone before." Unlike her.

Blushing scarlet, Kit shifted beside him then muttered, "Me either."

He gaped at Kit. She couldn't be a virgin too. "But you're a widow. *And* you courted the greatest rakehell in Ormas."

Kit grimaced, still blushing. "I despised kissing them, so I froze to stone whenever they did. When Lord Blaine saw that on our wedding night, he withdrew and never pressed for intimacy again. He was such a kind gentleman and still in love with his first wife, although I managed to temporarily dazzle him. After that night, Lord Blaine treated me much like he treated Elise and never reproached me for marrying him—he'd met Father when requesting my hand, so he knew how desperate I'd been to escape."

Mel swallowed, his chest aching at her desperation.

Kit sighed. "As for the Duke of Oakmoor, I avoided kissing him after the first time because I knew he'd refuse to marry me if he realized I couldn't return his passion."

Inhaling, Mel stared at Kit. So all those coy smiles with the duke that had made his stomach tighten with jealousy had been all pretense. He exhaled. After he'd realized she loved him, he should have realized that as well—Kit had never once used such flirtatious wiles on him. She'd been herself, not the fashionable Countess of Blaine.

Shaking her head, Kit sighed again. "A rakehell like the Duke of Oakmoor wouldn't want a wife who froze at mere kisses."

Smiling to hearten Kit, Mel threaded his fingers through hers. "You never froze at *my* kisses."

Kit leaned against him. "Yes, and my wild response when we first kissed made me realize I still loved you, even though I'd told myself for years 'twas nothing but a girlhood fantasy."

He wrapped his arm about Kit again, his pulse quickening. "Yet afterward, you pretended those kisses were insignificant and said we should forget they ever happened."

Humming, Kit placed her hand above his heart. "Our kisses upset you, and I was too proud to admit my love when I thought you didn't return it. When did *you* realize you did?"

Mel blew a laugh and laid his hand over Kit's. "Our kisses *should* have made me realize I loved you, but I refused to see it because I believed loving you was impossible since you couldn't want to marry a humble priest. Yet when I burned to strangle your father for raging at you, I could no longer deny how I loved you."

Kit smiled. "So we both required shocking emotions to admit the truth in our hearts."

He chuckled and kissed Kit's hair. "We're both stubborn. Fortunately, we now have each other to temper that, although our quarrels whenever we disagree shall be fierce."

Kit giggled as the carriage halted. "And they'll frequently end with wild kisses."

Mel grinned and risked a brief yet thorough kiss. "Not just kisses once we're married."

His grin deepened at Kit's eager blush. They were definitely going to enjoy being married. Too bad that was months away. He sighed then helped her alight, and they entered the Great Temple together.

EPILOGUE

On Summerday morning, Kit swallowed a laugh when Mel hauled her upright as soon as they'd finished eating breakfast. They were both desperate for the Goddess's approval to marry after waiting the past two months. Hopefully, they'd not need to wait long for the wedding ceremony, although the duchess was attempting to convince them they should have a grand ceremony before all of court.

She smiled as she and Mel strode beneath the covered walkways toward the Sun Chapel. They'd managed to restrain themselves to kisses so far, mostly by not spending too much time alone together. The most they'd been alone had been when he'd taken care of her during her megrims. Thankfully, those were still four weeks apart now that she wasn't forcing herself to deny her genuine self. And despite the pain during her megrims, she'd enjoyed being alone with Mel and his tender care.

She quirked a wry smile. Yet her and Mel being alone together wouldn't have been wise when she'd been well—they'd never have stopped at kisses. But their busy lives at the Great Temple helped distract them. During the day, she was immersed in completing her accelerated novitiate while he was handling his duties as the elder community priest of Calatini. Plus, they were overseeing the repair of Sutton Manor using some of Mel's inheritance so the people there could have a better life and their future children could have the estate one day. Then despite their many duties, most evenings they visited their families or Sarah and Deacon or Jemima from the Goddess's Refuge, who'd become a close friend too.

Kit grinned. Meeting her family in person had been wonderful, and she treasured the evenings they'd spent together. Mother still cried often, but they were mostly happy tears now, and she'd become friends with Lady Ducharme, even attending some of Lady Ducharme's fencing salons. Father Christopher treated Kit with the same love he showed his own children, and he, Hawke, and Hawke's merchant friend Mr. Buford had begun a profitable business venture involving Orandia. Plus, her three younger siblings were a delight. Thom, at sixteen, was a sturdy and warm boy very like his father. Chase, at fourteen, was somewhat wilder but still sweet. And little Lizzie, at eleven, was adorably vivacious and ingenious at charming others.

She squeezed Mel's hand as they entered the Sun Chapel. Besides visiting their families, the only court event they'd attended had been their betrothal fete last month, which had been even more well-attended than the duchess's usual events and was probably still being gossiped about. When Kit and Mel had arrived, court had stared at her youthful appearance as well as her novice priest robes over her crimson ballgown. Then they'd stared even harder when she refused to dance with anyone but Mel, except for a few dances with family. The erstwhile fashionable Countess of Blaine becoming a priestess and being besotted with her priest betrothed was not at all what court had expected. But 'twas a relief to ignore court's shallow games and focus on living a happy and fulfilled life with the gentleman she loved among people who shared their calling to serve the Goddess.

Mel glanced at her when they halted before the many Goddess laurels. "Before we summon the Goddess, I wanted to discuss our wedding ceremony. I was thinking we could ask Winifred to marry us at the Summerday festivities tonight. I'm certain she'd agree even though we didn't get handfasted last Summerday."

Kit tilted her head. Although a Summerday wedding ceremony was considered somewhat scandalous, 'twas *much* better than waiting for a grand ceremony before all of court. Plus, their family and friends would already be celebrating Summerday with them and wouldn't miss their wedding ceremony. She grinned at Mel. "I'd like that—and dancing around the Summerday bonfire with you, although I'd prefer making love for the first time in our bed rather than outside like Summerday couples usually do."

Mel chuckled. "So would I." He pulled her close for a hungry kiss. Lifting his head, he added, "But to prevent protests, we should wait to tell Mother our plans until 'tis too late to alter them."

Kit almost giggled. Probably wise. "We'll let her host another fete for us instead of planning our wedding ceremony. Now, are we going to summon the Goddess so we can finally get her approval to marry?"

Mel laughed again, then holding hands, they faced the many Goddess laurels. To summon the Goddess's presence, he spoke the Goddess's true name known only to her priests, and all the Goddess laurels rustled like during a warm breeze while their heavenly cinnaspice-apple fragrance flooded the Sun Chapel.

As Kit's lips parted, Mel squeezed her hand and said, "Goddess, Kit and I have come here today to request your approval for our marriage. Please speak to us through your Goddess laurels."

Their fragrance burgeoning, the Goddess laurels suddenly stilled, and with a poof, an impossibly beautiful lady of middle years with lush curves, golden skin, brown-green eyes, and wavy hair a glorious mixture of brown, gold, and black appeared before Kit and Mel. Her warm voice both old and young, she said, "I can speak to you more directly than that."

Gasping, Kit and Mel fell to their knees and bent their heads without separating their joined hands. A manifestation of the Goddess, even on a holy day, was as exceedingly rare as one of her spells. Her head whirling, Kit gulped a bracing breath. Neither of them had ever expected to meet the Goddess *in person*.

The Goddess's gentle laugh reverberated through the Sun Chapel. "Do not quake, my beloved children. Rise and face me."

Their knees trembling and still gripping each other's hand, Kit and Mel rose and gazed into the Goddess's radiant countenance as she commanded.

The Goddess smiled. "I am so proud of you both. You are compassionate and wise and strong and dedicated to serving others without neglecting your own needs—exactly like my priests ought to be." She turned to Kit. "I am especially proud that you have overcome your self-doubt and become who you were always meant to be." She sighed. "It grieved me to see you suffer as you did, but my high priests must know some suffering to be strong enough to lead."

As Mel clenched her hand, Kit wobbled and only remained upright because of him. "H-high priests?"

Inclining her head, the Goddess smiled brighter. "Yes, and you shall be one of the greatest I ever had." She grinned at Mel. "Although without you, she would never be as great."

Still dizzy, Kit swallowed and licked her lips. "Does High Priest Theodag know I'm his successor?"

The Goddess hummed. "From the moment I bestowed one of my Goddess laurel apples upon you, but he knew telling you then would only panic you and prevent you from becoming who you were meant to be. My beloved Theodag is uncommonly wise."

Kit exchanged a wide glance with Mel. No wonder High

Priest Theodag had mentored her and quit asking Mel to become his successor.

Beaming, the Goddess waved a hand, and the Goddess laurels behind her danced. "Now on to your request today—I most gladly approve of your marriage. I shall even marry you myself before I depart."

Kit and Mel exchanged another wide glance, then Mel said, "But our family and friends..."

The Goddess laughed. "Do not fret; everyone shall arrive shortly." She smiled at Kit. "Although before they do, I must do this."

As the Goddess pressed a finger on Kit's brow, warmth surged through her head, and she swayed, but Mel steadied her.

Her eyes crinkling, the Goddess nodded. "Your megrim four days ago was the last you shall ever suffer. A boon for your faithful service, my daughter." She winked at Mel. "Now you can use your massages for more pleasurable endeavors."

While Kit and Mel blushed, High Priest Theodag, Elder Priestess Agnes, Sarah, Deacon, and Jemima burst into the Sun Chapel. The five priests genuflected before settling in the pews. Then Mel's parents, Wren's parents, as well as Kit's mother and stepfather swept inside, followed by Aragon and his family with Kit's three siblings. Soon after, Wren, a newly pregnant Queen Kiera, and Lady Ravenstone arrived with their husbands and the twins. Finally, Elise, her family, and Pippa's brothers entered with Edouard and Pippa, who'd not been seen since they'd shocked everyone by eloping last month.

Once everyone sat, the Goddess began the wedding cere-mony by speaking about love and marriage. Blessing their marriage, the Goddess crowned Kit and Mel with garlands of Goddess laurels and bound their left hands together. Then the Goddess led them through their vows and gave them two tin necklaces with Goddess laurel apple pendants to exchange as wedding tokens. After the Goddess presented them as husband and wife, she vanished with a poof. While the other guests began to chatter, High Priest Theodag rushed forward and had them sign their matrimony certificate.

After many exuberant embraces and well-wishes, Kit and Mel finally hurried back to his—their—chambers. Her pulse surging, she wrapped her arms about Mel's neck when he pulled her against him and kissed her as if starving.

Eventually, Mel wrenched their mouths apart. Panting, he said, "I was wondering if we could skip the Summerday festivities tonight."

Eyeing his lips, Kit hummed. Festivities would just distract them, and they'd their duties to attend to tomorrow. "Yes, please."

Then she yanked Mel down for another kiss. She purred when he rumbled and swept her toward their bedroom. They needn't restrain themselves any longer. They were in love and *finally* married—with the Goddess's blessing no less.

Want more?

Sign up for my newsletter for a bonus epilogue about Kit's ordination examination and the surprising news the Goddess tells her and Mel as well as other exclusive stories and book extras, new book announcements, giveaways, and more.

And order the next book The Sun-Nymph Bride about Pippa and Edouard today! Keep reading to learn more about the next book in the Calatini Tales.

Like The Goddess's Illusion?

Please consider writing a review. Reviews truly help spread the word about the titles you love.

THE SUN-NYMPH BRIDE

In the Regency-inspired kingdom of Calatini, magic can complicate anything... even true love.

When Pippa Hawke sees Edouard, Lord Blaine, at a family wedding, it's love at first sight. Sunny, cheerful Pippa charms

Edouard unlike any lady has before, and she's just as enthralled. But Pippa has yet to be introduced to society, with her reclusive father intending to keep it that way. And Edouard is too conscientious to court a lady as young as Pippa before her debut, no matter how much he loves her.

Yet Pippa knows that Edouard is the gentleman she'll marry, regardless of the many others attempting to court her. She sends heartfelt letters and arranges intimate outings that deepen their love, until serious, careful Edouard is taking delicious risks that cause her father to denounce him as a rakehell and forbid their betrothal.

But Pippa's father isn't the only threat to their courtship. In Calatini, magic is real... and sometimes, it's a curse that destroys even the strongest love.

THE SUN-NYMPH BRIDE IS A COZY, **fairytale-inspired low spice historical fantasy romance, perfect for romance lovers looking for a little extra magic. Fans of Robin McKinley's fairy tale retellings will fall in love with the Calatini Tales.**

WANT MORE? Order **The Sun-Nymph Bride** *today!*

CALATINI TALES

The enchanting Calatini Tales includes...

The Spellbinding Courtship (Book 0.5)
The Enchanted Bird (Book 1)
The Nightmara Affair (Book 2)
The Secret Soulbond (Book 3)
The Goddess's Illusion (Book 4)
The Sun-Nymph Bride (Book 5)
The Beast Curse (Book 6)
The Lethe Elixir (Book 7)

ABOUT KATHERINE

A lifelong creator of her own bedtime stories, **Katherine Dotterer** writes cozy tales of fantasy romance inspired by Regency England. Born and raised in Maryland, she still lives there in an almost cottage surrounded by trees. When not writing, she enjoys reading anything she can find, singing in local choruses, hiking in nearby parks, watching the wildlife outside her windows, and cuddling with her cats. Visit her at Katherine-Dotterer.com to learn about her book releases, read her many book extras, and sign up for her newsletter.

www.ingramcontent.com/pod-product-compliance
Lightning Source LLC
Chambersburg PA
CBHW061541190726
48289CB00004B/1128